Once in a Lifetime

a novel

Suzanne Mattaboni

EMPHASIS PRESS

[READ!—WE MEAN IT]

ONCE IN A LIFETIME
Suzanne Mattaboni
Published by Emphasis Press
Northampton, PA

Copyright © 2024 Suzanne Mattaboni
All rights reserved.

ISBN-13: 979-8-9889675-0-7

This is a work of fiction. Names, places, characters, and events are fictitious. Any similarities to actual events and persons, living or dead, are purely coincidental. Any trademarks, service marks, product names, or named features are assumed to be the property of their respective owners and are used only for reference. If any of these terms are used, no endorsement is implied. Except for review purposes, the reproduction of this book, in whole or part, electronically or mechanically, constitutes a copyright violation. Address permissions and review inquiries to suzanne@mattaboni.com.

Editor: Jenn Haskin
Cover Image: Braxton Kocher, Bandt Agency

Visit the author's website at www.suzannemattaboni.com
www.onceinalifetimenovel.com

@suzanne.mattaboni X @suzmattaboni @suzannemattaboni80s suzannemattabonibook

[2nd Edition with Foreword/Author Q&A/short story]

Printed in the United States

Awards for ONCE IN A LIFETIME:

2023 "IPPY" Independent Publisher Book Award Medalist

2023 International Book Award, Finalist, Best New Fiction

2022 Pencraft Award Winner, Women's Fiction

2022 Paris Book Festival Award Winner, General Fiction

2022 Fall Bookfest Winner, Romantic Comedy

Congrats for Suzanne Mattaboni, author of ONCE IN A LIFETIME:

"Congratulations on the launch of *Once in a Lifetime*, Suzanne ... that is a huge accomplishment ... All the very, very, very best... **You're an absolute dreamboat!**" – *1980s Film Actress Lea Thompson (via Cameo)*

Praise for ONCE IN A LIFETIME:

"Mattaboni's prose is rich with sharp dialogue, musical references, and painterly details ... **ebullient and engaging** ... An enjoyable, starry-eyed coming-of-age tale." – *Kirkus Reviews*

Five stars. "Mattaboni perfectly captures the era ... Lyrically written, *Once in a Lifetime* is **a celebration of female friendship**." – *Suzanne Kamata, author of* Screaming Divas

"Mattaboni **masters the complications and daily nuances of female friendship** while emphasizing women's dreams and opportunities in a vibrant cultural moment." – *BookLife - Lightning Bolt Review*

"A **smart and entertaining** read, **the writing shines** with engaging imagery and insights about the nature of creativity ... a romantic comedy that's not all about the guy." – *Los Angeles Wire*

"*Once in a Lifetime* is **a fun, irreverent, yet intelligent read**, achingly full of the things young people yearn for when it's time to launch themselves into the adult world." – *Entertainment Monthly News*

"The novel .... plays out against a vibrant background of 1980s new wave music and art, with a tone that combines a much-needed pop-culture sensibility and snarky wit with an **intelligent, literary edge**." – *New York Weekly*

Five stars. "Suzanne Mattaboni ... has expertly woven numerous themes throughout her book *Once in a Lifetime*, in a flawless way ... *Once in a Lifetime* is **an incredible book that has thrilled and amazed me**." – *Red Headed Book Lover*

"**I absolutely love this book**! If *The Sisterhood of the Traveling Pants* and 'The Breakfast Club' had a love child, it would be this." – *Renée Night Owl Loft Reviews*

"Wow. What a read. The characters are **rich and in-depth** ... Suzanne has captured the essence of the timeless struggles of youth and opportunity."
-- *The And I Thought Ladies Literary Community*

Once in a Lifetime

Dedicated to all the people I love:
John and my family, my ex-roommates.

And to New Hope of the '80s.

FOREWORD

By Annie Zaleski, Rock Journalist

"I want it all. Isn't that what they told us we could have? We're the women of the '80s. We can have it all. No one mentioned what would happen if we got it."

As I was reading *Once in a Lifetime*, these lines stood out to me like they were a bright, flashing neon sign. Growing up in the 1980s, I never felt like I had to choose between achieving just one thing. School, jobs, relationships, family, adventures—everything seemed within reach, and I didn't have to sacrifice one of these to have another. Our generation was encouraged to be ambitious and dream big.

Perhaps that's why '80s music also felt like a time bursting with immense possibility. The decade's mega-superstars—Madonna, Prince, Michael Jackson, Bruce Springsteen—offered any number of tantalizing fantasies. But '80s music was also intertwined with reinvention. Disco and punk received a new wave makeover. Hard rock developed a flashy, polished edge. Synth-pop became seductive, not robotic. Goth rock often had a moody pop sheen. Even Roxy Music and David Bowie evolved from art rockers into (respectively) suave sophisto-pop mavens and a tanned MTV star.

That artists felt emboldened to transform themselves and push boundaries was fun and exciting. But it was also empowering to music fans, especially young women. And the characters at the heart of *Once in a Lifetime* certainly also saw nothing but potential on the horizon—starting with Jess, a talented artist who's working all summer as a waitress to earn money to live and study in London. To her, the city is a coolness Utopia full of cutting-edge art, music and fashion, a place where her creativity can run wild.

Getting to London won't be easy, however: Not only is waitressing full of stress, but she's navigating a new relationship with a hunky musician named Whit while sorting out her confusing feelings for her high school boyfriend, Drew. Her friends are facing similar romantic tumult—including abusive (or dishonest) boyfriends—and navigating roadblocks to having it all: work stress, mental health challenges, and financial woes.

Throughout the book, Jess also encounters people who don't always respect her dreams or understand why she needs to go to London to cultivate her passions. These negative attitudes are another downside to striving for it all: Motivated young women in the '80s often had to fight against outdated expectations, ingrained gender stereotypes, and people who tried to put a damper on their ambition. Sadly, of course, this wasn't necessarily a new phenomenon; the thoughts, desires and feelings of young women had long been looked down upon as being frivolous or unimportant.

But here's where '80s music also shined. Young women supported the burgeoning alternative music underground and helped propel unique artists like Duran Duran, Culture Club, George Michael, and Cyndi Lauper to pop stardom. Their unwavering belief in these artists—all of whom didn't fit into a neat sonic *or* sartorial pigeonhole—represented the power of possibility. Fans had permission to be their unique selves because their idols looked *and* sounded different. Not only did this music provide emotional solace and unstoppable dance grooves, but it also served as a blueprint on how to march to the beat of a different drummer—and stay focused on a future you define on your own terms.

Annie Zaleski, February 2024
Music Journalist [*Rolling Stone*, NPR, Salon, Rock and Roll Hall of Fame]
Author of *Duran Duran's RIO: Celebrating the 40th Anniversary of the Classic Album*

CHAPTER 1

AUGUST 1984—Delaware River
Psycho Killer

The Camaro spins into a U-turn, tires wailing against the water-flushed road. A scream comes out of me like a full-throated siren. The car revolves across the asphalt into the opposing lane in an eerily smooth path, like some unseen hand is turning us. A truck horn blares and headlamps beam into my eyes, shining against the windshield through a curtain of storming rain.

We veer off the pavement, a fender slicing through the guard rail, metal screeching. The car shunts down a ravine. Its headlights bleach skinny trees as we lumber sideways, clunking, bending branches. I lift out of my seat to the sound of the windshield *snapping*. A crack zigzags from one side of the glass to the other like a streak of lightning.

Silver fizzles across my vision, even when I close my eyes.

I wonder how close the river is. I can hear it, rushing.

MAY 1984—Capresi's, New Hope, PA
London Calling

I'm starting to taste desperation on my lipstick. I'm not a good enough bullshit artist to snag a job on the river side of New Hope, where the *real* waitresses work. I suck at waitressing. I'm Danger Girl, constantly tripping over myself. So, I'll take whatever job I can get.

A restaurateur in a lavender silk shirt interrogates me at Capresi's Continental Restaurant, sheltered between The Canal and a creek that meanders as if it's lost its way. My roommate Trina the Waitressing Goddess calls this town Pennsylvania's version of San Francisco, where the lifestyle choices are as assorted as the menus. This is the seventh place I've applied to today.

The restaurateur taps a finger against his lips. "What's your name, dear?"

"It's Jessi—"

A crash like a steel drum falling off the back of a truck comes from the kitchen behind us. My cheeks clench against the bar room chair I'm sitting on.

The restaurateur's jaw tightens. He raises a finger, nodding for forgiveness. "*One moment*," he mouths.

I hear a pot scrape against industrial shelving, ringing through a kitchen pass-through window behind us. A woman's voice rises over the squall. "*Teddy, would you get a grip?*"

The restaurateur rises from our table and heads to the pass-through, motioning me to follow him. He smacks his palm against a bell on the sill. "Behave back there," he calls. The bell drowns out my favorite Spandau Ballet song, drifting from a tinny transistor radio in the kitchen. "We've got company, Bernadette."

A woman with hair the consistency of a wire sponge and a face scrubbed clean of make-up flashes past the cut-out window. Her oven mitt-of-a-hand whisks to the pass-through and stifles the ring.

"I hate that bell, George."

"Gior-*gio*." He turns to me, wrinkling his nose. "Not George. I hate George."

The bell whines like a piccolo twisted in a knot as Bernadette drags it off the sill. "*We're even.*"

I nudge my application along the counter towards Giorgio the restaurateur. Let's not forget, I'm here for a job. I've got to come up with a security deposit in a week, not to mention study abroad tuition to save for, if I want to spend a semester in London junior year like I've been dying to. I want my real life to start, already. I've also got an hour left before I meet the girls for a ride back to Trina's parents' house. I can feel the sweat beading under my spiky bangs.

Giorgio lifts the sheet of paper. "What did you say your name was?"

"Jessica Addentro." I finger the bangs out of my eyes as the heat of the kitchen bends toward me. I subtly push the rest of my hair off my shoulders, not wanting to show a shocking lack of restaurant etiquette, which I'm guessing includes keeping my abundant hair off the countertops.

"Ad-*den*-tro." He repronounces my name with an Italian flourish and looks up from my application. "Do you know what that means?"

I recall my high school Italian lessons. "Inside?"

"More like, versed in." He turns his free hand in a circle. "Or, full of insights. Does that sound like you?"

"Depends on the subject." When it comes to waitressing, I'm full of something, all right.

"Do you live here in town?"

"I just finished my sophomore year of college. My roommates and I are moving into a place on Main Street next week for the summer." Then life will begin.

"What did you study?"

"Abstract painting. And I've recently decided to get into glass mosaics. I'm multi-media."

"*Ah.* How visionary. I can see the creativity in you." It's like he's reading my tea leaves instead of a job application. "As an artistic spirit, can you be happy as a waitress?" His eyebrows crush down as if he's bracing for the 15 terrible lies I'm about to tell.

I give him a smile that fits like a surgical glove over a watering can.

3

"Waitressing is *fun*." Trina the Waitressing Goddess told me to say that. "I like working with people and helping them enjoy their lives." My inability to bullshit bears down on me like a smoldering cigarette butt.

Giorgio the restaurateur flutters his eyelashes at me. "You don't have to say that, you know."

"I'm saving for a semester overseas," I admit.

His eyebrows relax back to their rightful position. "That sounds more honest."

God help me, waitressing is a means to an end. I'd much rather sit in a corner and sketch people than serve them—or talk to them. But it's a skill I'll need to ace if I want to fund my Exciting Life Plan and emerge from a European study jaunt as a New Wave-inspired, multi-media art sensation. *I hope—I hope—I hope.*

I've always been told my generation is lucky. The women of the fifties and sixties were stuck with lackluster contraceptive options, painful bullet bras, and spinsterhood by age 22. They gave birth to us liberated girls of the eighties. The world is ours if we work hard enough, we're told. We can have it all—careers, sex, adventure, friendships, love. Meaning.

Right?

Time to see if that's true—and to kiss up to a clairvoyant restaurateur with a penchant for lilac silk.

"So where are you planning to study?" Giorgio perks up. "Rome? Florence?"

"London. I want my art to reflect New Wave culture. I can take some awesome mosaic courses over there, plus photography and lit."

He leans an elbow against the pass-through sill as if waiting for me to finish. As if there's more.

And there is.

London. It's where all the coolest alternative music and ultra-creative post-punk sensibility is coming from. It's where guys with bulked-up shoulders, tight-waisted jackets, and mega hair sing with guitars slung across their bodies. Where slam dancers in shredded clothing and chains jostle for position in front of dark stages, buzzing with deafening feedback. I want to recreate that shoulder-padded, safety-pinned, gelled-together world, through abstract shapes, swipes of color, and vivid bits of broken glass, and make it twice as beautiful on canvas.

That's not too much to ask, is it? This life is out there. And it's all going on without me.

"London's where everything's happening. How am I supposed to create anything worthwhile if I don't . . . experience the world? The study abroad program is way above my budget, though," I add. "So here I am."

If I don't find a way to cut it in this town, God knows where I'll end up. Probably back in the sardine can of a bedroom I grew up in at my grandparents' house, which is really just a paneled-over TV room I inherited after my mother died and my dad surreptitiously disappeared. As well as they handled the situation of me landing in their laps, being raised by grandparents is something like being taken captive by the year 1954.

It beat the hell out of floating through the foster system as a hapless orphan. But not exactly an upbringing worthy of *Interview* magazine.

There in the restaurant, a series of lanterns and suncatchers revolve above us like some tacky rip-off of a Calder mobile. Happy laughter drifts in from the *al fresco* dining patio. I squint to see a couple lunching beyond a brick archway that marks the end of the bar room. Cool and verdant foliage waves beyond the patio railing as forks clink against stoneware.

A glass suncatcher in the shape of an owl glints light into my eye.

Giorgio smiles and runs his finger down the front of my application. "How old are you?"

"Twenty."

"As of when?"

"Tomorrow."

"*Oooh*! Happy birthday!" He lets go of my resume, which flits to the counter like a shed leaf. "Bernadette!" Giorgio stretches for the phantom bell, smoothing his hand against the contact-papered sill instead.

Bernadette's bushy head reappears in the kitchen pass through. "What now, Georgie?"

Giorgio clears his throat. "It's this young lady's birthday. Can we manage a piece of cake for her?"

A waft of garlic and mellow butter tickles in my nose. I stretch on my tiptoes for a look into the pass-through. Bernadette blots her hands with a crushed dishtowel and juts a palm at me to shake. Her grip is aggressive.

"Happy birthday. *Sheesh*," she says. "Are you even old enough to work here? You look like a baby."

"*Babe?*" A well-bellied, hairy guy in a white uniform shoulders his way into the window frame. "What babe?"

"Ba-*by*," Bernadette corrects, shirking her head my way. "A waitressing applicant." She retreats to the range tops, sliding heavy pans along the grates two at a time like a magic cup trick. Sparks kick-up from underneath.

The burly guy swings a wooden scepter of a spoon at me. "Never seen you in town before."

"She's from *Pittsburgh*," Giorgio mock-whispers to the guy, as if it's a sickness I have.

"New York, originally," I say. "I go to college in Pittsburgh."

"New York?" Giorgio looks me over. "That explains a lot." He's known me 20 minutes.

The burly guy sticks his wooden utensil through the window at me. "I'm Teddy."

"Jessica." I nod at him, acknowledging the spoon that's pointing at me.

Teddy swipes his implement at Giorgio. "Hire her. She's cute."

I try not to roll my eyes. If *cute* will keep me out of my grandparents' house and gets me to the study abroad program I've got my heart set on, then I'll be fucking Minnie Mouse for these people. But in truth, I hate *cute*.

Cute is not punk.

Bernadette emerges from a walk-in fridge the size of a woodland cottage, a bakery box in her arms. "Take it easy, Romeo." She drops the box on a butcher block counter.

Teddy gestures with the spoon as if to whack her one. She paws the end of it with her mitt-like hand, wrestling the spoon away. They're a bizarre, unkempt Punch and Judy, going at each other through the proscenium of the pass-through. Teddy elbows the cake box, which almost topples off the butcher block.

Bernadette straightens the box, pulls it open, and carves off a slice of cake. She tosses a plateful of triple-layer cheesecake onto the pass-through sill. The dish spins like a quarter dropped on the sidewalk. Giorgio shoots Bernadette a look that could wilt tulips. "*Careful.*"

"Wait!" She stabs the cake with a stubby birthday candle. "*Youth,*" she says to me. "Enjoy it while it lasts." Then she vanishes behind the stainless-steel armaments of the kitchen.

Giorgio extends an arm toward a bar room table, inviting me to sit back down. He delicately places the plate in front of me, then a dessert fork.

"We have the best Neapolitan cheesecake in New Hope." The dessert has a pink, a brown, and a yellowish layer, thick and textured. "I dare you to find better."

Sweet cheese melts against my tongue like heaven on a fork.

"*Oh my God,*" I mumble through teeth gummy with cheese. I push the gelled section of my hair back behind my ear, nodding.

"Now you know I don't lie." Giorgio smiles and steps toward the stacks of dishes and repeating rows of salt and pepper shakers. "As you may have guessed, this is the waitress station. Silverware, condiments, stoneware . . ." I rise and follow him again, abandoning the hunk of cheesecake. He pulls open a metal bin. "Here's the bread warmer, although we just got a microwave."

I rest a hand on the toasty metal ridge of the warmer. Giorgio whirls away from me and the hinged door of the bread warmer snaps shut.

Pain zings through my fingertip as it's nearly sacrificed to the Bread Warmer Gods. I stifle the urge to yowl like a police car. My cuticle starts to well-up with crimson.

Bleeding is likely against restaurant decorum, especially in this age of deathly infection. *AIDS*. *Herpes*. I shudder. Our generation hasn't had a good time when it comes to fucking health crises. But we're dealing. I pop my finger into my mouth.

"Rickie can show you where we keep the linens, out here in the chifforobe."

I can only imagine what a *chifforobe* is. Giorgio strides toward the patio, which is beaming with sunlight beyond the archway that divides the two areas.

"Are you available Wednesday?" he asks over his shoulder. "We need you right away. We lost someone recently."

I hope it wasn't due to a bread warmer incident. I hide my hand behind my back and eek-out a smile. "Does that mean I have the job?"

"Come in at 11:00 a.m. sharp and we'll see how it goes." Giorgio's eyebrows raise. "Are you all right?"

"Absolutely." *I am* not *committing a health code violation as we speak*, I think to myself, squeezing the wound. Psychically willing it not to drip on the carpet. "I'll be here."

"See you soon, Miss Art Student." Giorgio excuses himself through the proscenium to the patio, receding like a mirage I can't completely focus on. Suncatchers sway in his wake.

My muscles unclench as I mentally exhale. *I get to pay my rent!* And maybe afford London.

I think of Mosaic studio art classes with my morning tea and a view of the Tower Bridge. Celebrity sightings of Boy George as I drink-in the club scene. Me touring museums full of European Neo-Expressionist art. Me filling my suitcase with post-punk clothing from Malcolm McLaren's SEX boutique on King's Road.

Snagging a boyfriend with Sting-like cheekbones.

That is, if I can figure out how to waitress without bleeding out.

I startle as Teddy shoves open the kitchen door, gripping its wooden edge with sausage-like fingers. "Congratulations." He shoves a stash of cocktail napkins toward my bloodied hand. "*Wear something short.*"

The galley door swings closed again, joints moaning.

I better find a freaking Band-Aid.

CHAPTER 2

MAY 1984—Route 611, Doylestown
Young Americans

Our every possession is squashed into the back of a 1978 station wagon. The total collected belongings of all four of us girls can fit into the space of a standard refrigerator.

I tighten my arms around our record collection, in a cardboard box in my lap. A Flock of Seagulls. U2's "War." The Police. The Pretenders. I guard this box more carefully than anything else we own.

I know my priorities.

Trina spits out an expletive as the car wallops over a pothole. The glass chunk of an ashtray on the top of my box momentarily skitters away from my fingertips, showering grey flakes onto my roommate Kimmer's shoulder. She blows the flakes off her skin since her arms are busy holding a collapsible desk lamp and a milk crate full of nursing textbooks.

Trina honks as a driver ignores the double-yellow line that threads alongside the Delaware River. A Datsun whizzes past us. "Screw off!" Trina chastises out the window. "I remember my first car ride, too, asshole!" She lays on the horn.

My third roommate Audrey drapes herself over the front console, reaching toward the back seat, and shifts my ashtray into a more accessible position. Trina's mom got rid of the car's original ashtrays, but that hasn't stopped us from smoking. Have ashtrays, will travel.

"When we get to the apartment," Audrey says to me, tobacco smoke adding a nasal tinge to her voice, "don't cry." She blasts a column of smoke against the worn velour ceiling. Even with her head tipped back, the stiff, Red Zinger Tea-colored spikes of her hair radiate upward, as if magnetized.

"Is the place that horrifying?" I ask.

"It's a dive," Trina blurts, her insidious grin flashing at me in the rearview mirror. In addition to being the Waitressing Goddess, Trina is the Empress of Inappropriate Smiles. "A dive in a basement, next to a biker bar."

"What do you want for four-hundred bucks a month?" Audrey adjusts her inside-out sweatshirt, whose sleeves she chopped off in an impromptu fit of fashion design last week. The girl is dangerous with a scissor and a fist full of safety pins. "We're on a shoestring budget."

Kimmer blows a fluff of blonde hair off her lips that keeps sticking to her formidable pink lipstick. The desk lamp shifts in her lap. I shove its metal hinge away from my rib cage. "Four hundred for all four of us?" I ask.

"Yes," Audrey says. "It's more like a dental floss budget."

Audrey studies economics, although econ isn't what you'd expect from a girl who can dance Cyndi Lauper under the table. Economics is more for a girl who's never experienced the cool buzz of a man's electric shaver against the back of her neck.

"Brace yourselves," Audrey goes on. "The place is tiny."

"And ugly," says Trina.

"And don't forget filthy," says Audrey. "We're talking multiple bottles of 409 cleanser."

"I'll clean for five bucks an hour," Kimmer pipes up. Rows of Bucks County elms stream past outside, throwing animated shadows through the car.

"*Some things are good filthy.*" Trina laughs. "And Kimmer, I don't believe you'll clean a thing. Even for a hundred bucks."

"Who cares if we have to clean?" I say. "As long as I can freaking get out there and live, like a real adult." The river glitters at me through the brush

Once in a Lifetime

outside, guarding New Jersey like a moat. "I'm tired of everything cool in the world happening without me."

Trina glances over her shoulder. "Is that why you agreed to venture into food service?" She rounds a bend like we're in an Indy roadster instead of a station wagon. "To be an *adult?*"

Kimmer bolsters an arm against the passenger side door. "I thought it was about money for study abroad." The cargo on Kim's lap shifts.

I hug the record box tighter as we swing out of the curve. The road is bordered only by wild bushes and a tumultuous drop into the river. "It's not just the semester abroad. I want to get out into the world. To be inspired. I want to see *life-as-it-is.*"

"Ha!" Trina huffs. "Good luck."

"That's why I'm shooting for London. Instead of, say, Poughkeepsie."

Audrey reaches over and taps her cigarette butt into my ashtray. "We'll make sure you get to England, Jess. Even if it means we have to live without you for a while. That's how much we love you." She slides back into her seat and bats a finger against a globe-shaped compass that's suction-cupped to the dashboard. The floating ball spins till the letters blur like a 1960s Batman scene change: *N-E-S-W N-E-S-W N-E-S-W.* "Waitressing in New Hope is your best bet to make enough cash for that. But personally," she says over her shoulder, "I'm not ready for that *adult* shit yet."

"You'll officially get there before me," I say.

"What else is new?" Audrey says. "Your parents really screwed up having you the year after our parents had us."

"Sorry," I say. Audrey, Trina, and Kimmer were transfer students when we got thrown into the dorms together, so they're already heading into their senior years. As a soon-to-be-junior, I'm always catching up.

Kimmer shifts under her load of boxes. "I'm *almost* ready to be an adult," she says. "Maybe. Sort of. I want to have a little fun first. Can we take a raincheck on adulthood for the summer?"

"I'm not patient enough for a rain check," I say. "But fun is on my list, too."

The bells of a Madonna song tinkle to life on the car radio. Audrey hard-pokes her index finger against a station button in the dash to change the channel. "No Madonna *ever*." She punches the buttons until she finds a more appropriate song by The Smiths.

"You definitely deserve a good time after all that *Drew* crap that just happened, Jess," Trina says. "Are you two still a couple?"

"Not exactly." I wipe a gray shadow of cigarette ash off my fingertips and onto my shorts. It leaves streaks as if someone's pawed at me. "We're *semi-dating* now. It's complicated."

"*Semi-dating?*" Trina's voice kicks up half an octave. "You just made that up."

"Life, meet Jess," Kimmer says, fidgeting in her seat. "Her relationship calls for its own terminology." The metal cone of the desk lamp swings forward and whacks her in the knee. "*Ow.*"

"Drew doesn't see the point of doing a long-distance thing if I go to London," I say.

"Or while you're in New Hope, with us?" Trina asks. "You self-absorbed, ambitious little slut?"

"Yeah, right. That sounds like me."

Audrey laughs. "Thank God you're spending the summer with us." She cracks the window, dispersing the cloud of smoke settling around her spiked hairdo. "Makes me feel better. Someone else without a conscience."

"Or a foreseeable romantic future," I say. In reality, I'm on the market for the first time in almost three years. I shudder.

Trina's thick thigh shifts as she modulates the gas pedal. Her hand leaves the wheel long enough to finger the golden razor blade charm that's strung around her neck, a tribute to a morbid David Bowie lyric. Bowie is God, and we're convinced we're the Young Americans. "Welcome back to the dating world." She smirks like the Cheshire Cat in the rear-view mirror. "*It sucks ass.*"

Once in a Lifetime

Training at Capresi's restaurant begins at 11:00 a.m. The brick sidewalks of Main Street are calm, still missing the stream of tourists that are due to materialize. A creek beyond the patio railing glides over flat planes of shale, sloping under felled trees tinted with green lichen. The dining room patio is scattered with naked plywood tabletops waiting for me to dress them.

Rickie the waitress has obsidian pixie hair and stubby, bruise-colored fingernails. She rests a tray of bud vases on a table and gawks at the jumble of utensils and glasses I just placed around a stoneware dinner plate at the "deuce" she asked me to set.

She shakes her shorn head and stifles a laugh. "First, the tablecloth goes *this* way." She rotates the burgundy cloth so the pointy ends drape in the middle.

Rickie wears black jeans and running shoes instead of the standard waitressing skirt. "And the utensils go like this . . . forks on the left, knife and spoon on the right." She reorganizes the utensils obediently into size order. "Dessert spoon at the top."

I blanch at having arranged everything so thoroughly wrong. I should have requested a tutorial from Trina The Waitressing Goddess.

I suck at this.

"Where did you work before?" Rickie asks.

Birds trill in the tree limbs beyond the patio railing. They might as well be circling my head like a Bugs Bunny gag.

I served drinks at the Up Your Alley bowling parlor the week their regular waitress went on her honeymoon. The league ordered a row of flaming Sambuca shots. One emptied fire extinguisher and an emergency services vehicle later, it was the end of my waitressing career.

Danger Girl.

"Lemme guess." Rickie pulls a plastic bin full of utensils from a low shelf. "You never did this before?"

"Sure, I have." I try to brace for getting through this gig without dying of embarrassment.

London, I think. I picture myself cheering through a Police concert at Hammersmith Odeon. I can do this. "*Umm* . . . I was a waitress for one day."

Rickie laughs at me.

"Christ, you won't tell Giorgio, will you?" I ask. "I'll figure shit out. I promise. Is it that hard?"

Her muscles flex as she tosses the plastic bin onto the next deuce. Flatware rings. "Fuck if I know. I'm the dishwasher."

"*What?*"

Rickie gives a deep chuckle. "Giorgio put me on the floor 'cause the last two girls quit on the same night," she says. "Welcome to Capresi's."

She pulls a 2 x 4-foot chalkboard from behind a podium. "Here's the menu board. You need to write up the day's meals by hand, every morning." The metal legs of a white mesh patio chair scream against the uneven floor as she wings it in front of me, balancing the chalkboard on its seat. "Here's how you show it to customers." The board shifts. She straightens it with a kick of the chair.

"Are you serious?" I ask.

"Giorgio says the menu is a living thing, different every day." She pulls a tray of Creamsicle-colored jar candles from the storage cabinet and flings it onto a tabletop as easily as if it were a Frisbee. "The menu has to be written in chalk, so he can change it, whenever."

"Every table in the restaurant gets a board?"

"Nope. There are two." She shoves up her sleeves. "For the whole place."

"That's insane."

She slaps my back with the vigor of a truck driver. "You *do* learn fast."

CHAPTER 3

ALMOST JUNE 1984—The Sandler Apartments
Girls Just Want To Have Fun

Our apartment is a jumble of cardboard boxes in a room that's tighter than our quad dorm room back at Pitt. The wall's marked by a water stain resembling a four-foot-tall, mutant ringworm. I wonder if the river has made its way inside the building.

Today's objective: to test out New Hope's nightlife, especially since the town's star alternative club is in walking distance. Trina says Drazine's has got a dance floor the size of Columbus, Ohio, accented by the town's premium river view.

Getting ready to go out is half the fun, and it requires use of the whole living room.

Behind two panes of window glass coated in an earth-tone spatter, the grill of a Buick stares into our basement apartment window. A duck waddles past the rusted chrome of the car's bumper, stretching its neck at us in the almost-dark.

Hairbrush in hand, I stop short in the middle of the room. "What the fuck?" I say, gawking at the white bird staring at me. It pecks at the window screen, making metallic music.

A live *duck*.

Audrey spreads her arms and cants a knee, spokesmodel-like. "Welcome to Sherwood. Have you met our mascot, Frank?"

Kimmer strides in from our only bedroom, trailing a line of cigarette smoke, searching for the can of Aqua Net that has been making the rounds through the apartment. "You named the duck?" She laughs, grabbing the can off the arm of our sofa bed and giving it a shake.

"He was here when Trina and I rented the place." Audrey leans against a stack of boxes. "At least I think it was him. He looks like a Frank."

The duck honks at me through the grimy window. I back away, stepping past an ashtray the size of a pie plate that's sitting on a box in the middle of the cut-shag carpet. We don't own a coffee table.

I head to the narrow coat closet by our front door, which Kimmer and I have to share as a clothes closet. The two of us have to sleep in the living room on a hideous, orange pull-out sofa bed that spent the last 20 years in Trina's parents' basement. Trina and Audrey claimed the one bedroom, since they found the apartment. They've piled comforters on foam mattress toppers that resemble egg cartons in there, which is as close as they'll get to having beds.

Last summer at the shore, Trina and Audrey slept in sleeping bags the whole time. In our quest for independence, we're a step above squatters.

But we don't talk about The Shore anymore.

Kimmer fluffs her hair, throws her head askew, and attacks her golden waves with a fog of Aqua Net, plastering its crimpiness all on the left side. She pulls herself upright again. "I feel a little imbalanced," she says.

"What else is new in Kansas, Dorothy?" Trina applies lipstick thick enough to wax a Corvette, staring into a make-up mirror that's balanced on the arm of the sofa. She gags as Kimmer sprays more Aqua Net. "I'll need a gas mask if you don't ease up on that shit."

"Keep the spray away from the cigarettes," says Audrey. "It's a fire hazard." She adjusts the hem of her red sweatshirt dress, which reaches halfway to her knees.

Kimmer stands on the sofa bed to view her reflection in our smudged living room window. She taps the can against the glass, shoo-ing away Frank the duck, then fluffs her gold waves. She sprays once more. "Does Aqua Net work like mace? Maybe I'll bring some to The Boat Haus to fend off Karl's *dogs.*"

Kimmer got hired at a pricey establishment across the canal from Capresi's, which is done up like an old boating dock.

"Are those animals still threatening you?" I sit down in front of our tiny closet to rummage for my spiked-heel ankle boots, the ones with the scrunched leather cowls. "Who the hell keeps Rottweilers in a restaurant?" I pick through a hoard of sandals. Our combined shoe collection is a mound of leather, jutting heels, and straps, all piled at the bottom of the tiny closet.

"Dogs? That's gotta be a violation," says Trina. In addition to being the Goddess of Waitressing, she's gearing up for law school.

"Karl swears they're harmless," Kimmer says. "Meanwhile, they've got fangs like Jaws revisited."

"You should file a complaint," Trina orders, dragging on a cigarette. Clouds of hairspray offend her. Clouds of tobacco smoke, not so much.

Kimmer the nurse-in-training hops down from the sofa bed and mimes a phone call in her faux geriatric-patient voice, dialing a finger in the air. "*Helloooo, New Hope Better Business Bureau and ASPCA?*" she mocks. Then back to her real voice: "Karl will throw me out if I report him, and I need the job."

Audrey twists a black leather sash around her glaringly red sweatshirt, instantly chic-ing up the outfit. "You could get another waitressing job in a minute, Kim," she says. Unsatisfied, Audrey tosses the sash aside.

"*Maybe* I could get another job," says Kimmer, shaking her head to test her hairdo. Her teased hair gleams but doesn't budge. "Or maybe not."

"You've been hanging around restaurants with your dad since you were a kid," I say.

"Don't be so afraid of rejection," Trina demands. "Unless you're into self-torture. In that case, go ahead and stay at The Boat Haus." Of course, Trina already snagged a job at the best restaurant in town, *La Chambre Rose*, right along the river on the outskirts of Main Street.

"I'm not afraid of rejection," says Kimmer. "I'm afraid God will strike me down for no apparent reason. Or because I was bad."

"Bad? Oh, come on," I tell Kimmer. "You're never that bad."

"Just ask my brothers and sisters," she says. There are eight of them, and she's the baby of the brood. After about kid number five, Kim says, her parents gave up on them and went dysfunctional.

Audrey retreats to the bathroom, sneering at her reflection in a mirror glued to the inside of the door. She rifles through the Army duffle bag that currently serves as her dresser, then joins us back in the living room with a fist full of crescent-shaped shoulder pads.

"That shirt's already padded," I say.

"Not enough." Audrey stuffs the foam cut-outs into her sweatshirt. "I have too much neck," she announces, securing the pads with safety pins.

"No one has too much neck," says Kimmer. "Trust me, I take anatomy." Nursing is part of Kimmer's life-long effort to *fix* everyone. Since she couldn't fix her parents.

"You're tall and regal," I tell Audrey. "Like a queen."

Audrey lets her upper half droop, accentuating the slope of her shoulders. "More like a coat hanger."

"Don't fight Audrey on the neck thing," says Trina. "It's a deep-seated insecurity. Try to convince her otherwise and she'll crawl into bed for a week."

I dig through the shoe pile and pull out a "tenny runner"—the cheap, fake Keds sneakers we bought at a discount store specifically for waitressing. It's part of the *de rigueur* uniform: white shirt, black skirt, white tennies.

We're penguins.

This tenny runner is three shades grayer than it should be. I dangle it from my index finger. It drips.

"Girls, why are our shoes *wet*?" Then I notice two sweaty copper pipes running down the back of the closet.

Audrey sticks her head in to take a look at the damage. "Oh, cripes," she says. "Between the water stains and this, the plumbing in this place is out to get us."

I pluck my beloved scrunch boots from the clammy mound of shoes.

Once in a Lifetime

"*Damn.*" I try to rub them dry with the sleeve of my mesh tunic, but mesh isn't designed for housework. It's really just meant to look cool over a black tank top and drop-waist mini. The boots are still dry inside and will function for tonight since it's important for me to pretend to be tall. "We need a spaghetti pot for this leak," I say.

"We're lucky if we can boil one potato at a time," says Trina. She pokes her hand into one of our boxes, coming out with a tiny, enameled camping pot, which she thrusts next to my head. "But have at it."

I stick the pot under the pipe and crawl out of the closet, taking a seat on our oatmeal-colored carpet right next to the satellite-sized ashtray. Water pounds against the pot's metal bottom like a tom-tom . . . three feet from where I'm sleeping tonight.

"Ha! That'll keep you up at night," says Trina. "That's what you get for claiming the sofa bed."

Kimmer comes to my rescue with a towel bearing the likeness of Kermit the Frog. She yanks a set of beaded sandals from the closet and starts shining them dry. "Is this place like *The Plaza*, but different?" she jokes.

"Very different." I flop onto my back on the carpet. A hand-made poster stares down at me, badly secured to the popcorn ceiling with Scotch tape. Trina wrote it up last year, borrowing a page from my mega sketch pad. It beams lyrics from the Talking Heads' magnificent ode to confusion, "Once in a Lifetime," in electric blue marker. David Byrne's language always made us feel understood in moments of bewilderment, as we contemplated our under-developed roles in this whacked-out world.

Or to chastise us when we passed out on the floor. I've woken up more than once staring at the poster—my brain blazing with a hangover.

I shift my back against the prickly carpet and point to the message on the ceiling. "Time to play our theme song!"

Audrey slips a record onto the second-hand stereo she's owned since middle school, the one with the arm that holds multiple LPs. I pull myself off the carpet to dance around our smoke-pit of an ashtray to the *Remain in Light* album. Kimmer joins in, drawing indecipherable circles in the air with her cigarette as she swings her arms over her head, as David Byrne asks how we got here.

So where the heck are we going, and how *did* we end up here? I ask myself this every day as I wait around for my life to start, like some bundled nomad at a transit stop wondering when the beeline to Fame and Fortune is finally going to materialize and whisk me off. I'm a half-formed mosaic, dancing around in a world full of indecision and New Wave anarchy and the mystery terror of AIDS. It's anybody's guess where we girls will come out of this twisted, post-adolescent funk, like some cosmic game of Spin the Bottle.

Dancing helps, at least. When all else fails, we dance.

Audrey slinks gracefully past the stereo. "How did we get here? Let's face it, Jess." Our milk crate storage unit judders just lightly enough to avoid making the record skip. "You and I would never have met if we hadn't faked our housing applications. Both of us were pretending we didn't smoke."

"I just didn't want my grandmother to find out."

"Ditto for my mother. But that's the reason we got plunked together in the dorms," says Audrey.

"It's true. Our friendship is based on a big, fat lie designed to fool our parental guardians," I say. "That, and on A Flock of Seagulls."

Audrey throws her head back at the memory, laughing. "Thank God for those wild-headed freaks!"

Our first day in the dorms, Audrey stared at my New York-savvy record collection as if it invented fire, having just escaped a sleepy little back-to-the-fifties town where Bob Seger's "Night Moves" was as close as music got to subversive.

"You have the Flock of Seagulls record?" she gasped. "Not a single station in my hometown will play that!" No one in her town understood her haircut, either.

Back in the basement in New Hope, we circle the ashtray, bouncing to the Talking Heads, still half-dressed, like Lord of the Flies on mescaline.

"We have Beatrice to thank, too," I remind Audrey as I spin past the living room windowsill, which is eye-level for me. I swipe a hand at our hideously cheap curtains with my arm, accenting the deep plucks of Tina Weymouth's bass line.

"You mean, Be-a-Priss?" Kimmer does a turn, her cigarette still wiggling high in the air. David Byrne garbles on about water, which is appropriate theme music for New Hope. Everywhere you go, water is all around you. The Canal. The Creek. The River, which laps at the edge of the apartment building's parking lot. Who knew we could afford such a view?

Trina jumps into our dance circle, swinging her arms from side to side, balancing on her toes. She has no pants on yet. "Always remember: If one of us could even mildly stand Beatrice's guts, we girls never would have bonded," Trina says.

I think back on Beatrice, the fourth victim to be stuffed into our quad at college, even before Trina transferred to Pitt. Be-a-Priss wore pearls and Chanel blouses, worshipped Debbie Gibson, and was ticked-off-as-hell over being saddled with three working-class, punked-out roommates in mini dresses. Audrey and I put on fishnets, turquoise stilettos, and denim skirts to head out to parties. She wore docksiders, silk tops, and pleated IZOD Lacoste trousers to preppy-girl sorority mixers.

Audrey and I watched a different guy complete Beatrice's homework every week—then disappear. It was an Orient Express of vanishing exes. Tired of Beatrice's upturned nose and her Boy Toy Parade of doomed groupie boys, we resorted to musical espionage.

"Remind me: How many times did you play 'I Ran' before she put in for a room transfer?" Audrey asks.

I stop dancing. "Two hundred and twelve." It was Death by Seagulls.

Audrey lets out a deep laugh and not a single spike of her stiff red hair moves. "There you have it, ladies. The history of chaos."

That's how we came to be four girls prancing around an ashtray the size of a hubcap, on a shag rug old enough to have witnessed the moon landing. Staving off closet leaks with second-rate kitchenware and stomping in circles to the Talking Heads.

Waiting to see where in the scheme of the world the spinning bottle will land.

Ain't life grand?

I dance over to the bathroom, and for the sake of nostalgia, I vaporize myself with the first gift my ex, Drew, ever gave me: an atomizer of perfume I've had since prom. Despite it having since degenerated into nearly pure alcohol, it masks the apartment's faint but lingering scent of mildew. Trina dances past me to the bedroom and hops into a pair of black Capri pants.

I dig my arm into a box—marked *Jessica's crap* in clumsy Magic Marker—and rifle through batches of crumpled newspaper and art supplies, pulling out a swollen manila folder and a roll of Scotch tape. The folder is mostly filled with snippets from *Rolling Stone* and *Interview* that used to hang on the corkboards and cinder block walls of our dorm. I carefully rest the collection spread-eagle along the cushions of the sofa bed. "Girls, it's time to Christen this place," I say. Trina comes back into the living room and arranges three boxes into a chair.

I lift a prized black-and-white ad from my pile of tear-outs, tweezing the magazine page reverently between my fingertips, displaying it for everyone.

Trina sinks against the stack of boxes like it's a throne. Audrey pulls the stereo arm abruptly off the *Remain in Light* album for a moment of silence and holds a hand over her heart. Kim reclines against the sofa cushions.

We sigh as one.

The Soloflex Man.

In the ad, a male torso worthy of a Renaissance sculpture sheds his tank shirt, bathed in half-light, his image imposed over a workout machine. The guy's buff arms are suspended above his head. His face is blocked by the stretched cotton of his shirt, shielding him from the adulation of the millions of women whose pulses have been raised by this photograph.

I tape the corners of the glossy page against our kitchen cabinet door, then stand back to admire the view. We bow our heads in awe.

"Look at him," I half-whisper. "He doesn't even need a face."

Audrey blinks. "We're home now."

"Should we give him a name?" Kimmer asks. "How about Gus? Or Jack?"

"He's too perfect for a name," I say.

Kimmer rambles on. "...Toby? Tony?"

"NOT Tony!" Trina and Audrey shout.

I pitch the roll of Scotch tape at Kimmer's feet and she bolts upright on the ugly orange sofa bed. We don't talk about hot punker boy Tony from The Shore anymore. Not when Trina is conscious, anyway.

"*Whoo*-ny?' Kim says. "I didn't say Tony. It's a mean and terrible lie. I forgot myself."

"I'll let it go this time," says Trina through tight teeth, pushing herself off her mound of boxes. "One more thing." She rips a shining bottle of Johnny Walker Gold out of one of our cartons, unscrews the cap, and swigs. "*Now* we're home." She slams the bottle against the countertop.

"HEY, ladies!"

A man's voice resonates from our front doorway, far too loudly. The four of us startle like frogs. My heart ping-pongs in my chest. Audrey adjusts her sweatshirt dress. Trina finishes buttoning her pants.

"You girls pledgin' allegiance to the gym?"

A lanky guy in a flannel shirt rubs his palms together in front of us, standing in our tiny foyer. Feathered hair falls over a wide set of plastic-rimmed eyeglasses. He's tall but hunched over like he doesn't have the confidence to stand up completely straight.

"Geez, are you trying to send us through the roof?" Audrey says.

"Technically, we'd hit the first floor," says Kimmer, kicking her legs against the sofa. "This is the basement."

Trina lunges forward. "What's your deal, pal, and who the hell let you in here?"

"You left the door open." The guy's face goes pink. "Sorry to rattle you, *neighbors*. It's just I saw you four girls carrying a couch through the hallway yesterday, which is something you don't see every day. So, I thought I'd stop in and say hi." He smiles.

We don't smile back—except for Trina's smirk, which shows itself even in the most questionable of circumstances.

"I'm Russell, from A3," he says. A faint air of marijuana rises from his flannel as he reaches to shake hands. "Glad to meetcha." He pumps Trina's palm, then works his way around the room, tripping on the corner of a box marked *Unmentionables*. "It's not a bad shit-show around here, as long as the river doesn't come in. *Huh, huh*." He shakes with Audrey.

"Does that happen?" Audrey flexes her palm as if something sticky has tainted it.

"Not this year." Russell claps his hands together in front of himself. "So which one a' you lives here?"

Shoulders shrug around the room like a chorus of ejected Pop-Tarts. "All of us," I say.

"*All four of you?*" He pushes his glasses further up his nose.

"Don't tell the landlord," Audrey begs. She and Trina are the only two on the lease. It took some doing to get Trina the future lawyer to falsify a document, but she made the compromise.

"You're gonna be *all sorts a'* cramped." Russell laughs.

"Maybe," I say. "Just don't rat us out, huh?" I feel the ghosts of 20 dust bunnies climbing up to my elbows, and I sneeze. "Although if you have a vacuum cleaner, we may need to borrow it."

"Fella, we're a little busy painting ourselves up," Audrey says, ushering him to the door. "Next time, knock first, instead of invading the apartment."

He turns his back to the green hunk of a door. "Right. If you need any little thing, you can come a-knockin' upstairs," he says. "Or you can find me working at the motorcycle shop on Bridge Street."

He doesn't look like a biker, but what the hell. I wonder about any person who lives in this building for anything other than a strategic summer gig.

Audrey swings the door open wider for him.

Russell's goofy grin fades as he ambles into the hallway, trailing his aura of cannabis. "By the way." He pulls a mini baggie over the hem of his pocket as he backs into the hall. "Lemme know if you're up for a *Welcome to the Building* Party."

Audrey shoves the door closed.

"Well, whistle my Woodstock." Kimmer lifts our flying saucer of an ashtray off the floor. Ashes dance downward in a twist. "Did you get a whiff of that guy? How many terrariums do you think he's growing upstairs?" She heads to the garbage can to dump the ashtray. The entire kitchen consists of a few cabinets, a hefty refrigerator, and a mid-century range. No dishwasher. Which is ironic in a restaurant town.

"He was interesting," says Trina.

"The only *interesting* thing is that he didn't bother to help us with that couch," says Audrey. "Thanks a lot, guy."

"Let's file him away." Trina flips open an imaginary lockbox, sliding a non-existent index card inside. "Russell, A3. He might be useful."

I'm not sure what *use* Trina might be planning for Russell. Especially since she doesn't own a motorcycle.

CHAPTER 4

STILL ALMOST JUNE—Drazine's
Sunglasses At Night

We finally perfect ourselves and clomp down the street, where the sprawling synthesizers of Depeche Mode rattle the glass windows of Drazine's front stairwell. This place is the jewel of New Hope's various riverside attractions, which include bars, galleries, antique shops, drag venues, and a first-rate regional theater.

The stairwell gets darker each step we take up toward the club's entrance, which is guarded by a set of over-muscled henchmen at the top of the stairs. Trina plants her hands on her hips as we scale the landing. "Joseph Keller!" she calls.

A black-bearded, concrete wall of a guy wheels around. "Trina Moran!" She's engulfed by his bludgeon-worthy arms.

"Are you back at The Helena?" asks Joseph. The Helena Inn is a converted, historic farmhouse rumored to be haunted by the spirit of a little girl. Everything in New Hope has had another life: A church rebirthed as a restaurant. A tree fort converted into a biker bar. You can enter here as one thing and emerge as whatever you like.

"I'm at *La Chambre Rose* this year," Trina announces. Her chest literally puffs out, showing off her bleach-splattered t-shirt under a denim jacket full of metal pins. Or maybe she's just showing off her boobs.

Joseph takes a step back. "*La Chambre Rose?* Top of the pack, now, aren't we?"

"I don't like to make a big thing about it," she says.

"Yes, she does," says Audrey, extending a hand. "Audrey Mallick. Nice to meet you." Audrey decided to go with the leather sash after all, cinching her sweatshirt dress tight enough to make Norma Kamali jealous.

"Nice to meet you, too," Joseph says. The dim obscurity of the club's dance space looms beyond his boat-like shoulders, as a whacked-out Haysi Fantayzee song starts playing on the sound system. A screen the size of a drive-in movie projects music videos on the back wall.

"Who are these lovely women you've brought us today, Trina?" Joseph asks.

"This is Jess." Trina points and I nod my head, trying to get a look at what video is playing. It doesn't match the song. "And Kimmer."

"Kim-a-*whatter?*" he laughs.

"Kim Meredith Thorsen," Kimmer corrects, extending a hand. Joseph pulls the back of her palm to his lips and kisses it.

He squeezes her tiny fingers. "Awesome," he says.

"Excuse me—why aren't you intimidated?" Kimmer asks, staring at him through an abundance of black kohl eyeliner. "Do you know how long it took me to get my hair to do this?"

"Beautiful *and* funny," Joseph says. "Next time don't keep your friends a secret, Trina."

"*Hello?*" Trina sputters, waving her fingers between Kimmer and Joseph, breaking his stare. "We haven't been hiding. We just moved into an apartment on Main."

Joseph lets go of Kimmer's hand. "Not the Sandler apartment building on the corner of Waterloo?"

"What's wrong with the corner of Waterloo?" I ask. Just what my over-developed sense of danger needs to hear. We've moved into New Hope's version of The Overlook Hotel. *Abandon all hope, ye who enter with boxes of art supplies.*

"Are you in the basement?" Joseph asks.

"*Shit.*" I stamp my scrunch boot.

"Anybody can climb through those bottom-floor windows," Joseph tells me. "And keep an eye on your neighbors. Do you girls pack?"

"We haven't even unpacked," says Kimmer.

"I mean weapons," says Joseph.

"Oh, please," says Audrey. "We're college students, not warrior tribeswomen."

Joseph waves us inside, gesturing an okay to his bouncer brethren. He knows Trina is legal already. Little does he know I'm not. This is convenient since the name on my very impressive fake ID doesn't match the introduction Trina just made. The jig would be up for me.

"I've got something for you ladies. Be right back." He tweaks Kimmer's shoulder, then heads to the other end of the club. We file against the dark bar as a Howard Jones song asks us to contemplate the meaning of love.

"Is he serious about the danger level around here?" I ask Trina. "I thought this was basically a safe town for women."

"Jess, relax. You're running the feature film in your head again," she says.

"But what if some lowlife breaks in and loots my tuition savings?" I ask.

"You don't have any tuition savings," Trina says.

"I still can't cope with a home invasion."

"No one's getting invaded." Trina smirks. "At least not without an invitation. Or a condom."

"We certainly won't be molested in *this* place." I look around the cavernous dance floor at the small scattering of well-groomed men who are completely ignoring us. "I know the culture around here is pretty alternative, but have I *open-minded* myself into a heterosexual romantic wasteland?"

"Not if Joseph is any indication," says Trina. "And so what if the bar's empty? That means we own it."

"And we can hear each other," shouts Audrey. "Sort of."

I notice my section of the bar is wet and lean past Trina for an all-purpose cocktail napkin.

Her nose twitches. "Oh God," she says, pulling a section of my hair toward her face. "Are you wearing that God-awful *Eau de Prom Night* shit again? You reek like a fire at the Love's Baby Soft factory."

"Hate to say it, but I can smell twelfth-grade prom from here," Audrey adds.

I whip my hair away from them. "No insulting Drew's perfume. Your olfactory senses need to stop working overtime."

"Sorry," Audrey says. "I forgot you were still Drew-sensitive."

A Thomas Dolby staple drones on about *SCI-ence!* Kimmer shimmies onto a stool between me and Trina, leaning over to get the bartender's attention. He's in a lustrous, smoke-colored shirt pinned with a name tag that reads "Reg." He disregards us, even though we're nearly the only people in the place. I shoot him a smile as he cleans a line of rocks glasses with a linen napkin.

I poke Trina with my elbow. "Do you know this guy?"

"No." She squints into the darkness as synthesizers zing through the air around us. "But I bet his name is Reg."

"Too bad," I say. "I like having an *in* with the bartender." This typically includes flirting with said bartender. "What percentage, you think?"

"Twenty percent," says Trina. Chance. Of being straight. This is New Hope.

"I'm not convinced yet," I say. Reg stops wiping a bar glass long enough to acknowledge me. "How much is a VO and ginger?" I ask him, leaning over the bar. In a low-cut, mesh-covered tank.

Reg smacks the glass on the countertop and rolls his eyes, exhaling exasperation. "How much have you *got?*"

A shot runs through my gut. Every ounce of sexy-girl power I ever possessed drains through the soles of my boots. Blood whirs in my ears, accentuated by the electronic drums of a Pat Benatar anthem that starts bleating in the background.

It's one of those moments when you realize you must have said the *stupid* thing. Because you don't know any better. It becomes clear to me in this moment that grown-up people in sophisticated restaurant communities don't ask how much the drinks cost. They just drink.

I want to know better. I want to at least be mature enough to sit at a bar and order a decent whiskey, without inspiring disdain over how pathetically broke and childlike I am.

Reg shakes his head, blond Duran Duran hair bobbing. "Forget I said that."

"*How much have I got?*" I repeat, still absorbing how clueless I must look to him.

"Forget it, really," he says, running a hand through his John Taylor mop. "VO and ginger coming up."

"If that's okay," I say, slinking back into my bar stool.

"It's fine," he says.

Audrey and Trina order Scotch on the rocks. Kimmer gets wine. None of them are idiotic enough to ask for pricing or to beat their lashes at a guy who doesn't prefer their gender in an attempt to curry his favor.

Joseph Keller swaggers back to us, tapping a baseball bat in his palm. It's splintered on one side with a chunk missing from the bottom grip. He extends the Louisville Slugger to Kimmer. "For you."

"God, am I *up?*" she asks, swooping a lacquered tidal wave of blonde hair out of her face. Her black cardigan sways open, showing a white button-up blouse underneath, sparkly brooch at the top of the collar like an accent mark.

"I'll feel better about you girls if you keep this thing in your house," says Joseph.

I run my fingers across the rough lines of the bat in Joseph's hands, paint thinning along the veins of wood. "Is this really necessary?"

"Put it by your window," says Joseph. "And steer clear of Dean Clayton upstairs from you. He's a bruiser."

I've been hearing some thumping through our ceiling at night. I wondered if it was one of New Hope's famous ghosts. Instead, maybe it's Dean Clayton.

"We haven't met a Dean," says Audrey. "We met a Russell. Strange guy. Says he's a biker."

"He reeks of weed," I say. "Kind of creepy."

"Russell Lee's not a biker. He's a mechanic," says Joseph. "He's harmless." Joseph sidles closer to Kimmer's bar stool. She kicks her pumps against the foot rail. "Anybody bothers you, you crack their skull," Joseph tells her, slapping the meat of the bat in his palm.

"Skull-bashing goes against Kimmer's oath as a nurse-in-training," I say.

"The oath is for doctors, not nurses," Kimmer says, sipping wine. "But I'm still not up for skull-busting. I'm a nurturer."

A Dead or Alive song kicks into gear on the sound system. On the video screen behind us, groupies with spidery, black cotton-candy hair sing along with Pete Burns in a stadium full of flags.

"Something's calling us," Audrey says, gesturing toward the unused space of the dance floor. "Nature abhors a vacuum."

"Yes. Time to dance," I tell Joseph. Audrey, Trina, and I start to gravitate toward the floor, leaving our drinks behind. Kim takes a step to join us, but Joseph grabs her arm.

"You're staying with me," he says.

"I am?" says Kim.

"How about we get to know each other?" asks Joseph.

"*Okay.*" She relaxes against the bar.

We girls dominate a bunch of songs, all heavy techno guitar riffs and gummy-sounding English accents. The Cure. Siouxsie and the Banshees. And a screechy, early number by The Police. We ironically sing in unison about being lonely, swinging our arms and canting our knees until sweat builds under my piece-y bangs.

"We've gotta take you to The Fall Out Club in Philly," Trina tells me, her caramel-colored bob swishing. "They play true couch-breaking music. You'll find the best of everything there. Slam dancers. Punks. Hardcore types. Androgyny up the wazoo." Spotlights in red and blue wash past, dancing with us.

Audrey leans in toward me. "It's the closest you'll get to London around here."

"*When* are we going?" I ask, hungry to get out into the world. Where people are living. And partying. And making cool, gorgeous, artsy stuff. Not just *studying* about artsy stuff and getting rebuffed by stuck-up bartenders. Or spending time at my grandmothers, waiting for life to begin.

A guy in jazz pants elbows past me as we head back to the bar. He beats us there, hoisting his torso over a section of the Formica, babbling to Reg the bartender about the Canal Stage I. The two of them entwine tongues like they just met on a deserted island.

"Do you think that's core curriculum in bartending school?" I ask Trina, as Reg and his partner continue to swallow each other, half-draped along the bar.

"Welcome to *life-as-it-is*," says Trina. "This is what you wanted, Jess. To experience the world outside our college bubble."

"*Right.*" I hop back onto my bar stool. "We're very cultured and savvy members of the real world." The lights of the Lambertville Bridge bounce like Roman candles off the river through the windows behind us, all to the strains of "Rock the Casbah."

Kimmer digs a pair of oversized Ray-Ban aviators out of her purse, modeling them for us. "Absolutely. Aren't we sophisticated?" She grabs the corner of the frame with one hand. "Cultured and savvy and blind. I can't see a thing in these."

Trina tilts her head in recognition. "Wait. Whose sunglasses are those?"

"They were sitting in our kitchen." Kimmer reaches for the edge of the bar but misses it entirely.

"You didn't ask whose they were before you took them?" Trina asks.

"I thought maybe I loaned them to my other personality," says Kimmer.

Audrey leans over. "Trina, *you* know whose glasses those are."

"*Shit.* They're Tony's, aren't they?" Trina plucks the sunglasses off Kimmer's finely-shaped nose and gazes into the smudged lenses. "Did he give them to you, Auge, or to me?"

"He gave them to me," Audrey says.

"Lemme see," I grab the Ray-Bans and pop them over my eyes. The already-dark club turns the color of the Atlantic Ocean. At night. "Tony gave you a lot of things, Audrey." I laugh, spilling drops of my drink to the floor.

"Or more like," Trina says, straightening her hiked-up t-shirt, "he *took* something from you."

"And I never want it back!" Audrey shouts.

Trina whips the sunglasses off my face. The club becomes strangely bright again.

"I'm keeping the fucking frames." Trina zips them into her purse with finality. Kimmer shifts in her seat. I wince, not wanting to pore back over the forbidden *Tony* stories.

Tony was Trina's steamy-eyed, life-long, punker-boy crush and former neighbor. Last summer, she invited Audrey to move in with her, Tony, and a couple of other co-eds in an illegal studio apartment in Ocean City. A bunch of hot, sandy, post-adolescents, together on the Jersey Shore.

Things happened.

Trina gulps her Scotch. "Ten years living next door to the guy and all I get is a scraped pair of Ray Bans." She turns to Audrey. "You, on the other hand, got—"

"I thought we were never talking about that again!" shouts Audrey.

"*Fine*," Trina snips over the nasal rantings of the Ramones' "Rock and Roll High School." I choke on my drink and avoid eye contact. "Not another word," she says.

For a guy we're not allowed to talk about, we sure hear a fuckload about Tony.

CHAPTER 5

JUNE 1984—Capresi's
Dumb Waiters

It's time to put my restaurant training into action, although I'm not sure Rickie the Pixie Dishwasher's crash course in table-setting was exactly comprehensive.

The *alfresco* patio at Capresi's fills by the minute with youthful guests in formalwear. When it's 86 degrees out and people are in wedding clothes, no one wants to crowd into a humid bar room.

Giorgio mixes a rum and coke. "You've been a cocktail waitress before, correct?" he asks, spritzing soda into a glass with a sprayer nozzle. "That much of your resume is authentic?"

"I served drinks for my uncle's bowling league once." I don't mention the flaming shots, and the moment of distraction where my bony elbow toppled the glasses across the bar like incandescent dominoes. Blue and twisting Sambuca flames blaze through my memory with a hot *whoosh*.

"We'll be more crowded than any bowling night this afternoon," says Giorgio. He places the rum and coke amid five lovely daiquiris on a round tray in front of me. Glasses clink. So do my teeth.

"Here," he says, nudging the tray of cocktails at me. The glasses create the palette of a watercolor sunset, revolving around the Coke. "Lift the tray over your head."

"*What?*" The suncatchers wink in the rafters above me.

"Balance it on your fingertips." He pulls another tray from below the bar, "then lift it high." He spirals the empty tray into the air with the dexterity of a circus performer. "*Voilà.* You'll float past any obstacle."

People who know me don't ask me to balance things over my head. I'm an insurance risk.

"The heaviest drink goes in the middle," he says. "Work around a center of gravity. It's now or never, Jessica." The patio continues to swell with guests. "Think of how powerful you are."

I think of all the expensive things I want to do and see in England. I need to learn this if I want to earn my way there. Or *whoosh*, it all goes away.

Giorgio crosses his arms, waiting. I breathe deep and slide the tray of drinks onto my splayed fingertips. I push it toward the ceiling like the Statue of Liberty's torch.

"Keep your elbow soft and close to your ear," he says. "And *smile.*" My lips part to reveal teeth. He flicks his fingers at me. *Try it.*

I maneuver towards the patio, tray suspended, stepping around buzzing guests. I somehow keep control of my lanky and hazardous elbows. Suddenly I'm Miss America, striding, turning on my heels, pacing back to Giorgio, lowering the tray to the counter, drinks still intact. I smile widely.

He taps his hands together in applause. "Very good," he says. "If you spill, make sure it's just on you. Now go back out there and be my waitress."

The cocktails are a dreamy rainbow of icy delights, accented with swizzle sticks and striped straws. I slide the tray back onto the pads of my fingers, surprisingly without a wobble.

My free hand steadies the vaulted tray as I let out a few *excuse me's* and head toward a group of guests. The bride passes by me, wrapped in a bodice like a calla lily, drop-waisted ruffles descending to the floor. Giddy, overheated bridesmaids in blue satin dresses and pointy-toed pumps wander around the slate floor. People dip into serving dishes full of shrimp puffs at the dais buffet like gnats on the surface of a pond. I inhale the lacquered hair spray of each woman that drifts near me.

Surrounded by the crowd, I safely lower the cocktails and steady the tray against my rib cage. I distribute drinks to the correct people without even a spill. I start to believe in miracles. Towering ushers in matching cummerbunds pluck mini quiches off gilded plates on the dais behind me.

"Miss?" A bridesmaid with baby's breath in her French braid stops me. I tuck my empty tray into the crook of my elbow.

"What can I get you?" The tray dampens my blouse. I flip it over.

"Is this the restaurant where Jessica Savitch bought it?" She tugs her date closer by the arm.

"*Excuse me?*" I ask.

"Where did Jessica Savitch die?" The bridesmaid's date has lavender sweat crescents generating in the pits of his shirt.

Newscaster Jessica Savitch and her dinner date got confused in a rainstorm last year. They drove off a parking lot landing and plunged into the canal, drowning horribly in the mud. No one will stop talking about it. "That didn't happen at this restaurant," I say.

"Can you see the spot from here?" Braided Bridesmaid asks. The puffy, globe-like shoulders of her dress nearly skim her earrings.

I blink, incredulous. "That happened at *La Chambre Rose*, further down Main." My finger tilts in that direction.

Braided Bridesmaid smiles at her sweaty guy. "We'll have to go there." She chuckles.

I slowly back away from them. All around me, girls in custom-dyed, matching shoes order frilly cocktails. Guests jostle each other as the crowd multiplies.

I jot down orders, then turn on my tennies and head back to Giorgio, who practically hangs over the bar to greet me. "I knew you could do it!"

"It's a jungle out there." I tear a sheet from my pad. "But here's our next order. One couple asked me where Jessica Savitch died."

"*Horrid.*" Giorgio shudders. "They're running 'death tours' through town, if you can believe it." He pours vodka shots toward an array of glasses. "Don't mind them. Tell Teddy we need the blender."

I lean toward the waitress station. "Hey, Teddy!" I shout.

Giorgio cringes mid-pour. "In person. Do not *cat call* across the bar," he says.

Teddy the chef pops his head into the pass-through and waves for me to come into the kitchen. I grip my order pad and push through the doors, where chafing dishes brimming with scallops Mornay, chicken divan, and roasted asparagus wait to be taken to the patio. A mellow scent of butter and cream drift toward my nose. Teddy is nowhere to be seen, though.

I peek around a rack of metal shelving.

"Teddy, we need the blender out—"

A saucepan BONGS behind my skull with the force of the freaking Bronze Age, reverberating through my body. My order pad dances in the air before diving into the corner of a gelatinous chafing dish full of scallops, the pad now poking caddy-corner out of the sauce like a garnish.

When I swing around, Teddy holds a pot the size of a war helmet and an industrial steel ladle over his head in victory. His gut burbles up and down as he laughs at me. The ringing in my ears could drown-out the Mormon Tabernacle Choir.

He juts the ladle at my face. "*Ha*! I knew I'd get you!"

"*Oh, for Christ's sake!*" I pluck my order pad out of the scallop quicksand and wipe buttercup-colored Mornay sauce off the pages with a dishtowel. "Did I just destroy a whole tray of bridal seafood?"

Teddy sweeps a ladle into the dented corner of the Mornay glop, skimming up the tainted section and whapping it into the sink in one motion. The ladle bangs against the porcelain.

"*Fixed.*" Teddy smooths the disturbed portion with the flourish of a painter. He tosses the ladle back into the sink and hikes up his chef pants, belt buckle clinking. "Always keep your sense of humor."

"Get a real life."

"This *is* my life." He huffs out another laugh. "I like life. It makes everything ironic."

"Oh, please. I can't wait to grow up and never have to waitress again."

"*Lighten up.*" Teddy washes his hands and tugs his shirt straight. "The minute you grow up, you'll wish you were bumming around for the summer, in a place like this. Then you'll be sad you didn't go for somebody real, like me. Instead of your punk rock boyfriend."

"I don't have a *punk rock boyfriend*," I say.

I think of Drew, who's not at all Mr. Punk Rock. He's an astrophysics major and Led Zeppelin fan who thinks he can study his way to micromanaging the universe. But he's more Andy Kaufman than Andy Taylor. More David Lee Roth than David Bowie.

I'm shot back to the first day I brought Drew to my dorm, which I've named "The Ceiling Incident."

In our corridor, Drew took a long look at the cinder block walls of the cream-colored, tenth-floor hallway.

"Sturdy construction," he said, flattening a palm on each opposing wall like Stretch Armstrong, biceps straining under a Giants jersey. He nudged the toes of his Pro Keds against the cinder blocks and started to climb.

"Drew . . . must you?"

He let out an evil-scientist laugh, ascending into the dust-covered air ducts, gazing down at me, like God. Tendons tightened in his neck. In a fake bass voice, he said, "I watch you from on-high."

Audrey pulled open our dorm room door and peered into the hall as if prepping to cross the Forbes Avenue bus lane. "Weren't you bringing your boyfriend today, the Carnegie Mellon physics guy?"

I blinked and pointed upward.

She padded into the hallway, barefoot except for the bands at the bottom of her stirrup pants. Drew was hanging over the two of us like a window swag, his head between the ceiling pipes.

His eyes bulged. "I'm Spiderman."

I've always had a thing for strangeness. Zebra-striped pumps. Lene Lovich. Teal fishnets. And Drew.

But would Audrey feel the same way? There was a guy hanging from our ceiling.

She pointed to the grate that brushed against Drew's hair. "If you're here to clean the air vent, you missed a spot."

Drew wiggled his eyebrows and dropped to the floor next to me, lanky and crouched.

"She gets to live," he said.

Once in a Lifetime

A weird smile crosses my lips at the memory as Teddy the chef stares me down. I bite my lip, reminding myself that however brilliantly whacked-out Drew is, he's past-tense now. Our pairing has suffered a demotion to long-distance, semi-dating status.

"Aw, come on," says Teddy. "I know girls like you. Always hanging out with the rock-and-roll poster boys."

"*I wish.*" I take a heated step toward the kitchen out-door.

Teddy's barrel-like form blocks me. "Jessica," he says.

I plant my hands on my hips.

"Blender's on that shelf."

I gather up the appliance and push through the out-door, an electrical cord waving its tail in my footsteps. It's a struggle for me to keep the glass pitcher from toppling off its base. I feel my order pad sticking to the inside of my apron pocket as I slide the blender onto the counter.

Giorgio uses it to grind an attractive-looking fuchsia daiquiri, which he adds to my next tray of drinks. I balance the tray high and successfully deliver cocktails to three other sets of guests without any injuries or spontaneous flames. I pass a sign screwed to the wall that reads, "Maximum Capacity: 50 Persons."

"How many people are in this party?" I ask Giorgio, arranging the next set of glasses according to my tray's center of gravity.

"*Shhh.* Ninety. But you didn't hear it from me." He flicks his fingers at me again in a *go* gesture. I hoist the tray of pink and orange frothy things into the air and head out.

My *excuse me's* can barely be heard as I navigate the sea of people. They mill in a sweaty mob so tight the floor becomes a malformed blur underneath me.

"Coming through," I call. "Behind you." My free hand taps a few shoulders. Oblivious couples burst with laughter, standing in my way. The slate dips and pokes under my sneakers as I work the floor.

An absurdly tall usher throws his arm in gesticulation and bumps my tray, instantly apologizing. A shot of adrenaline zips through me as I grab the tray's rim.

I freeze.

For a split second, the tray is fine.

That moment ends.

A frozen strawberry daiquiri clunks top over bottom, surrendering icy fuchsia onto my shoulder. The next glass topples down my arm. The guests are so loud I can barely hear the breakage as the glasses hit the floor.

"*Watch out!*" I shout. There's no space to lower the tray without whipping the rest of the drinks onto fine gray suits and shiny pastel cocktail dresses with overblown shoulders. One by one, the drinks come down. I aim the downspout away from anything other than my mini-skirted penguin suit, shirk wet bangs out of my eyes, and make a desperate noise that no one hears but me.

Finally, the guests step back. A last drink falls, a baby bird tipping out of its nest. I catch the glass as it bounds off my shoulder.

Strawberry slush cascades down my blouse. It's like I'm suddenly in a wet T-shirt contest.

"Did anyone get splashed?" I ask. Spectators shake their heads. I hide my chest from view with the tray as blended ice seeps through my white waitressing blouse.

I imagine the pain my feet will be in when I'm forced to pound the pavement again in search of a new job, without even the benefit of a recommendation. *There goes my London tuition money.*

Giorgio's dumbwaiter of a jaw hits bottom as I re-enter the bar, trailing wet, pink splotches. In my mind, I see my mosaic art classes canceled . . . Adam Ant's chiseled and striped face receding away from me . . . my coveted King's Road shopping trips becoming more and more remote. . . .

"Don't tell me—" Giorgio gasps.

"Even with the tray in the air," droplets ping to the carpet around me, "the men are still taller." I shake melted daiquiri off my hands.

Giorgio passes me a nubby white bar towel. "How many dry-cleaning bills do I owe?"

"None. I took it all for the team." I try to figure out how to wipe the front of my blouse in the presence of a member of the opposite sex, orientation notwithstanding, without humiliating myself any further.

"Is the bride in tears?" Giorgio asks.

I dab my damp mid-section and squint past the ocean of guests on the patio floor. The bride and groom pose in our garden gazebo, ivy crawling through its gunmetal filigree. A photographer dotes on them. "I don't know."

Updates to my waitressing resume flash before my eyes. I pull my sticky order pad out of my apron and surrender it on top of the bar, hanging my head. So much for my semester of art classes in London.

Whoosh.

Giorgio sighs and rests a hand on my saturated shoulder. "Go home and change," he says.

I look up. "And then . . . *come back?*"

"Somebody's got to work the buffet tonight," he says. "*Rickie, get the broom.*"

The nightmare wedding party shift is over. I shove open our heavy apartment door, shower off the daiquiri juice, and change into a tiny pair of shorts. Giorgio gave me a few hours before I have to be back for the regular dinner shift.

I see that Audrey has tacked a poster of David Bowie from the *Serious Moonlight* tour on the living room wall across from the sofa bed, his fluffed, honey-gloss hair sweeping over his eyes. As I drop onto the couch, a corner of the poster unhitches itself from the wall, slinking in a triangular flap that obscures much of its subject's New Romantic physique. The mutant ringworm water stain on the wall peeks from underneath the poster.

The ringworm is eating David Bowie. I have to rescue him.

Being careful not to damage dear David, I untape the remaining corners of the poster, revealing the additional curl of stain on the drywall. The big, round blemish revolves like a hypnotist's wheel in my mind as I give it a stare, spinning slowly towards me.

I tug a cardboard box from behind the orange velour sofa bed. As I pop open the cardboard flaps, a mix of oil paints and brushes shine up at me. I finger the crinkled aluminum tubes of paint: Viridian. Lamp black. Prussian blue. They feel firm and cool against my palm. I pull brushes from the box like arrows from a quiver.

I head to the bathroom, unhook our vinyl shower curtain from the rod, and shimmy it along the living room floor in front of the stained wall.

Swooping, striping, following the inspiration of the stain, I spend an hour obliterating our wall-based parasite. I transform it into an Op-art vision of flying geometrics on a spiral plane with bright, illusory patches practically levitating off the wall. I accent the painting with shards of a smashed Welch's jelly glass that I sacrifice for the occasion—the one piece of glassware I've broken on purpose today—gluing textured mini-triangles to the surface. *Here begins Jessica's career in New Wave multi-media art*, I tell myself.

When I'm done, our shower curtain is a mess of ebony blotches and effervescent smears, wrinkled across the floor. My arms are cross-hatched with paint slashes that a psychologist might find disquieting. I lie on the sofa bed with my legs sticking up in the air, my head hanging off the bottom of the couch cushions, viewing the mural upside-down.

This gives me *perspective*. The swirls and streaks jostle each other in my mind.

Trina's hefty keys chime in the door as she pushes her way into the foyer. I toss myself off the couch and jump to standing, which gives me a bit of a headrush.

I'm in the middle of a downed shower liner, barefoot and besmirched with paint. Cheap plastic curtain rings are sprinkled around the rug like discarded bangle bracelets.

"Holy shit." Trina's purse thuds on the kitchen table. "Nice work, Mrs. Warhol."

I rub my thumb over a stripe of black paint on my forearm. "It's more Frank Stella than Warhol, actually."

Trina points. "Didn't that used to be a juice glass?"

"It went to a good cause." I step back and spread my arms toward the mural. "I call it, *Attack of the Wall*."

"Yeah." Trina folds her arms. "You realize you owe each of us girls a hundred bucks now."

"*What?*"

"Good luck getting our security deposit back with your *mixed media* shit on there."

The recognition clonks against my brain like a cartoon frying pan.

Trina smirks. "You're such an apartment virgin." She escapes into the bedroom, vanishing like my imaginary bank balance.

Whoosh.

CHAPTER 6

JUNE 1984—Sandler Apartments
Talk Talk

On a wooden garage-sale end table, our phone flares to life like a fire alarm, interrupting Audrey's Lysol-spraying session. A rag-tag headband suppresses the uncooperative spears of her hair, as wild sprigs of red escape the band and spill over her forehead. She mists every centimeter of our apartment.

Trina stops dressing for work long enough to pounce on our unmade sofa bed to get at the ringing phone. She swipes up the receiver on the second ring, her caramel bob swinging.

"Hell Hall," she says. "Reception desk." The metal legs of the bed squeak under her weight.

She listens, rolls her eyes, and tosses the receiver at me. An over-generous curl of phone cord flies along with it. "Jessica, you owe me five bucks. Payable immediately. I knew Drew would be the first one to call here."

"*I* didn't," I say.

Audrey stops Lysol-ing long enough to chime in. "Face it. He's a devoted guy, *semi-dating* or not." She sprays the bottom of our foyer closet as if a skunk has taken up residence in there.

I *shush* them and press the hunk of plastic phone against my cheek. "Drew?" I say. "Our phone service was only just turned on. How did you get this number?"

"Where else? Your grandmother." His voice is smooth like warm chocolate.

"That's absolutely devious."

"I'm a guy of many talents," he says. Like this is an ordinary call, in an unconfused relationship. One where no one is threatened by my designs on life.

I stretch along Kimmer's Strawberry Shortcake sheets, the only set we have that fits the pull-out.

"Tell me about the new apartment. Are you excited?"

"The place is filthy," I say into the phone. I study the concentric water rings on our ceiling. Their edges have been dappled with white latex house paint as if someone tried to kill them before they multiplied.

"As in *good filthy*?" Drew is versed in our roommate vernacular.

"As in water damage filthy."

He persists in trying to sound normal. "Have you been painting?"

"I camouflaged the wall with a not-too-terrible mural. But life's been getting in the way. I got hired at a smaller place in town," I say. "They needed me right away."

"Meaning, someone quit, right?" Trina shouts from the kitchen. "*We need you right away* is code for no one wants to work there."

I stifle the mouthpiece with my hand. "Do you mind, Trina? This is *my* conversation." She flashes a rude grin at me.

"Congratulations," Drew says.

I recall our final scene together in the dorms, elevator doors buzzing closed in front of his resolute face. *You can't have everything, Jess*, I can still hear him saying. *Let it go. We need a break from each other.* The elevator doors clomp shut in front of him all over again.

I do not.

I do not *let things go*.

He's out of line getting back in touch with me now. Making like nothing happened. I have to stand my ground. No matter how much his voice sounds like home.

"Drew, why are you calling me?"

He's quiet for a beat. "Can't we talk for two minutes before you bring the ceiling crashing down?"

"No."

"Jesus Christ, Jess."

"What are you looking for here?" I ask into the phone. "You're the one who said we needed to take leave of each other if I wanted to venture off to Europe."

Audrey flits past the sofa bed like a determined hummingbird, misting Lysol through the living room. I wave off the gust with my palm and flip onto my stomach, Strawberry Shortcake sheets wrinkling.

"*See other people*, not take leave," Drew says. "That doesn't mean we never talk to each other again."

"It doesn't?" So this is *semi-dating*. "Forgive me, I'm trying to keep up." I cough as Audrey spritzes our rust-plagued window frame to death. "So, what are the ground rules?" I say to Drew. "We date other people and then . . . what? Report back?"

"I don't want the gory details," Drew tells me. "But if you find someone else you think you belong with, you have to let me know. Agreed?"

"Do you think I'm planning to elope with some guy in London? That's not what the trip is supposed to be about," I say.

"No, it's about your compulsive need to experience the whole world before you're even a senior," says Drew, his tone rising a degree. "As if life won't happen unless you force it."

"How am I supposed to create anything if I don't find something to be freaking thrilled about?"

I want to be neck-deep in something that keeps me up all night. Something so cool I'll be petrified and sick to my stomach at the mere thought of it. I want to dance until I lose my breath. I want to absolutely fry in inspiration.

Then I want to capture the essence of those moments in oils and charcoals and bits of sparkling broken glass and display them to the world, in a piece of art that oozes magic and fear and grace and possibility. I want to find a city. An adventure. A song. *Something.*

To hell with the American Dream. I want a reason to kick and scream.

And as often as my grandmother cheered me on, saying I can be anything I want to be, we all know I'm not going to find those things in the tiny bedroom at the back of her house. And not in the dorms. Maybe not even in this country.

"Jess, life happens when you're not looking," Drew says. "Whether you like it or not."

I watch Audrey freeze mid-spray, fixated in our bathroom doorway. "Oh, for cripe's sakes," she says. "What the hell is with this ceiling?"

I stretch my neck but can't see past the baby-blue porcelain of the 1960's sink. "Drew, I gotta go," I say.

"Right," he answers. "Places to be. Wheels of creation to turn. I just wanted to make sure things were understood between us."

"They're not." I tug the Strawberry Shortcake bedding around me.

"Call me back," he says, "or I'll flood your basement."

"Please don't do that," I say. "I live in the basement." I clunk down the receiver and shut my eyes.

Ammonia pinches my sinuses. My eyelids open to Audrey's bottle of freaking 409 hanging over my face.

"Tag—you're it," she says. The white container dangles. "You get to clean the bathroom."

I accept the bottle of cleanser and roll out of the creaking sofa bed, my toes digging into the cut shag carpet. I head to the bathroom.

The sight of the ceiling stops me short. Panels slope above the tub area as if suspending something engorged. Audrey steps next to me, drying her hands on her oversized Bow Wow Wow concert tee. "I swear that was almost flat yesterday." She adjusts her headband. Spikes of hair shuffle for position.

"Is it even safe?" I peer at the obtuse sweep of ceiling and climb on the edge of the tub. Audrey holds me steady as my index finger makes contact with a bowed, tainted ceiling panel.

Vaguely soft, it diffuses a perfume of mold.

Disturbing.

This town better be a hell of a party, because the housing conditions suck.

CHAPTER 7

ALMOST JULY 1984—The Fall Out Club, Philadelphia
You Spin Me Round

We finally make it to The Fall Out, a punk club on South Street. It took us about two hours to get dressed into our most frightening outfits.

A guy with biceps thick like knotty tree limbs inspects my truly convincing driver's license at the door, flicking his eyes at me. For all intents and purposes, I am Julianne Wolfe tonight, age 22. I've memorized her birthdate and can even fake her signature if asked, after months of practice. I'm proud as hell of this fake ID, which is a necessity in my life since I hang out with girls who all turned 21 before me. This is one of the things that got fucked-up because my parents popped me out when the rest of my friends were approaching toddlerhood.

It's not the only thing my parents fucked up, since each of them then left my universe in their own way, but that's another story.

Meanwhile, God bless the ultra-talented MFA student at Pitt who artfully created a life-size template of the Pennsylvania drivers' license, stood me next to it, and snapped a high-quality instant Polaroid. It cost me 40 bucks for this finely laminated beauty, which keeps me in highball glasses next to my already-legal buddies.

The bulky monster of a doorman at the Fall Out glares at me. I'd smile, but that seems inappropriate for a place like this, where people dress in head-to-toe black, ripped tights, studs, and steel-toed combat boots to protest the sordid state of their collective youth. The girls want to show me hardcore *life as-it-is*, by way of a buzz-saw type band called Killing Joke that's scheduled to play tonight.

Guitar riffs strain through an obscured hallway, its walls plastered with Xeroxed 8 x 10 fliers for previous performers: The Circle Jerks, The Dead Kennedys, Black Flag. This place is what we New Wave types call *authentic*. None of that bubble-gum, Katrina and the Waves "Walking on Sunshine" shit around here. The Pretenders are playing here at the end of the summer. That show's been sold out for months.

A girl paces toward us in the dank hall, clomping in studded stilettos. She wears a leather jacket and a cap with chain links tacked across the brim, and leather ankle-length pants. Her face is a shambles of white powder and thick tracts of eye makeup.

"Ow!" barks Kimmer. "Excuse you. You stepped on my favorite foot." Leather Girl trudges on down the hall, not even gracing us with a glance.

Trina pulls Kimmer aside. "Will you get with the program, please? This is not a comedy club."

"And that wasn't a clown shoe," Kimmer says. "Unless it was the special dominatrix version." She limps her next few steps.

"Do I look severe enough to be in here?" I ask Trina as we navigate the shadows of the hallway. "I'm worried."

"You're always worried," Trina says. "Just keep your eyes low and your mouth shut." She turns to the lot of us. "Seriously—jokes are not *punk*. Don't embarrass me, people."

Audrey is Amazon tall. Trina's black eyeliner is angry, and her hair is blunt enough to be positively fascist. Kimmer is sprayed-up Debbie Harry gorgeous, so she doesn't need to be scary. I'm somewhere in-between, not brave enough to screw up my hair with dye or an overdose of Aqua Net. I gel it behind my ears for a swingy, geometric look and piece-y bangs. But I won't qualify as tough unless the Lollipop Guild shows up.

"Squint," Audrey tells me. "That usually adds an intimidation factor."

"That, or people will think I lost a contact lens." I yank at the hem of my leopard-print skirt, which hikes with every step I take.

"Think of it this way. You don't want to mess with anyone." I can smell the wax of Trina's lipstick as she leans over my shoulder. "Sid Vicious used to smash people in the face with drink glasses if they looked at him wrong. Then he knifed his girlfriend. *Allegedly*."

"Then he died," says Audrey. "So we won't be hearing from him tonight. Stay calm."

The Fall Out looks like someone's black-washed, Pirandello-esque nightmare, wallowing in cigarette smoke. It's a cavern with a stage knocked-together in the back, expansive and pitch. A few metalwork tables and blood-red diner chairs line the walls, their upholstery split open like reverse wounds. Kimmer and I elbow our way to claim two bar stools.

She pulls off a pump and rubs her pained foot. "At least my jokes don't injure anyone," Kimmer says. "Those spiked clodhoppers are first-class weapons."

"I'll behave," I tell Trina, as the wet bass notes of a militant Gang of Four song resound through the place.

"Just don't do a Nancy Spungen tonight, and we'll be all right," Trina says.

Even with my keen sense of danger, I think she exaggerates the unseemliness of the place because it makes her feel brave and superior. This is Chestnut Street. Not "The Hunger."

Audrey hails a lanky male bartender in punk guyliner whom I estimate at 40 percent. We're not that far from New Hope. She orders Scotch on the rocks and Trina orders the same, but with higher-shelf liquor.

"You're drinking Dewar's, Trina?" Audrey asks. "I wish I had your deep pockets."

Trina always seems to have more money than any of us. When we visit the campus mailroom, envelopes from her father materialize once per month. These usually signal the appearance of a freaky new blouse from a high-priced South Street New Wave boutique, or leather boots I beg to borrow. And she always snags the best jobs.

She smiles. "Working at The Rose has its perks. My buddy Bryan at the restaurant turned me on to Dewar's. It's smooth stuff."

"Bryan sounds like a buddy," says Audrey.

"He is. Please don't ask him to point out New Jersey, though," Trina says. "You'll forever be marked as a *tourist*."

A tourist is an ugly thing to be. We've quickly learned to identify ourselves as locals, if temporary ones. We've been indoctrinated into the faction of New Hope Servers, a special breed that passes no judgments, imposes no limits, and are all stunningly aware of the exact location of New Jersey.

"We're a pretty tight crew at The Rose," Trina brags. "When you pool tips, everybody pitches in. And Bryan is especially . . . helpful . . . to everyone."

"Everyone in a skirt?" Audrey asks.

"Okay, so he's a big fucking flirt," says Trina. "That shithead."

"*Triii-naaah*," Kimmer says as she adjusts her shoe, "sounds like you're falling *in like*." Sprays of inflexible blonde hair flop over her one eye.

Trina grins as if she's harboring something amusing. "No way," she says. "Like I need that crap." Under better lighting, we might witness some blushing here. But she'd probably whack me with her rocks glass if I pointed it out.

Instead, I pull a bill out of my ankle boot and order a whiskey sour. I'm perpetually on the tightest budget of us all, being the least experienced waitress.

I don't dare ask how much the drink costs this time.

Audrey sidles next to me, her eyebrows raised and ready for action. She leans next to my ear. "Twelve o'clock," she whispers. Well, anywhere else it would be considered a whisper. With the Buzzcocks' "Ever Fallen In Love" blaring in the background, it was still probably shouting. "*Someone staring at you*."

Adrenaline paints a stripe in my stomach. I stretch to get a better view across the bar, swiveling my vinyl barstool.

"*No*—" Audrey grabs my seatback, halting it mid-spin. "He'll know I tipped you off. Blond hair. Or . . . brunette-altered. Bleach streaks in the front."

The bar is lined with shoulder-padded men in brawny blazers. This uniform makes all guys look like brutes who feed at the Pitt football training table. When these jacketed types disrobe, they lose four inches of shoulders.

"Is he one of the scary ones?" I ask.

"Maybe." Audrey swirls her glass of Scotch. "Long earring, black jacket. Look . . . *slowly*."

"Every guy in here has an earring and a black jacket," I say.

"Everyone in *Philadelphia* has an earring and a black jacket," says Trina, elbowing between us. "Who are we scoping?"

"Bleach job due north," Audrey says. She points an unobtrusive pinky finger. "Semi-Adonis."

Trina's eyes dart toward the guy. "Huh. I wouldn't kick him," she says. Meaning, out of bed. Part of our roommate rating system. *I wouldn't kick him out of bed.*

I try to get a subtle, side-eye view of the somewhat-blond guy, who's leaning over his bottle of Guinness as if he's protecting it from danger. Amazing synths zing through the club as "Lips Like Sugar" discharges from the sound system. It makes the staring guy more exciting.

The guy-linered bartender hands Kimmer a Heineken then plants a highball glass full of foamy liquid in front of me, decorated with fruit and a swizzle stick. I offer him a bill, but he waves me away. "From that guy." He tosses a thumb over his shoulder.

Blond Streaks.

Now that I have an excuse, I finally take a better look. He has European-esque bone structure and a steamy stare ratcheted up to full power. The line of silver that swings from his one ear could break skin.

Audrey pushes herself off the bar. "Ten points for Jess."

I smile and mouth "thank you" at the guy, since there's no way my voice can compete with the club's speakers. Staring through platinum spikes of hair, he tilts the bottom of his bottle toward me, lifting just one eyebrow.

Trina leans in. "Wrap him in a bow and take him home," she says. "Or I will."

"You will *not*," I insist, checking out what I can of his physique. Under the big black jacket. "He's lovely, though, huh? *Lov-e-ly*."

I spear the cherry in my drink with the swizzle stick and raise it to my lips, *slowly*. I roll the edge of my tongue against the plumpness of the fruit, watching the guy all the time. Blond Streaks' gaze stays locked. As I methodically pull the cherry off the stick with my teeth, I imagine Drew laughing at my dramatics. A pang of guilt laces my stomach tight.

I shake it off. It's time to branch out. The cherry lingers between my teeth.

Blond Streaks' stare could melt my fucking highball glass. Cigarette smoke wafts across the bar space between us.

"Are you kidding with that fruit routine?" Trina says, jostling me with an elbow.

"Works every time," I say.

"Or you could go talk to him," says Trina.

I chew the cherry. "Let him come here." I swivel away from the guy and swig my drink. "Is he getting up?"

"Nope," Trina says.

Kimmer hoists herself onto a foot rail for a better look. "Maybe he's parked in a handicapped zone and can't walk." She slides back onto her barstool. "Anyway, Trina, tell us about this Bryan character."

Trina tilts back her Scotch and swallows. "He makes me laugh." She pulls her fingers through the bottom of her sprayed, brown bob. "The other night, some tourist ordered the braised Long Island duckling in rosemary glaze, and I'm trailing him," she says, sing-songing her way through the story.

"*Girls*," I say. "Is that blond guy getting up?"

"NO!" Audrey and Trina shout together.

"Anyway, Bryan picks up a plate full of duckling," Trina goes on, "balancing it like he's in the Russian Circus. He says, '*Okay dokes, who gets the fuck?*'"

Kimmer bursts into laughter, slapping her Heineken to the bar. I pretend to laugh, and instead swivel in my seat to steal another look at Blond Streak guy, still stooped over his beer bottle. No longer looking at me. "Jesus, he's really just gonna sit there?"

"I thought you were letting him come to you." Trina smirks at me.

"You got a drink out of it, no strings attached," says Kimmer. "Who can complain?"

"I can," I say. "Finally, a straight guy looks at me, and he just *sits there*."

Joy Division drones through the speakers and a few black-coated brutes gravitate to the dance floor. They plod gracelessly across the black floorboards, shaking and slumping.

"Oh, ladies, that is not attractive," Audrey says. She rests her Scotch on the bar.

"Looks like the Bozo Bus just let out," says Kimmer.

Audrey nudges Kimmer off her barstool. "Let's show them how it's done. Time to send the Bozos packing."

Kimmer limps, favoring her stomped-on foot. Trina drains her Scotch and shoves off the bar. She yanks my arm as the music hits full flail capacity.

"*But . . . but . . .*" I gesture vaguely in the direction of Lovely Blond Streaks, who's left a void in his place at the bar. A harrowing cultist-type moves into his seat, some guy in a black trench coat, thick chains, and Pete Burns hair reaching to the ceiling.

I gulp my drink and let the glass smack against the bar. Alcohol plods to the bottom of my stomach just as harshly, delivering a shiver. It buzzes in my brain, amping up the magic of the Aztec Camera song that starts playing.

Trina leans against my ear. "Jess, you can dance, or you can write that guy an engraved invitation on a cocktail napkin to come talk to you," she says. "Pick A or B, before the song ends."

"Let's dance." I leave my glass behind and head for the smoky plane of the dance floor. We girls assume our typical positions, a New Wave square dance, or a human compass. Cobalt and scarlet beams of light swipe past, blurring my vision. We swing our arms, bobbing through a sea of slashed black clothing, intimidating boots, and leatherware.

I revolve to see if Blond Streaks is watching, but he's nowhere.

"Don't worry about that bleachy guy," Audrey shouts in my ear.

"Maybe he's only 80 percent?" adds Trina, swishing her arms to pounding guitars.

I start to get lost in the whiskey-fueled buzz, the smeared starkness of everyone's black, white, and bruise-purple make-up, the fierceness of the androgyny all around. And my beloved synths pouring out of the sound system, racing through my body like blood. "I'm dancing now," I yell. "Nothing matters anymore."

The club distorts at its edges as I whip around the floor, absorbing the bass lines through my boots. We girls dance through two more songs as if our lives depend on it. Spotlights battle through the space like disembodied lightsabers. My arms mistakenly whack a guy whose bangs are a little too Flock of Seagulls for real life, sending half his drink flying. I always hit people when I dance. It can be dangerous.

I head back to the bar, side-stepping the scowl of Flock of Seagulls Guy. I sing along as Chrissie Hynde from the Pretenders devastates "Message of Love" over the speakers.

A powdered-up, skinny girl with a Mohawk and her strangely beautiful leather-wearing boyfriend lean against the bar where we were sitting. The girl has piercings threaded all the way up her nose, like stitches. I tweeze my whiskey glass out from between their two sets of shoulders and tilt back the watered-down remains of my drink, catching ice cubes between my molars.

I don't need that streaky guy, I think. *I don't need any guy*. I crunch an ice chip.

Through the lens of my tilted glass, a tall shadow moves into my light, blotting it out. "You do a hell of a Chrissie Hynde," I hear.

I almost spit out my ice shards.

CHAPTER 8

STILL ALMOST JULY—Still The Fall Out
Tension

Blond Streaks' eyes assault me with blue. He's a tall one, with nice shoulders, now that he's not slumped over a beer. I hope his deltoids are not all padding, courtesy of an oversized black jacket riddled with metal buttons up and down the lapels. I clear splintered ice out of my throat.

"I almost gave up on you," I say. An ice pain blares through one side of my head. Or a Drew-based guilt pain. I'm not sure which.

Trina comes up behind me as I rub my temple. "*Don't kick him*," she whispers over my shoulder, clutching her rocks glass.

"*You're leaving now*," I hiss back. She winks, then steps away, eyeing Mohawk Girl's leather-clad boyfriend before being engulfed by an ocean of black blazers. The English Beat spills out a musical confession in the background as she disappears.

I raise my empty glass to the streaky-haired guy in front of me. "Thanks for the drink," I say.

Blond Streaks lifts the glass out of my hand. An earring resembling a fishhook swings from his ear. A half-smile takes its time spreading across his face as he passes the glass back to our charcoal-eyed bartender friend, past the Mohawk Girl's formidably high hair. "One more of these," he tells the bartender. "And another Guinness."

What little illumination there is in the place slides along the guy's smooth cheekbones. He's got a horizontally striped T-shirt underneath the blazer; very Sting, 1978.

"What took you so long to say hello?" I ask.

"I had to gear up for it." Spiky hair falls in front of his eyes.

"To talk to *me*?" Maybe I look rowdier than I thought.

"A good-looking girl who can dance like that? Absolutely." The shoots of his hair quiver when he nods.

"*Huh*. In that case, I forgive you. And keep talking."

"I'm Whit," he says. "As in Matt Whitlan." The Sex Pistols belt out Anarchy in the UK through the sound system as he talks.

"So why aren't you Matt?"

"My roommate is Matt, too. We need to differentiate."

I look over the buttons on his hulking blazer to get a take on his character: Joy Division's Ian Curtis gripping a mike. Generation X. Oingo Boingo. All acceptable post-punk paraphernalia. Except for one tiny button featuring a blonde woman in a bowler hat....

"Wait . . . *Bananarama*?" I say, pressing the tip of my finger on the aluminum button, against the lead singer's smirk. I'm not convinced those three girls do anything other than lip-synch, which annoys me. "Did some *bubble gum chick* give you this one to wear?"

"Well, a girl did, yeah. How'd you guess?" he says, futzing with the button.

"Get rid of it!" I demand. "Bananarama's just not worthy."

He tilts his head at me and gathers up the lapel, clamping an impressively straight set of teeth against singer Siobhan Fahey's smug face. He yanks his chin until the button rips off in his jaw, taking a piece of lapel with it.

A ribbon of laughter sifts up from my chest, flowing like filter bubbles.

"Better?" he mumbles. His smile wraps awkwardly around the metal, tweezed between his incisors.

My breath returns. "*Much*."

He spits Siobhan Fahey across the floor, where she skitters under the heavy boots of terrifying punkers. "I wouldn't want to offend your musical sensibilities," he says. Whit leans to my eye level, being significantly taller than I am. "What's your name again?"

My insides tingle, like snow crystals climbing a window. "I didn't say."

He puts a hand against his ear. Rowdy types in torn clothing begin whipping themselves around the dance floor behind us. Slam dancers, with clothing all safety-pinned and shredded.

"Okay. I'm Jess."

"Tess?"

"*Jess.*"

"*Distress?*" he says, stepping away from a slam dancer who nearly tosses himself between us.

I rise on my toes, resting a hand on his arm. "*Jess.* As in Jessica."

"I heard you the first time."

I bite my bottom lip. "*I know.*"

A sticky-slow XTC song drips down around us. "Jess, you've got a great laugh," he tells me.

"Thanks. And you've got," I run my finger along his lapel, "a rip in your jacket."

The bartender passes our refills over a few sets of shoulders at the bar and Whit hands me my glass. "Jess-as-in-Jessica, want to get a table?"

I glance over my shoulder at the girls. Kimmer blows cigarette smoke and makes a kissy face full of red lipstick. Audrey waves me away. Trina ties an imaginary bow.

I push my hair behind one ear and accept his outstretched hand. We trail away from the bar through rows of partiers, some of them spasmodic and dancing. I notice the back of Whit's hair is dark, getting paler as it reaches the front. He's gradient.

Whit claims a scrap metal table near the stage. "Good thing that guy didn't knock you flat when you hit him. You really take over the floor, don't you?"

"You caught that?" The cracked red vinyl of the seat nips at the undersides of my legs as I settle in. I sip sour mix and harsh, low-grade Canadian whiskey. "I'm an enthusiastic girl."

"I noticed," he says. "What else do you do with yourself? Besides play with fruit."

He caught that, too. *Works every time*, I think. He wears a leather studded bracelet with triangular taps that knock against the table.

"I'm a waitress at the moment. I'm in New Hope for the summer."

"New Hope?" he repeats. "Isn't that place a little . . . *off-the-wall*? Unless you're an actor. Or an artist. Or gay."

"*Bingo*," I say.

He pushes back against a bench seat. "Wait—which one?"

"Artist," I say.

He exhales. "I thought I might be hitting on the wrong girl for a second." He guzzles opaque brown beer.

"Right, sorry." I laugh. "Artist, with a minor in music. I'm also a vocalist. I sang in a couple of cover bands."

His eyebrows arch. "*Hmm*. A Renaissance woman. Have you sung anywhere I've heard of?"

"Have you heard of Open Mike Night at The University of Pittsburgh?" I laugh. "Or my drummer's garage back on Long Island?" I tilt my pretty drink and sour mix sends fumes down my throat.

Whit takes off his slightly compromised blazer and slings it along the bench seat. His shoulders are the real thing, having benefited only slightly from the jacket. He runs a hand through his hair, which flexes back to rest in front of his eyes again, barely rearranging. "So, New Hope, Pittsburgh, Long Island, Philadelphia—"

"London!"

"When were you in London?"

"With any luck, next year. I've got a lot of double shifts in front of me if I want to afford the semester overseas I'm planning for junior year. Are you in college?"

He winces. "Nah. I majored in business for a couple of semesters at Temple. You know what I learned?" He downs lager, slapping the bottle to the table. "Business sucks. Now I work on a loading dock at IBM in Center City. And I'm . . . waiting for things to happen."

"Like what things?"

"Life. Magic." A smirk wanders across his face. "I don't know, but something's out there." His eyes catch the overhead lights as if distracted by the *things*. I notice how cut his jaw is; he's kind of John Taylor-ish—which is about as good as cheekbones get in this life.

I wonder if he's searching for the same things as I am. If he's waiting for the *incredible moment* that always feels like it's just about to break.

It's like I'm always on the brink of something awesome, on the other side of a membrane that my scrappy nails can't pierce. Like someday I'll burst through and join this elite class of famously creative souls who are *out there*, beyond my fingertips. . . .

Is that what he's waiting for?

"So wait—" He looks at me sideways. "You're not even a junior yet? How'd you get in here?" he asks. Behind us, a guy with Cher-black hair tapes down cables around the stage.

"*Shhh*," I say. Vinyl shrapnel bites at the back of my thighs as I dig into my boot for the driver's license. I slap my card in front of him. "This little baby is foolproof."

He lifts it to the gel lights in the rafters of the stage, then taps it against the metal tabletop, staring at it ten different ways.

I swipe it back. "Can you please not draw attention to my fake paperwork!"

"You're not kidding. This thing's professional. Where'd you get it, *Julianne*?"

"I've known some very talented art majors. Now let me see yours."

"See my *what*?"

"Your ID. I'm carding you. Hand over your license." Let's see how he likes it.

He extracts a wallet from the back of his jeans, passing me his card. In the picture, he wears a casual smile. His signature is neat and linear. He's got a desirable Main Line address.

And dark brown hair. At least his name is real. And he's not afraid to dye.

I hold the card level with his head. "*Ahem*. Not much resemblance."

"*Shit*. You caught me." Whit closes his palm around my wrist and pulls me close to his face. "Don't spread it around," he says in my ear, "and I'll keep you in whiskey sours the rest of your life." His chest rises as he breathes, lips barely open. That melt-ray in his eyes begins to charge.

Warm places in my body fizz to life. I want to draw his finger against my lips and into my mouth. His finger is . . . right . . . *there*. My teeth part. I can smell his leather bracelet as he leans closer.

Some ruffian swipes past us and knocks his knuckles against our table, making my glass jump. "*Come on*, man," he whines at Whit.

I throw myself back against the crimson diner chair with a mega exhale.

Whit gives the guy his least desirable finger.

"How can you afford to live in King of Prussia?" I ask. I paid attention to his license. On the stage, the roadie with the carbon-black hair taps microphones and adjusts equipment. He and Whit exchange nods. Lights flicker in the overhead beam as the guy tests the system. A crowd is starting to thicken by the stage, shouldering each other to the sound of The Stranglers. Synthesizers drone on; The Stranglers sing something about Trotsky and Lenin.

Whit laughs. "My mother got remarried a few months ago and moved out, and I needed a place to crash. She's letting me use her condo."

He's got a mother he's willing to reference in public. He's got a job with a real company. He's got a good dentist. And it took him half an hour to gather up the guts to talk to me. Not as scary as we girls predicted.

I decide to let the Bananarama thing slide. In fact, he can slide wherever he wants.

Audrey sidles up to our table, her heels whacking the floorboards. "You two coming to dance by the stage? We better stake out some territory before the opening band starts."

"I don't dance," Whit says. "But nice to meet you."

"Charmed." Audrey bends to my ear. "Although he loses five points for not dancing."

Once in a Lifetime

A guy in a cut-up tank shirt climbs on stage and tests the toms of a drum kit. He nods at me in recognition and I haven't a clue why. I don't know any Philadelphian drummers.

Whit stands and reaches for his blazer, crumpled on the bench. "I gotta go."

I blink so hard you can hear it. "Do you have a date or something?"

"No—well," he backs away from the table. "You could say that."

My chair squeals against the floor as I stand. "I was kidding."

"I'll talk to you later, I swear." He edges past me and disappears among the many ghastly bodies gravitating toward the stage.

I stand there, gaping.

Audrey and Trina come to meet me. "That is one undecided guy," Audrey says as the stage lights dim. "*Come on.* We'll never get a good spot if you wait for him." The lights swell, red and cerulean. Guitar chops begin as the opening band starts playing. Their vibrations tickle the soles of my boots.

"Jess—*oh shit!*" Audrey shakes my arm.

I look up, and there's Whit on the stage, a bass guitar slung across his body. He's washed in cobalt gel lights like some luminous New Wave alien.

"*Oh shit is right!*" I shout. He looks at his strings, adjusts the pegs, turns in place.

Trina leans against my shoulder. "Isn't that. . .?" She points with her free hand, balancing her rocks glass. Judging by the glassiness of her eyes, I estimate she's on her third Dewar's.

"It's him, all right," I say.

"*Big points,*" says Audrey. "This is big points."

The muscles in Whit's jaw tighten as he plays. The bass sound is strong and plush. Light catches his spiky mess of bleached-out hair, draping his eyes in shadow. He turns to mess with the knobs on an amp and I get a spot-lit view of how starkly the back of his hair contrasts with the front.

His band sounds like a guitar-heavy New Order. They play danceable, gorgeously oversaturated guitar riffs, complete with brush cymbals and real lyrics, not emotional whining. A chill darts up my spine as Whit leans toward a battered mike stand and his eyes flick toward me for a split second. The crowd is a shifting sea of bobbing heads—a swelling, undulating mass. Slam dancers jettison themselves above the horizon of the crowd every few riffs. We girls dance in what sweaty space is available, molecules colliding like we're some wild splatter of New Wave protoplasm.

Whit is talented. The band is fun. I'm wired.

I elbow my way to the front of the crowd, past various black jacketed monsters that I hope won't hurt me. Whit's lip curls just slightly when he sees me against the rim of the stage. The set breaks and the lead singer starts prattling to the crowd.

Whit bends to the edge of the stage, his guitar balanced on his knee. He leans to my ear. "You enjoying yourself?"

"You could have warned me!"

"Where's the fun in that?" His lip hitches upward, like a tell-tale punctuation mark.

"And you let me go on about open mike night like a fucking idiot."

"Open mike night sounds awesome. Next one, I'm there." He turns a guitar pick in his fingers, then presses it into my palm. "Hold onto this." I turn it in front of my face. THE RILERS is scrawled across the red plastic triangle.

I press my waist against the stage. I've spent a full year of college drooling over the gorgeous bone structures of guitar players staring out from the backs of record albums. Men who melt my heart, oozing the mystique of a 60-frame-per-second, slo-mo video shoot. They're fellow brooders, wielding instruments like axes, gelled-up and safety-pinned to oblivion.

In a spark of a second, Whit leans in and presses his lips against mine. Sheer stage light burns through my eyelids as they flutter closed. A rush of heat rises from deep springs in my body until he breaks away, *slowly. . ."*

"Wait for me after the set?" he asks.

There's suddenly less oxygen in the room. My brain spins.

I think I've waited for this my whole life.

I brush my lips against his ear, his sweat sticking against my cheek. "*I can do that*," I say breathily.

He stands to finish the band's opening set. I join my roommates, dancing in what little plot of floor they've been able to carve out.

"I saw that kiss," Audrey shouts in my ear.

"It was *a beautiful fucking thing*," I say.

"Yeah, the whole club saw that kiss. You're famous now." Trina raises her empty glass over the crowd and swings around toward the bar. "Who do I have to sleep with to get a refill around here!" she shouts.

"You know what this place needs?" Kimmer chimes in over my shoulder. "A waitress."

We fight our way past the dancers and back to the bar as the band wraps it up, slicing a few extra wild guitar riffs at the very end, before the lights drop. I back against the bar and try to slip Whit's guitar pick into my boot without falling over. Hopefully, it won't pop free when I reach for my money. I'd rather lose the money than the pick.

I look back toward the blackened stage, but there's no more sign of the band or Whit's tall shadow. I hate to unfold a twenty from its resting place against my ankle, but I need to keep this buzz going. I wonder if Whit will offer to buy me another drink, or if I'm about to get blown off for some blonde groupie chick who loves Bananarama. I squint towards the stage again.

I don't see anyone I know.

Trina elbows her way between two black-shouldered punkers and smacks her empty glass in front of the bartender. "*Thank-you-sir-may-I-have-another*," she says, slurring.

I lean to Audrey. "Did Trina forget she's driving? Should one of us volunteer?"

Audrey lifts her Scotch. "I'll arm-wrestle you for it." *One of us driving* would mean me or Audrey. Kimmer's parents became alcoholics by the time she was sixteen. They never got it together enough to teach her.

I hail the bartender and he mixes me another whiskey sour. I could stop drinking, except I don't want to.

A tap on my shoulder makes me hop.

"You couldn't wait for me to get the next one?" Whit points to my whiskey.

Me of little faith. "I didn't want my buzz to wear off. Now stop sneaking up on me."

Whit's hair has taken on a bit of a sexy wave, sweat dissipating the magic of whatever hair product he uses. From somewhere behind his nice shoulders, musicians from the headlining act start to populate the stage. Harsh feedback rips from one of my eardrums to the other as chords chop against a brain-splitting drumbeat. It's true couch-breaking music.

Trina argues with the Mohawked chick at the bar. Seems she accidentally doused Mohawk Girl's Pleather sleeve with a healthy dose of Dewar's. I pull Whit back towards the dance floor. You never want to be in the nuclear blast range when Trina goes off.

Killing Joke continues blowing wild guitar chords and big, flat drum beats through huge columns of speakers. The wild-eyed lead singer makes me wonder if he's made too many hats in Jolly Olde England. The crowd morphs into a group of men-only, slam dancers thrashing in a mindless clump, all in Stephen Sprouse-looking street garb. A few of them drop to the floor, then spring back up and toss themselves across the mosh pit.

"Come on, we can get closer." Whit inches us toward the mosh.

The danger alarm pulses in my head. "Are you kidding?"

"Not to worry." He leads me forward by the shoulders. As reckless as they seem to the naked eye, the slam dancers make space for us.

"They're being so *obedient*," I say.

"It's not a British soccer game." Whit laughs. "It's just Killing Joke." I remember news footage of UK soccer fans struggling against a chain-link fence until some guy's cheek was squelched against the mesh like Jell-O. Then he died.

"Now I know why you don't dance, if this is what you listen to," I tell Whit. We watch a burly roadie throw a brazen slam dancer off the stage.

"They're not who I listen to," Whit says. "They're who the club let us open for. Why'd you come here if this isn't what you listen to?"

I look up at him and laugh. "*To see if I'd survive!*"

He presses against my back like a fitted garment. Warm. Monolithic. His arm wraps around my waist from behind. I start to think I might even like this obnoxious frigging band. For a second. Maybe. In some other life.

Once in a Lifetime

Glass shatters at the bar behind us and Whit's grip tightens around me. I hear: "Well *fuck* if you think I'm cleaning that up!"

It's not Sid Vicious. It's Trina.

"What are you looking at?" Trina howls at the bartender. "Suzie Mohawk with the scrub-brush hair bumped me!"

Suzie Mohawk takes a clod-hopping step toward Trina.

"She's good! We're good," Audrey says, holding out hands of peace between Trina and Mohawk Girl. "Tri', you need a valium."

This isn't the first time Audrey's been called upon to put a stopper in a potential brawl for Trina. I'm thrown back to a party at the Phi-O fraternity house.

Trina couldn't resist bitching-out a brother who ignored her hardcore flirting. If you know anything about Greek life, you don't call House Vice President Brent Fox a fucking ass and a half.

Audrey's arms rolled like a watermill in front of a frothing Brent, as if she could paddle back his outrage and reverse the slew of insults he spewed onto the party floor.

"Git her outta here," he drawled in his middle-of-nowhere accent, heaving alcohol-drenched breaths. "I don't like nasty girls calling me out in my house. I don't like big girls in my house."

Audrey kept trying to make peace. To somehow stick the seams of the evening back together like Peter Brady's badly-repaired vase. Just as Brent's bile started to ease, Trina lunged and spit a stream of beer against the front of his button-up shirt.

We were escorted out of the Phi-O house that night. Little-Sisterhood at a fraternity can be a fragile proposition.

Back at the Fall Out bar, Trina is still in attack mode. "She doesn't own this place!" Trina shouts toward Mohawk Girl. "She's just a skinny bitch full of holes!" Trina points at Mohawk's model-like boyfriend. "That goes for you, too, Adam Ant!"

Audrey wrestles Trina to the other side of the bar. Suzie Mohawk growls at Audrey with a voice like a bad muffler. *"Tell your friend to watch herself,"* Suzie says. Her skin is pallid as a German impressionist painting. She could pose screaming on a bridge. Yet she hesitates, listening to Audrey's hands of peace. Her gorgeous boyfriend watches with barely a tick of facial expression.

"Isn't that your friend?" Whit asks me.

"She gets this way."

"This isn't the best place to throw a tantrum," he says.

"It'll only go downhill from here. And she's our ride home."

Whit takes the bar glass out of my hand. "I'll drive you girls home. But we better go now, before things get extreme." I grab Audrey and talk in her ear. She gathers up Trina.

I fetch Kimmer from behind a wall of hulking guys, and the bunch of us head for the door. A tube of Trina's lipstick spits out of her purse. She kneels on the filthy floorboards, grappling for the lipstick between people's feet. "Where are my effing keys?"

"I stole them half an hour ago." Audrey picks Trina up off the floor.

"Good plan," says Kimmer, carrying her shoes in one hand. "You win Nurse Kimmer's Extraordinary Foresight Award." Kimmer's feet are left in nothing but black knee-highs, one toe jutting through a hole in the nylon.

Whit shoves open the club's blacked-out door and we pile into the late-night mischief of Chestnut Street. Trina stumbles in a line that wouldn't qualify as straight in a police stop. She looks up at Whit. "What's he doing here?"

"He's driving your car home." My boot heels clomp on the pavement. A gaggle of punker girls in ripped tights march past us.

"To my *mother's*?" Trina asks.

"To our apartment," I answer. "And you're going to lay off him."

"Oh yeah?" Trina mutters. "I'll lay whatever I want to lay on him." She giggles.

"Trina, shut up and walk," says Audrey, guiding Trina's arm like a rudder. "You're killing my buzz."

"*Fuck 'em* if they can't take a joke," Trina says.

Audrey plants Trina's jangle of keys into Whit's palm. "I forgive you for not dancing."

CHAPTER 9

STILL ALMOST JULY—Route 476
Drive

Whit drives for-shit, but better than Trina would have. She lasts three minutes in the back of her mother's station wagon before passing out on Audrey's shoulder. The car's worn struts bounce us around as Whit negotiates a cobblestone side street somewhere off Rittenhouse Square, heading away from The Fall Out Club. I'm next to him on the tan vinyl of the front seat.

"You wanna hear something weird, Jess?" Audrey talks low, trying not to rouse Trina. "That Mohawked girl's boyfriend in the leather vest at the bar?"

I turn around. "Yeah?"

"A dead ringer for Tony," she whispers.

"*Tony* Tony?" asks Kimmer.

"What other Tony is there?" Audrey says.

Whit glances back at Audrey as he clicks the car's blinker. "Who's Tony?" he asks.

We three girls ring in: "*We don't talk about Tony.*" Not when Trina's conscious, anyhow.

"*Whoa.* Forget I asked," Whit says.

The car strays from its lane for a second and I clutch the dashboard. I grapple for a decent radio station, poking buttons in the dash as the other girls fall off to sleep in the back seat.

"Maybe it's late to ask," Whit says to me. "But is it safe to say you don't have a boyfriend?"

A dart finds its way into my stomach, scraping at me from the inside. I've answered this question the same way for two years until this moment. Drew still has *My Boyfriend* stamped all over his image in my head, as if no one else could wear that suit. I wonder how long it will take for that to fade. To stop feeling like a betrayal I have to kick under the seam of a rug.

"We're *seeing other people*." I stretch my feet, which throb from standing all night in heels. "It's an experiment. He's back home on Long Island for the summer."

Whit stares. His guitar pick rattles under the arch of my foot. "I'm trying to be open with you," I say. "What do you think of that situation?"

His body shifts. Highway lamps sweep over his face, filling in smooth planes and angles as he drives. "I think Long Island's pretty far away," he says.

"I wasn't sure this seeing other people thing was such a hot idea," I say. "But I'm forcing myself to warm up to it."

Adrenaline seeps out of my body as I relax in the quiet of just me and this new guy. "How come you don't have a girlfriend?" I ask. "Half the women in the club would probably throw themselves at you, seeing as you're in the band."

"I'm not looking for a *groupie*, if that's even the right word." His fingers whiten around the steering wheel, taut as the faux stitching molded into the plastic. "I just broke up with someone. Two weeks ago."

"*Two weeks?*" I notice my jaw hanging slack and snap it closed. I wonder what fresh crap I just stepped into, smearing figuratively under the soles of my scrunch boots.

He breathes deep. "It was brutal. I came home and found two people in my bed. Neither of them being me."

"That so sucks." The gearing-up-to-talk-to-me thing doesn't seem as strange now.

"I thought I'd had it with women for a while," he says. Headlights whip past us, throwing patterns through a repetition of slats along the top of a concrete highway divider. It's like watching a movie through a running fan. "But maybe that's stupid," Whit finishes.

I gasp as he swerves toward the divider, then corrects course. Air returns to my lungs.

"Maybe we both need to branch out a little," I say.

"How about we go out together and see what happens?"

"If you're good with this whole arrangement. How far is King of Prussia from New Hope?"

"Oooohhh . . . about 50 minutes."

"*No way*," I say. "You're willing to drive that far?"

"Could be." The pink highway lights glow through the car, swelling with each passing streetlamp. He initiates a nod that slowly recruits the rest of his body. "Okay, *definitely*." He smiles. "And if we have a good time together, that's what matters."

He parks with the grill of the station wagon pulled up against our apartment building. Trina groans in the back seat. Audrey opens the heavy car door and pulls Trina out of the vehicle.

Kimmer slides out of the car, jostling Trina's free arm. "You're a trooper," she tells Whit. He and I stay in the front seat. Kim's gold waves kink in all the wrong directions now. "If I had to listen to that band one more minute, I would have gone up in flames." She hauls Trina's arm over her shoulder.

Trina wrangles free, yanking open my car door and tossing her weight on it. She giggles.

"*Jessss*-ica." Trina slurs. The sharp edges of her hair swipe across her mouth and cling to her dark lipstick. "*Never fuck a guy in a station wagon*."

I palm my face.

Audrey and Kimmer drag Trina off the car. Kimmer pushes the hunk of door closed with a nearly-bare foot.

"Say goodnight, Trina," Audrey says.

"Goodnight, *Treee-na*," she moans at my window. The girls stumble away toward the back of the building. I listen to Trina's voice echo across the narrow parking spaces. "*Whaaaat?* Advice from the master!" She sings Clash lyrics about life by the river and laughs far too loudly.

Whit and I are alone in the car. The amber of a new streetlamp falls over his face.

"This was really nice of you," I tell him. "I'm too exhausted to be more articulate than that."

He leans back against the headrest. "You're doing pretty good for three in the morning." It's like I can feel his pulse from across the front seat, infusing itself through the muggy air.

Crickets buzz loud enough to be heard through the closed windows. "So now what?" I ask. We didn't plan on how he'd get home.

Whit looks at me like I'm that girl he had a crush on in fifth grade, suddenly sitting next to him on the school bus.

He blinks, exquisitely slowly, then bends toward me in a slow arc. His lips touch mine, warm and tired and unbelievably perfect, moving. He kisses deep and without reservation. Like I ordered him to fit, from some personalized boyfriend catalog.

His palm glides across my shoulder blades, the other smoothing its way up the small of my back, fingers spreading, displacing clothing.

Synapses prickle up and down my body, like when I used to run my bike over cap gun strips as a kid. I snake my arm under his jacket.

Did someone tell him exactly what kind of touch does it for me? *Did I conjure this guy?*

I snap upright, a sheet of my hair smacking his jacket. In two minutes, we've created score-fog on the windows. He loosens his hold on me, looking the way I feel. As if neither of us knows exactly what just happened.

He says, "*You're good at this.*"

"*So are you*," I say.

I've known him for four hours.

His hands linger. I shimmy out of his grasp, adjusting my shirt. "I have to get out of the car."

"Okay, I get it," he says.

"I can't leave you out here. Can you come in—I mean, without anything else . . . happening?"

"I hope so. Otherwise, I'm sleeping in the back of this wagon." He bangs a palm against the inhospitable steering wheel.

"We'll drive you home in the morning," I say.

He twists Trina's mega keyring out of the ignition and hands it to me. "I promise not to attack you," he says as the keys chime in my hand, cool metal poking my skin.

"Good. Because I promised Trina I wouldn't end up like Nancy Spungen tonight." I shove the keys into my purse and smooth my skirt, which has hitched to an inappropriate level. "I'll have to trust you."

The river gurgles behind the building as we climb out of the vehicle. Crickets sing in phrases. The rest of the street is quiet. I point toward the apartment window he's parked in front of, where a pair of matronly eyelet curtains stretch across a tension rod. Ugly as original sin, but they were all we could afford. And it was better than draping a sheet across the window.

I point to the curtains. "See that? Welcome to my living room."

I click on the foyer light switch to see Kimmer already tucked into the pull-out. She yanks a Strawberry Shortcake sheet up over her head. I kick her discarded Capris and oversized 1960's bowling shirt under the bed with my boot.

Whit grabs two fugly orange sofa cushions and rearranges them on the floor. He gets a dim view of my Op-art ringworm mural.

"Your work?" he asks, gesturing at the illusion corkscrewing toward him. I nod.

"Pretty fucking wild. I'm impressed." He smiles, then stretches out on the cushions and rolls to face the wall. "Don't mind me," he mumbles over his shoulder, waving a hand. He's still fully dressed, including combat boots and the black blazer. "Nothing to see here."

I move the ashtray off our end table so I don't have to smell it all night. Two slips of paper flutter from underneath, scrawled with the same message in clumsy Sharpie. "DREW CALLED." Another pang invades my gut and I don't know how to distract myself from it. I pick up the paper scraps and crumple them in my fists.

I hear Trina shuffle into our apartment's only bedroom. "Hey, Jess," she mock-whispers, thumping a hand against the wall between us. "*Don't you kick him.*"

She cackles like a madwoman.

CHAPTER 10

JULY 1984—Capresi's
Accidents Will Happen

Four days. Whit didn't call.

I shove my order pad into my apron and wonder why I didn't take his number instead of just giving him mine. That is, if I could muster the guts to call a guy who hasn't bothered to call me.

One who kissed me like I was his life's lost passion.

I smear sweat off my forehead and unfold the crumpled paper reproduction of today's menu, spreading it on a butcher block counter. Giorgio and Teddy flank me on either side. Pans sizzle behind us.

"Can't I laminate this paper instead of using the chalkboard menus?" I ask Giorgio.

"Oh, how tacky. *No.* Now: Chicken Francaise," he coaches.

"Chicken, dredged in flour and special house seasonings, in white sauce with lemon, garlic and . . . red paprika."

"Very good," Giorgio says. "Say it's a *delicate* white sauce."

"Delicate my ass," says Teddy, slicing away at garlic cloves with a scary knife. The blade taps against the butcher block.

"Scampi," Giorgio goes on.

"Cream sauce with lemon and wine?"

Teddy hangs his head. "You have *eaten* in a restaurant before, right?"

Giorgio shudders. "Wine and lemon curdles cream."

"Sorry. No curdling. I'll get it." Strands of hair fall loose from my mandatory ponytail. I whisk them back.

"Alfredo carbonara," Giorgio says.

"Fettuccine in cream sauce, with *prosciutto* and garden-fresh peas."

"Lovely pronunciation," says Giorgio. "We appreciate your Italian heritage in this restaurant." He is, after all, Giorgio *Capresi*.

Teddy does kissy lips. "Say *pro-jshoot-tow* again?"

Bernadette rushes to the range tops and grasps a pan handle in each palm, shaking the metal. Mushrooms swirl in an arc. Garlic fumes waft. "Teddy, make yourself more useful," she snaps.

He waves the knife at her. "What? We're training the new girl."

"Bernadette's right," Giorgio says. "Keep prepping." He shoos Teddy back, returning his attention to me. "Beef Capresi."

"Beef tips in burgundy. Portobello mushrooms, capers, and . . . onion?" I hope no one asks what a caper is.

"Sirloin," he corrects. "Tell people it's a varietal of the classic Bourguignon."

"Bor-gon-*yone*." I sound it out with the precision of a first-grader. Teddy laughs at me.

"We're depending on you to communicate the essence of the menu, Jessica," Giorgio says. "Dining is an *experience*."

Teddy peers through the kitchen pass-through, eyeing a few groups of diners that Rickie the dishwasher has already seated on the patio. "Brace yourself," he says. "We could get a crowd tonight."

"You can do this, Jessica." Giorgio places a hand on my back and makes eye contact that almost hurts. "*Believe in your own power*. No one can defeat you but yourself."

Teddy folds the paper cheat sheet and tucks it into my palm. "Yeah. Power. And keep this for emergencies."

I follow Giorgio as he pushes through the kitchen doors, wondering what waitressing emergencies I've got in front of me. Whatever they are, I'm sure they'll be *varietal*. On my way through the bar room, I'm stopped by the sight of a brand-spanking white gazebo in the courtyard.

"Wasn't that gazebo gray when we closed yesterday?" I ask Giorgio.

Teddy waves from the pass-through, dragging his finger frantically across his neck in a cut-your-throat gesture.

Giorgio sighs. "That's the second repainted item this week."

I head onto the patio and grab the chalkboard menu that's leaning against the wall. My sneakers scuff on the uneven slate. I think of Giorgio's teachings as I step in front of a pair of customers at deuce number one.

Smile. Introduce yourself. You're entertaining people. Forget that this is drudgery and you're intimidated to death. And remember: *Communicate the essence.*

"Hi, I'm Jessica and I'll be your waitress." I extrude a smile.

A forty-ish couple smile back, including a woman in chunky jewelry and a zebra print dress in size *this-is-too-young-for-me*. Her husband is rail-like and graying at the temples. It's a mystery to me how well-to-do people are always thin. Especially since they spend so much time in restaurants.

"Well, hello, Jessica." Zebra Woman is overly cheerful. I'm tempted to curtsey, but that wasn't part of my training. I take drink orders, then drag a skittering, white wire chair from a neighboring table and mount the chalkboard menu on it.

Zebra Woman stares into the courtyard. Rows of lights wind their way up the trees as if an artist sketched them in sparkles. The breeze nuzzles the leaves, twirling them into disorderly patterns.

The woman points to the creek behind the newly-white gazebo. "Is that the Delaware Canal?"

"No. The canal is the other way." I point over my shoulder. "That's just a creek."

"I thought we might have a view of New Jersey," she says.

"New Jersey's on the other side of the river," I tell her, "across the street."

The woman crinkles her nose at her husband. "Maybe we should have picked a place on the river."

"You can always walk along the river later," I say. "You can't miss New Jersey around here." Although plenty of people do, based on how many require the wait staff to point it out.

"Can we have menus?" the man asks.

A streak of panic paints my guts, me not knowing how to defend the restaurant's chalkboard policy and still earn a tip. "This *is* the menu." I point to the board propped on the chair.

They squint—a gesture I worry I'll become acquainted with. I'll have to write up the menu in bigger print next time. It's hard to retain all these details when my mind keeps returning to the front of Trina's station wagon, washed in streetlight the color of rose quartz. I can still feel Whit's newly-familiar fingers on my back, the heat of intent boiling through the car.

"A menu on a chair?" Zebra Woman stares.

Not my idea. I get the sinking feeling I won't ever make enough money to afford that London tuition bill. That my paneled-over high school bedroom is calling me back. Yet I keep smiling. "Our menu is different each night. We write it up special to reflect whatever local ingredients the chef gets in daily. It's a new encounter for every diner, every time." How's that for *communicating the essence*? "I can give you some time."

"That'll be fine." The man leans against the table and it rocks to one side. "This is a little unstable," he says.

You're not kidding, I think. I tear the cardboard backing off my order pad and get on my knees to shunt the wobbly leg.

I'm on the ground in a mini skirt, under a table.

I poke my head out from underneath the plywood. "Better?" The man shakes the tabletop and his place setting stays put. He nods.

I crawl back to standing and retrieve the second chalkboard, lugging it to the next active table and displaying it in front of them. They're a family of five, including an infant. They request a highchair. I have no idea if the restaurant has one but swear to get it straight away. My drop-waist ruffled waitressing skirt flounces against my legs.

"You're very kind," says Mom, bouncing junior, who chews her stringy mommy hair.

Zebra Woman and her husband order veal and sausage dishes. I scuttle away—tennies catching on the floor, chalkboard smacking against my thigh—and wonder why I didn't apply somewhere with more carpeting.

As I approach the waitress station, I see Kimmer standing by the pass-through. She's supposed to be working a shift at The Boat Haus across the canal. Her eyes are puffy as if she's the one who's been squirted with mace, not the owner's duo of dogs.

As I get closer, Kimmer throws an arm around me and bawls in my ear. My pencil topples out of my apron. I would worry about money falling out of the apron, but I don't have any.

"*How can I go back in there?*" Kimmer moans in my ear.

"Whoa." I seat her at a bar room table. "What happened?"

"The rottweilers! You'd think my name tag says *Kibble*." Kimmer blows a lock of hair off her face. It drifts back onto her forehead.

I take her hand. "Kim, start from the beginning."

"This nice older couple ordered cherries flambé. The whole reason Karl gave me the job is because I had experience lighting Cherries Jubilee."

"You're one dedicated waitress," I say. "Flames are out of my pay range." And they've gotten me fired once already.

"I brought out the cart and tossed a shot on the cherries. It lit like a pro. You should have seen it, Jess. It was dessert poetry." Kimmer's eyes start to well again.

"Let me guess," I say. "Rottweilers don't love fire?"

"They went charging through the restaurant like wild horses. I dropped my shit and *ran*."

"*Holy crap.*"

Teddy eyes us through the pass-through. "Jess, you got anything for me?" he asks.

"Right." I rip a sheet from my order pad and shove it through the window. I can smell sausages broiling.

Teddy swipes the order slip off the sill. "Who's your friend?"

"Later, okay?"

He glares at me, then tilts his head toward the waitress station. "Bread, babe. Feed these people."

Duh. I load up a wicker basket with bread and give Kimmer a wait-a-minute finger. "I need a highchair for table eight," I tell Teddy.

"We don't have a highchair," he says. "This is a restaurant for grown-ups."

"They've got a baby."

"Tough luck." He laughs. I leave to distribute baskets full of homemade sour dough bread, swaddled in baskets and magenta napkins like Moses. Wiser already, my fingers narrowly avoid getting slammed in the bread warmer.

Giorgio seats a new couple, making it four full tables full of diners now. And one me.

I remember my pencil is missing when I ask the family of five for their orders. I apologize for our lack of a highchair. I memorize their dinner requests and prop the chalkboard menu in front of the next four guests, starting them off with soft drinks.

I grab my pencil off the floor by the waitress station, scribble my latest orders onto the carbon-backed order slips from memory, and head to the bar.

Kimmer sits at a bar room table and knots her disheveled ponytail into a smooth bun. "I've never walked off a job before in my life." She sniffles. "They'll hate me."

"Let them," I tell her. "It's that or be eaten."

Giorgio sits next to Kimmer and runs a finger along his chin. "Is everything all right, young lady?"

"Giorgio, this is my roommate Kimmer."

"One of the four waitresses," he nods. "Of course." Giorgio takes Kim's hand in both of his. "Have you seen a ghost, my dear?"

Kimmer gets as far into the story as *The Boat Haus*, and Giorgio gasps. "Karl Volmer's dogs!"

"You know them?" Kimmer wipes an eye.

"We've been trying to run those animals out of town for years." He eyes the patio, then me. "Jessica, get drinks and dessert for that deuce by the railing. I told them about our house peach Melba."

"Yes. Melba. Vanilla ice cream, fresh peaches, and raspberry sauce, right?" I say, pointing my pencil at him.

"Good work. But tell Teddy to drizzle a shot of peach Schnapps over them." Giorgio shoos me toward the dining room. I welcome the new couple, deliver more bread all around, and serve salads to Zebra Woman and her mate.

Giorgio comforts Kimmer. I scramble from table to table, slinging veal dishes and baskets and rearranging chalkboards. My head spins. Teddy constantly asks how I'm doing.

When the action breaks, I see Kimmer standing by our vintage bookshelves, arms out to her sides like airplane wings. Giorgio wraps a black apron around her waist and ties it ceremoniously.

"I want you to remember something," he says to Kimmer, who nods at him. *"No one can make you feel inferior without your consent,"* he goes on. "You know who said that?"

"Not a clue," says Kimmer.

"Eleanor Roosevelt."

"Did she own Rottweilers?" Kimmer asks.

Giorgio takes Kimmer by the elbow and walks her toward me. "Don't ever underestimate yourself," he says to her. "And don't let anyone dictate your value. Not Karl. Not anyone."

"I like that." Kimmer tugs her apron straight. "Thank you. Honestly."

Giorgio hands Kimmer off to me like an Oscar statuette. "We've arrived at a solution," he tells me. "Please familiarize your friend with the menu."

I shrug. "Wow, Kim. Welcome to Capresi's." She gives me a Hollywood smile, wiping away the last of the eyeliner drip from under her fluttery lashes.

"In that case," I continue, "can you please get two glasses of Merlot for that deuce by the rail? I'm losing my shit here."

"Absolutely." She salutes me and heads to the bar.

Behind me, Teddy pats the bell and places a row of pastas and saucy dinners along the ledge.

"Table eight—*up*," he calls.

For the first time ever, I unfold a metal stand big enough to accommodate a suitcase, top it with a wide oval tray, and arrange dinners on it.

Kimmer comes up behind me, Merlot bottle in hand, and whispers in my ear. "Heaviest plates go closest to you, or the tray will flip."

"I'm *so-so* glad you're here." I crouch down, settling the tray on my deltoid, gripping its damp rim. Rising tenuously. My free hand lifts the stand, which snaps closed as I pull it against my hip. My feet begin to compensate for the dips in the slate floor. Kimmer trails me and reopens the stand, helping to guide the tray to a soft landing.

"Behind you," she whispers as she steps around my back. Waitressing code. So we don't smack into each other. I place each dinner in front of the correct person. I accept that there are such things as miracles.

Kimmer and I practically skip back to the waitress station in celebration of my first time delivering a tray of dinners. She jumps with me. "You did it!"

Teddy's growl from the pass-through stops us. "Cute," he says, pointing a knife our way. "Betty and Veronica." Kimmer and I look each other over, a side-by-side blonde and brunette, dressed identically. Like salt and pepper shakers. We laugh.

"Teddy, I need that pair of peach Melbas with Schnapps for table two," I tell him, pointing my pencil, glad to have some kind of implement of authority to wag at him. "They're already into a round of Merlots."

"C'min here," he says.

I push through the kitchen door. Teddy waves me to the butcher block. He's got a peach pinned under his fingers, split up the middle, a wet knife gleaming at its side.

"You want a peach?" He spreads the sides of the pithy fruit and rubs his index finger up and down its pit-less center. "I've got a peach for you."

I cover my eyes. "Oh, for the love of whatever, Teddy!" I should know never to enter the kitchen when he says *C'min here*.

"What? This is great technique, believe me."

"I'm not serving that," I say, looking away.

He laughs from his gut. "Hey, is your girlfriend single, by the way?"

Bernadette appears behind Teddy. She's taller than he is, even without her squalled-up mound of a hairdo. "Teddy, you're a P-I-G!" She pulls the ribbed hat off her head and beats him with it. He howls and shields himself.

I slink through the out-door as the hinges moan behind me.

"*Giorgie-oooh!*" Bernadette calls, leaning through the cut-out, huffing a dragon-like breath. She bangs the pass-through bell a bunch of times. "I can't take any more!"

Giorgio races to the pass-through. Bernadette pelts her chef hat at him. He catches it before it whaps his clean-shaven face.

Giorgio motions for me to make myself scarce. "Go take dessert orders on four."

Kimmer whispers in my ear as I pass her. "Is it always this crazy?"

"This is my first dinner shift, remember?"

I enter the patio in time to see Mommy with junior laid out atop table eight. She unsnaps the baby's overalls. Wind kicks up in the trees in the courtyard, causing the Melba-and-Merlot couple by the rail to adjust their cardigans.

"Um, ma'am," I say as Mommy wrestles a hand under the baby's bottom.

Before I can lift a finger, junior's diaper is open. In the dining room. Where people are eating.

The diaper is full of crap.

The man at the Merlot table rises to standing. His eyes bulge. "Oh . . . my . . . *Lord!*" He raises a pointy finger like a quivering tree branch.

Mommy recoils. Her children freeze. The mullet-haired Dad stands up, his chair bumping behind his knees and scraping against the slate.

Giorgio rushes to the Merlot people by the railing. "I apologize. Please, sir, we'll take care of this."

"I've never seen such a thing in a nice restaurant!" Merlot Man bellows. Giorgio takes him by the forearm and turns him to face the creek. He's surely offering to pay the man's bill.

Mommy shields her half-naked son. I place a hand on her back. "Ma'am, maybe you can take the baby into the ladies' room?"

"No she won't!" shouts the husband. A vein the size of an earthworm pumps across his brow. "Elizabeth, let's get out of here!"

I haven't given them the check yet.

The family gathers up its brood of shaken children and clears out of the patio area, creating a cacophony in the bar room. Giorgio tries to follow them. He's blocked halfway by Bernadette's bulky frame, her white coat balled in her fist.

"I'm outta this place!" She shoves her uniform at Giorgio, who clutches it against his chest. "It's a mad house."

Bernadette stomps toward the exit, behind the skulking family whose infant bawls like a car alarm. His tiny overall straps are flailing. Kimmer steps back, a hand sealed over her mouth, making way as the family lumbers through the lobby.

"What the hell-in-a-handbag is going on out there?" Teddy calls from the pass-through. "Can't I leave you people alone for ten minutes?"

Giorgio marches to the pass-through, pressing a hand to his forehead as if preventing his brain from leaking through his upper palate. He shoves Bernadette's chef coat into the cut-out.

"Astonishingly, Teddy," Giorgio announces, "you've been promoted."

A strip of sleigh bells jingle on the back of the lobby door as The Crappy Diaper Family escapes up the garden stairs, cowering like fugitives in the whirling wind. Bernadette helps them.

Shit happens.

Kimmer and I walk past the Canal Stage theater, which is currently running a production of *Guys and Dolls*. She whips a scrunchie out of her hair and gold locks topple down her neck. "I've been working since 11:30 this morning. I'm Coma Waitress." She stretches out her shoulders. "Glad to have a new job, though."

"See? We said you could get another waitressing gig anywhere," I remind her. "I hope you're not disappointed it's at Capresi's."

She laughs. "As long as no one else treats the patio like a baby-changing station."

"Okay, so the place is insane," I say. "But it's home for me now. No one else offered to hire me."

We cross the concrete bridge over the creek. The water underneath cascades down a drop toward a slowly churning waterwheel outside the theatre. Lily pads dot the surface of the pond in pale, lopsided circles.

Kimmer's sneakers slap the pavement. She walks in scissor steps, squeezed into a black pencil skirt worthy of Kate Pierson of The B-52s. "So did this Whit person call you?"

"Nope." Lights hop along the river behind Main Street, connecting the dots between us and the next state. "It's been four days."

"Did he mention he was going on vacation? Or into suspended animation?"

"Nope," I say. "No life-threatening illnesses, either." A maple leaf the size of my head revolves toward the waterfall, joining a procession of reedy pond debris.

"Did you two suck face?" Kim asks.

"Kinda-sorta."

"Was it nice?"

"I melted like a pat of butter."

I remember the morning after Whit slept on our floor under my *Attack of the Wall* mural, when Trina and I drove him home.

I climbed out of the car to say goodbye in front of an upscale-looking condo complex. His fingers smoothed the scrap of receipt where I scrawled my phone number in bad, moving-vehicle handwriting. He folded the paper into the pocket of the night before's blazer.

"Let's do something this week. Whatever you want." His warm fingers ran through one side of my hair, flaking away the last semblance of gel and hairspray over my ears. "I'll call you. Soon," he said.

I tilted my face up to him. There we were again, in the dizzy center of a kiss that made me wonder what past life I knew him from. I caught my balance against the car door as his lips separated from mine.

Whit's eyes opened slowly, the color of that beautiful day people sing about in musicals. *Blond spokes of hair fell in his eyes.*

"I'll call you tomorrow," he said.

Never one for patience, Trina laid on the horn.

Kimmer's laugh jerks me back to the Main Street overpass. "Aw, Jess, don't get all bent out of shape," she says. "You didn't even know him a week ago, right?" Insects hum as the creek spills underneath us.

"I guess. But it's not every day a guy kisses you and turns you into a frigging Dali watch."

"A *dolly what?*"

"Salvador Dali? *Persistence of Memory?*"

"I'm still working on my organizational skills. Please don't get on me about my memory," Kimmer says.

"I mean the painting with the melting watches," I say. "I've got a textbook at home. I'll show you."

"So your textbooks don't have photos of aneurisms in progress and genital warts in full color?" She laughs. "I'm in the wrong profession."

I bump her shoulder, disturbing the rhythm of her steps. "You're in the totally right profession. You want to repair everyone, whether they deserve it or not," I say. "Were you really going to stick it out at The Boat Haus with that creep-ola guy?"

"I don't want Karl to hate me," Kimmer says, gazing at her tennis shoes.

"He almost served you to his dogs, Kim."

"Even so."

"Let's focus on what's important," I say. "You've got a new job for the summer, and I made it through my first dinner hour."

"You're right." Kimmer unzips her purse and yanks out a fist full of bills. "Look what we did tonight!" Her free arm wraps around me. "Fifty dollars apiece for Betty and Veronica, Capresi's new waitressing duo. And it's not even the weekend yet."

I crunch her bills with my fist, taking in the visceral crispness of them. "Ooo—*they feel good.*"

She stuffs them back into her bag. "*That'll* get you to London," she says. "Now let's go home and put our feet up. Forever."

Kimmer is a good nurse.

I stop at the Milano Art Gallery before my next lunch shift. It's a hole-in-the-wall, repurposed farmhouse located right before the stairwell that leads to Capresi's courtyard. The screen door is framed in gray driftwood. Talk about rustic.

Milano's interior is modern as hell, though. Its walls swim in an ethereal periwinkle straight out of one of Monet's lily ponds. A vaulted ceiling and I-beam rafters glow with white high-gloss interior paint. The place is flushed with light from a high row of windows.

The artwork features trees drawn in impossible colors, the frames of each painting floating against the periwinkle, each tree bending in a different direction. A tufted black leather chaise lounge sits in the middle of the space for viewing purposes.

An oil painting stretches across the far wall showing a forest of birch trees with papery trunks in vibrant hues. Violets. Emeralds. Cerulean. Their branches are done up in rich tertiary tones, all surrounding a patch of snowy earth. A beam of teal light radiates from the back of the birch forest, piercing the foreground like a glint off Excalibur.

My pulse flutters. I could walk through this landscape forever, following the shoots of light to the vanishing point where all troubles disappear. Art is like an out-of-body experience.

It's what I want, all the time. For my whole life. With New Wave music mixed in.

"*Hello there*," a voice sounds.

I trip onto the chaise lounge.

A gray-haired man in wire-rim glasses leans against a podium. "Isn't this a brilliant piece?" He steps toward the birches.

"Fabulous," I say, pulling myself off the chaise, ignoring the fact that I was just practically lying on my back in public.

The man hands me a card with the artist's information. "Are you looking for anything in particular?" I read the prices under each item. Even the smallest collage exceeds an entire semester's expense budget.

"Hmm. What am I looking for?" I say. "How about . . . my future. I think it's somewhere back there." I point to the ray of light that skewers the center of the painting.

Someday, I think, *what a life this will be.* Someday when I'm done scraping my way down a rabbit hole of acrylics and pastels and tile fragments, I'll produce something *visionary*. I imagine mixed-media mosaics hung on cathedral-worthy walls, sparkling like a Swarovski avalanche. Someday, when my work delivers chills through bodies unknown, as patrons waltz through climate-controlled galleries sipping long-stem glasses of sauvignon blanc. What a life I will have, that day.

When I come out of this *spin*. This is what I want.

"Ah," says the gallery attendant. "We're always happy to inspire." He smiles and steps back behind his podium, next to a terrarium shaped like an industrial-sized brandy snifter.

I spend the rest of the afternoon downstairs at Capresi's slinging spinach pastries, panini sandwiches, and Teddy's special gazpacho. But through the whole shift, my mind lingers in the impossible birch forest.

I dip my wrist into leftover ketchup more than once.

I'm a long way from my future.

CHAPTER 11

JULY 1984—Sandler Apartments
Should I Stay Or Should I Go?

Six days. I resign myself to the fact that no matter how long you stare at the phone, it doesn't make it ring. Picking it up and slamming it down again is just as ineffective—and it scratches the end table.

Audrey sits at the one chair we've added to our possessions, a hand-me-down (and down and down) wooden spindle-back thing with a loose spoke. She's finishing a Mary Shelley book at our kitchen table. Her eyes well-up, little fountains to throw itty-bitty coins into.

I fluff our hideous throw pillows. "Are you getting emotional over *Frankenstein?*"

"It's so *sad*." She whimpers. "Have a heart, will you?"

"Sorry. I didn't realize monsters could be so sympathetic." As I dust our milk crates with a dishtowel, something taps along the outside of the living room window.

I freeze. "Did you hear that?" The dishtowel prints a dust crescent on my tank top.

"All I hear is George Thorogood at Jan's biker pub down the street."

"*Shhh*—" Sounds rasp against the pane again. My insides tighten like a guitar string. "*That*," I say.

Audrey bookmarks *Frankenstein* with a paper napkin. "Jess, it's broad daylight. And we have nothing to steal."

"I'm from New York. We don't take chances." I reach for Joseph the bouncer's bat in the corner, positioning the thick of it behind my head, motioning for Audrey to join me. I choke up on the handle.

"You're not a jock at all, are you?" Audrey laughs, adjusting the club in my hands.

"My batting stance is not the issue here," I fake-whisper. "How about you throw back the curtain on three?" She pinches a corner of the badly embroidered panel.

"One . . . two . . . THREE—"

Audrey tosses the curtain. A duck on the other side of the glass honks at us then pecks at the half-opened pane. I drop the Louisville Slugger with a thud.

Audrey laughs hard and slides the windowpane. The screen behind it falls off entirely, waggling to the ground. The duck stretches his beak at us.

"Aw, come here, Frank, baby," Audrey says. "Can I get you some toast or something?"

"Frank's lucky he still has a head," I say. The duck cranes his neck as if to sneak a look at my mural on the wall. He quacks in indignation.

"Everyone's a critic," I say.

"Hey, high art is expensive, Frank," Audrey says, "and we're broke. Don't disrespect *Attack of the Wall*."

"Lucky Frank doesn't understand my aesthetic," I say. "Let's hope he doesn't end up on a plate garnished with fresh parsley. This is a rough town for ducks."

"*Someone's* feeling a little dramatic today." Audrey heads back to the kitchen, plucking a box of cereal from a cabinet. It barely rattles when she shakes it, her chopped-up sweatshirt sliding off one shoulder as she tilts the box. "Frank may have to go hungry."

I continue dusting, lifting the oversized tea mug full of junky mementos that's resting on a crate underneath the mural. Old beer caps and seashells jangle as I swirl the contents with my finger. I notice the guitar pick that Whit pressed into my palm last Friday. I pluck it out of the mug and flop onto our sofa, holding the pick in front of my face. "*Huh*. . ." THE RILERS is emblazoned across the front.

Audrey flops down next to me. "Wait . . ." She twists my wrist to reveal the opposite side of the pick.

Printed on the back. . . .

Is . . . a. . . .

Phone number.

"Oh, shit!" I pull myself upright.

Audrey shakes my shoulders. "Now you can call him."

A thought hits me and I slump back against the squishy cushions. "*Hmph*."

"Is there a problem?" Audrey asks.

"I'm not calling a guy who has officially blown me off for almost a week. He's had my number this whole time."

Audrey's jaw hangs. "You're joking, right? We're *modern women*."

I blow scrambled bangs out of my face. "We are?"

"How do you expect to take the world by storm if we can't even disrupt a few Chauvinist stereotypes? Why do you think our mothers and grandmothers sent us to college when they didn't go themselves?"

I roll my eyes. "So I could call guys?"

"So we don't have to be *dependent* on guys for stuff. Jessica, if you don't dial that phone, I'll sentence you to three straight hours of Kimmer's Madonna album."

"No Madonna—*ever*!" We're devout members of the Anti-Madonna Club.

Audrey picks up the phone and thrusts the receiver at my face. "Happy Sadie Hawkins Day."

The dial tone hums like a dare as I press the chunky plastic receiver to my ear.

"*There's* my favorite post-modern feminist roommate," Audrey says, heading to the kitchen. She starts rooting through our meager fridge.

I dial wrong, twice. An answering machine for the band picks up on my third try.

"*Umm*, this is Jess." I sit on the arm of the beat-up sofa, unprepared to be recorded for posterity. "I'm looking for Whit." The armrest is stiff as a concrete block under my ass. "I mean Matt. Not the drummer Matt. The bass guitarist Matt. We met at The Fall Out Club." It's as if someone's tightening a choker around my neck. "So, give me a call. Back. Okay?" I clunk the receiver back into its base with both hands.

I'm sweating. We have no air conditioning, but still.

Audrey stops poking through sparse containers of the refrigerator long enough to look at me. "You okay? Do you need water or something?" She tosses a take-out carton into the garbage. "How does Trina afford this crap?" she mumbles.

"That was torture. Women suck, putting men through that all the time."

"Well, you pulled it off."

"Was it that nerve-wracking the first time you tried it?" I ask her.

She freezes. A container drips in her hand. "I'll let you know."

She ducks but can't avoid the Strawberry Shortcake pillow I pitch at her head. The pillow's no match for her spiky hairdo, a field of sunset-colored wheat that continues to reach for the sky.

It's my first night off all week. The apartment's lonely once Audrey and the rest of the girls leave for their dinner shifts, and the yelling and thumping noises in the apartment upstairs are unsettling.

I decide to paint something to distract myself. Even if I dab an abstract onto some cheap canvas or let the ducks stamp across it to make web-footed prints, that'll at least produce something interesting.

There's a mom-and-pop craft store on Ferry Street and a thrift store at the edge of town. That'll work.

I climb into a pair of two-tone acid-washed shorts and a deep fuchsia V-neck. It's refreshing to stroll through town in something other than black and white.

Springsteen's "Born in the USA" pours from the sound system as I pass Jan's Pub, where motorcycles are racked outside as usual. Bikers with unruly beards and scraggly ponytails populate Jan's deck. It could double for Paul Bunyan's front porch.

Two guys wolf-howl as I pass. A man hops on his leather saddle and revs his engine loud enough to make me stumble. He laughs at me.

Charming. 100 percent. Jackass, that is.

Sparing our shower curtain this time, I spread a thrift-shop bedsheet on the asphalt behind our building, with a view of the riverbank. I've spent a good amount of tips on new shades of blue paints, from deep sapphire to a dusky slate. As I set up my workspace, the river rebounds light back toward the sky. Shades of magenta stick to the bottom of the clouds. The Delaware is painting, too. Go, nature.

I don't so much decorate the canvas as seep into it, directing the brush until the pigment smears in a way that reminds me of breathing. I'm in that *zone* where my brain blots out details like rent and screwed-up dinner orders, or well-shouldered men who don't call me. Every hint of energy works to commit the perfect streak of dawn sky onto the canvas. I sprinkle some sand and pulverized bottle glass onto the wet spots for texture and add a tinge of slate gray to the cloudy shapes, like the edge of something ominous is lurking.

Blue splotches collect on my arms like bruises. I take a few steps back. The canvas has been turned into a smudgy, boundless horizon.

Next, I trowel plaster over a distressed wooden plaque and smash apart some old glass tumblers, piercing my finger in the process. I incorporate blood into the design, rearranging and juxtaposing shards until some mysterious impulse between my ears says it's *done*.

I stare at both creations. My lungs can somehow fit more oxygen in them than before.

The girls amble in after their dinner shifts end, all within the same half-hour, swinging our clunky door back into its frame with a rumble each time. My artwork vibrates with every slam, azure and animated, their edges resting against the wall underneath David Bowie. I bought hooks to hang them, but we don't have a hammer. I've gotten comfortable in just a long T-shirt screen-printed with a Howard Jones album logo, which I usually sleep in.

Kimmer stares at my canvas. "Wow. Nice. It's so *blue*."

"It's an abstract sky," I say. "It's prettier in daylight."

"Definitely original," says Audrey, unzipping her black penguin skirt. "'Bout time we got some grown-up décor in this place. You did that one, too?" She points to the mosaic.

"I re-imagined some old glassware from the thrift store on Bridge Street." I suck on a cut finger. "Maybe I'll gift it to the restaurant."

"Interesting." Audrey crawls out of a pair of pantyhose, then steps in front of my mosaic and tilts her head. "Kind of *The Wizard of Oz* meets *Godzilla*."

"This one's stillness," I mumble, my finger between my teeth, "and that one's anarchy." Anarchy is big in the New Wave universe. It's a motivating factor behind most of what we listen to. It's why these cracked-up pieces of glass and ground sand feel so personal to me. They're about purposeful chaos.

Kimmer pulls my blue forefinger out of my mouth. "And this," she says, wagging my own finger in my face, "we call *Ode to Bacterial Infection*. Go wash it out."

"Speaking of thrift shopping," Trina says, pulling her waitressing blouse over her head and flinging it to the sofa. "My dad's been cruising garage sales for us. He found a dresser." She pulls on a neon turquoise T-shirt that hangs to her knees.

"I can't picture your prosecutor dad at a garage sale," I say. "God help anyone who has to haggle with him."

"We've officially become a pro-bono case, girls," says Trina. "I'll give you each a drawer if you're nice."

Audrey pulls on a pair of shorts then puts Spandau Ballet's "Gold" on the stereo.

The glass of our living room window scrapes.

"Wait," I say. "*Listen.*"

"Oh, for cripe's sake," Audrey says. "You know it's just Lucky Frank the duck." I grab Joseph's bat anyway.

"Are you running the Feature Film in your head again, Jess?" Trina asks.

The windowpane squeaks like someone's yanking at the frame. We all stop still.

"That doesn't sound lucky to me," Kimmer whispers.

The thick of the bat teeters in the air next to my head. Our white curtain visibly puffs with air from outside. The pane screeches with movement.

"I'm calling Joseph!" Kimmer shouts, grabbing up the phone.

"*Who the fuck is out there?*" Trina calls, backing toward our front door. "And what apartment is Russell the mechanic in again?"

The window glass creaks in its track and a hand peels back our curtain. Shaking like a vibrator, I pull back on the bat in cave-girl fashion, ready to strike. Blood sings in my ears.

"Whoa, hey—cool out, there, ladies," comes a guy's voice.

Whit from the Fall Out Club pokes his bleachy head through the window frame. The ugly eyelet curtain rests on the shoulder of his olive-drab Army jacket.

Kimmer thumps the phone back onto the end table with an off-key ringing sound. I let the bat clunk to our dingy carpet. "Are you out of your *mind?*" I flex my fingers as feeling returns to them.

"*Surprise.*" He juts his torso through the window.

Trina shudders with nervous laughter. "Haven't you heard of this thing called a door?"

He shrugs. "Where's the fun in that?"

"How . . . what the hell are you doing here?" I stammer.

"I came to see you." Whit salutes the other girls with two fingers. "How many points for this?" he asks Audrey.

She scoops her shed pantyhose off the rug. "I'll let you know when my heart starts beating again."

"You didn't leave me much choice," Whit tells me. "The front door of the building is locked." He swings his legs through the window, scuffing his boots on the wall and hopping into our living room. My art pieces judder.

"You could have called." I straighten my hair with my fingers. I haven't so much as caught a glimpse of myself since before my painting spree. Blue splotches still crisscross my arms.

"Right. There's this other thing called the telephone," Trina snarls. "We've got one right there."

"Yeah, about your number—" Whit pulls the crumpled slip of paper I handed him last week out of his pocket and passes it to me. "Thanks a lot."

I unwrinkle it and recite the scrawled number out loud, then whap my hand over my mouth.

Kimmer drops to the sofa, chuckling. Audrey shakes her head and disappears into the bedroom, pantyhose wilted in her fist like a molted snakeskin.

The last two digits are reversed.

"I thought you gave me a fake number," Whit says. "And you're not in the phonebook."

I shrug in embarrassment. "We only had the line turned on a few days before. I guess I hadn't memorized the number yet." And let's not forget I had a crippler of a hangover the morning we dropped him off.

"Our manager called me this afternoon," Whit tells me. "He said a girl with a New York accent was looking for me on our machine."

"Wait," I say. "*When* did you get the message?"

He peels off his jacket to reveal a green T-shirt with the sleeves sliced away. "A couple of hours ago." The jacket lands on our sofa.

Trina yanks her shed blouse out from under his jacket. "But you live an hour away," she says.

"Right," he answers.

"What'd you get the message and jump in the car?" I ask.

"*No, no, no,*" he says. "I took a shower first."

He slides his hands along the sides of my arms, squeezing me like I'm a cute loaf of Wonderbread. "So, what are you doing tonight?" he says.

I realize I'm standing there in a T-shirt and underwear. "Getting dressed?"

CHAPTER 12

STILL JULY—Main Street
Fascination

Once I change into a party-worthy halter top and shorts, Whit and I head out. We settle into a bar down the far side of town called Tijuana Brass known for its kick-ass margaritas. People don't come here to rock out, though. They come here when they actually want to talk to each other.

He drinks a bottle of Corona with a lime stopped in its glossy neck. I sip from a glass the size of an overturned sombrero. The place is done up in shady yellows, palm fronds, and fake tropical accents. Rattan ceiling fans. Silk dahlias.

"Are margaritas too girly for you?" I ask.

"I'm a beer guy. But this is still in theme." He tips the bottle toward me and his lip curls, the same way he swung the bottom of his Guinness my way when I first met him at The Fall Out.

"This glass is totally out of control." I swirl the cloudy margarita. "I feel like I shrunk two sizes." I notice the bar tiles have cartoon-like scenes scribbled into their blue and white glaze.

Whit laughs. "You're pretty miniature as it is."

I roll my eyes.

"It's cute, though," he says.

"*Please*. Kittens are *cute*," I say. "Cute is not New Wave." Maybe I should break down and dye my fucking hair. For the moment, though, I'll run with the fact that he finds my size endearing. "Come to think of it, there's nothing to play with in this drink," I say. "My glass feels naked without fruit slices."

Whit flags the bartender, a middle-aged woman in a turban that matches the pattern of the wallpaper, and asks for a lime wedge. She slides one toward us on a cocktail napkin.

I run the fruit along my lips. The lime stings but I don't care. I bite the wedge.

"The point is to eat that *with* the margarita," Whit says, eyeing my lips.

"Fuck margarita etiquette." I down more of the cocktail and watch Whit fight back a turned-on smile. Cloudy liquid washes over the salt crystals along the edge of my glass, dissolving them.

This is actually the most disgusting margarita ever.

Whit's tall enough that he towers over me even when we're sitting. "So you don't do things the everyday way, huh?" he says.

"No. But not always on purpose. I think it's an artistic brainwave thing. Or undiagnosed dyslexia." I haven't decided which. But I know that my *do things the weird way* gene also accounts for why I do stuff backward, and trip over things that aren't there. "Maybe we creative types are all just defective and trying to compensate."

"So how did you end up in this town?" he asks. "Did you come because of any . . . tendencies?"

"Meaning do I like girls, too?"

"Just wondering. This is New Hope."

"Nope. Never felt the urge. And there are just as many screwed-up girls out there as screwed-up guys, so why switch over?" I laugh. "If I were a guy, though, I'd marry Audrey."

"This is confusing," he says.

I smile. "Not so confusing. I know what I want."

I notice the tourists flowing past the front window of the place, mostly young types like us, propelling the party world forward. Girls with magenta lipstick and inches worth of rubber bracelets and winged eye make-up that I wish I could pull off. Guys in Doc Martens and two-toned jeans, clasping hands with chicks who look like they'd knife you in the back for your Menthol Lights. I want to embody their narrative and churn them into art. That's what I want—it's everything. And that's what everybody always said I could have, including my grandmother, who wanted me to have everything my mother never went after.

"I want to learn people's stories. I want adventure. Inspiration. Experience."

"In *Pittsburgh*?" He laughs, clanking his beer against the tile. "You had the beach. And Manhattan." Spikes of hair fall in his eyes.

"All right, so I'm still ironing out the details," I say. "Understand, New York is what my whole family always had. It's not all Manhattan parties and Broadway shows. It was more like me stuck in a low-end town where no one really amounted to anything exciting, with sweet but over-protective grandparents whose hearts I didn't want to break by being caught up in rebellion. Yet I was always dreaming of the day I could break out and express myself. So far, Pittsburgh has been a good time."

He raises an eyebrow at me.

"*Cold*. But fun," I say. "It's a step on the way to somewhere like London."

Whit rocks a bit in his seat as if sitting still isn't his thing.

"New York warps your perspective," I go on. "It makes you think every city is frightening and overwhelming. The first time the girls took me to downtown Pittsburgh, I thought, *Is this all of it?* It's like eight buildings. Manhattan goes on forever. You could get lost in there for weeks. And you'd come out dead."

"What do you think of Philadelphia?" he says.

"It's not too big, it's cool, it's punky. People talk to you on public transportation without looking down your dress," I say. "I love it here."

"See? That's why I don't leave," says Whit. "That, and the band's starting to pick up momentum. There's a great music scene here. Bowie recorded 'Young Americans' here."

"*Fucking A*—really?"

"Between gigs during the Diamond Dogs tour."

For a moment, I think, *what if this guy's onto something?* Margarita salt numbs my tongue. Which isn't good, since I might need my tongue soon. "So what's your gig?" I ask. "Are you resisting the suburban throng like in *Synchronicity II?* Were your parents upstanding Pennsylvania types who attended PTA meetings?"

"My parents divorced when I was four," Whit says.

There I go again. Saying *the stupid thing.* "Oh, shit. Sorry. I thought I was being amusing."

"What about your parents?" He dries margarita splashes off the bar with a cocktail napkin. "Did they stay together?"

"If you want to call it that." I breathe deep and kick my chair rail. "I'm one of those babies that were born to keep the marriage together."

He shifts back in his seat. "Really?"

"Guess what? It doesn't work," I say. "It's a lot of freaking pressure. And it makes everybody miserable to the point of wanting to die. Which my mother did. Then my dad just *disappeared.* And my grandparents stepped in."

"Oh, shit—my turn to apologize," he says. "That's a terrible story."

"You don't have to be sorry. It's not your fault." I shrug. "It's taken me a long time to face the fact that they made their own choices in life."

As I edge toward this adulthood thing, it dawns on me that my parents could have done whatever they wanted. They could have lived totally different lives, separately. They chose instead to keep true to the hypnotic vapor trail of a post-war society that told them divorce was B-A-D. *Bad.*

My generation? We're free to do whatever we want, for the first time ever. *Oh, the choices I have.*

I lift the lime wedge back to my lips. "I'll tell you a secret," I say. "One day my parents had a screaming fight and my mother threatened to leave. I emptied my fold-up Barbie carrying case, the one with the tiny orange plastic hangers full of mod paisley outfits. I stuffed the case with my own clothes and stood by the door. My mother asked me what I was doing. I clutched the Barbie case and said, *I'm ready to go.*"

I can still smell the white vinyl veneer of the case, slim as paper, ripped in one corner and showing gray cardboard underneath. "I was always looking to take off and start again, somewhere better."

The studs of Whit's leather bracelet scrape the bar. "I moved around a lot with my mother," he says. "It's not such a great sitch', believe me."

"Do you like the guy she married?"

"It's complicated." His dyed spikes spill forward again as he looks to the floor. I want to stretch my fingers through the gelled scramble of blondness.

"That sounds like a no," I say. I catch a glimpse of a scar on his forehead, shooting diagonally above his eyebrow. It must have been painful once.

"He's some rich guy," Whit says.

"So you're a trust fund baby, pretending to be a punk?"

He laughs. "Get that right out of your head. I told you, once my mother's lease is up, I'm on the street." He looks away for a moment, then knocks his knuckles against the bar tiles. "This is her fourth marriage."

"Her *fourth*?" I choke.

Bubbles tumble to the overturned bottom of his Corona as he drains it, then whacks it back against the ceramic. "Her fourth in five years. This new guy was married to somebody else . . . a couple of months ago."

"Uh huh. I get it," I say. "So, which of us do you think had it worse? The one whose parents stayed together for no good reason and are now out of the picture, or the one whose parent stuck around but kept switching partners?"

"Hard to say. Maybe we're all just fucked-up and trying to figure shit out," he says. "The world won't know how screwed up us kids from broken homes are . . . maybe for years."

Whit gets it, I think. Drew's parents were Leave it to Beaver types. He was convinced my stories of angry parental fits and abandonment issues were all fabricated drama. What he doesn't get is that theatricality sometimes stems from dark places.

I try one more swallow of my oversized drink and think of how to lighten the mood. "I'm sorry, I have to bail on this atrocious margarita." I laugh.

Whit straightens in his chair. "Do a shot with me instead." He waves to the turbaned bartender, ordering two shots of Jose Cuervo.

"I'm not much of a shot girl. And isn't a tequila shot the worst kind of margarita?" I ask.

"Keep your mind open," he says. "This is a night to try something new."

"I can handle new things." I perk up in my seat. "I live in New Hope!"

The bartender arranges two squatty glasses in front of us and overturns a bottle of Cuervo, filling them instantly. A saltshaker slides to a stop in front of Whit. Next comes a saucer of lime wedges.

He hands me a glass. "Come on. You and me." His warm hand lands on my knee, fingers spreading . . . moving. The studs of his bracelet contact my bare skin. It's like reading Braille with my thigh.

And what the fuck, I've got to put my trust in *somebody*.

I accept the glass. "I know there's a procedure for this," I say. "Will it keep me from spitting tequila across the room in a fit of nausea?"

"A *procedure?*" He laughs as he unscrews the top of the saltshaker, spilling crystals against the tile. "You make it sound so clinical." He closes my fist, creating a loose ring with my fingers, then does the same with his own hand. "Watch and learn."

Whit licks his hand between his thumb and index finger. "The salt has to stick," he says.

I wet the space between my fingers with my tongue and surrender my fist to him. He dispenses salt on both our hands, whitening the damp spots.

"Salt, shot, lime," he instructs. Mariachi music drifts in from a speaker hidden in a fake palm tree behind us.

"Isn't this what people do when they need to vomit up poison?"

"You gotta work with me a *little*." He laughs. "*Salt. . .*" he says. He licks the white shit off the side of his fist. I follow his lead, slurping crystals off my hand.

"*Shot. . .*" He throws his back. Mine takes effort; I can't do it all at once. "Come on, tilt your head," he coaxes. I almost spit the stuff out.

"Lime!" I call out. Pulp squirts against my teeth. The tequila makes a slow play down my throat, hot despite the citrus. I shudder as warmth generates in the core of my body. Juice spritzes the bar, sticking against my arm as I steady myself. "Hardly worth the mess." I wipe my lips with the back of my hand.

"You'll feel it in a minute." Whit blots the spill of salt and juice in front of me with a stack of napkins. "It's like speed-drinking." He motions for the bartender.

Turban Lady refills our shot glasses and flicks her head toward Whit behind his back. She winks at me. *Nice*, she mouths.

"I feel it already," I tell Whit. "If I throw up, it's your fault."

Whit draws an X in the center of his shirt with a finger. "I'll take full responsibility. I'm the upstanding guy who slept on your floor the other night, remember. *Innocently*."

"You're also the guy who I almost decapitated with a baseball bat tonight."

"*Come* on." He arranges my fist just so, pouring salt for both of us. "One more." I stare him down and click my miniature glass against his.

Instead of licking his own salt this time, he swipes his lips against my hand and licks mine. I swirl my tongue along the side of his fist in return. We tilt back the shots and attack the lime wedges. I laugh.

He leans in and kisses me mid-giggle, tasting of citrus, making me forget the sting along my lips, drawing me to the edge of the bar stool. Heat pulses through my body. My hand is in his hair. His palm moves along my thigh. I expect at any moment someone will shout for us to get a room.

The warm hum of his lips move against my ear. "I'm *really* glad you called me," he says. Ten points for the disruption of Chauvinist stereotypes.

Whit deals a few bills onto the bar tiles, slides off his wicker bar stool, and takes my hand. "Let's get out of here."

CHAPTER 13

STILL JULY—Still Main Street
Catch Me I'm Falling

The two of us spill onto the uneven brick sidewalk outside Tijuana Brass, avoiding the trees growing out of decorative grates in the pavers. We've become one with the party-going chronicle of the street. I trip on a metal grate that seems to be bolting down the roots of an elm. One appears on the sidewalk every few yards. "You're right about that speed-drinking thing," I say.

"Told you." Whit quickens his pace and I kick my legs into gear to keep up with him. New Hope at night is punctuated by neon shop windows, strains of jazz drifting from recessed entryways, and the postered-up windows of Lopito's music club. "What else is down this way?" he asks me.

"Everything. The Canal Stage, Bennett's Taverna, Andrea's Bakery." I tick off places with my fingers. "The leather crafts guy. The Asia gift store. And of course, Jan's biker bar, which is right by my building."

"You live next to a biker bar?" He turns around and walks backward, facing me.

"It's entertaining," I say.

"Where's your restaurant?" His hair springs as he walks, and he almost steps on a flighty-looking couple carrying to-go bags.

"The place has been closed for hours."

"Take me anyway." We turn onto the concrete overpass that crosses the Delaware Canal, which runs right behind Capresi's.

Whit stops in the middle of the bridge, leaning against its concrete guard rail. The canal threads underneath us, churning toward the green paddles of the watermill. The Canal Stage theatre glows with incandescent floodlights across the water.

I lean next to him, against the rough concrete. "This town is gorgeous in the afternoons," I say. "Every day, pink light bounces off the river and collects under the clouds. I'm convinced that land-locked places never see that kind of sky. Long Island was like that. And New Hope is like that."

"*Beautiful*," Whit says.

Water gurgles, shoving the scent of green murkiness up at us. Whit leans over the concrete. "How far of a drop do you think that is?" It looks deep enough to pour a car into.

He hoists himself onto the concrete abutment, catching his boot on a crack.

"*Whit. . .*" I say.

Slowly, he stands upright, extending his arms for balance. "The view is great from up here." A breeze rifles his hair. He turns, scuffing his combat boots against the cement. "I can see where the creek empties into the river." He steadies himself. There's a man-made plunge underneath us, where the canal waterfalls a good ten feet before it floods into the Delaware River.

"That's a little ballsy after several shots of tequila," I say.

The gold haze of the Lambertville Bridge blurs into the night sky. Whit stretches his hand to me. "*Come on up.*"

I laugh. "I can't even climb the steps of my apartment building without tripping."

"I won't let anything happen to you." A dusting of stars shows through the willow leaves behind him. I suddenly remember that he manages to play complex bass lines with those hands.

I grab his palm. He pulls me onto the concrete as if I'm made of paper.

I yelp as he faces us both toward the river, my back against his body.

"You're fucking nuts," I say. The breeze shifts the bottom of my halter.

He secures an arm around me from behind. "Nothing bad is going to happen. I promise." I grip him as if he's more rooted than I am, the two of us suspended on a strip of concrete not much wider than a sidewalk curb.

He closes the sides of his Army jacket around me. "You don't have to worry so much," he says. "Take a minute to take things in. *Process* stuff."

If we go into the drink, I think, *at least we'll go together.*

His arms draw around me and I feel him breathing. I'm sure he can sense my nervousness, gathering under his Army surplus jacket. "Listen to what the world is trying to tell you." His voice is like sedation, evening-out my pulse.

Frogs, cicadas, dragonflies—everything buzzes and screeches from obscured muddy places along the banks of the water. I inhale the smell of green things rushing under us.

"Why did you decide to become an artist?" His tone vibrates against my ear.

"I didn't decide," I say. "I just am. I want to meld everything I see together with some new idea and turn it into something else."

"I like that," he says.

Chills run through my body as I take in the coolness of the night, soft like a mist evaporating against my skin. "I wrote poetry for a while," I say. "But with writing, everything starts as a scribble on a page, and the words have to combine to create an image. Art hits your brain with *urgency*." Normally I'd underscore this kind of statement with hand gestures, but I hold back. "Art doesn't have to be words first."

"I knew you were a poet," he says. "I could tell by the way you talk about the sky."

"Yeah?"

"And the Barbie carrying case."

The judder of my laughter is petrifying all over again. I wasn't built to teeter. His jawline brushes against my temple, a steadying force.

"Here's a question," he says. "If the thing that inspired you already exists, why recreate it?"

"To share my vision of it." I stretch an arm toward an invisible subject and notice it's easier to balance this way. "To reach people with that moment and make it permanent. Besides, the source material has to sift through my weird, transmogrifier of a brain. It never comes out the same way."

He exhales, slowly. "Let's listen for inspiration, then."

Cicadas scream. I tuck my arm back inside his jacket.

"Why did you decide to play guitar?" I want to look up at him but I'm worried we'll tip.

"I think it decided to play me, you know?" he says. "I knew there was something I was supposed to *do*. Then my uncle handed me a guitar, and I knew that was *the thing*. As if it was in my head the whole time."

"*Wild*."

"That and I wanted to be Paul McCartney."

We shuffle; my adrenaline spikes.

"Playing out with the band is awesome," he goes on. "But I can't do it forever."

"Who says? You're talented," I tell him. His heart beats against my back. "You can do whatever you want."

"Nah. I'll see where the music thing takes me. But real life is coming."

"*Real life*," I echo, staring into oblivion. "I'm still looking for mine."

"I want to run this whole guitar thing into the ground before mine gets here."

I watch the stars hanging above the bridge as if my real life is hiding there, waiting to stage an ambush. Soon. We listen to the river burbling under the glint of the moon.

"Are you ready?" he asks.

"For what?" I can't really move; I've enveloped myself in his jacket. "Ready for *what*?"

He doesn't answer. We tilt. The horizon of the river slinks to one side.

"Oh, FUCK—" I yell. My sandals slip as gravity yanks us . . . toward the sidewalk. I cling to Whit and my feet clunk to the ground. My left sandal slides off completely.

Whit's arms are still wrapped around me. He pulls me back to a full stand. My one foot is bare. "*We're fine*," he says. "Like I promised."

I stoop to grab my cast-off sandal. The sidewalk scrapes underneath my foot, cool and hard. "One stagger in the wrong direction, we'd have been duck food," I say. "Which would be ironic in this town."

He laughs. "You still don't trust me?"

I shove my foot into my sandal but the shoe won't cooperate. A strap may be broken. "*Cynical New York bitch, here,*" I say.

He presses his hot face against my ear. "*You're not in New York anymore, remember?* Now, where's your restaurant?"

We turn down Mechanic Street, past Bennett's Taverna and the leather craftsman's rough-hewn storefront. Capresi's courtyard is set back from the street, below the art gallery. Guests have to navigate stairs and an overgrown S-path to reach the doorway, past sage bushes and day lilies. It's the secret on the other side of the wardrobe.

Whit follows me downstairs and across the walkway, pebbles crunching under our feet. The restaurant comes into view, all blue and black shadows. Strains of big band music rise from a radio playing in a patch of salvia plants, ninja-like under the cover of night.

I stop, stretching an arm in front of Whit. He takes the cue.

A shadowy man is stationed next to Capresi's brick wishing well, a chipped structure that greets diners as they wander toward the door. A stepladder and a bucket sit next to him.

My eyes adjust to the light.

The man is painting the bricks.

I back away, hauling Whit with me. Shadow Man doesn't notice us. Whit and I shuffle up the garden stairs to street level, me stumbling on my broken sandal.

"Was that guy doing yard work?" Whit asks.

"*The Midnight Painter!*" I giggle. "Someone keeps appearing at the restaurant overnight, painting things."

"You mean like vandalism?" Whit asks.

"No, like redecorating."

"Is that the New Hope version of vandalism?"

"Maybe." We turn onto Mechanic Street, heading back down the cobblestone pavers toward a still-active Main Street. He digs his hands into the pockets of his Army jacket, coming down from his A-D-D party boy high. Or maybe he's just metabolized some of the tequila. I'm still feeling its glow.

"This town lives up to its reputation," he says. "*Off-the-wall.*"

"Welcome to my life," I say.

Along Main Street, zinnias bloom silently in railroad-tie flowerbeds, petals stretching in the moonlight. I give Whit a walking tour past each restaurant, boutique, and bar. He tells me their lead guitarist used to play at Lopito's on Main when the place first started offering live music. It was a nice scene.

I discuss the mystique of *La Chambre Rose*, which marks the end of downtown New Hope. I explain about Jessica Savitch's fatal accident. He remembers the news stories.

As we stroll to my building, my apartment windows are blackened. I lead him around back, running my hand along the grainy bricks. At the edge of the parking lot, scrub bushes border the pavement, dropping off toward the water. Always water.

"It's not much of a building," I say, "but we've got a kick-ass backyard. Who knew a bottom-dollar apartment would come with a beautiful riverside view?"

He presses me against the bricks. "Right. *Gorgeous*," he says in my ear.

I point over his shoulder. "It's that way."

"*To fuck with the river.*"

The bricks tingle my shoulder blades. My skimpy halter doesn't protect much of my skin.

I tilt my face up to him. Secret confession: The one thing I adore about being smaller than almost all men is the tilting-back, the moment of surrendering up to that *kiss*. That ignition of intensity and splendor you can't let go of. His hands flatten against the bricks at my sides.

To fuck with the river is right. The world beyond his punked-out warmth is a blur I can't decipher, Army green and black and bleached.

He breathes into my ear. "What are you doing Saturday?"

"Working. Gotta save money," I say. "Goals to meet."

"What nights do you have off?"

"Mondays."

He hangs his head with an audible exhale. "I could come Saturday and wait at one of the bars in town for you to finish."

"We have a bar in the restaurant. You can wait there." I slide my hand across the heat of his back.

"Perfect. Then we can drive out to my apartment. Find someplace that's open late. Get something to eat."

"You want to take me to a *restaurant*?" I laugh. "How novel."

"You can't be ruined for restaurants all summer." He moves his lips against my ear, sounding like my own personal thunderstorm. "Promise you'll come out Saturday night."

"Wow, you are *Speed Dater*." The tequila hums in my head, as thick and muggy as the banks beyond the parking lot. Whit brings my fingers to his mouth and sucks on them one by one, running his tongue along the soft pad of my index finger.

"You're only here for the summer," he whispers, "and we've already lost a week. Don't make me wait till Monday to see you again."

My breath hitches in my throat. I can't help but arch when he touches me. "*Whatever you want*," I say, breathily.

We stay there until my hair is a mess and his palms have basically imprinted all over me, until I decide I have to go inside.

I unlock the door and toss my purse against the wall, regretting the thwack it makes. Kimmer is a mangle of covers on the pull-out, quiet in the center of our dim apartment. I remove clothes that Whit has been shuffling with for the past hour and pull a T-shirt down over my head.

We have the loudest phone in the world.

I yank the receiver off its cradle as it rings and loud-whisper: "*Hello* and what-the-*bejesus!*"

A cheer bleats through the earpiece. "*Jesssss!*" Drew slurs. "It's a good thing you're awake."

My head swims in pheromones and residual tequila and the artificial light of bridges that played across the surface of the water all night. The ceiling revolves; the Talking Heads' Magic-markered lyrics call down at me accusingly from our DIY poster, blurry and drained of contrast in the moonlight, making me question my place in the world.

"What if it's a bad thing I'm awake?" I say.

The receiver bangs on Drew's end. I imagine it swinging at the end of its metal coil, clonking against the plexiglass of a phone booth.

How does he know to call at this moment? Do pheromones cross time and space, rivers and landfills and highways when the former object of one's affection is in the throes of an emotional compromise?

"Jess," Drew says, "I gotta question for you." The regular, daylight-worthy Drew doesn't scrunch words together like *gotta*. Only the beer-saturated, post-2:00 a.m. Drew does that. My gut lurches as I try to guess what his question could be.

One of his buddies screams in the background for him to get off the phone.

"You're quite trashed," I whisper, trying not to wake Kimmer.

"I am," he says. "Back to my question. Are you ready?"

"God, no." I burrow into a fetal position under the cartoon sheets. "But go ahead."

Drew clears his throat. "Jess, *why is the universe here?*"

"What?" I flip over on the bed, dragging the sheets with me. Kimmer rustles next to me and pulls them back. "This is why you're calling me in the middle of the night?"

"I look at the stars, and I miss you," he says. "And I wonder how the hell we got here, what *fucking phenomenon* made the planets come into being to bring us to this moment. You and me. It's *assssss*-tounding."

I separate the phone from my ear as his volume peaks. "It's *assssss*-something, all right."

"It makes me need to ask," he goes on, "Why is the universe here?"

I smack my forehead with my palm. "Because it has no place else to go!"

Kimmer snickers and the sheets jiggle.

"Good answer." He switches to a news commentator voice. "*Judges, what do we have for this young lady?*" He breathes deep laughter through the receiver.

"You always have the right comeback for my bits," he goes on, dropping to a whisper. "*I freaking love you.*" The sound tiptoes across my eardrum, triggering chills.

"Is there such a thing as a Mad Physicist?" I ask. "Because I think you are one."

"Maybe. But I know what I'm talking about," he says. "Jess?" Shuffling noises bounce across the line. "Anything to report?"

A dart game zips into session in my stomach. There's some kind of intramural tournament revving up in there. "Drew, it's late, all right? I've got to work tomorrow. Can we contemplate the universe during normal business hours?"

"*Fine,*" he says. "Be that way. While you're on your summer adventure, don't forget what guy convinced you to enter your sketches in County Fest, when you'd never won anything before in your life," he says, half-mumbling. "And who dragged that abstract sculpture you made with him to two different colleges after I graduated. And who was the first guy—"

"—Drew, come on, you're really wasted right now—"

His voice goes deep. "*The first guy to touch you. . .*"

I press my hand against my eyes. Goosebumps rise on my arms, responding to memories I'm not ready to revisit at this moment.

"Don't you forget," he says.

I won't ever forget that stuff. I hold myself, since he's not here to do it. Yet I still feel Whit's handprints all over me, glowing like guilty trails of phosphorus in the opaque night of the room. Like spots worn shiny on the neck of a guitar.

"Jess. I know you heard me."

He waits for it.

I squish a fist into my pillow and mentally crowbar the night's activities into a separate boyfriend compartment in my brain, dousing paths that still smolder in soft places on my body. The airy fill of my pillow pushes against the side of my face.

"I love you, too," I say.

"*You better.* Or I'll,"—he breathes a throaty laugh into the phone—"I'll de-al*ffff*-abetize your address book."

The line goes dead. I smell the phantom mist of *Eau de Twelfth Grade* as my hair swishes against my face.

I cry against Strawberry Shortcake's cartoon cottage.

CHAPTER 14

JULY 1984—Sandler Apartments
Master And Servant

Our new dresser is the size of a Buick. It's painted black. *Black*. It's a cult-dresser.

I pull open the solitary drawer Trina assigned me, uncrumple a stack of tank tops and halters from a cardboard box, and start stuffing. My clothes give off a whiff of laundry rooms past. "This is no way to live."

"'Tis a far better drawer I give you," Trina says, "than the cartons you had before."

She's right, if overly poetic. The drawer beats the Dickens out of the cardboard box I've been using. Even if it's drowned in a gothic coat of latex house paint.

I fill the drawer in five minutes since I don't own much clothing. I stash the few items I won't need on a regular basis in my art supplies box and shove it back behind the sofa.

"That was my last box!" Kimmer cheers. She stamps a cardboard carton with her foot like Godzilla decimating Tokyo. But in a dainty tennis dress.

The front door clicks open. Audrey strides in, dressed in an unusually preppy blue silk blouse, her hair modestly slicked back.

"What'd they say?" asks Trina.

Audrey clasps her hands together, prayer-like. "I start tomorrow! Thanks for recommending me, Trina."

"Hell yeah!" Trina lunges through the kitchen and wraps an arm around Audrey's neck. "You're gonna love *La Chambre Rose.*" She plucks at Audrey's serious collar. "Now never wear anything this preppy again," she says.

"It did the trick, though. I'm the latest waitress at the most expensive joint in town, thank you very much." Audrey fans herself with her hand. "My shit officially no longer stinks."

I hug Audrey. "Now you can afford take-out, too." Although frankly, we don't need take-out. We're fed by our employers. Nothing as fancy as what they serve the guests, of course. We get reject food: plain chicken lacking its savory herb breading, reheated pasta with butter, whatever ingredients are otherwise about to go into the dumpster.

"We should go celebrate at The Rose," Trina announces.

Audrey kicks off her pumps. "I just came from there."

"So? Let them wait on *me* for a change," Trina says. "I'll introduce you to Bryan. You two coming?" she asks me and Kimmer.

"I've got a date," Kimmer says. The kitchen faucet gurgles as she fills the carafe of our coffeemaker.

"*Ooo,*" coos Audrey. "Joseph again?"

"Yeah. That big lug," says Kimmer. "He wants to go driving in his Jeep." She reaches for a coffee mug with a rooster painted on it. The rooster pines for a country kitchen we're just not in. As Kim slides it out of the cabinet, she bumps a red punch glass that rolls off the shelf and smashes on the counter, spreading grains of scarlet glitter along the Formica.

"Dammit! There goes my favorite family heirloom." Kimmer roots under our sink for a dustpan. I stare at the crystalline pattern formed by the blood-colored shards. In my mind, red circles start to emerge from the sprinkles.

Kim comes out from under the sink with a hand broom.

"Wait—" I shoot an arm in front of her. "Let me save that stuff. I've got an idea."

"Uh oh," says Trina. "See the smoke coming out of Jessica's ears? You just supplied her with her next art project."

Kimmer shrugs and passes me the hand broom. I sweep the fragments onto a paper towel and put them aside.

"So did Joseph buy a nice utility vehicle that can fit his huge body?" Trina asks Kimmer. "Or does he still own that pitiful little sideless thing?"

"It has *sides*." Kimmer inspects the rooster mug and runs it under the faucet. "They're plastic and held together with zippers. But they're sides."

I picture Magilla Gorilla in a Hanna-Barbera cartoon racer. "How the hell does he not fall out?" I ask. Kimmer shrugs.

Trina points to me. "How about you? You coming to The Rose?"

"I can't blow all my tips on lunches like you rich girls," I say. "I need to save for study abroad money."

"You can order tea," Audrey says. "Tea's cheap."

"Won't they throw me out for ordering nothing but a glass of hot water?" I ask. The bartender at Drazine's already has me on the Low-Shelf-Liquor Watch List. I don't want any more trouble.

"You'll be fine," Trina says, changing her clothing. "I'm *Chambre Rose* family." She pulls a blouse out of her assigned dresser drawer. It's a screaming tomato-red clingy number with zig-zag slashes across the neckline, as if someone took a razor to it. "I'll spring for chocolate mousse cake." She tugs the blouse over her head.

"I never say never when it comes to free chocolate," I say.

Kimmer searches our sparse cabinets for a bag of sugar since we don't own a sugar bowl. "I can't come," she says. She spoons sugar into her coffee straight from the bag. "If Joe says we're going driving, that's what we're doing."

My eyes narrow. "What does that mean?"

"He's used to being in charge, that's all. He has a strong personality. People listen to him."

"People like you?" I ask. A memory flashes of Kimmer returning home from a late-night wedding in a cab, solo. Her date, a bio major named Ray, had gotten himself arrested. For beating the pulp out of a guy who dared to eye Kimmer's V-neck dress, which Ray insisted was too sexy for her to wear in public.

Ray wouldn't even let her wear red.

Before it was over, Ray was responsible for increased security at our dorm. We finally convinced Kimmer he wasn't the guy for her.

"Joseph just needs a little affection," says Kimmer. "He's had it rough."

"Rougher than *Kimmer of the Eight Sisters and Brothers*?" I ask.

"At least my sisters took care of me after my parents went off the deep end. He's been supporting his family since he was 15."

"Where are his parents?" asks Audrey.

"His father's disabled and does nothing but drink," says Kim. "And his mom's been out of the picture for years."

"Join the club," I say. "Don't you think it's strange that Joseph keeps one-upping everyone's hard-luck stories?" I ask her.

"That's ridiculous." She blows on her coffee. "He's just had some bad breaks. The poor guy's starving for some understanding, so he doesn't have to be the tough guy all the time." *Blow, blow.* "He thinks I can help him."

"Funny how all your boyfriends need help," I say. Kimmer rolls her eyes behind the rooster-themed coffee mug.

Trina wags a finger in Kim's face as she sips. "Don't let him boss you around." She turns to me. "*You*, get ready. If we high tail it, you can make it back in time for your dinner shift."

I would point out the irony, but I don't want to bite the hand that buys me chocolate. I whip on a blouse accented by functional zippers. Their silver teeth streak diagonally across the shirt's checkered front, which resembles a racing flag.

Guys love the zipper shirt. They all want to know if the zippers work.

The walls at the *La Chambre Rose* are covered in green toile wallpaper straight out of a Jane Austen story. Vintage crystal chandeliers hang from the ceilings.

Ironically, nothing is rose-colored. The place buzzes with guests, far outpacing the typical lunch crowd I'm used to at Capresi's. This restaurant outsizes mine by two full dining rooms.

Trina greets the hostess at a podium, a tawny willow of a woman whose nameplate says Lima. A gleaming layer of ebony hair slides down her back as she reviews the hunk of a reservation book. It's the *David Copperfield* of ledgers.

"Trina Moran, you're not working this afternoon," Lima notes. Her painted magenta lips don't display anything resembling a smile.

"I'm visiting." Trina peers over a brass reading light attached to the hostess podium. She lifts a pen and starts darkening a dog-eared corner of the reservation page.

Lima reaches across the book and takes the pen out of Trina's hand. "Is this honestly where you want to spend your free time?" Lima turns over the defaced page to reveal a clean one.

Trina grins. "It would be an honor to be served by our staff."

Lima taps a flawless manicure in frosted mauve against the wood of the desk.

"Can you seat us in Bryan's section?" Trina asks. "We're celebrating."

Lima comes out from behind the fortress of the desk, pulls a set of menus from a stack, and motions for us to follow. She glides to a far-removed table, her shantung dress clinging to her every epithelial cell as she moves, arranging menus against the etched stoneware place settings. I contemplate ordering tea early to thaw the chill that creeps up the windows as she passes.

"Enjoy your lunch." Lima flips her hair and deserts us.

Trina holds a menu to the side of her face and faux whispers, "Bryan's ex, also known as the Queen Bitch."

"Why doesn't she just model?" Audrey whispers back.

"Daddy wants her in med school," Trina answers.

The windows reveal an expanse of river lined by rolling hills of tufted foliage, dappled in shades of green like an impressionist masterpiece. A cloud-spattered sky stretches over Jersey. Mallards ding their beaks against the surface of the Delaware River as it clings to banks that slide out from under the restaurant.

"Jess, you look like a tourist pressed against that window," Trina scolds.

"*Never.*" I pull my head off the glass. We are locals. Dammit.

Trina tosses her menu towards an empty place setting. "I've got this thing memorized."

"I should study up," says Audrey, opening the bulky triptych. She gulps, running her fingers along a sepia-toned page. Her complexion begins to lose luster. "*Holy crap.* You didn't tell me I needed to speak French."

"The menu's not that difficult once you get used to it," says Trina.

I flip toward the dessert section. Overblown prices flash at me. "*Whoa.* This place makes Capresi's look like an Army mess hall." One with a chef who molests produce for shock value.

"I'm so below this place. I don't think I can cut it here," Audrey whispers, her eyes taking on a tell-tale glassiness. "It's intimidating as hell."

"Auge, *stay with us.*" Trina gives Audrey's shoulder a rustle. "People are banging down the doors to waitress here. You can rake in the bucks. Don't stress."

The pink sifts further out of Audrey's cheeks. It's a look she gets right before she crawls into bed. For a week. I reach for her hand. "Audrey?"

"I'm all right." She remains entranced by her new sepia-toned enemy.

"Please don't turn this into one of your flash-fire, I-hate-myself episodes," says Trina.

Audrey leaves us now and then. You never know what little hangnail of self-doubt will start the process, where her psyche becomes a Rube Goldberg device full of curved tracks and tapping metal pendulums that can rarely be stopped. At the end of that domino trail, Audrey ends up wadding herself into bed, barely able to speak, as sheets of the calendar rip away in the wind. Sometimes we can head off the reaction, at least for a while, if we stabilize her early enough.

"You're in control," I tell Audrey. She stares at the Persian carpet. "It's just a job," I say.

"*Oh, boy,*" says Trina. "Here we go."

"You're stronger than a freaking menu," I tell her.

"You're *what?*" A sunny blond guy in black-and-white appears at the table, holding a finely-sheathed order pad. "*You are* ... three beautiful women ready for drink orders." His uniform is rescued from the ordinary by a cummerbund and formal bowtie. He's part penguin, part Chippendale's dancer. And his leather-bound order pad is dressed better than I am.

"*Heeeey,* Bryan," says Trina. "My usual, right away."

"You betcha. A Scotch-rocks for Trina Babe." The gravel in his voice makes you want to draw close enough to be sure you heard him *just right.* Audrey straightens in her chair, letting the menu drop to her plate. I snap the fucking spellbook of a menu closed and pull it out of her reach.

"The roommates, right?" Bryan tips a glistening pen at me and Audrey. Even the writing implements at The Rose are levels of fineness above what I'm used to.

Trina rests her chin in her hands, displaying a gentleness I've only seen her offer her parents' Irish setter. "Yep," she says to Bryan. "At long last, this is Audrey and Jess."

"Is bachelorette number four workin' today?"

"She's on a date," says Trina. "But Audrey just got hired here. She's one of us, now."

"No shit!" Bryan says. His eyes dart around to see if anyone heard him swear. "Welcome to the asylum."

What does he know about crazy? I think. It's hard to picture someone unwrapping a shit-filled diaper under these crystal-ridden ceilings.

Bryan gives Audrey's shoulder a squeeze and flips open his order pad. Trina lifts her chin out of the complacent sling of her hands. "*Ahem,*" Trina says. "Can you bring my alcohol so we can celebrate Audrey's new position?"

"I'll celebrate any position you want." Bryan tucks his shirt more snugly into his cummerbund. "Sounds fun."

One hundred percent, I think.

The glow flickers back into Audrey's cheeks. She stretches taller in her seat.

"Bry', tell Audrey this place isn't so rough." Trina shakes her blunt hair. "One look at the menu turned her white as a sheet."

"I'm having a moment," says Audrey.

"*Aww.* Don't let that French-fried menu rattle you," Bryan says. "It's kids' stuff."

"It better be," says Audrey. "I failed out of finishing school in Monaco."

"No problem," Bryan says. "We support each other around here. Right, Trina Babe?"

"You bet your bow-tied ass," she answers.

Bryan swings his attention back to Audrey. "What can I get you?"

"I'll take coffee," she says. "Black."

He bends to Audrey's eye level, slithering an arm along her padded shoulders. "You sure about that caffeine, love?" His surfer boy charm beams at her. "It's not great for nerves."

Audrey meets his eyes and places a hand on her hip. "You're right. Scotch here."

He pings his sword-like pen against the pad. "Care to make it a Dewar's, like Trina?"

"Sure," says Audrey. "Dewar me."

I feel the sudden obligation to interject something sweet, to counteract Audrey's upgrade from caffeine to stiff alcohol. "*Um*, let's remember we're here for cake."

Trina clears her throat, rattling Bryan. "We'll have the *Gâteau Mousse au Chocolat* all around," Trina says. She's developed a decent French accent without any of us realizing. "And tell Reese at the bar not to cheap-out on my drink. At least two fingers."

Bryan looks my way, pointing his pen. "And you?"

"I have a question first." I gesture toward the rolling foliage that borders the riverbed, then let my best New York accent fly: "*Waiter, is that New Jersey?*" Clouds sift themselves together over the horizon outside. New Hope may be in for some rain.

Bryan places his hand over mine. "No, Miss. *That's Afghanistan.*" His sandy voice tickles my ears.

"Cake, then," I say. "Cake is good."

Bryan retrieves our menus. "By the way, great shirt," he says to me. "Do those zippers work?"

I tug the shirt straight. "I'll never tell."

"I'll be back with *Gâteau au Chocolat.*" Bryan's accent could melt the sauce off a *duck à l'orange*. He leans to Audrey's ear, lowering his rasp. "See? *Kids' stuff.* You'll catch on." He disappears.

Audrey leans back in her chair and taps her chin with a finger. "Trina, do you like him?"

"What? *No.*" Trina says. "We discussed this. He's my friend. I don't *like* him."

"Why not?" says Audrey. Waitresses scurry past as the volume of guests begins to swell.

"You saw the evil-eye Lima gave me for even requesting Bryan's section," Trina snaps.

"*Uh huh,*" Audrey says.

Trina shifts in her seat. "I like my job. And Lima practically runs this place." The crowd murmur intensifies behind her.

"You're intimidated all of a sudden?" Audrey swishes a hand through the top of her hair. It hardly moves. "You were as subtle as a speeding truck at frat parties all year."

I smooth a wrinkle out of the tablecloth. "You do talk about the guy a lot," I say.

"I talk about you, too, but I don't want to fuck you." I can almost feel Trina's Scotch-ache as she strains her neck to get a view of the bar.

"Do you recognize him, Jess?" Audrey lifts the end of her dessert spoon to her lips. She bites the utensil the same way she chomped down on the end of the giant Pixy Stick we bought one day at—

"The guy from *Clovers*," I call out. "He almost stepped on me in the aisle."

The week we moved in, we hit Clovers discount department store to buy supplies. I hopped on one foot in the aisle trying on a new pair of tenny runners between the narrow troughs of merchandise.

When I looked up from the cheap gum soles of the tennies, a wall of tanned chest in a white muscle shirt was in front of my nose. Audrey pulled me upright.

"Whoa, sorry," said the husky voice of a surfer-looking guy with hair gelled way past oblivion. On closer squint, his hair might have been wet.

We performed that momentary you go that way, I'll go this way *dance. I pressed myself against a counter full of jelly shoes to let him past, savoring a whiff of hot salt as he glided by.*

"Casual Male *Sale?*" *Audrey mouthed behind his back, recounting the message on a retail sign we had laughed at in the parking lot moments before.* "Ooo, good. Let's buy one!" *She snapped a fallen bra strap back under her blocky sweatshirt and bit down on the end of the mega Pixy Stick, hard.*

Back at the *La Chambre Rose*, Audrey lets the spoon leave her lips and taps it against the sage-colored tablecloth. Slowly. "Trina, you're sure you're not into him?"

"We're done with this line of questioning." Trina props herself taller. "New subject. My dad set me up with an interview for an internship at a law firm tomorrow." She waves a butter knife at Audrey. "*You* will loan me that blue silk blouse until I have a chance to go shopping."

"A law office, huh?" I say. "Is this the part where we stop being New Wave post-punks and take our places in polite society?" I tilt an empty teacup, my pinky extended.

"Nah," says Audrey. "Who would we use as fashion role models if we stopped being New Wave punks?"

A youthful busboy arrives, placing drinks on the table. Trina swirls her glass with a flick of her wrist and takes a swig. "What happened to Bryan?" she quips at the busboy.

"Lima needs him in the main room," he says.

"See?" Trina points accusingly across the table. "She won't even let him wait on us. You'd think the world would explode into social disruption if he did."

I raise a water goblet. "How about a toast to unfettered views of Afghanistan?"

Audrey raises her Dewar's. "And to a welcome social disruption."

"Jess, where's your alcohol?" Trina asks.

"I'm on the dinner shift in an hour."

Trina slurps gold liquor. "Never stopped me." She grins, a force strong enough to twist the room like a kaleidoscope.

The next morning, I glue-gun shards of Kimmer's red punch glass together, combined with a couple of metal washers I found in the back of our kitchen drawer. They construct a freestyle pattern of angles and orbs. I string the piece in our bedroom window with a thread and a thumbtack.

The glass piece shoots streaks of aberrant ruby light across the room, beating the pluck out of the suncatchers that spin in the rafters at Capresi's. I call it "Disruption in Scarlet."

CHAPTER 15

LATE JULY 1984—Capresi's
Hanging On The Telephone

I'm ready for duty, apron slung over my arm, carrying my mosaic as a gift for the restaurant. A man and woman are perched at a table as I enter, embellishing the space like a rhinestone brooch at the top of someone's collar. The late afternoon light has barely found its way into Capresi's bar room, so my focus is a little soft.

"Hi there," I say. "We're not seating anyone for dinner yet." I place my angst-ridden mosaic on a bookshelf, in front of a row of sundry European travelogues and cooking manuals. My fingertips leave trails in the dust on the shelf.

I hit a wall switch and our lanterns flick to life.

An empty sequined dress is pooled across the table, shimmering like a disco ball. Dots of light bedazzle the face of a tall, late-twenties-type guy in snug jeans. With the dress rippling into his lap, his spindly fingers reattach sequins with a sewing needle.

The guy's moussed hair waves obediently over his head like Morrissey's. *He can't be wait staff*, I think. *He's not in a penguin outfit*. He's in a kick-ass pair of Billy-Idol-black boots I'd love to borrow, though.

The man cuts a length of thread with his teeth. "You're Jessica the waitress." His needle hand waves at me.

"Jessica the art student," I say, gesturing to my mosaic like Vanna White. "But yeah. *Um*, do I know you?"

A middle-aged woman in multi-colored capri pants springs out of the chair next to him, her clothing screaming in a palette of early Kindergarten paint box. Her purply makeup hits my eyes before the rest of her.

"Giorgio gave us a full briefing on you, dear," the woman says. It's rare that I meet an adult this much shorter than I am. "We've been waiting for you." She shakes my hand with both of hers and shows me to a seat, as if she works here, not me. "I'm Nena Love. But you can call me *Miz* Love. M-I-Zeee. That's my stage name."

"Aha. Do you work at The Canal Stage?" That might explain the theatrical greasepaint.

"Oh, no," she shakes her head, then shoots a smile toward the sewing man.

The guy extracts himself from under his spangled yardage, resting the dress on the tablecloth. He stretches his fingers as if they've been cramping then extends a hand to me.

"I'm Tye." He puts his back into a hearty handshake. Except his fingernails are Barbra Streisand rapiers whose tips poke the back of my hand. "Tye Madera. Direct from Oregon." He settles back down with the gown, repositioning the fabric. The patio isn't fit for formalwear right now. Its chairs are still mated upside-down on naked plywood tables.

I rest my apron on the burgundy-colored tablecloth, steering clear of the glistening dress so I don't contaminate it with my clumsiness. "Is that your stage name, too?" I ask the guy.

"That's my real name," he says, slinging an arm over the chair back. He crosses one leg over the other, swinging a boot. "But honey, nobody has only one name in this business."

"The restaurant business?"

Miz Nena Love elbows Tye. "Tell her your stage name."

"*Babylonia*." His smile is high-wattage.

"Like the skater?"

Tye and Nena smirk at each other. "Not exactly," says Tye. "More like, I give *historic* performances."

A pan clangs in the background and I turn to see Teddy craning his neck in the pass-through. I salute him a hello. He points a long utensil at me and scrunches down his eyebrows, then disappears.

Nena flattens her hand along the tablecloth in front of me. "We're the entertainment," she says.

The three of us rattle in our bar chairs as a glass item in the kitchen shatters.

"*I'm on it!*" comes Teddy's voice.

Tye lifts a panel of the gown to view his handiwork. The hypnotic sparkle of sequins sprays over me. "You're not going to ask what we do?" Tye asks. His eyebrow lifts.

"Something very glamorous, I'm guessing. Unrelated to skating."

Sleigh bells jangle and Giorgio strides through the lobby clutching a grocery bag. Something in the courtyard catches his eye as the hydraulics of the door hiss to a close. He stares at the brick wishing well, freshly painted in white high gloss.

Giorgio waves a thought away with his palm and paces toward the bar. The tail end of a crimson silk kimono ripples behind him. "I'm glad you've all met." He empties items onto the bar: limes, lemons, a jar of maraschinos. "Jessica, how are you this morning?"

"I'm learning a few things."

"Jessica's been telling us she's a fine art student," Nena interjects as if bragging about a grandchild. She pats my hand. "What medium do you work in, dear?"

"I paint. And I've started getting into glass mosaics. Giorgio, I brought one for you." I motion to my piece on the bookshelf. The glass chips embedded in the plaster spit back fragments of light, a rough-hewn version of the sequined dress on the table.

"So deconstructionist." Giorgio smiles. "I knew you were talented."

"Have you been to Italy?" Nena asks me. "You need to see the stained-glass windows in the churches of Venice and Florence."

"Italy's on my list. I've seen the Tiffany windows at MoMA, though. They're outrageous."

Maraschinos spill like squishy red marbles as Giorgio empties them into a glass container. "I appreciate you sharing your gifts with us, Jessica."

"You didn't tell me we were adding entertainment," I say.

"I've been contemplating it for a while," Giorgio says. "Then I heard Tye was looking for a venue."

"We're a venue?" I ask.

"You will be." Tye winks. He places his sewing notions in a storage case, popping the gold thread onto a spindle.

Giorgio sits next to me. "Jessica, Tye does a Diana Ross revue."

"Diana. Cher," Tye says. Soft crow's feet bend around his eyes. "If you're tall and beautiful, I'll do you." This statement would have an entirely different meaning at a frat party.

"How do you feel about serving during a drag performance?" Giorgio asks me.

"A *quality* performance," Tye adds.

"Tye is *very* high-class," Nena says. She flicks her hair with Shakespearean drama.

Giorgio leans to me. "Are you good with that?"

Tye and Nena hold their breath like toddlers.

I shrug. "This is New Hope, isn't it?"

"Excellent," says Giorgio. Nena and Tye exhale. "I wasn't sure how comfortable you'd be."

"You were worried about *me*? It's your restaurant."

"But you're part of the family now," Giorgio says. My heart does a mushy little thump in my chest.

Miz Love taps a hand to her sternum. "Isn't that sweet?" she says. "It's wonderful to be accepted whole-heartedly, right dear?"

Tye stands to his full and impressive height, draping the column of gold dress along his frame. He tosses a swingy panel of fabric along his legs. "In that case, what do you think of the gown?" He's more statuesque than any runway model I've ever seen.

"It doesn't go with the boots. But you certainly have the figure for it," I say.

Tye nods at Giorgio. "*Keep her*," he says.

He steps toward a coat rack in the corner of the room and arranges the gown on a hanger, smoothing it under a sheath of dry-cleaning plastic. "Not too flashy?" he asks, finger to his lips.

"The dress is good by me," I say. "I'll be disappointed if you're not a good singer, though."

The three of them chuckle. "That's so cute," says Tye.

Heat flushes my cheeks. Sometimes I want to smack myself.

"*Oh shit*. I don't want to be cute," I explain. "I want to be mature and knowledgeable." And un-stupid. "What did I say wrong?"

"We don't sing. We lip-synch." Tye sinks back into his chair. His fingernails glow with opalescent polish. "If I could sing like Diana, I'd be doing Vegas instead of New Hope." He folds a linen napkin into a perfect square against the table, more precisely than I could ever hope to. "No offense," he says to Giorgio.

"If you could sing like Diana Ross, I'd be your manager. No offense." Giorgio comes around behind Nena's chair. "Did you know Nena's one of the most accomplished lounge acts in the Pacific Northwest?"

Nena fans her face with her hand. "Well, I don't like to boast."

"Yes, you do," says Tye.

"You're absolutely right, I love to boast," she says. "I also do readings. Palms. Tarot. It's a gift. And every little thing helps pay the bills."

I notice a beaten upright piano has appeared at the back of the patio, topped by a tarnished candelabra. Like Liberace's lesser-appointed cousin is visiting.

"Where'd that come from?" I ask. It's amazing, the laundry list of things that appear at Capresi's overnight.

"There are lots of antique dealers in town," says Giorgio. "And I know every one of them."

"You mean thrift stores," corrects Tye. He heads to the bar and plucks a lemon wedge out of a plastic container, then pops it into his mouth. He's a fellow garnish-eater.

Giorgio walks behind the bar and grabs the soda sprayer, filling himself a glass of sparkly Coca-Cola. "One man's thrift is another man's antique."

"So true. Sounds like my last two husbands," laughs Nena. "Plus my one un-lawfully wedded wife. At my age, spouses start out as fine antiques. Then they *devolve* into thrift."

Tye wipes his fingers with a cocktail napkin. "Oh, Nena—where did you find the time for that many marriages?" He crosses toward the winter room, which is where people dine once patio season wraps up. "Excuse me," he calls back, "I've got a few more costumes to inspect for wear and tear." I catch a glimpse of a portable garment rack full of dresses, set up beyond the interior fireplace.

Giorgio takes me by the shoulders. "Please confer with Teddy on today's menu while Tye and Miz Love get familiar with the place."

I grab a mini legal pad and a golf pencil off the corner of the bar, then push through the kitchen in-door.

Teddy sweeps fragments of a broken coffeepot off the floor. The disembodied, green plastic neck of the carafe sits on the counter, ringed by a crown of broken glass. He brushes shards through a puddle of brown swill with the broom.

"So you heard the latest," he says, working the dustpan. Glass fragments tinkle and scrape. "Miami Night every other week."

"Works for me. *Life as-it-is*," I say. "What's today's menu?"

"I gotta get out of this place," Teddy slams a pan full of jangling glass particles into the trash. "I'm trying to build a reputation as an *artisan of cuisine*, here. Suddenly I'm a chef in Vaudeville."

"Don't you dare quit," I say, wagging the legal pad at him. "I'm certainly not taking over in the kitchen. We don't even have an assistant back here."

"A *sous chef*," he pronounces. "*Sous-sous-sous*. How can you waitress and not know this stuff?" He sets the dustpan under a counter and rinses his hands. Such is life at a restaurant. We wash our hands six times per shift.

"What does *sous* mean?"

"It means second banana. And until recently, it was me. I thought this was my chance to move up in the world."

I won't touch his banana reference. "Question for you," I say.

He scrunches a dishcloth in his fist and leans in.

I go on, "I was down here late the other night with a date—"

"A date? Where'd you find a date?" He pokes my side with his thick finger and I whack him with my notepad.

"In Philly."

"Figures. So you brought him *here?*" Teddy swipes dots of water off the butcher block with the towel before tossing it over the spigot.

"He wanted to see the restaurant," I say. "When we came down the front path, there was a man outside, in the dark. Painting the wishing well."

Teddy's eyes widen like one of our stoneware saucers. He pulls me closer by the top of my arm, his hand still damp. "*Shhh,*" he whispers. "Don't bring that up."

"But I saw The Midnight Painter!"

"*You didn't see a thing.*" A tea kettle whistles behind us, which he yanks off the flame. "That's Ernest." The whistle trails off like a dying bird. "He owns half this place with Giorgio, plus the gallery upstairs. They used to run things together, as a couple."

"Giorgio owns the gallery?"

"Keep it down." He glances through the pass-through to make sure Giorgio isn't in range. "*Half-*owns. After Giorgio and Ernest—" he mimes a stick snapping, "as a couple, Ernest became a silent partner. But he sneaks around here at night and changes stuff. It's Ernest's way of showing he's still in charge."

"I *knew* that gazebo was gray before."

"So, did you and some guy sneak in here and do it on one of the deuces or some shit?"

I pummel Teddy a few more times on the side of his arm. I'm the new Judy to his Punch. "All I'm putting out on those tables is silverware," I say.

"Poor guy. Too bad for him."

Meanwhile, I can still feel the tingle of the bricks along my shoulder blades from when Whit pressed me against my apartment building. I hide a smirk from Teddy with the back of my wrist.

"Would you read me tonight's menu, please, *Chef Artisan Cuisine?*"

He straightens his chef's jacket and pulls a metal stool out from under the butcher block. "Calm your jets and sit." He prattles off the night's dinner offerings, me scribbling on the yellow pad to keep pace with the herbs, light reductions, and organically grown, locally sourced this-and-that's, so I can transfer the information to the chalkboards.

"Try to move the tuna," he says, knocking a knuckle against the counter. "We gotta get rid of it."

"Move the tuna," I repeat, dropping the pencil into my apron pocket. "Of course, that means people will be eating old tuna tonight, correct?"

"Don't get smart," he says.

"Too late." I spin on my tennies and head out to the dining room patio, where naked tables cry out for me to dress them.

Miz Love is already banging out selections from *Pippin* on the well-used piano. She plays with her eyes half-closed as if her hands are being yanked from above by some puppeteer. Maybe that's how all artists feel, as if guided from on-high. She sings in a thick, vibratoed voice that's nearly a man's baritone. I snap fresh linens smooth on top of the plywood tabletops in rhythm with "Corner of the Sky."

I see Giorgio signaling me from the archway. I stiffen in place, a tablecloth melting to stillness against my side. He tilts the phone toward me, its curly cord bouncing.

I step slowly; the piano music vamps.

"A gentleman caller," Giorgio whispers. "Literally." I wonder if my grandfather has tracked me down to tell me not to wear such a short skirt. Giorgio hands me the hunk of plastic and leaves me alone in the barroom, lanterns swaying in the rafters.

"*So when do you get off?*" I hear in my ear. Whit's voice is as deep and compelling as a U2 bass line.

"That's a loaded question if I ever heard one."

He laughs. "Seriously. I can get there by ten tonight."

"What happened to 'Hi, Jessica, how are you?'"

"Hi, Jessica. I miss you. Let's get together tonight."

The tiny scrapes on my shoulder blades sing under my blouse. "I don't know if I'll be done by ten."

Tye whips through the room like a blur and I shelter the mouthpiece with my palm.

"How about I wait for you at the bar, like we planned," Whit says in my ear.

"I was drinking when we made that plan. But sure. Come down for a second date." I twirl the cord. The black loops create a tube around my index finger.

"You mean a third date," Whit says.

"Third?" My elbow digs an impression into the padded black vinyl as I lean against the edge of the bar. "We only had one date so far."

"You don't consider my sleeping on your couch cushions a date?"

"One-and-a-half dates, then. But who's counting?"

"Me," he says. "I'm counting."

I remember counting the days when he didn't call me. They ticked down in beats like water torture, me wondering if I'd get to feel those fingers sketch warm stripes across my back again. "*Okay*. I'm glad you called."

"I'm glad you answered," he says, "because no one ever picks up at your apartment."

At least he didn't crawl through the lobby window.

I clunk the receiver into its cradle on the wall. Tye sprints behind the bar, quick enough to almost leave a cartoon smear in his wake. He starts filling condiment containers in front of the beer taps. "I didn't want to interrupt, kiddo," he smiles.

"What are you doing back there?"

He leans on one elbow. "Word is you need a bartender."

We do. Sorely more than we need Diana Ross.

Tye is actually a decent bartender, clicking his long nails musically against the glasses. He gets all the orders correct. And he's fast.

Meanwhile, I wait for Teddy's dinners to emerge from the kitchen. And wait and wait. Four tables' worth of meals are not forthcoming.

Miz Love tinkles out romantic lounge numbers from her musical post on the floor. Marvin Hamlisch. Burt Bacharach. Cole Porter. It's not cool. It has a certain torchy, Rainbow Room charm, though. Tye pours a martini behind the bar as I duck away from a set of diners whose summer squash ravioli should have been in front of them 20 minutes ago.

I hop on a bar stool, stealing a look through the pass-through window. Teddy's nowhere to be seen. Neither is his culinary handiwork.

Tye places a glass of Coke in front of me. "So you can stay sharp." He smiles.

Sometimes it's the little things that keep you from losing it. "Thanks." My shoulders gradually unclench as I sip.

"I'm glad, by the way," Tye says.

I tilt my head. "*About?*"

"About the fact that you're not . . . apprehensive. About my show."

"Do people still act like that, even around here?"

"People still do it *everywhere*. Don't you watch the news?" He begins slicing lemons into wedges, collecting them in a ramekin on the counter. "And if you bailed on this job, I'd have to turn into a waitress." He licks lemon juice off his fingers. "No offense. But that would suck balls."

"None taken." I laugh. "So, you and Nena don't perform together?"

"Rarely. Babylonia is a one-woman show." He smiles with shiny lips. "Nena and I have been roommates for a few years. She's been in this business a lot longer than I have. She helps me. But believe me, I do all right on my own."

Tye pulls a scrapbook off the counter near the register and spins it to face me. The brown textured cover reads *Babylonia!* in loopy, gold cursive.

I flip through pages of Tye as Babylonia, dolled-up like a showgirl, or a towering Grecian goddess in a high wig and headdress. She cavorts with men in retro Chicago gangster attire here, smokes long cigarettes with a Tony Bennet look-alike there. She poses on a billiard table in a plunging emerald gown, surrounded by body builder types, revealing more cleavage than I have.

"How did you do that?" I tap at the boobs in the shot.

"Make-up." Tye's tan skin crinkles just sightly around his eyes. "Tape.

And lighting." He lingers on the photo a minute and raps a fingernail. "That was a hell of a night."

"Can you teach me?" I giggle. "I can use all the help I can get."

"Stick with me, kid. I know all the tricks." He has one of those noses so straight I wonder if someone sculpted it. But this is New Hope. We don't judge.

The bell at the waitress station finally sounds. "Apps on seven—*Up*," Teddy calls. My shoulder muscles tighten two notches as I head to the pass-through. Two plates of Portobello mushrooms and fresh mozzarella with arugula and special dressing are lovingly arranged on stoneware plates on the sill. These are not the dishes I'm looking for.

"Portobello salads?" I stick my face into the window frame. "What happened to entrees for six, four, and eight?"

"I'm working on it," Teddy huffs, facing the grates of the range. His back shifts in and out of my view. Flames hiss like ghostly jumping animals as he shakes a series of pans.

I slide the salads off the ledge and deliver them to table seven. Multiple diners follow me impatiently with their eyes.

Giorgio appears by the waitress station, still wearing the red silk kimono.

"Are things supposed to take this long?" I ask him. Guests peer around the arch of the bar room entrance in an effort to make their dinners materialize. "Table six has been waiting 40 minutes for entrees." I'm glad there's nothing sharper than a butter knife in front of our diners, since one of them might attack me.

Giorgio tilts his head. "Did everyone get salads?" Lanterns spit flecks of light against his face.

"Twenty-five minutes ago," I say. "The whole floor hates me. I'll have to swim across the Atlantic at this rate if I want to make enough tips to get to London."

Giorgio's spine straightens. He pulls his kimono more tightly around him and places a hand on my arm. "Bring them more bread." He disappears, red silk waggling behind him.

I scoop a loaf of Giorgio's sour dough into a wicker basket. The sides of the bread warmer are . . . cool.

Teddy works four pans at once as I push through the kitchen in-door. The temperature is 15 degrees hotter on this side of the barrier. "The bread warmer has stopped warming," I tell him. "What's the procedure?"

He doesn't even raise a hand to acknowledge me.

"Are you good in here?" I ask.

"*I'm working*," he says. I recognize the first of the many entrees I'm waiting for, sliding in a pan.

"Can I help you with something?" I ask. "My tables are getting impatient."

"You can get outta here. *FUCK*—" Teddy ducks as an arm of fire spouts at him. I slink away through the out-door.

"Jess." Teddy finally acknowledges me through the pass-through. "Warm the bread in the microwave twenty seconds. Then keep your little butt out of here."

I decide to handle all further bread issues on my own.

My grandmother hasn't even gotten a microwave in the house yet; I've barely worked one before. Regardless, I pop the wicker basket with the bread in and press some buttons. I fold a magenta napkin over the hot loaf and carry it to a starving four-top of all men.

The Alpha male at the table grinds his eyebrows as I draw closer. I urge myself to be strong. "I'd like to offer you some additional bread," I say. "Your dinners will be out shortly."

"Will they?" says Mr. Alpha. He's not the same laughing sophisticate he was when I sat him down, joking about the real estate market. He's imposing even when seated, dressed in a hunter green turtleneck and a blazer reminiscent of a 1970s television henchman.

"Apologies from the kitchen. We're shorthanded tonight."

"Please get on it," he says. His friend across the table shifts in his seat. The clear Christmas lights in the courtyard twinkle like they're laughing at me.

A woman at the next deuce hails me, rocking her table on the bricks. I crawl under the table and shunt its foot with a matchbook. Guests stare bullet holes through me as I escape to the dimness of the bar room. I wonder how well the chalkboard menu will perform as a shield.

Giorgio leans through the pass-through, eyeing Teddy's progress.

"One table is re-stuffed with bread," I tell Giorgio. "Three to go."

Giorgio turns to me and folds his arms into the gaping sleeves of his kimono. "I wish the crowd warranted this much trouble. The patio should be brimming on a Saturday."

"Can you help Teddy?" I ask.

He shakes his head, *tsk-tsking*. "Not my job. That's why I hired a chef."

"A *sous* chef," I say. "In fairness, that's what he was until recently."

"I need him to step up," Giorgio says.

"And these customers need to eat before they wither."

"*Guests.*" Giorgio corrects me. He bites his lip and shoves off toward the kitchen.

I don't follow him. I want to spend less time in the kitchen. It only leads to hot trouble.

Against my better judgment, I head back outside to check the status of the *guests* on the patio. Nena's chords tickle the soles of my tenny runners as I pass the piano. The '70s TV henchman in the blazer waves me over.

"Your dinners will be out next, I swear it."

"That's not the problem." The edge of his turtleneck skims his chin as he speaks. The piano transitions, and The Girl from Ipanema starts a-walking.

The guy grips the football of a sour dough loaf and bangs it on the table in front of me. "Hard as a doorstop," he tells me. *Some things are not good hard*, I think.

I sigh, apologize, and lift the wicker basket. Henchman drops the rock-loaf into it. A second member of his party presses his Oscar Goldman-ish hands against the tablecloth. "Try again, sweetie," he says.

Lesson of the night: Never warm bread in a microwave unless you want it petrified.

CHAPTER 16

LATE JULY—Still Capresi's
Girl U Want

The turtlenecked cast of The Six Million Dollar Man is now drunk on gin and tonics. They sing along to a Ray Conniff piano standard. Teddy may be a slow-as-shit cook who can't handle volume, but his meals are ridiculously delicious.

Mr. Alpha Henchman hands me back a gilded plastic check tray with several large bills and tells me to keep the change. I fold the money into my apron. This is the last table left on the floor.

As I decrumb a tablecloth, I see Whit standing in the bar room. I'm suddenly aware how much of my hair has frizzed out of its ponytail holder. I swipe at whatever makeup must be smeared under my eyes.

Whit's smile takes its time crawling across his face as I come through the archway. He's in his Army jacket, complemented by jeans with a ripped knee and his hulking combat boots. His six shades of gradient blond hair is tousled, blender-like. I want to ruffle my fingers through it. I resist the unprofessional urge to roll him under a bar room table. Instead, I hit him with a quick kiss hello.

Tye wipes down the surface of the bar as Giorgio spray-rinses the sink underneath.

"Giorgio, Tye, this is Whit," I announce. "He plays bass guitar in a band in Philadelphia."

"Ahh." Giorgio nods.

Whit shakes hands with each of them. "Matt Whitlan," he says. "Nice to meet you." I wonder if Tye's nails jab Whit's hand like they did mine.

Giorgio leans back against the counter near his register. The wall behind him is racked with liquor bottles under colored lights, like a heathen pipe organ. "Our gentleman caller from this afternoon?" he asks.

Whit looks behind him for whoever else Giorgio might be talking about. He lets a laugh slip, flashing straight teeth. "I guess that's me."

The spectrum of liquor bottles glow beyond Giorgio's shoulders. "Jessica doesn't call you Matt."

"Whit's short for my last name," he explains, shoving his hands in his pockets. "It just stuck."

"Very mysterious," Giorgio says. "Are you hiding something? Or is that a stage name?"

"*Giorgio*," I warn.

He smiles my way. "It's good to get to know people," he says, eyebrows raised. "He's a performer, too. Correct?"

"Yeah," says Whit. "But I don't hide much."

Giorgio bites his lip. "If you say so."

I pull a black vinyl bar seat out for Whit. At least these seats are intact, unlike the cut-up diner chairs that bit my ass at The Fall Out Club. "We thought he'd have a drink while I finish up," I say.

"That's wonderful," says Giorgio, pushing himself off the wall. "Tye, can you help Jessica break down so she can leave?"

Tye whips a hand towel into the sink and steps out from behind the bar. "Notice I don't have a problem switching roles on the fly." He winks at me.

"Have you got any lager back there?" Whit asks, leaning his forearms against the bar, showing off those brooding shoulders. Like the night I met him, hunched over a beer bottle.

Tye rubs his hands together. "Come on, kid," he says to me. "I'll help you close up, then it's time for a shift drink."

"A shift drink?"

He stops. "Haven't you been doing a shift drink every night?"

"We haven't had an official bartender until today," I say.

"Oh, honey, learn to make demands," Tye says.

"*Eh-eh!*" Giorgio motions to Tye, waving a finger. "No shift drink. She's underage."

"God, you're strict." Tye gives Giorgio a weird combination of a glare and a smile. He turns to me. "Sorry, kid."

"Thanks for nothin'," I say. I guess my bullet-proof ID can't save me here.

Tye tugs my elbow, heading toward the patio. I lean to Whit's ear. "*I'll be quick,*" I whisper before I go.

Giorgio pours Whit a frothy beer from the tap. "You were telling me how you came to play guitar," I hear Giorgio say, handing Whit the over-full glass.

Whit sips to keep the foam from spilling. "I was?" He wipes his lip with the back of his hand.

I head off with Tye, trying to maintain a cool workplace demeanor. He steals a last glance at Whit before we step through the archway.

Tye shakes his fingers at me. "Nice," he says. "*You sure about him?*"

"One hundred percent," I whisper back.

As I break down the last four-top, I tamp back the thrill of knowing that a heart-stopper guitarist is waiting for me at the bar. One who's passed a bonafide hardcore litmus test of opening for a punk band whose songs I have on a mixtape and everything.

I can't decide if that makes me turn neon chartreuse with envy, or hot as hell over him. Maybe both. I try to keep my impure thoughts from contaminating the linens as I close things up.

Eventually, Miz Love packs sheet music into a scuffed leather valise and I restock the last of the condiments at the waitress station. Teddy's face greets me in the pass-through as I swish a hot towel across the Formica countertops.

He bangs the bell on the sill, sending me into the air. "*Bingo,*" he says. "I knew it!"

I stifle the ring with my palm. "Huh?"

"Punker . . . boyfriend," Teddy says. Steam rises from the deep sink behind him, releasing a cologne of vaporized cleansers.

I snap my towel towards the window. "Not another word out of you."

Back at the bar, Giorgio's kimono hangs on the coat rack in the corner. He leans against the counter under the wall of liquor bottles, nodding intently at Whit.

Whit's glass is void except for lacy lines of foam. He tilts back in his chair as if picturing the whole world at once. "The future . . . is totally unknown," Whit says. "It can be anything. That's what makes it amazing."

"In the abstract," Giorgio says. "But your *individual* future," he raises a finger as if discovering a new scientific theorem, "*that*, you have to *make* happen."

"I know," Whit hangs his head, spikes pouring forward. "I'm on it. Really. I need time. I can't hammer in the tent posts yet."

"I know you think you have forever," Giorgio goes on, leaning over the beer tap. The light of the bar sink reflects up against his pastel shirt. "But time passes more quickly than you're going to anticipate."

I'm in awe of how Giorgio can extract a person's every hope and ambition and anxiety and fling it into open space, all in less than a half-hour of meeting them. Whit doesn't seem to mind it any more than Kimmer and I do. It's like free therapy.

I clear my throat. Both men turn their heads to me.

"Am I interrupting?" My hand goes to my hip, feet apart. I recall how the hands-on-hips pose motivated the fraternity brothers to nickname me *Scary Sister*. Whit lets his tilted chair reconnect with the bar room carpet.

Giorgio smiles. Liquor bottles diffuse colored light behind him. "We're getting along nicely."

"Can I have him back now?" I ask Giorgio.

Whit pulls me to him and folds an arm around my neck. "Great girl you've got here," he says. His palm runs along my shoulder blades, reminding me how nicely his touch connects with the contours of my back. As if he carved me himself.

"Great girl *you've* got there," Giorgio responds. "Why don't you two get going?" He flicks his hands at us.

Whit slides off the bar stool. I slink an arm inside the warmth of his jacket, feeling the back of his muscled ribs, washed in a familiarity that by all rights should take more time than this to build. As if he's just . . . mine.

We head for the red lobby door, sending the sleigh bells ringing to life. I wave goodbye over my shoulder.

Giorgio gives me an okay sign. "*Nice*," he mouths.

This seems to be the consensus. Snagging a guy like Whit is *nice*. As in, *nice trick, Jessica*. Twenty points for the aspiring mosaic artist temporarily masquerading as a waitress.

I take a minute to compare Whit to Drew, who's so intellectual and intense, even weird. (Some things are *good* weird.) More than anything else, though, my relationship with Drew has been . . . steadfast.

As I thread my finger through a belt loop at the back of Whit's jeans, I wonder where steadfast begins to slake its way toward being rote. Like the times tables I learned in third grade.

Whit is the most exciting, hot, and volatile thing I've wrapped myself around, maybe ever.

I lead him up the garden steps as his hand works its way underneath the back of my waitressing blouse.

We reach the sidewalk. "I'm sorry you had to—"

I'm cut off by his whole body, engulfing me in a kiss that feels like it's been trying to bust free from a padded cell.

When he finally steps back, I have to remember how to walk.

The Thompson Twins yammer over WMMR radio, pulsing electronic drum sounds through Whit's roughed-up dashboard. He twists the volume

Once in a Lifetime

knob down. "That's enough *dance pop*," he says.

"Don't get all hardcore snobby," I say. "You should try dancing." I wonder why he insists he can't dance. I have an intuition that he can truly move his body.

"I'll stick to driving," he says, "and the driver picks the music." He sweeps a hand along the place on his forehead where I've noticed a scar.

Whit owns an old-model Camaro that's missing cloudy circles of paint on one side. A line of rust, craggy as a mountain range, showed itself above the footrest when he opened the door for me.

The white concrete highway zooms with traffic, this being a Saturday night in the Philly suburbs. Whit drives as if every bit of his pent-up energy needs to be processed through his exhaust system. I inspect the dark labels of the tape cassettes that litter the floor of his passenger seat, plucking them off the mat. Echo and the Bunnymen. Bauhaus, which is pure gothic punk. Modern English, which is smoother and more danceable.

"So is this when you tell me?" I ask. Plastic clicks in my hands as I shuffle the cassette cases like a deck of cards.

Whit looks at me, then at the windshield. I offer half a smile as I look up from Echo and the Bunnymen.

"When I tell you what?"

"About that girl you were seeing." I tap the corner of one cassette against the other. "The one who almost made you give up women."

His body stiffens as he pulls in a breath, shoulders rising. "Oh, *that* girl."

"I bet she had a name."

He stares at the road. We've got a lot of time for the drive. He can't escape this conversation.

"Delilah," he says. The transmission groans as he switches gears in preparation for an off-ramp.

"*De-li-lah?*" I lose my grip and the Echo tape rattles to the floor. "You're making that up."

"Would I make it up?" He palms the wheel, hand over hand. I brace myself against the passenger window as we cloverleaf.

"It's just so . . . biblical."

"*Not exactly.*" He stares at the unresponsive highway. "One of my friends was kind of a slacker. I let him stay at my apartment when he lost his job. Dee worked weekends, so she practically lived with us during the week." He lowers the volume on the radio. "He was home all day. With *my* girlfriend." I watch his knuckles blanch around the steering wheel.

"That so sucks." It *sucks balls*, as Tye would say. I scrape a fingernail over the molded faux stitching in the dash. "How long did you two go out?"

"About six months."

"Sorry." I open his glove compartment and stack a few of the tapes inside. "Well, I'm not *that* sorry," I shrug. "You know what I mean."

The cassette deck in his dashboard is mounted kind of crooked and is in a finish that doesn't match the rest of the car. Rather than fix the rust rot, it seems, he installed a cassette player. Whit lifts the Modern English tape out of my lap and flicks it open with one hand, sliding out the black cassette. He notices a loop of tape sticking out of the bottom of the plastic casing.

"*Shit.* Fucking ruined." He tosses the cassette back to me, eyes rolling. I catch it between my two hands. "Things started getting weird when he moved in," no longer talking about the cassette. "I should've noticed from the start. I developed temporary blindness. You can bet that won't happen again."

I turn one of the plastic gears in the Modern English cassette with my pinky finger in a sad attempt to rewind the loop back into the casing. The brown strip of tape has developed a kink, though, which means it'll never play right again. Whit pulls the cassette off my finger and pitches it hard into the back seat, where it ricochets off the triangle of the far back window.

"Some things are unfixable," he says.

"*Right.*" I cross my cassette-less hands in my lap.

"Those two live together now." Whit shudders like he's expunging a vision of his girlfriend in a jumbled sex knot with his roommate. In his bed.

"I didn't mean to dredge up bad shit," I say. "I just want to know what I'm dealing with." Because of course, it now falls to me to erase that vision.

Whit half-smiles and twists the radio volume back up. He clasps a hand against my thigh. "It's all right." He sings along to a grating number by the

Dead Kennedys, his head bobbing until the spikes of his hair vibrate like tuning forks. "She wasn't *the* girl, you know?" he continues as guitar feedback zings through the car speakers. "I thought she might be the Long-Term Girl. But she wasn't."

"How will you know the Long-Term Girl?"

"Not sure," he says. "But I've got time to find someone who's worthy."

"Ah," I say, folding a leg underneath myself. Miniature girls like me can collapse themselves just about anywhere. "So *worthiness* is the key."

He laughs. "What about you? How will you know *the guy*? That 'seeing other people' guy of yours in New York, he's not *the* guy?"

I'm silent for a beat, trying to ignore the other *boyfriend* compartment in my brain. I bite my lip, choking back images of Drew that make my heart suddenly ache.

"Oh, fuck," Whit says. His hands tighten further around the steering wheel. "Don't tell me."

I shift in my seat. "No, you don't understand. I'm trying to figure this all out, too," I say. "That's what the 'seeing different people' thing is supposed to be about." I remind myself that I was the one resolved to leave the country, which is what set the whole rift with Drew in motion. I decided to venture out. Drew just went with it.

I twist the tuner knob in the dash in search of something more soothing than the Dead Kennedys to diffuse the tension. Nothing suitable presents itself. We're stuck with "Holiday in Cambodia."

"I'm being as up-front as I can," I remind Whit. "*Guys. Life.* It's all a fucking jigsaw puzzle that somebody threw in the air. Every day, I wonder when all this is supposed to assemble itself into my life. Are things any different for you?"

"Not really," he says.

"Right. So yes, I'm still searching."

"Wow. *Honesty*," he says. "What a concept."

"Just because I don't have all the answers doesn't mean my feelings aren't valid," I say. "They're real. And they matter."

"Your feelings about what?"

"About everything." I twist a lock of hair in my fingers. "Maybe about you. How about this: I think *the* guy is the person you want holding your hand when you die. If I were going to kick off tomorrow, who could make that moment bearable? I don't want anything less than *that guy*." I pound a finger on the dashboard.

"No pressure, huh?" Whit laughs, shifting between watching the traffic and watching me. "You're breathing pretty heavy, there, Jessica."

Dial it down, I think. *Don't become Scary Sister*. "Can't help it," I say, swiping hair out of my face. "I need to know how you feel about this shit. Otherwise, we may be wasting our time."

"I feel this shit is . . . intense." He bobs his head to a couple of beats of The Dead Kennedys as obnoxious guitars give way to DJ chatter. "But in a good way."

"*God*—I need a drink." I pop his glove compartment back open, riffling through the cassettes. "Have you got any vodka stashed in here?"

"You know something?" Whit laughs. The amber of the streetlight slides gracefully over his cheekbones. "You're the coolest girl I know."

My waitressing skirt shifts under his palm. This is more the level of friction I was picturing for tonight. I shimmy closer, the stick shift a rigid barrier between us. I want to do things to him that will send us careening over the median.

"Do me a favor," he says.

"Whatever you want." I think about that answer and push back into the bucket seat. "Well, *maybe* whatever you want. *What do you want again?*"

"About that guy in New York . . ." Whit's fingers trace a line along my jaw, then down my neck. "Don't tell me another thing." Peter Gabriel's synthesizers saturate the air around us.

"Fine." I close a hand over his, just before it slips under my clothing. "Now watch the road, will you?"

CHAPTER 17

STILL LATE JULY—King of Prussia
Melt With You

Whit's apartment is huge by college standards. A chocolate suede couch and a futon float in an L-shape in the center of the space. You wouldn't expect a New Wave musician to "float" furniture. But there's still an air of make-shift throughout the room: A desk made of a sheetrock panel mounted on construction horses. Foldable metal snack tables from 1976.

No New Wave posters. No amps. Instead: earthy neutrals, glass knick-knacks, photographic prints by Ansel Adams and Georgia O'Keefe. I wonder if his unfaithful ex-girlfriend was an interior designer.

"My mother," he says. "In case you're wondering."

"Is that who does your decorating?" I let my purse drop to the warm yellow wood of the floor. A couple of throw rugs are scattered around, and tall, potted plants guard a sliding door to a balcony behind us.

"Maybe I should shit the place up more," Whit laughs.

"No, no," I lift a seashell made of amber-colored glass from a curio shelf, inspect it, then put it down. "It's like an *adult* lives here."

"I'm not sure that's a compliment." Whit tosses his keys onto a snack table and slips out of his jacket. "The place is going up for sale, so I can't change anything." He undoes a couple of notches on his gray button-up, revealing a Violent Femmes T-shirt underneath. This is the first time we've been alone together outside of a vehicle. I make myself at home on his surprisingly clean futon.

"You want to watch something?" Whit flicks on the TV and plucks a hand-labeled videotape from a stack under the TV stand. "You want to live in England, right?" He fits the tape into a boxy VCR player. "Have you heard of The Comic Strip?"

"Is that like Ziggy, but different?" I notice a copy of *TV Guide*, a beer can, and a half-empty pack of Dentyne gum on his coffee table, aluminum wrappers scattered like fallen leaves. Finally some evidence of *guy* in the room.

"This is a bootleg tape from a club in London where they do alternative comedy sketches. Kind of like *Monty Python goes punk*."

I sit upright. "That I've gotta see."

The grainy recording looks like it was filmed by a guy hiding behind a ficus tree. A pair of freakishly skinny types in suits inhabit the stage, abusing each other with power tools, squawking in urban British accents I can barely understand. Cigarette smoke obscures parts of their performance.

Whit sits on the floor, pushing back against the futon. He slides an arm across my legs. A Johnny Rotten wannabe in a bad three-piece suit on the TV screen slams himself through a wall. "*The Dangerous Brothers*," Whit explains.

"They certainly are. Where did you find this?"

"A record graveyard on South Street." He runs his hand along my thigh. I wish I had enough foresight to have changed into something other than waitressing clothes before coming here. "I'll take you there some time," he says.

"I'll hold you to it," I say. His hand radiates heat along my calf.

The Dangerous Brothers scream the kind of bloody murder that only bloody Britons can scream. "Maybe this doesn't strike the mood I was thinking of," Whit says.

He pulls a blocky remote control off the coffee table and punches the volume down to nearly imperceptible. I process the fact that not only do we not have a TV with a remote control in my apartment, we don't have a TV.

"Let's try something." Whit lifts himself off the floor and heads toward a console. He fishes out a record album with an ethereal cover in clouded blues and yellows. "The Dangerous Brothers meet Roxy Music." He spins the vinyl in his palms and sets it on a turntable sunken in the console.

Bryan Ferry sings "More Than This," from *Avalon*, which drifts from a tall set of speakers: romantic, flighty guitar and thick, dreamy Eurotrash vocals. It makes for an ironic soundtrack as one Dangerous Brother unsuccessfully launches the other from a cannon.

Whit moves the coffee table out of our way.

I kick off my scuffed tenny runners and stretch my toes. "I've been on my feet since two. Capresi's patio isn't gentle on them."

"Your feet hurt, do they?" He fakes a reasonably good British accent, the kind that has played a huge role in my overseas daydreams. "We can't have that," he says, shoving my empty tennies aside. He cradles my feet in his hands. A guy can hardly do a greater thing for a girl who's been standing for eight hours than rub her feet. They tingle with every press of his thumb. Goosebumps spread across my body like crops budding in the spring.

The skinny guys on the TV set each other on fire.

After making mush of my soles, Whit's palm finds its way back to my legs. When he runs his hand upward, his fingers spread apart. When he smooths them downward, they close. It's like he's studied *Effective Ways to Melt Jessica 101*.

I spill to the floor next to him, my hair flowing down the upholstery. The red-headed comedian on the TV screen wails, his pin-stripe suit scorched and ragged.

Whit drapes himself over me, his body hovering but not touching me yet. He presses his lips against mine, I roll his button-down off his shoulders. I want to wrap myself around him, pull him flat against me, and claim him for my own. I've barely felt this way about anyone. . . .

Except Drew.

I snap that thought out of my mind like the click of a View-Master, off to a separate mental boyfriend compartment.

Whit's faux-British accent vibrates in my ear. "Too *beau*-ti-ful." He swishes a mermaid-worthy section of my hair out of the way and runs his lips along the side of my neck. *"Too beau-ti-ful for sore feet on a Saturday."* His body molds against mine.

My toes curl. "That accent thing is *so* unfair."

"Yes." He unbuttons me, his lips drawing lines along the dip in my neck, nudging aside fabric, sliding away straps. Dampening warm stretches of my skin. "But is it working?"

I push my hips up to meet him. "You think?"

He touches me in places that make it difficult to keep my composure. I arch my back and twist my hands through his multi-colored hair, which springs between my fingers. Roxy Music's otherworldly guitar riffs descend around us like mist. My muscles cinch when the cool, triangular studs of his leather bracelet graze my stomach, the linen of my waitressing shirt having been peeled away.

He sings in my ear, his Bryan Ferry-washed accent dissolving me.

I'm a canvas being painted.

I don't ever want to do anything but this again for the rest of my life.

I pull his Femmes T-shirt over my head. It snakes down my torso as I step barefoot toward the hallway bathroom. In the process, I mentally tiptoe through a slow fermentation of guilt. I made Drew wait months for a moment like this. Not three dates. The disparity between being 17 and being 20 is more jarring than I anticipated. Like hurtling myself across the Grand Canyon.

I wonder if sexual permissiveness just naturally skyrockets as we move toward this *adulthood* thing. And if this is why Whit was literally counting dates with me. Because a certain amount of dates lead to sex.

I pass a bedroom filled up by an iridescent drum kit, copper cymbals hanging over an unmade mattress on the floor. The next bedroom has a full bed in it, with a tufted comforter and a respectable-looking dresser. Whit could have invited me into this room, but he didn't. We stayed on his living room floor.

The porcelain in the bathroom is actually clean, not some spectrum of grays that need to be scrubbed away to reveal white. Did he scour the place before he invited me, or is he just not gross?

I lock the bathroom door and peel down black lace underwear that I inadvertently put back on inside-out. The fabric clings to my body a little too enthusiastically. *Hmmm.*

I rest a foot on the tub, reaching for the places where he had so nicely been playing.

My finger hits something that is not me.

I contort myself to view a region of my body that I otherwise have no desire to see. As aesthetic as the female form can be, this section of our anatomy could pass for a pile of fish bait if you ask me.

I glimpse a vibrant blob of pink, a color that no woman has ever been in real life. When I pull it, I feel distinct, tiny pinches of pain as it lifts from my skin.

"*Oh, Holy God!*"

I shuffle backward, whacking an elbow against the papered wall. A bottle of Nivea topples from a shelf behind me and clunks to the floor, its push-spout clogged with yellow gook.

Whit calls from the living room. "You good in there?"

"*Not exactly.*"

I swing open the door. Whit's at the end of the hall, hopping into a pair of sweats.

I root myself in the rectangle of the hallway, hands on my hips. I imagine myself lit by the brazen white glare of the bathroom fixture. *Scary Sister.*

I raise a harsh eyebrow. "*Ahem.* This is a good one."

His collared shirt is flung over one shoulder. His chest is still bare. He shakes his head at me.

"Are you missing something?" I ask him.

Whit stuffs an arm into his shirt and pulls the fabric up his back. He shrugs. "Are you gonna make me guess?"

"*Gum!*" I say.

His eyes search the ceiling, hair riding in front of his eyes.

"You were *chewing gum*?" I exclaim. "Do you realize where you frigging left it?"

Whit wipes his palms on the corner of his unbuttoned shirt and stumbles toward the aluminum garbage can next to his construction-yard desk. He lifts the can and spits a pink gob to the bottom of it, which makes an ugly drum sound.

"*No gum*. It's gone." He stifles a laugh. "You didn't notice all night, babe."

I fold my arms into a pose that has petrified many a frat brother. "I'm going to murder you slowly."

"How's tomorrow night for that? I have practice in the morning."

I whirl back into the bathroom. My reflection greets me in the mirror, hair all over, eye make-up almost vanished except for a powdery veil. I hang my head and *laugh*.

"*Sorry*," Whit calls. I hear the trash bucket topple and ring out a steel drum noise as it rolls along the floor. "I'm glad you're keeping your sense of humor."

I suck in a breath. "You got me into this. You need to get me out. I mean get . . . *it* . . . out."

"Okay." Metal scrapes against wood as he rights the trash bin. "I'm coming."

"Bring scissors!" I call.

I'm slumped against the cold porcelain of the sink when he comes in with a comically huge pair of knife-block scissors. "How, um . . . what do you want me to do?"

"Holy Mother, don't point those things at me." I push the blades away. "You don't have anything more petite? Maybe one of those little jobbies with the plastic safety handles?"

"*Petite*?" he says. "This isn't kindergarten. Or France."

He kneels and I brace my foot on the edge of the tub, gripping his shoulder for balance. He flicks on a second light fixture, flooding the room with day-worthy brightness.

It's like being probed by aliens.

I stretch past his shoulder trying to snap off the light; my fingers don't reach. "This isn't how I pictured our first night of nakedness," I say over his shoulders.

"Hold still. *Please.*" I grip an overhead shelf, hoping not to yank it out of the wall. A shadowbox full of dried flowers slaps face-first onto the floor. A second container thuds against the tiny octagonal floor tiles, spinning.

I laugh. "Welcome to my nightmare game of Twister."

"Jessica, you've *gotta stop giggling.*" He snips with the scissors. Delicately.

I notice his ceiling has far fewer water stains than my apartment. I hold my breath in a futile attempt to stop laughing.

"I'm begging you," he says. The scissors make a swishing noise. I flinch when the cold metal taps my skin.

His hand reappears with a spot of pink matter between his fingers, which he quickly tosses into a garbage can. I try not to look.

"Better?" He rubs my legs. I take the scissors from him and slide them into the sink.

"*You're so fucking lucky I like you,*" I say.

His face flushes red. "I owe you one. Okay?" He yanks at the T-shirt I'm wearing and smirks. "You look cute in my shirt." He twists the excess fabric into his fist. The cotton slides up my back.

He skips band practice the next morning. I snatch what's left of the pack of Dentyne gum off his coffee table as we leave the apartment. When I razz him for timing things badly and missing rehearsal, he insists it's fine, that the band moves practices around all the time.

I pitch the pack of Dentyne into a trash can in his lobby.

CHAPTER 18

AUGUST 1984—Sandler Apartments
Is She Really Going Out With Him?

Audrey and Trina slam their way through the apartment doorway like heavy artillery, making me wonder whether the front doorknob has dented the wall. I duck as they clomp past me, huddled in the foyer. I stop rummaging through our closet shoe mountain in hopes of helping Kimmer find a missing tenny. Kimmer's on the floor, searching under the sofa bed.

"When I need help, I expect to get it." Trina kicks one of my sandals out of her way and across the living room. "I taught you that damn menu when you were freaking out, Audrey." She rips a black mesh headband out of her hair that's a little too Madonna for her. Such is waitressing life; we have to compromise our post-punk fashion sense to comply with food service conventions. "I was stressed to the max today and you didn't offer a hand once."

"I was assigned to Lima, not you," says Audrey.

"You avoided me." The headband flies through the bedroom doorway.

"Oh, please." Audrey tugs open the refrigerator door and grabs a half-empty bottle of Coke, unscrewing the top. She takes a swig. "Reality check in aisle four." She shoves the fridge door closed.

Kimmer's head is halfway underneath our sucky orange sofa, searching for her sneaker. "*Uh-oh*. Maybe working with friends is like borrowing money," she says. "Don't do it."

"You and I are doing it," I remind her.

"Oh yeah."

"See?" Trina points at Kimmer. "Some people respect the working relationship."

"Why don't you tell them the real problem?" Audrey leans against a kitchen chair, stressing out the loose spindle.

"I don't have a problem," says Trina.

"Bryan asked me out," Audrey tells Kimmer and me, sipping soda. "We're going dancing at Drazine's. And he's been hinting about taking me to Cape May for the weekend." Audrey holds the soda bottle in front of her eyes, swirling the remaining Coke. "This is flat as Kansas," she says, spilling it into the mint-toned sink.

Trina turns her back on us and clomps through the bedroom. A dresser drawer bangs shut. I follow her.

"You all right?" I ask Trina. I'm distracted by the bathroom ceiling looming in the background, ringed with more brown loops than ever, like a 1970s wallpaper pattern. Just add Mylar.

Trina strips out of her uniform with a vengeance. "I'm absolutely fine," she insists, wearing only underwear. "Some people think they don't need to reciprocate when other people help them," she shouts toward the kitchen.

"*You swore you didn't like him,*" Audrey calls back.

"I don't like him. Do what you want." Trina climbs into a T-shirt with a giant skull screen-printed on the front. She stomps across Audrey's egg crate mattress to pull the bedroom curtains closed, knocking the tension rod askew in the process. My red glass suncatcher swings like Tarzan.

Audrey rests against the bedroom door jamb. "I'll blow him off if it bothers you," she says. "Just say the word."

"Nothing bothers me," Trina shouts. She sticks her arm into our scary black dresser and comes out with a tape cassette box in her fist.

"By the way, waitressing is total bullshit." The cassette case clatters like a maraca. "Now that I've got an internship and a stipend, maybe I don't need New Hope." She zips herself into a snug pair of shorts, struggling with the snap. "Maybe I'll commute to Fox and Rascowitz from my parents' house."

Kimmer pokes her head into the bedroom. "But who'll pay your share of the rent?"

"*Thanks a lot*," Trina says in a huff. "The more I learn about the firm, the more I think waiting tables sucks."

"You were the one to make like waitressing was the end-all," I say, "Miss Waitressing Goddess." I reach to stop my suncatcher from spinning in the window frame.

"I didn't ask for that title," Trina says. "It's not like I get to walk the Waitressing Red Carpet or something. Come off it, girls. There are better things to aspire to."

"You mean like waitressing in Atlantic City?" asks Kimmer. "Wait, *there* it is!" Kim darts over to Audrey's foam mattress and pulls her missing tenny out from under it.

"No. I mean law school. Or at least a real job." Trina pushes past Audrey in the doorway, cassette box prattling in her fist.

"Real jobs are hard to come by," says Audrey, "I need to make some cash for the summer if I'm going to be able to afford books for school in the fall. And an alcohol budget."

"And I'm not even halfway to the extra grand I need for London tuition," I chime in, trailing Trina into the kitchen. "Not to mention expenses."

Trina pulls a knife out of a drawer and splits open the Scotch-taped cassette case, just missing her thumb. She bangs the case against her palm, shooting a selection of black tablets into her fist. She pinches two in her fingertips, tosses them into her mouth, and shoves her face under the kitchen faucet, gulping water.

Kimmer comes up behind me. "Was that what I think it was?" she whispers over my shoulder.

Once a semester, Trina receives a delivery of rattling cassette cases.

Sometimes she loans the contents to girls on our floor during finals or sells them. Black pills. Blue pills. I'm not sure which ones do what.

Trina slips the cassette case into her pocket, a rectangle bulging in her shorts. She yanks a violet button-up cardigan out of the closet even though it's 80 degrees outside. The sweater belongs to Kimmer.

"Where the hell are you going?" Audrey asks.

"Off the wall," Trina says. "I'll go to a movie. Or maybe I'll move out."

"You're getting all sorts of upset over nothing," Audrey adds.

"Have fun with Bryan at Drazine's." Trina grabs up her purse, throws open the front door, and disappears into the hall with a slam. A strange set of banging and grunting noises follow.

We girls head to the foyer and swing open our front door. I look for the trick panel in the floor that Trina must've just fallen through, because she's vanished.

In Trina's place, a washed-out blonde woman is on her knees at our threshold, gathering a jumble of vegetables off the tiled hallway floor. From her bone structure, I'm guessing she eats once a month.

I remember getting a brief glimpse of this woman the day we moved in. Her husband whisked her past us quickly. I've barely seen her since.

She's on her knees cradling an eggplant. Kimmer sprints to the doorway. "We're so sorry," she says, helping the blonde lady gather a stray zucchini.

I help rescue a cucumber as it rolls across the floor. "Should we go after Trina?" I ask Audrey.

"She needs some cooling-off," Audrey says.

Our neighbor rises to her feet, a floral dress draped on her meager frame. Circles shade underneath her eyes.

Audrey quickly adopts a waitressing smile. "Welcome to The House of Rage. Did you have a reservation?"

"You'll have to excuse our friend." Kimmer rests a zucchini on the kitchen counter. "She was recently possessed by her evil twin."

"We're kidding," Audrey says. "Please come in. Have we met?"

"Not really. I'm kind of a homebody," the woman says, swiping a string of hair behind her ear. "I'm Paula from A4." She offers a handshake. Paula has a hint of discoloration on her cheekbone, like a thumbprint of smeared eyeshadow. "I've got a garden growing on the west side of the building. I thought you girls might like some fresh vegetables."

"Didn't we see you when we moved in, the day our sofa nearly got wedged in the stairwell?" I ask.

A smile of recognition lights her face. "Was that you ladies?"

Audrey pulls a garage-sale Tupperware bowl from a cabinet and places it on the table.

"I'm surprised the ducks haven't eaten these," I say, settling a couple of vegetables into the bowl. This is as close as we've come to having a centerpiece since we've lived here. I jumble a few veggies around to see what arrangement looks most attractive. It looks more like a salad than a piece of decor.

"The ducks do get into things now and again." Paula's accent is pure Pennsylvania cornfield, bubbly and without inhibition. "That's why I thought you girls might as well have some. There sure are a bunch of you squished in here."

"Fewer every minute," says Kimmer.

"*We're fine*," stresses Audrey. Kimmer grabs some mismatched drink glasses from our dish drain and puts them back into the cabinet, suddenly aware of the state of the kitchen.

"What I mean is," Paula's voice drops to a whisper, "there's only supposed to be two adults livin' in these units at a time."

Audrey freezes. "You won't tell the landlord, will you?" she asks. I bite a nail.

"I wouldn't do any such thing," says Paula, waving the notion away with her palm. "But I figure if you're jammin' four people into a place like this, you might be in a bad straight. And groceries help."

"I'll make soup," says Audrey. At least somebody knows how to cook around here. I never appreciated this talent so much before in my life. My thoughts drift to the brown, garlic-soaked goodness of my grandmother's homemade lentil soup, which rivals Teddy's special gazpacho.

I curl up on our sofa. Instead of warm Italian bean soup to comfort me, I have nubby tangerine throw pillows. "How long have you lived here?" I ask

Once in a Lifetime

Paula.

"Since Dean opened a cigar store on Main Street last fall," she says.

Kimmer freezes, the cabinet door handle still in her hand. "Dean?" she repeats. "Dean Clayton?" She sets a gas-station tumbler back in place on a shelf.

"Do you know Dean?" Paula fingers a delicate chain around her neck.

"Uhhh, no," Kimmer says. "I'm having a psychic vision." She taps her fingernails on the counter. "Or maybe I saw the name on the mailbox upstairs."

"I've seen him around," says Audrey. "He leaves in a pick-up truck in the morning."

"Sounds like him. *Ooo*—those are some cool numbers on the wall." Paula gravitates to my mural, then points to the abstract canvas. "Did you buy this one in town?"

I join her in front of my work. In my head, we're viewing the pieces in some metropolitan gallery. "No, I painted it. That one's supposed to be a sky."

"I see clouds!" She smiles with teeth that could've used braces.

"I'm flattered you think it's salable," I say.

"Sure," says Paula. "People shell out cash for all sorts of junk in New Hope."

"*Right.*" My shoulders slump. I pull a pillow off the couch and flop to the floor. Kimmer joins me with the ashtray.

"Sorry we don't have much seating around here," Audrey tells Paula, taking a seat on the floor, "but you're welcome to a spot on the rug." Paula claims the fourth space in our roommate square around the ashtray, typically occupied by Trina. "It's nice to have girls to talk to in the building," Paula goes on. "This place seems to attract loners."

I steal a cigarette from Kimmer's pack and light up. We offer Paula one, but she waves it away. I guess she gets enough smoke in the cigar store.

"Speaking of girl-talk, Jess." Audrey sidles closer to me on the distasteful shag. "How'd it go at Whit's apartment?"

"It's his mother's condo, actually," I say.

"You have a new boyfriend?" Paula asks.

"Pretty new." I try to keep from hyperventilating as I picture him, all bleach streaks and cheekbones, adrenaline, and creativity. *Too beautiful*, he called me.

"He's pretty *and* new," says Audrey, tweezing the Virginia Slim out of my fingertips. She takes a long drag. Our cigarettes have become communal. Some roommates synch periods. We synch tobacco products.

"The place is decorated like his mom still lives there," I say. "Classy. And suspiciously clean."

"I don't need the decorating report," Audrey says, blowing smoke at me. "Unless his ceiling needs painting."

Kimmer coughs. "Don't hold out on us," she says. "If we don't live vicariously through each other, who will?"

Audrey points the glowering orange eye of the cigarette at me. "How many ceiling tiles did you count?" she asks. I hug a throw pillow like a shield.

Paula gazes at us, thrown by the roommate vernacular. "Sorry, girls, I don't get it."

Audrey hands the cigarette back to me and drops to her back against the carpet. "There are certain moments when we women are in the position to . . . survey the ceiling. If you're not completely engaged in this activity, your mind wanders," she points to imaginary panels above our heads, "and you count a lot of ceiling tiles."

"But if the guy knows what he's doing," I add, "you stop counting." Light dawns on Paula's face and she nods until her lackluster hair swings.

"*Spill*," Audrey says to me. "How many tiles?"

"Um, it was the floorboards, and the wall, and the bathroom wallpaper . . . and okay, *sometimes* the ceiling."

"The bathroom wallpaper?" Kimmer laughs.

"*Don't ask.*" I don't mention the gum. I'll never mention the gum. I consider it a bonding experience between Whit and myself.

Paula readjusts the collar of her dress. "It's been a while since I've been in the middle of *this* kinda talk." Her collar bone is as defined as the piping along the edge of the sofa cushions.

"So, what's the verdict?" Audrey demands, jostling me.

I squish the pillow in my forearms like it's being punished. "Somebody obviously taught him something, girls," I concede. "His talents go well beyond just playing the guitar."

"I knew it!" says Audrey. "You could tell by the way he *looks* at you."

"It's a good thing you didn't knock his block off with the bat that one night," Kimmer says.

"You're not kidding." I pitch the orange pillow at the baseball bat positioned in the crook of our living room wall. It topples over, clunking against the shag. "Meet our friend Louisville Slugger," I tell Paula.

"You play baseball?"

"I play 'Let's be prepared in case we ever need to bash some skull.'"

Paula gulps hard. "You must've been a heck of a Girl Scout."

We gab with Paula for a while, then see her to the door.

"By the way, Jess." Audrey wrestles an overstuffed garbage bag out of our trash can and holds it in front of me. "It's your turn to take out the trash. The joys of apartment living."

I follow Paula upstairs, hauling a trash bag that smells of cigarettes and old lettuce. "Maybe you could come out with us some time," I say as Paula reaches her apartment.

She opens the door scarcely wide enough to fit her body through, like a Paula-sized mail slot. "We'll see." She slips inside. "Thanks for the invite."

I shoulder my way past The Sandler's glass front doors and hurl the trash into a ripe-smelling Rubbermaid receptacle, then head back inside.

I hear Trina's laugh. She stumbles out of the apartment across from Paula's, sliding an arm into the violet cardigan sweater. A man's arms reach for her through the doorway. She swats him away.

Russell Lee, the stoner who made a play to hang out with us the day we moved in, grabs at Trina. He looks younger without glasses. Trina smacks him off her waist, laughing.

They see me and freeze in place. Pink rushes across Russell's face like someone just smacked him with a bouquet of roses. Trina tugs her shirt toward her beltline.

"Thanks for visiting, Miss," Russell announces, too loudly. His apartment door rumbles shut. Trina pulls the cardigan closed with both fists.

She paces toward me, barefoot, her cat-eye liner looking angry. "You didn't see a thing."

"I didn't?"

The metal fixture hanging over her head darkens her eye sockets. "*Not even a shadow.*"

"I don't care, you know," I tell her. "Who you like. Or who you fuck. Go ahead, already."

"*Cut the shit*, Jess." Her sweater falls back open.

Audrey's not here to raise the hands of peace. I have to manage Trina myself. "Are you all right?" I ask.

"See, there you go again—like something's *wrong* with me." For once, she isn't smiling.

"I didn't say that."

"But you're thinking it. Not everybody has the luxury to be Miss Discerning, like you. Not everybody is a little size five, with a new guy eyeing them on every dance floor. Or with Drew to use as a back-up."

I push myself against the wallpaper. "*What?*"

She wags a ringed finger at me. "You think it's all right to jerk guys around because you *care* about . . . every . . . one." She presses her hands together under her chin, mock praying.

"So it's bad that I care about the guys I sleep with?"

"Why don't you ask *them?*" A tang of weed rises from her clothing. "If you supposedly care about *all* of them, they cancel each other out."

I push off the musty wall. "*Bullshit.*"

"Fine. Just don't expect them to care back. At least not for long. They'll figure you out sooner or later." She circles around me, making me revolve like the center of a merry-go-round. "I'm going downstairs now," she announces, "and you're not going to say a word about this." Bare feet slap the tiles as she trots through the hall, her bobbed hair mangled in the back.

"Trina," I call.

She whirls, grabbing the stair rail. "*What?*"

"Your shirt's inside-out."

She tightens Kimmer's sweater across her chest and stomps down the stairs, leaving the hallway quiet.

I knock on Russell's door, which flies open with a croak. "Hey, could you—" he says. He's in boxers. "*Oh.* Howdy, neighbor. Thought you were Katrina." He blushes and fixes his feathery hair. He has nice eyes, when not outlined by tortoise shell frames.

The apartment reeks of sweet smoke. "When Trina was, um, borrowing a cup of sugar," I say, "she left her shoes. Do you see them around?"

"Hold on a minute."

The seams of the cheap wallpaper curl as I wait. Russell reappears, back in his glasses and a pair of Levi's. He hands me Trina's baby-blue plastic jelly slippers. "Hey, Jessie?"

No one's called me that since fifth grade. But then again, no one calls my roommate Katrina, either. Except her dad. "Can you keep this a secret? She made me swear not to tell anyone about us."

I cross my heart with the jelly shoes. "Not a word."

I head down the hall. He shouts a thank you and I raise the shoes in acknowledgment.

Downstairs in our apartment, Audrey washes dishes to the accompaniment of The Police's *Zenyatta Mondatta* album.

I find Trina in the bathroom fiddling with the soap dish and my Eau-de-Prom atomizer, repositioning the bottle on the sink. She hurries to the bedroom, plopping down on her foam mattress. Shirt righted, hair detangled. I sit next to her and place the jellies in her lap.

"Peace offering." Her denim comforter feels rough under my fingers.

"Really?" she says. "I don't deserve it."

I bump my shoulder against hers. "I'm the forgiving type."

She lets out a long breath. "You know I was just spouting off, right?" She straightens her puckered bedding, not looking me in the eye. "I'm a hostile bitch when it comes down to it."

"Good thing I love you anyway."

She lights a butt, tossing the match into a cereal bowl next to her bedding. "Russell's not exactly Richard Gere," she says. "And he's no fucking physicist." The smoke lends her voice a nasal twang. "But I bet he won't pin my underwear to a dartboard like the frat brothers did. And that counts for something."

"I don't judge," I say.

"Yeah, you girls do." She Cheshire-Cat grins at me. "But I'm learning to live with it."

CHAPTER 19

AUGUST 1984—King of Prussia
Who Can It Be Now?

Whit picks me up again after my next dinner shift. We find a restaurant near his condo open late enough to serve us this weird beer-batter cheese fondue thing he likes. It leaves my fingers sticky. We launch into a game of Truth or Dare that makes us feel like middle school students. I let it slip that in seventh-grade health class, I fainted during the tourniquet portion of a first aid film. I find out that he had such a violent and mortifying case of the hiccups in ninth grade that the nurse sent him home.

I feel like I've known him my whole life. Except he's barely heard any of my stories.

The next morning, he sits on the suede futon in only jeans, an acoustic in his lap. We still haven't slept in his bedroom.

He picks at the guitar strings with agile fingers, sometimes barely touching its neck, coaxing exquisite bell tones out of it like a magician. *Harmonics*, he tells me. The sounds remind me that piano music actually happens on strings, beaten with tiny, felt-covered hammers. His bare feet shift the coffee table just slightly as he plays.

"Very cool." I sit on the floor, sketching on a blank sheet of typing paper. I haven't lifted the pencil nearly as much as I planned to this summer. It's concerning, the way having fun hinders the artistic process. I may need an influx of heartache and destruction in my life to earn the right to be creative.

Whit lets a slo-mo smile crawl across his lips, while his fingers climb and drop against the neck of the guitar. I scrape the pencil against the page. He turns his face with each chord progression.

"I can't capture you if you keep moving," I say.

His eyebrows arch. "*Capture* me?" A string vibrates, caught against a fret, crying out a high note under his finger. "Interesting choice of words." The coffee table rasps along the floor as his foot stretches.

He moves on to a classical guitar piece I don't recognize. My pencil recreates the strips of hair that fall over his eyes, the route of the scar that tiptoes along his brow, the sinewy line of his jaw as he clenches in concentration. It gives me a rush to fashion something out of nothing, something that looks like him.

"When did you first start playing?" I smudge pencil.

His shirtless torso rocks. "My uncle played. We used to visit him when I was maybe ten years old." The strings squeak as he presses them against diamond-shaped inlays. "I'd sit on his bedroom rug and listen."

"Was he talented?" My pencil point scuffs sideways against the page. Fronds of tall potted plants sway on the balcony outside, as if they hear the music. Filaments deep inside my body vibrate to the same rhythm.

"He was *awesome*." Whit's voice continues as I focus on the image I'm drawing, as if the sketch is talking to me. "When I was thirteen, he gave me a beat-up six-string and taught me some basics," he says.

I smudge the graphite, creating shadows with my fingertip. "Did it take long to learn?"

"Nah." He watches his own hand change position. "I ran with it."

The tune transitions to a more modern piece, full of lilting sharp notes. He taps the body of the guitar, adding his own percussion.

The gray tones of my sketch pale compared to the depth of his eyes. I can't do them justice. I'd need to use a far more dimensional medium. Jewels. The stratosphere. *Kryptonite.*

I let my pencil stop. "What song is that?"

He smiles like he's keeping a secret. "I'm just making shit up for you, now." He plucks a couple of gorgeous notes, and that *stare* of his locks down on me. Pieces of his hair skip past his irises. Blood rushes in my ears. I'm a needle stuck in a scratch in a record, hitching in place.

"How do you *do* that?" I finally sputter.

"Do what?" The taut strings shudder under his fingertips.

"Look at me and make time fucking *stop.*"

The guitar music cuts out and he reaches an arm to me. Deep and slow as the chords of a deathly-sick Cure song, he breathes, "*Come here.*"

My pencil and pad drop. Strings squeal as I pull the acoustic out of his hands, his fingers surrendering the fretwork. I balance the guitar in a stand next to the futon and climb into his lap.

His hands ring my waist. The guitar and I seem to be interchangeable when it comes to his ability to play both instruments. I swing my hair, snaking my body against him. His eyes fall closed, then open again.

"How did you get so good at this kind of thing?" he whispers.

"*Instinct.*" I toss my head backward, laughing. "I actually haven't done all that much of this kind of thing."

"Are you sure?" He rifles his hands underneath my balmy tank top.

"Okay, I have done a lot of this kind of thing," I correct myself, "just not with that many *people.*" Really, just one person, but he doesn't need to know that. "Finding the right guy is like finding the right pair of shoes. You don't need to own a ton of shoes to know a great pair when you see one." I lace my hands behind his neck. "But once you find them, you want to wear them. *All the time.*" I arch my back. "Because they make you feel fabulous."

"Are you using me for sex, Jessica?" he asks. "The guys in the band think I'm your summer boy toy."

I stop.

"Is that what you think?" My face hovers over his. "You don't understand," I go on, letting my hair drape in his face. "With shoes, it's not so much that you love the walking." Tendrils of hair stroke the side of his jaw. "It's that you *love the shoes*."

I twist my legs around his waist and squeeze. "Do you *get it?*" His eyes roll back.

"*Yes.*" He breathes a low moan that I wish I could record and listen to all day.

"Then count your blessings," I whisper.

His eyes could steam linen. The front of his hair begins to take on that *sex wave* it gets when he's overheated, ruining his normally spiky look. As if his true nature can't help but emerge when he's turned on.

He pushes my tank top over my head, thick palms drawing lines along my skin, his lips following. I yelp as he flips me on my back. It amazes me how deftly a guy can squirm out of clothing when the moment calls for it.

Whit doesn't even flinch when the guitar slides off its stand and bongs against the yellow floor planks. We defile his furniture.

The phone rings on the counter. I motion jokingly over his shoulder at the noise. He pins my waving hand against the upholstery. "*Can't hear it*," he says.

I hear it, though. Barely. A woman mumbles on the answering machine, shooting a tinge of angst through my gut. Maybe someone's calling about the noise. Or about something else.

The answering machine clicks quiet. Whit breathes in my ear and makes me forget whatever clever quip I was planning next.

I let go . . . of the voice on the machine, of waitressing chaos, of guilt and inhibition and anxiety over what the hell my life is supposed to be. I melt against the suede of the futon, dissolving into whatever dimension he takes us to.

It's a fucking thing of beauty.

He heads to his bedroom to change, leaving me alone to find what happened to my clothing. I locate my tank top between the cushions of the futon. As I reassemble the furniture, the orange light of an answering machine blinks like a traffic flare on his kitchen countertop.

I gravitate to the machine, loitering over the light. The hairs on my arms raise.

The "Play Messages" button is flat and warm as I trace my fingertip against it. I think of the female voice that garbled in the background as Whit and I shifted the couch, my heart ping-ponging in my ribcage, the ceiling all a blur.

I don't know enough about answering machines to screw with it. Not without him noticing.

The light flashes.

I back away and straighten my tank top.

CHAPTER 20

AUGUST—Capresi's
Party Out of Bounds

The party at Capresi's tonight must be a reunion of a football team and a cheerleading squad. Every woman in attendance has hair that radiates a sheen of light, and legs curvy as a Rodin nude. The men boast gym-worthy biceps barely contained by their sleeves.

Kimmer leans against Capresi's bar room archway, oblivious to the handsomeness of the crowd. "When Paula told us she was married to that Dean Clayton guy the other day, I almost spit out my false teeth," says Kim.

"Your teeth are real." I stash a few extra jar candles in the sideboard. Since this is a closed affair, we don't have as many tables out as usual. "You're letting your geriatric patients rub off on you again. But okay, what made you almost lose your imaginary dentures?"

"Dean Clayton? You don't remember that name?" Kimmer asks. "Joseph warned us about him when we moved in."

I think of the list of dangers Joseph went on about the night we met him. "Right," I say. "What did he call that guy again?"

"A bruiser," says Kimmer. "Did you see the mark under Paula's eye?

And she jumps any time a door closes. Plus, we girls look like fattened chickens compared to her."

"You think she's anorexic?" A table of pretty people erupts in laughter and I accidentally drop my pencil, which dances against the slate.

"I think Dean Clayton must be a tough guy to live with," says Kimmer. "That, and Paula's anorexic." She picks my pencil off the floor, groaning as she bends. She really does let her patient base influence her too much.

An unfairly attractive blonde woman hops onto the dais table and dangles her legs. The nametag on her blouse says "Joanne." A mustachioed guy next to her waves for me, muscles rippling.

"*Showtime*," I say, shoving off the archway.

The men at Mustachio Guy's table chant, "Wai—*tress*. Wai—*tress*!!" I notice a podium and a microphone near the dais.

Blonde Joanne crosses her gams, which look as if they've seen some beach time. The mustachioed guy, whose nametag reads "Jeff," gestures me closer. "You know why we like waitresses?" Jeff says. "Because they bring alcohol."

"Right. I'm Jessica." I pluck the order pad out of my apron. "What can I get you?"

"Who's that cute number there?" He points to Kimmer in the archway. She waves hello, ever the polite hostess.

"That's Kim," I tell the guy. "We'll be serving you tonight."

Blonde Joanne pushes the ball of her foot into the back of the hulking guy nearest to her. "Luke, order me a Manhattan," she says.

Luke wears a polo shirt with a popped collar; very preppy. And antipunk. Personally, I'd like to scrape the Izod alligator off the chest of every prepped-out guy who dares to come near me. With guests, though, I let these urges pass.

Joanne's strappy shoe drops off her foot and clocks against the floor. Luke picks it up with a chuckle, then tries to fit it onto her sole. He has no aptitude for applying women's shoes.

"One Manhattan," I say. "What else?"

"A Michelob." Luke laughs, leaning back for a view of my rear end.

"And a handful." His pals guffaw.

I flatten the back of my skirt. Managing unruly customers without ticking them off is a talent I haven't fully developed yet, but I'm working on it. "One Michelob," I say. "Period." I giant-step away from him. "*Next order.*"

"*Ooooo,*" moan several guys at the table.

Luke sways in his chair, looking less than steady. He may not need a Michelob. "Can't blame a guy for trying," he mumbles.

I surely can, I think.

"Don't mind him," says Mustachio Jeff. "We're good guys. We'll have," he counts heads, "eight Michelobs, and a Manhattan for the lady."

"What lady?" Joanne laughs. She leans back on her palms like the dais is her personal lounge chair.

I walk away backward, careful not to provide any further views of my ass. My foot snags the slate floor and I catch myself on the edge of a wire chair, apologizing to the man whose back I just molested.

"It's gonna be a long night," I tell Kimmer when I reach the bar room. "This crowd has been lit since before they got here."

"Maybe Teddy should put the buffet out early," Kimmer says. "Otherwise, they'll be downing more alcohol on empty stomachs."

Tye enters the bar room, stashing an overstuffed duffle behind the bar and hanging a garment bag on a coat hook. The guests on the patio roar at someone's joke.

Tye peers through the archway as he tends to his bag. "What a live bunch tonight. Is it a Ken and Barbie convention?"

"Private party," I say. "Tables one and two want a round of Michelobs and a Manhattan."

"They're not booked for the whole night," says Tye. "I'm doing a preview of the Babylonia show at 11:00 for a few special guests." He grabs condiments from the mini-fridge and arranges them along the bar. "You girls want to stay and watch?"

"Can't tonight," says Kimmer, flipping a tablecloth to its cleaner side. "Joseph the Bouncer is picking me up."

Tye nods, filling a Lucite container with swizzle sticks. "Right. A hot date beats a drag show. Even one of my fine performances." He fans the sticks into an obedient swirl.

"Kimmer, what if you and Joe stay for the show?" I'd like to support Tye but would rather do it with company. Otherwise, I'll be a lone chick at a private drag show. "Joe's worked in town for years. He must have seen it all by now."

"That's not the problem," says Kimmer, moving on to the next tablecloth. "He likes hanging out at the river with a group of friends who . . . do his bidding. It's funny."

I squint my eyes as I help her straighten a wine-colored cloth. "What bidding?"

"They bring him six-packs. And last time I was there, Joe dared one of his friends to punch out the other for fifty bucks."

"How is that funny?"

She swipes a wrinkle out of the linen with her hand, not looking up at me. "He'll be here in an hour. If he wants to go to the river, we're going."

"He sounds like a tyrant to me," says Tye. Michelobs clack as he lines them along the bar, pulling a cocktail tray from a shelf for me. Then another. It's a multi-tray night.

I grab Kimmer's arm. "Kim, you don't have to do anything you don't want to." I look her in the eye. "Remember Ray?"

She waves her hand at me. "Joseph is nothing like Ray," she insists. "Ray was a textbook alcoholic."

Laughter booms from our rowdy patio. Polo-Shirt Luke shouts for his Michelob. Tye points to the drinks he assembled.

"Shit—the Ken patrol is getting restless," I say. "Kimmer, can you follow me with the last few Micks and the Manhattan?" I position a tray on my fingertips, channeling a plate-spinning acrobat. Kimmer grabs the second tray and navigates behind me.

Luke ogles Kimmer as she moves from guest to guest. "No bending over tonight," I say in her ear. "These guys will look up your skirt in a heartbeat."

We head inside to talk to Teddy. As we swing into the steamed-up realm of the kitchen, I notice there are no dinner buffet trays in sight.

"Looking good today, girls," Teddy says. Kimmer and I look each other over. We look like waitresses. "Does this crowd realize this isn't some rowdy sports bar?" Teddy asks.

"You noticed, huh?" I say. "They worry me."

"Everything worries you," says Teddy, wiping a knife with a dishtowel.

Kimmer moves closer to Teddy and his cheeks go pink. He drops the knife and swipes the dishcloth over his brow. He doesn't do that kind of thing with me.

"We should get some food into these guests early," says Kimmer, "so things don't get . . . louder."

Teddy smiles. "Maybe if you ask me extra-special-nice."

"*Pleeeeease?*" Kimmer tosses her ponytail. "I don't mind begging if it's effective."

"Awww. That was beautiful," Teddy notes. "But the trays are still in the oven." He tilts open the heavy metal door, exposing its glowing interior. I peek inside; a whoosh of heat attacks my face and nearly curls my eyelashes.

Kimmer folds her arms. "Did I just waste a perfectly good, drawn-out 'please'?"

"It wasn't wasted," says Teddy, letting the oven door bang closed. "I really enjoyed it."

Kimmer looks around the kitchen for ideas on how to pacify the crowd. There's nothing but equipment in view: chafing dishes. Sterno cans. A steel tub full of butter. "Can we get them some apps? Maybe some *crudité?*" she asks.

"They didn't pay for apps. But that's pretty nice catering talk," Teddy says.

"My father owned a restaurant," Kimmer says.

"Around here?"

"Outside Pittsburgh," she answers.

Teddy backs against the sink. "That's awesome."

"Not so much. It went under. Sad, but it was a long time ago," Kimmer says. "I'm better now."

"I hate to interrupt, but what's a *crew-de-tay?*" I over-pronounce for effect.

Teddy and Kimmer turn to me at once. "Vegetable platter," they answer, synchronized.

"Jinx!" Teddy raises his hand for a high five. Kimmer slaps his palm, her ponytail swinging. She heads to the walk-in refrigerator, grabbing its door handle. "What have you got in here that will work as edible crowd control?"

"There are plenty of vegetables we can get rid of, if you girls prep them." Teddy gestures at me with a long metal spoon. "Jess, get the veggies. Kimmer, let's teach Jessica here how to use a knife without hurting herself."

I head to the walk-in. "How about this? You give me a cooking lesson," I call to Teddy as I poke my head around the walk-in shelving. I can see my breath. "And I'll consent to be the assistant kitchen girl tonight."

"*Sous chef,*" Kimmer and Teddy say in unison. Kimmer laughs.

I pull a bin of vegetables and the cold metal stings my palms. "I got this," I tell Kimmer as I plunk the bin on the counter. "Why don't you deliver more drinks?"

Teddy's eyes follow Kimmer as she pushes through the out-door. His hand grabs for the knife he left on the counter, but he overshoots.

I wave my palm in front of his eyes. "Ground control to Major Teddy?"

"All right," Teddy says, snapping up the knife. "Chop the carrots and cucumbers in sticks and rounds." He fishes an industrial-sized peeler out of a drawer, pulls an intimidating blade from the knife block, and places it in front of me. I lift it by the handle, turning it in the air.

"Jessica, put the weapon down." He takes it from me, sighing. "Wash your hands first."

There's that rule of food service again: *Always, always, always* watch what you do with your hands. I wash up, grab two chilly cucumbers, and pick up the knife to start chopping.

Teddy groans. "Did your house even *have* a kitchen?" He shakes his head.

"My grandmother did all the cooking. She never let me touch the stove." I chew my fingernail.

"You gotta peel stuff first." He pulls my finger out of my mouth and grabs a second peeler from a squeaky drawer. "Move over." Utensils rattle as he shoves the drawer closed. "Notice I didn't crack a joke about the cucumbers."

"That must have been hard for you," I say. "I mean *difficult*."

"Shut up and peel." He nudges my elbow.

Teddy denudes carrots like an automatic machine gun, spewing peel along the counter. "Here's your lesson." He cleaves an onion with a whack of the knife, turning one side of it against the butcher block. "Always cut on the flat, or the vegetables will roll away. And the secret to how much to cook," he wags the knife at me, "depends on whether your ingredients shrink or expand. Vegetables shrink."

He decimates the onion. "Pasta expands." He swishes the bits onto the blade and slides them into a sauté pan, followed by a knife-swipe of butter. The onions hiss and exhale sweet steam. "Meat stays basically the same."

"That's more than I've learned about cooking my entire life," I say, inhaling a mellow waft of caramelizing onions. "Between this and memorizing the menu, I might actually be able to prepare a meal soon."

Teddy tips his chef's hat. "Wonder of wonders."

I leave the kitchen, remembering that we have vegetables from our neighbor Paula's garden at home. I look forward to cutting them on the flat.

Our vegetable platters don't do much to curtail the head-start these guests have on alcohol consumption. Finally, the buffet is ready.

I fit a tray of chicken divan into a stand, and Kimmer follows with shrimp marinara. The patio sounds as if someone has cranked the crowd volume up to eleven.

Tye lines drinks along the bar. "I don't usually complain about customers. They pay my wardrobe allowance," he says, neatening a row of glasses and beer bottles. "But it's like open mike night on the docks out there. They're running some kind of dirty poetry contest. And they're *blitzed*. This is the last round. I hate to be a bummer, but I'm closing the bar."

"I won't fight you on that." I stock my drink tray and truck it outside, where Kimmer navigates a table full of jocks. She avoids the bulky arms that sweep toward her waist as she collects empties. The girl is skilled.

At the dais, Mustachio Jeff passes the microphone to two pals who recite an off-color limerick to the accompaniment of a boombox. The crowd belly-laughs. Guests stomp toward the newly-opened buffet, filling stoneware plates with saucy mounds of scarlet shrimp and sepia-toned chicken dinners.

"While you enjoy the eats," Jeff says, tapping the microphone, "please welcome your favorite and mine, Joanne Curry Kennedy." The crowd applauds. Joanne pops a tape into the boombox. She bounces to a twangy beat in front of the dais and sings, breathily:

There once was a girl, kept her cooter in a bucket.
So damn ornery a dog wouldn't fuck it.
A guy reached in,
Thought what's the harm?
Now old Stumpy's got a fake right arm.

The dining room howls. Someone tosses a spoon, which hits a woman on the other end of the patio in the head. "Howard, you bastard!" the woman screeches across the dining room.

"Holy shit, these guys are out of control," I say, gripping the archway for balance. A soundtrack lush with fiddles gets louder in the boombox.

Tye emerges from the bathroom as alter-ego Babylonia, in a green column gown and a voluminous black wig, curls winding down to her tight-as-a-drum rear end. She tosses her wig-hair behind her shoulder à la Cher, showing Kimmer and me a canted-knee pose.

"What do you think, girls?" she asks, falsetto lilting. She gives us jazz hands. A recessed fixture above her head spills light down her curls. I recognize the Grecian emerald gown from her photos.

She's the Statue of Liberty with an obsidian spiral perm.

Crash. A stoneware plate disintegrates against the slate patio tiles.

"What the hell?" Tye bellows, voice dropping back down to a baritone. She springs toward the archway, curls waving magnificently in her wake. I peek around her near-bare back.

"Whoa!" Tye yells as a teacup comes flying toward us. She grabs me like a soldier would clutch a combat buddy, shielding me with wide, spaghetti-strapped shoulders. She shoves my head against her semi-buff chest. The teacup smashes on the bar room rug.

My nose is stuffed into the fake bosom of a seven-foot-tall guy in a spiral perm and sequined dress. Thank God.

Tye reaches for Kimmer and pulls the three of us to the floor behind the bar.

"Stay here," Tye says, barring us with an outstretched arm. "I'm goin' in." She springs to full height and bounds toward the patio. A frenetic instrumental squeals on the boombox outside, as if Charlie Daniels can't get down to Georgia fast enough.

Kimmer and I kneel on a wet rubber bar mat that smells like LaGuardia Airport. I poke my head around the wainscoting and glimpse the edge of the patio, where a rugby-shirted guest pisses over our railing.

Tye bursts back from the patio, dragging two men by their up-turned collars. Her leg pops through the slit in her gown with each lunge forward. She tosses the guys into the lobby, where they bluster and straighten their shirts. Tye heads back to the patio.

The lobby door swings open and Kimmer's date Joseph Keller steps into the chaos, all mountainous NFL shoulders. Kimmer signals to him, peering from behind our shelter. The two men that Tye just bowled through the room dash past Joseph and out the front door.

"The party's gone out of bounds!" Kimmer shouts to Joseph. "Can you help us?"

Tye emerges through the archway again, grappling with another muscled guest's collar. "Consider yourself ejected, sweetheart," Tye says. The muscle guy jerks his clothing back into place, flexing his arms. As he pulls himself upright, his eyes meet Joseph the Bouncer's . . . chest.

Muscle Guy thinks about it for two whole seconds before darting out the door.

Tye swipes a curl out of her face and stands eye-to-eye with Kimmer's date. "Let me guess," she says. "You're Joseph the linebacker."

"Bouncer," he says.

"Close enough," says Tye.

"You're not a bad bouncer yourself," Joseph says. "Do you have any experience?"

Tye rights a fallen spaghetti strap on her broad shoulder. "Lebanon, 1982," she says. The two of them march into the madness of the patio.

Kimmer and I brush off our sticky knees. "See?" Kimmer says to me as we unfurl ourselves back to standing. "Joseph is a good guy to have around."

Tye and Joseph usher men out of the restaurant three or four at a time as Kimmer and I straighten up the place. Several female guests follow the men out, heads drooped, hair bedraggled.

Teddy pushes through the kitchen out-door and grabs the phone off its cradle so hard it makes a bringing noise. He dials, stretching the cord into the kitchen. I hear him explain the situation to Giorgio.

Finally, the guests are gone. Patio tables sit crooked. A starburst of broken stoneware marks the slate.

Tye collapses into a chair and tries to right her frizzed-out curls. "So much for a preview show tonight," she says, peeling off a fake eyelash. It drops to the tablecloth like a dead centipede. "I have some calls to make."

Joseph pulls a seat away from the table and joins us.

"You guys were great out there," Kimmer says. Joseph's cheeks burn rosy under his beard. Kim has a way of making men go pink in the face.

Joseph wraps his steam pipe of a bicep around her neck. "I didn't know this was a dangerous place to hang out," he says, his bellows of a chest heaving. "I may not let you work here anymore." Kimmer shifts under the weight of his arms. He rubs the top of her head.

"Hey, easy, there," I tell him.

Joseph releases his half-headlock. I exhale. Kim smooths her hairdo.

"Kimmer, help me a sec with the condiments?" I say. She gets up, untying her apron as she follows me to the dimmed waitress station.

I take her arm. "You'd tell me if Joseph was . . . getting *rough*, wouldn't you, Kim?"

She looks at me like I'm from Neptune. This is harder than I thought.

"Are you kidding?" she says. "He's a teddy bear."

"Bears can get unruly," I whisper.

"He just needs some understanding," she says. "Remember?" She flashes me a winning Colgate toothpaste smile. "You have to trust people, Jess."

She steps back toward Joseph, who folds her into his waiting biceps. She's Mini Barbie compared to him. She waves to me and mouths, *Trust*.

I slump back into a chair next to Tye, who's busy wrangling a broken acrylic nail off the tip of her index finger.

"By the way," I ask Tye as I whip the ponytail holder out of my hair. I blow a misplaced lock out of my eyes. "Did you say *Lebanon*?"

"Nice to meet you." Tye reaches a hand to shake mine. "U.S. Army Reserves."

Tye and I re-assemble the dining room. A siren sounds on the overpass above the garden stairwell; blue and red lights flicker through the front courtyard.

I make a dash for the kitchen pass-through. "Shit, Teddy—you called the police?"

He comes out from behind a metal rack. "Giorgio's orders."

"Damn! I can't get involved in a police report," I say. "I've gotta pass a background check for my study abroad application. What if this shows up in the check?"

"You didn't *do* anything," Teddy says. Through the lobby window, I see boots shuffling down the front staircase.

"This is a competitive program I'm looking to get into."

Teddy sighs and heads into the bar room. "Hey, Lieutenant Diana Ross," he says to Tye, who's busy finger-combing knots out of her spiral wig. "Can you stall these guys?"

Tye straightens her ruined mass of curls. "On the job." She salutes and strides to the door.

Teddy waves me into the kitchen. "Move your tail," he says, ushering me past cauldron-sized pots stored on industrial shelving, continuing toward the back of the kitchen. He yanks open the rear door. "You're off the hook. Get outta here."

"Really?"

"I'll tell the cops the rest of the help ran out on us," he says. "That way this dumb-ass party won't ruin your big plans." Teddy lifts a windbreaker off a peg by the door and slings it over my shoulders. "Run straight home. Do not pass go. Do not collect 200 dollars. Got it?"

"Teddy,"—I tighten the windbreaker around me—"are you being *nice?*"

He rolls his eyes. "Don't get your panties in a bunch."

He nods goodbye and closes the door. I scurry past the dark Canal like a rat.

I come home to another late-night phone call from Drew. "You heard right," I say into the receiver. "A guy in a Goddess gown bounced a room full of drunken men out of the restaurant." The sofa bed creaks underneath me. At the sink, Trina washes out a glass that until moments ago held two fingers of Scotch. The only light in the room is a kidney bean-sized bulb over the kitchen basin. "Giorgio might bring them up on charges. One guy knocked a bathroom sink out of the wall."

"Admit it," Drew's voice growls in my ear. "You love the drama."

I stare at a water ring that decorates the popcorn ceiling like a bullseye and wonder if he's right. If that's why I'm here.

"I've always been up for a good drama. But only if it's fictional," I say. "This town out-dramas even me."

Trina glances over her shoulder from her spot at the sink. "Like *that* could happen." I roll to face away from her.

"I could use a little more drama on my end," Drew says. "The world is too one-note over here. My frat brothers aren't here. You're not here. You're never around when I call."

My thoughts cloud with visions of why I'm not around when he calls. The tequila-shooting, jaw-clenching, melody-conjuring reason. The one who shares my inexplicable drive to *create*. And who can flip me on my back and make me forget how to speak English.

"I work a lot of doubles," I tell Drew. I bite the inside of my cheek. The pain seems appropriate.

"Is that what it is?" he says. "*Work?*" Last time Drew called, Audrey told him I was serving at a late-night party. She swatted me with a copy of *Their Eyes Were Watching God* the next morning for making her lie.

The sofa bed rocks as Trina suddenly climbs over me on the mattress. She yanks the phone out of my hand, spilling a curl of cord to the floor. "Yes, the theatricality of this woman," she tells Drew. "Be warned, as her official roommate, it's tough putting up with her."

I reach to pull the phone back from her. "Geez-us! Must you?"

Trina stiff-arms me away. "Every moment with her is a star-studded docu-drama, Drew," she says.

I hear Drew's voice burbling in the receiver.

"Colorful or not, she can keep it to herself," Trina says.

I wrestle the receiver out of her grip. "*You have to stop doing that*," I tell Trina through tight teeth, shoving her to the edge of the mattress with my feet. "And no crawling into my bed unless you buy me dinner."

"Technically, it's my bed, from my mother's basement." She slaps the mattress and hops away, disappearing into the bedroom.

"Jess, I've got some news," Drew says. A twinge nips at the pit of my stomach. "I'm moving to California for the rest of the summer."

I bolt upright. "Cali-what? Get outta here." The ache in my gut mangles into something more like John Carpenter's *The Thing*.

"I'm going bat shit living at home," he goes on. "My cousin Danny's in a summer film program in Los Angeles. He invited me to crash with him for a few weeks."

"Not fair. That's *my* thing, running off to cool locales." The sheets rumple as I fold my legs underneath myself.

"You can't call dibs on excitement, Jess."

"Will I see you before fall starts?"

"Did you plan on seeing me before you knew I was leaving?" he asks.

"I thought you'd be there if I wanted to." For a moment, Trina's voice reverberates in my head, the overhead light of the upstairs hallway beaming between us. *Not everyone has a Drew to use as a backup.*

"I'm leaving next Friday," he says. "If you want to get together, now's the time."

I run scenarios: I could take NJ Transit from Trenton to New York if I could convince Trina to drop me off at the station in Jersey. "I can come Sunday night."

"*Nice.*" Drew's voice takes on that honey-coat it gets when he imagines us twisted up together. Naked. "That sounds nice."

"In that case, you're taking me to the beach." I picture miles of pebbled

Long Island shoreline, its faded mauve snow fences half-buried along the dunes of the North Shore.

Home. The real thing. "I can smell the beach in my head," I say.

"You, and the beach," he muses. "Maybe the two best things about Long Island. That is, if you can tear yourself away from all that *work*."

The monster in my stomach does another cannonball dive. I pull the mess of excess phone cord into my lap like I'm weighing an anchor.

"Jessica?" Drew hesitates. "Anything to report?"

There are some people in life you just can't hide things from. Not even across two states and a half-mile of tangled phone cord.

Our apartment doorknob jangles, the hinge squeaks. An overhead fixture firebombs the place with light like a Steven Spielberg finale.

I cover my eyes. "Are you trying to blind me!"

My vision adjusts. Kimmer leans against our closet door. Water drips from her elbows. Her hair is a drenched tussle.

"I have to go," I mumble to Drew, clunking the receiver into its base.

Kimmer stares into nowhere, stiff as a statue in dirty tenny runners. Her soaked blouse is plastered to her skin. A triangle of collar sticks flat against her throat.

Trina wanders back in from the bedroom, now in pajamas. "Shit, Kim, is it raining?"

Kimmer shambles toward us, clutching a purse that trickles brown water from the bottom corner. She sobs.

I hop off the bed and lead Kimmer back to the mattress, shoving away the top sheet to keep it dry. Trina pulls Kimmer's keys out of the doorknob and tosses them onto the table. The phone topples off the bed and clunks against the carpet, generating a dial-tone noise.

"Kim . . . what the hell happened?" I search her face for marks, but nothing presents itself. Dark waves of chalky mascara have sketched themselves down her cheeks.

Audrey appears, wearing only a T-shirt. She hangs up the buzzing phone and kneels in front of us. "What's going on?"

Kimmer rips into tears, hugging the wet purse to her gut, folding like a Swiss Army knife. I coax her back up.

She sniffles. "Joseph said he bought the Jeep because it was light." She cries, trembling. I grab her cold hand as she continues. "He said the plastic sides made it like a big bubble."

"What does that have to do with the price of bananas?" asks Trina, joining us at the edge of the bed. "*God*—were you two in an accident?"

Kimmer shakes her head, spritzing me. She sucks in air and tries to draw her fingers through her hair. Wet knots stop her.

She dangles her feet off the side of the sofa mattress. "Kimmer," I ask, "why are your sneakers *green?*"

"The river!" she screams, splaying her hands over her face, trembling.

Audrey leans against the mattress. "*What did Joseph do?*"

Kimmer dabs her face with a bunched-up section of Strawberry Shortcake bedding. Audrey takes the purse out of her lap. It draws a squiggle of brown liquid on the rug.

"Did he hurt you, that big fucking ogre?" Trina pounds a fist on the bed and the sheets puff with air. "I'll kill him!"

"His friends were getting on his case for being this huge guy in a tiny car." Kimmer sniffles. "His buddy Jake said he'd give him 100 bucks if he proved the Jeep could float."

"Oh, for cripe's sake, no," says Audrey.

"Joseph got this *look*. He threw the car into gear and gunned it." Kimmer sobs, melting forward. The three of us pull her upright again. "Water came through the floor," she says. "It came through the dashboard. It spouted out of the radio!"

"Did you mention that your parents never taught you to swim?" Audrey asks.

"Yes!"

"But you made it out of the car," I say, wrapping the cartoon sheets around her shoulders. "Thank God."

"I climbed onto the hood," Kimmer says. "Jake followed us into the water and helped me back to the riverbank. Joseph stayed in that damn Jeep until it almost turned over."

"What a psycho," I say. "You're a brave girl."

"I screamed the whole time."

"Brave and loud," I add.

Kimmer rubs the tattoo of gray make-up from under her eyes. "Why did I go out with him? You and Tye both said it. Tye called him a dictator."

"A tyrant," I say. "But close enough."

"This is no time for semantics," Audrey says. "All that matters, Kim, is that you're safe."

"I'm a drowned rat," she snivels, "and an idiot."

"Not drowned," says Trina. "Soggy."

"And not an idiot," I say. "You're just inclined toward those 'fixer-upper' guys."

Kimmer sputters out a laugh. Audrey hands her a tissue box. She plucks out a fistful of tissues, sending a bunch fluttering down her legs. "I should know better by now."

"We always think we know better," says Audrey. "How come it's never true?"

Kimmer stretches her toes, studying her algae-colored footwear. "There go my tenny runners." She kicks them to the floor with a bang.

"We'll buy new," I say.

"Clover's discount rack, here we come," says Trina.

"It's late, Kimmer." I lean her damp head on my shoulder. "Why don't you change and we'll get some sleep."

Trina clicks off the foyer light. "We'll think of how to get back at Joseph in the morning." The room retreats back to quiet dimness, the kind in which you can hear your friend's clothing dripping on the carpet.

Kim peels off her shirt and digs through her purse for a hairbrush, yanking it through her tangled mop. She lets go of the brush. It sticks in place on her head, hanging there.

I tug a loosened sheet back over the corner of the sofa mattress. "Kimmer?"

She hiccups, wearing the brush like a giant barrette. "What?"

"You get the wet spot."

Once in a Lifetime

A saturated waitressing blouse whaps me in the head. It smells of river scum.

CHAPTER 21

AUGUST 1984—South Street, Philadelphia
Punk Rock Girl

If it were outdoors, the Record Graveyard on South Street would barely qualify as an alley. The place reeks like a thousand radio station storage closets, buzzing with the energy of as many unsigned bands. Who knows what underground gold we'll mine here, hidden in the rows of cardboard record bins?

Album jackets checker the walls: The Cramps, The Cars, Devo, Blondie. Red-headed Bowie defaced by a lightning streak. Joe Jackson's pointy white oxfords, half-lit against a somber stretch of sidewalk.

A framed poster for a punk show at The Ritz in Manhattan hangs in the stairwell that leads up to the street, screaming with blocked type and alternating red and blue splashes of color. A rush of New York haughtiness washes over me.

I poke Whit's thick shoulder. "Have you been to The Ritz? I saw the Ramones there last summer," I say. "I was almost crushed by a mob of drunken leatherheads."

Whit raises an eyebrow as he flips a Ministry album over on its back. "Must be nice to turn legal at 18." I realize that means I officially became legal almost the same time he did, even though he's got two years on me. God bless the lax drinking laws in New York State, which are going down the tubes this year. At least it gives me a reason to feel superior, despite always hanging around with people who are a year or two further along in life than I am. I turned legal back in New York. I only need the fake ID here in Pennsylvania where the drinking age is 21.

I take a look at the album jacket Whit's holding, which shows a dead rose against black marble.

"Wait—Ministry *bonus tracks?*" I grab the album from his hands. These are the kinds of unique scores you find at a second-hand record store. Listening to them is a trophy in itself.

The store clerk eyes us from behind an antiquated cash register. He wears a shock of black cotton-candy hair and a nose piercing that resembles a barbell. A cross the size of a boat anchor hangs around his neck. Very Cure-like. Although an aging version, which makes me wonder why he's here. Clerking at a second-hand record store past the age of 30 isn't exactly an enviable position.

Sometimes I wonder about the downside of this scene. There's a thin line between looking *authentic* and being permanently screwed up. I flick my chin toward Clerk Guy. "How does someone ever get a job anywhere but *here* looking like that?" I whisper.

Whit fingers his bleached spikes. "Some people say that about me."

"Oh, come on." From my point of view, Whit is worthy of a *Rolling Stone* photo spread. But on further thought, I wonder what they think of his hair at the IBM loading dock. Maybe he slicks it down for work. That tub of BOY London gel in his bathroom is depleting fast.

"You haven't spoken to my mother about this subject," he says.

I wonder if that was her on Whit's answering machine the other day. Or . . . someone else.

Clerk Guy emerges from behind the brass cash register and asks what we're looking for. A New Romantic frill-of-a-sleeve hangs out of his jacket cuff.

"Any Icicle Works around here?" Whit asks.

The guy thumbs through an unmarked box and whips out an EP, passing it across a row of bins. The otherwise-plain cover features some kind of tree sculpture. Whit turns it in his palms, smiling. "I've been looking for this one."

"It's a 4-song Extended Play from the UK," Clerk Guy says.

I sidle closer to Whit, eyeing the album. I've never heard of this band, and I make it my business to at least *hear of* as many New Wave acts as possible.

Now I've heard of The Icicle Works.

Whit stretches an arm around me and Clerk Guy backs away, his poet sleeves waggling. The guy drags a step ladder toward a TV that hangs perilously from two ceiling brackets. He slaps the side of the TV, making me swear it's about to crash down right there in the aisle.

A fat screen blinks to life and a video clip starts: A nearly adolescent Clash bursts into "Train in Vain" on some European TV program. Their wired-up enthusiasm lets you live the desperation of the lyrics, which I suddenly realize borrow from Ben E. King's "Stand By Me." On the screen, Mick Jones and Joe Strummer bend their emaciated knees inward and stomp on a stage the size of my foyer. They bounce like dots of oil on a grill; a sweaty, cokehead seizure.

Whit presses against my back, one hand sliding over my shoulder while the other rides low around my waist. Between him and The Clash video, I'm not sure which sends chills up my spine quicker.

Yes I do. Whit wins.

"You hold me like I'm a guitar, you know that?" I tell him. "One hand here,"—I reach up to the right, matching Whit's hand with my own—"and the other here." Like he wants to *play me*.

Whit laughs, deep and rumbling. "Babe, it goes this way." He reverses my hands.

"*Oh, fuck.*" I bury my magenta face against his T-shirt. The screen-printed lines of a Joy Division T-shirt undulate like a mountain range across his chest, blurred in my peripheral vision. I feel waves of our own creation beaming off him, vibrating through me as his hands run across my back.

Whit murmurs in my ear. "I think the cashier's eyeing you." He subtly inches my V-neck backward to cover more of my skin.

"I think you misjudge the object of his affection," I whisper back, yanking my neckline to its original position. "He's eyeing *you*."

"I don't—wait, you think?" Whit says.

The clerk retreats behind the register and counts receipts, a reluctant bystander caught in our fog of pheromones. It pulls oxygen out of my lungs and makes blips of silver flicker in front of my eyes.

I shake it off and lead Whit toward the glass showcase full of metal buttons, sharp earrings, and S&M-ish wearables. A less lethal-looking version of his studded bracelet is stretched out in the case. "I need one of these," I say.

Whit waves the clerk back over. The video on the TV changes to Siouxsie and the Banshees doing a cover of the Beatles' "Dear Prudence," mashing together my childhood with the present.

Clerk Guy places the bracelet on top of the glass display case for me. It looks a little like a dog collar. Whit slides a few bills to the clerk and their pinkies touch.

Whit snaps the leather strip around my wrist, watching it slink against my forearm. "I like it. That reminds me." He pulls a narrow envelope out of his blazer. "I have something else for you."

Adrenaline zips through my body. The envelope practically glows as he passes it to me.

"Careful," he warns as I rip it open with my chewed fingernails.

Two tickets to the Pretenders' show at The Fall Out stare up at me, printed in shades far more vibrant than any post-punk concert material deserves to be.

He takes my hand. "Jessica, will you see Chrissie Hynde with me?"

My mouth hangs open. "This show's been sold out since before the summer started."

"I know a few people at the club, remember?"

"No shit!" I stamp a foot in the aisle and the record bins shake. "Oh, you are getting the full boyfriend treatment for this!" I wrap my arms around him.

"You're not a subtle girl, are you?" he says.

I press my face against his ear. "Costuming, choreography, everything," I loud-whisper. The clerk rolls his eyes.

"Maybe let's take this outside?" Whit says. Clerk Guy waves the Icicle Works EP in the air as we streak past him and head up the stairs, ignoring him.

I'm hit with oppressive August heat as we burst onto South Street, emerging next to a punky clothing place called Zipperhead. Whit corners me against the warm shop window. The cartoon likeness of a guy whose brains are being zipped out of his skull hangs over us like a billboard. Metal zipper teeth cleave down the guy's giant, hand-drawn forehead, and the rest of the building-front is done-up with humongous, crawling ants.

"What was that about costuming?" Whit asks, wrapping me in his blazer. In the window behind me, mannequins in paint-splattered clothing pose among signs for BOY LONDON and Vivienne Westwood.

I finger the tickets as my new leather bracelet rattles on my arm. "I can't believe you got these!" The afternoon mugginess and Whit's persuasive hands work their way under my clothing.

"*You're fucking lucky I like you,*" he whispers, his teeth nipping at my ear.

When I turn my head, I'm face-to-face with a female mannequin wrapped in a magenta overdose of a satin party gown, topped by a pageant sash. A second manne-girl lounges underneath her wearing paint-splashed lingerie, spiraling her plaster hand up Pageant Girl's dress.

In nearly illegible scrawl, Pageant Girl's sash reads *Miss America 1984*.

Pictures from a lesbian photoshoot featuring this year's lovely winner, Miss Vanessa Williams, recently surfaced in *Penthouse*. She was forced to turn in her tiara. I quick-wonder if it will ruin the poor girl's career.

"Stay with me tonight," Whit whispers, distracting me from the lascivious mannequin pageant party. "I want you for a whole 24 hours."

I think of my work schedule, which dampens the sex-buzz growing in my body. I let a pouty moan slip past my lips. "You promised you'd have me home by four o'clock for today's dinner shift."

"Ditch it. Get Kim to cover." His hips pin me against the showcase window.

"Kim's not in a great place right now. And I want to keep this job. I need the money."

He loosens his hold on me. "Oh yeah," he says. "England. The beeline to fame and fortune."

"It's the whole reason I'm waitressing." I start to sweat, all this hair like a scarf around my neck. "I can't jeopardize that." I fluff hair off the window, igniting a crackle of static.

Whit hangs his head. "Am I still just a piece of your jigsaw puzzle?"

"Is that what you think?"

"That's what you said." He stares at the mannequins doing each other in the window.

I step away from the glass. "I said that weeks ago. Sort of."

Whit laces his hands behind his neck and gazes at the awning above us. His blazer rides his shoulders, flashing a blood-red lining at me. "Fine. Forget I said anything."

"You're crapping up a nice moment, here."

"You're right. I'll take you home. *Now*."

"I don't want to leave *now*," I say. A rusted chain bangs against Zipperhead's front door as a shop-keep in bleached cornrows gives us the eye.

Whit pulls a set of keys out of his jeans. "You've got things to do, Jessica. Let's go."

Where have I heard this song before, I think? It's the latest version of *You're Frigging Threatening Me, Jessica*. Special Extended Play version from Philadelphia.

Whit swerves through a lane change, making me decorate the Camaro's armrest with the imprints of my meager fingernails. He doesn't cut the engine when we reach my parking lot.

"You're mad," I say, pulling the door handle.

"I'm not."

"You have no right to be upset, you know."

He doesn't look at me. "I know," he says. "That's why I'm *not mad*."

The passenger door sticks, leaving me to bang it with my shoulder as Depeche Mode pounds out "People Are People" through the car speakers in the background. "Would you *just*—" I slam my shoulder once more. "If you're pissed off, just *say it*."

He rolls his eyes and leans across me, shoving the door open and dropping back into the driver's seat, not even meeting eyes with me. This from a guy who can stare me into fucking disintegration.

I climb out of the car and he pulls the heavy door shut behind me.

"Good thing you're not mad," I shout, standing in the street.

He pulls away, muffler roaring.

I flop on our sofa. Kimmer joins me, propping herself on the floor against the couch. She holds a bowl of ice cream as pretty as a modern sculpture: Shiny white mounds speared through the middle with a sleek, pink plastic spoon.

"Weren't you on a date?" she asks me.

"*Was* is the operative word."

She spoons ice cream into her mouth. "Sounds like you could use some totally unnecessary calories." She lifts the bowl and hands me her utensil. "Vanilla cookie-dough ripple?"

I scrape a spoonful and suck frozen dairy off the bubble-gum-colored plastic. "This is *great*. Where'd you get it?" I stick the spoon back into the mush and stare at my ringworm mural on the wall. It practically spins of its own power.

"I told Teddy about my unplanned swimming trip the other night," Kimmer says. "He bought me a sundae at The Scoop."

"Teddy did that?" I ask. She nods, digging for her next mouthful.

The phone screams to life a few inches from my head, sending me and the couch cushions jumping. I'm not sure how Drew knows to call whenever I'm in the middle of a romantic upset, but he does.

I scramble for the receiver, ready to hear Drew's warm-as-toast vocals, his humor like the proverbial shoe that fits. I hold the phone to my face.

"*Hey*," I say.

"Hey back. I'm sorry I sent you home."

"*Whit?*" I right myself on the couch, redirecting the crossed signals in my brain to the proper boyfriend compartment.

"That was unfair," Whit says.

Kimmer hops away, retreating to the bedroom with her sundae. I straighten my hair as if he can see me.

"Holy shit," I say. "You can't have gotten home already. Please tell me you didn't drive that fast."

"I'm at a gas station in Doylestown," Whit says. "I didn't want to wait to talk to you." Traffic noise sifts through the background, Doppler-ing under his dialog. I picture him leaning against the blighted glass of a telephone booth, alone, the Camaro resting in the afternoon sun.

"It wasn't exactly cool," I say.

"I know you have a lot of priorities," Whit says.

I bite my lip. "I can't apologize for that."

"No, it's good. That's what singles you out. It makes people want to be around you. You're this *force*. But. . ."

I hold my breath.

He goes on. "Jess, I can't be last on your list." Car noises rumble behind him.

My stomach pangs again. Call it a Love Cramp. "It's really not like that," I tell him.

The mural on the wall suddenly reminds me of a metal spring in an exploding clock, spitting broken watch innards at me.

"You know what happened to me, Jess," Whit says. I picture him, tired after a warehouse shift, stepping into his oddly quiet apartment. Chatting, he thinks, to the friend he was nice enough to let stay there. Turning a corner into his bedroom. . . .

Being confronted by legs and nudity and the slacker roommate tangled around his girlfriend. In his bed. A woman he thought might be the Long-Term Girl.

She wasn't.

I imagine the reality of that moment raining down on a person's body until you want to scream yourself into an alternate universe.

I know this is why we always sleep in the living room.

"Listen, I love how awesome we are together," I say. I pull the Pretenders' tickets from my pocket, thumbing open the envelope, rubbing my fingers against the brightly-printed paper. "It's amazing that you bought us these tickets," I say. "You're not last on my list. Far from it."

The dial tone clicks momentarily, signifying that he just shoved a coin into the payphone. Then another. The ache in my gut loosens.

"All right," Whit says. "Let's be awesome together. Let's go to that concert." I feel the world slip back toward semi-normalcy.

Whit and I talk until he runs out of change. I slide the receiver back into its cradle. Kimmer ventures back to the couch, carrying a fat manila envelope.

"Something came for you today." She tosses the parcel at me, covered in a mosaic of postage stamps. I rip it apart.

A perforated nylon sports jersey unfurls in my lap, followed by a strip of spiral notepaper, frilled at the edges. I lift the note, penned in boy-writing:

This is to compensate for an unfortunate
inconvenience of geography.
Don't you forget about me.
— DREW

Drew's oversized high school football jersey drapes itself across my thighs. I pinch it by the shoulders and hold it up to my chest, then show the back of it to Kimmer. Drew's last name screams across the mesh fabric in white capital letters: ELLISON.

Kimmer's eyebrows raise. "Subtle, isn't he?" she says, pulling me up from the floor.

I head into the bedroom and tuck the jersey into our ominous slab of a dresser, which sits there like the Monolith from *2001: A Space Odyssey*. A mini-golf pencil rests on top of the dresser, as well as my *Eau de Prom* perfume, making rings on its surface. Trina doesn't like when I leave the atomizer on our too-small sink. She keeps putting it on the dresser.

The huge, blank slate of a dresser. . . .

Hmm. My ears ring. In my mind's eye, superimposed over the dark surface of the dresser, silver tines materialize: moving, zipping together . . . assembling an animated shape.

I put my perfume back in the bathroom and swipe the scatter of pennies and dimes off the dresser top.

I spin the diminutive pencil in my fingertips. My red suncatcher revolves in the nearby window, bouncing ruby sparkles along the carpet. My hand begins to trace a silvery "Y" shape down the front of the dresser, like a zipper sliding open. The lead absorbs light from the window, turning my sketchings the color of mercury, shining like they're rising off the canvas. Um, *dresser*.

"Hey, Kim," I call into the living room. "Is that drop cloth I bought still under the couch?"

Half an hour later, the front of the dresser-monster is transformed into a big, half-open zipper. A track of silvery teeth are painted up the length of it, accented by the broken bits of a rocks glass that I smashed behind our building. The mega-zipper slides open to reveal a field of spattered fuchsia against receding mist-gray clouds. It's something Jackson Pollock might have painted if he listened to The Dead Milkmen.

I entitle it *Tribute to Zipperhead*. The girls will get used to it. Although we're getting lower on glassware every week.

CHAPTER 22

STILL AUGUST—Sandler Apartments
Do You Really Want to Hurt Me?

Audrey tosses an Army-issue duffle bag in front of our newly-painted dresser. She pulls clothes out of what is now a startlingly elaborate drawer and shoves a series of androgynous shorts and tops into the bag.

Kimmer and I stand at the kitchen stove, warming a camping pot whose bottom is filled with a millimeter of oil. Our Winnie-the-Pooh cereal bowl holds a pile of fresh breadcrumbs that Kimmer squirreled out of Capresi's in a Ziploc. One of Paula's zucchinis and a bowl of beaten egg glop sits on the counter. It's time to cook veggies.

I've never fried anything before in my whole existence. This is trial by olive oil.

Audrey pulls a swimsuit out of her drawer and inspects it. Trina has stationed herself against the dresser like the Garment Supervisor. "How many bathing suits do you think you need for one God-damn weekend in Cape May?" she says.

"Do they enforce a swimsuit limit?" Audrey unfurls a one-piece that offers as much coverage as a national flag. "I need options in case I get self-conscious."

"I'm sure Bryan will make you feel validated," Trina says, poking into Audrey's drawer.

"Hey, hands off the merchandise." Audrey plucks Trina's wrist away. "And have you met *me*? Validation doesn't come easy. You said you were fine with me going. So get off the rag train, sunshine."

"I'm perfect with it." Trina pushes herself off the dresser, making it shake. "Some of us have to work for a living this weekend."

"You're not the only one who needs to keep their status in the job market," I call from the kitchen, holding a steak knife. I notice an ironic spot of rust over the words *Stainless Steel* that streams across its blade. "I need at least four hundred bucks more to meet my study abroad budget. And the summer is ticking away."

Audrey stuffs a magenta scarf into her duffle bag. "Ladies and gentlemen, I give you Jessica's jet-set countdown."

"If I were rich, it would be jet-setting," I say, scraping a thumbnail across the orange stain embedded in the steel. The oxidation doesn't budge. "I'm poor. So it's studying. And it's probably the only way I'll ever see Europe."

"You don't know that," Audrey says. "What if you marry a wealthy foreign oil magnate?"

"Because that always happens," Trina adds.

"I'm not out for the M.R.S. degree." I laugh, rinsing the knife.

Our pot sizzles as Kimmer shakes it against the burner grate. "How about you worry about cutting the zucchini right now?" she says to me. Kimmer whacks the vegetable in two, shoving one side toward me. "Focus. Otherwise, some ER doctor will be studying how to reattach your fingers."

"Why doesn't anyone trust me with sharp implements?" I slice the zucchini directly against the counter since we don't have a cutting board. Teddy's cut-on-the-flat rule floats to mind as the vegetable shifts. I dredge a slice in the egg goop, then in the breadcrumbs.

"Jess, how many bathing suits do you go through in a weekend on Long Island?" Audrey asks.

"We don't go to the beach *every day*." I plop the slice into the hissing yellow pool.

"Drop it *lightly*," says Kimmer.

"But if it were a beach weekend, how many suits?" Audrey continues.

"I've never owned more than two at a time," I say.

"See, I'm telling you, Audrey," says Trina. "You're packing all wrong."

"You think I do everything wrong," Audrey says, stuffing a fistful of shoulder pads into her bag.

Trina smiles. "I think you can predict economic trends like a pro. You've realized your calling as an econ major."

"I wish I had a handle on my economic trends," says Kimmer. "I don't even know if my loans have come in for next semester."

I poke at the browning zucchini with a fork. A slice spits oil onto the top of my hand. "*Ow*—the vegetables are angry."

"Cold water." Kimmer shoves my hand into the sink and turns on the spigot.

"What's this about your loans not coming in?" I ask. Kimmer shifts the pot away from the sink.

"My sister forwarded me a bunch of official-looking crap in the mail. None of it looks good." She pulls a plate out of the cupboard. "I'll drain the zucchini." She spins a paper towel off the rod and arranges it on the dish. "You keep that hand under the water so you don't blister."

"You don't miss a beat, Nurse Kimmer," says Audrey. "Why don't you just proceed right to med school?" Audrey pulls a violet cardigan from the foyer closet, the same one that Trina wore to Russell's. Which I haven't mentioned to anyone. Audrey shoves the sweater into her duffle bag.

Trina stomps into the kitchen. "You're going to set yourselves on fire with the flame that high," she mumbles, turning down our burner. She grabs her purse and heads for the door. "I'm outta here. I can't watch Audrey pack ass-backwards." She stops in the foyer. "Audrey!" she yells.

Audrey whips around, craning her neck.

"Bon fucking voyage." Trina whirls out the door, which rattles in its frame.

"Maybe *she* should spend some time under cool water." Kimmer wraps my hand gently in a dishtowel. "Be careful, you. No more battle scars."

In 20 minutes, two plates of fried zucchini are piled high on the counter.

The stove looks like the Baby Oil Gods have been playing in a fountain. I taste a slice, letting the savory warmth dissolve on my tongue. "*Mmm*. Not exactly Capresi's, but I'll take it."

Audrey hauls her overstuffed duffle bag onto the couch and looks at the pile of fried veggies on the counter. "So, who's gonna eat Mount Zucchini?"

Kimmer smiles. "I've got an idea."

Audrey, Kimmer, and I stroll past rows of Harley Davidsons adorned with miniature Union Jack flags and bandanas outside Jan's Pub. The machines run the gamut from an unpretentious, spattered dirt bike to souped-up chrome monsters that look like they've swallowed a Mack truck. We girls each carry a folded aluminum foil envelope full of fried zucchini, still hot.

Leather-vested men sit around redwood picnic tables on Jan's deck. A denim-clad bartender blinks in bewilderment as Kimmer explains our intentions. The bartender shrugs, then lowers the musical strains of ZZ Top on the stereo system.

"Ahem," Audrey announces. "Gentlemen, we live here in town, and today we're in possession of far more fried zucchini than we could ever eat."

Men lift their heads from their beer mugs, gaping as if we just shot out someone's Michelins. I swallow hard and raise a foil packet of zucchini slices, facing off against the bushy eyebrows of every guy on the patio. "So we're going to share."

A man with a fat cigar in his fingers pushes back his chair. He sports a long, gray ponytail. "Are you off your rocker, Red?" he asks Audrey.

"We're not crazy," says Kimmer. "We're waitresses." A guy in a vintage Indian Motorcycle T-shirt laughs and turns his back on us.

Audrey unwraps her foil packet in front of the ponytailed Cigar Man, revealing the golden slices. He balances his stogie in an ashtray and pokes the zucchini with his finger. "*Damn*, that looks good."

I fold back a sheet of warm foil. Several bikers leave their beers long enough to pinch a few pieces.

"That's tasty stuff, young lady," Cigar Man tells Audrey. The four tarnished rings across his fingers could pass for brass knuckles. "You girls coming back tomorrow? I don't mind home cooking."

"No. But here's what you can do for us," says Audrey, taking a seat. "Next time you see us walking past, how about you don't whistle, or howl, or rev your big engines."

"Then next time we cook appetizers," Kimmer says, "maybe we'll come back."

"I'll take you up on that," says Cigar Man. He shakes Audrey's palm and leans in closer. "And thanks for noticing the size of my engine." He winks.

Kimmer gathers the empty sheets of tin foil. "How about you keep an eye out to see that no one bothers us?" she says to Cigar Man, balling up the foil. "It can get rough around here after hours."

Cigar Man raises a beer mug. "Will do, little lady."

We head home.

Audrey shoots her crinkled tinfoil ball at the garbage can when we enter our kitchen. The hinged plastic lid of the trash can flaps. We girls get as far as the kitchen table—then we freeze in place.

A torn paper towel is taped to the refrigerator door, off-kilter. A message streaks down the quilted paper in Trina's titan-sized scratch:

"IT HURTS!"

We stare at the paper towel.

"Aw, fuck," says Audrey. Kimmer clunks her purse on the flecked Linoleum floor.

I check the bedroom to see whether Trina is hiding in there. Audrey untapes the message and folds it into sections. She slips it into our dresser like she's archiving a veteran flag.

"Who was I kidding? Trina's got it in for Bryan," she says, slumping against the bright panels of our dresser.

She hauls her overstuffed duffle bag back to the bedroom and it hits the floor like a corpse. Audrey yanks the zipper pull.

She unpacks in silence.

I tip-toe behind her. "No more Cape May?" She shoves a pair of two-toned acid-washed denim shorts back into the drawer.

Kimmer pokes her head through the bedroom doorway. "Trina could have admitted she had the hots for the guy weeks ago," Kimmer says. Audrey doesn't answer.

"You're not gonna beat yourself up about this are you, Auge?" I ask. A ruby beam of light hits my eye from the suncatcher in the window.

"I'm not beating anything, I'm just not going." Audrey tugs the zipper. It jams halfway open, gobbling the corner of a scarf. "God dammit!" she shouts, digging both hands into the bag. "You know what? *I knew*!" She tosses a jumble of garments in the air like some fashion-forward version of confetti. "Tell me we didn't all know she was crazy about him."

Kimmer peels a pair of Audrey's buttercup yellow underwear out of her hair. I kick a camisole off my toe.

"*We knew*," the two of us mumble.

Audrey shakes the rest of the contents of the duffle onto the shag. A toiletry bag splits open, and a not-so-discreet pink plastic diaphragm case skitters along the rug. Audrey kicks it.

She kneels, surrounded by the gray and red tones of her wardrobe, then looks up at us. "What are you two doing today?"

I'm sitting in the middle of a pile of randomly tossed clothing. "What do you need?"

"I have to go talk to Trina at The Rose." Audrey reaches her long arms across the rug, gathering up garments.

Kimmer's shoulders deflate. "*Grr*. I promised Teddy I'd help him organize inventory today," she says. "I have to be at the restaurant."

"Since when are you an *organizer*?" I fold one of Audrey's shirts into a rectangle.

"I'm much more coordinated with food service than I am with house keys. Or school loans," Kimmer answers.

Staring at Audrey's garments, I flashback to my clothing-stuffed Barbie case from second grade, the one I filled in preparation for running away from home with my mom but was thwarted. After my mother marched me back to my room, I clicked open the case's silver-tone latch and watched the cascade of my daisy-patterned shorts, girly T-shirts, and pink ruffled nightgowns tumble to my bedroom throw rug. Next thing to drop: The realization that I wasn't going anywhere. Not until college, anyway.

"I need you to come with me to The Rose," Audrey says.

I pull myself to standing. "I'll get my shoes."

La Chambre Rose is as frenetic as Penn Station, penguins commuting past us in both directions. This kitchen makes Capresi's look like an abandoned walk-in fridge in comparison. We cross a dim, paneled corridor leading to the next dining room.

Trina smiles at patrons as she places fancied-up club sandwiches around a table for six. A penguin-suited busboy shadows her, nimbly filling water goblets with a swish of a metal pitcher. Mozart plays through the ceiling speakers.

Trina stops dead when she sees us. Her smile evaporates. She excuses herself to meet us in the hall.

"We got your message," I say, tugging at my collar. The hallway seems to be lacking airflow.

Trina wipes her hands on the linen napkin that rests on her shoulder. She juts her jaw at Audrey. "I'm not sure what to say to you."

"I'm not going," Audrey blurts out.

Trina blinks. "You're what?" Glasses tinkle in the kitchen behind us, which beams like a beacon of high-speed chaos, compared to the relaxed sophistication of the dining area.

"I said, I'm not going to Cape May with Bryan."

"You'd do that for me?" Trina asks. In the darkened hall, I can nearly see her wine-colored lip do an imitation of paper caught against a fan. It's a rarely seen phenomenon, like a UFO.

"If you weren't such a stubborn ass, I would have blown him off from the start," Audrey says. "No matter how cute he is."

Trina leans a shoulder against the hallway paneling. "We all know I'm a thick-headed bitch," she says. "But so are you. So we're even."

Audrey brings Trina in for a hug, sending Trina's waitressing blouse halfway up her back. I yank the shirt down. "*Aww.* I love you guys," I say, joining the hug. "This is such a Waltons moment."

"Shut the fuck up," Trina mumbles against Audrey's shoulder. She laughs and swipes at her eyeliner.

As I pull out of the hug, my vision adjusts to the glow of the nearby kitchen. A sunny-haired blond guy comes into focus in a corner. He grabs Lima, the raven-tressed hostess and med student, as she sweeps past.

Bryan and Lima suck face.

My jaw falls open. "*Holy shit.*"

Audrey shields her eyes from the kitchen glare. Lima squirms out of Bryan's grasp and trots away toward the front dining room, leaving him alone in the corner.

As we girls step closer, Bryan's smile dissolves. He blocks his body with his hands as if he can feel us staring a chasm into his torso. "Oooh, *crap,*" he says.

Audrey tugs her blouse straight, leaning as if she's about to blast off. Rather than bulldoze him, she stomps past in a seething cloud of woman-done-wrong. Bryan gulps air like a fish.

Trina drags me with her in Audrey's footsteps, smacking Bryan across those tanned cheeks with her linen napkin on the way. We ladies pile out the double doors into the slanted sunlight of The Rose's parking lot, between the canal and the river. Right where Jessica Savitch's car plunged into the water, to be slurped into its viscous bed and filled with muck.

Audrey runs her hands through her red spiked hair. "You knew about this, didn't you, Trina?"

"Not for sure," Trina says. "I tried to warn you."

I step between the two of them. "Why do you both like this guy again?"

"Not helping," says Audrey, who starts to cry.

"It pisses me off all-to-hell, too." Trina turns in a 360, holding her head in her hands. "I can't go back in there. I can't even decide which of you sons-of-bitches to be pissed at."

"Can I make a suggestion on that?" I say.

"NOT HELPING!" both girls snap.

Audrey and Trina heave in ragged breaths. Sunlight splinters through the trees along the river beyond us, thickening into the natural pine forest that marks the official end of downtown New Hope.

Audrey collects herself with a sputtering inhale. "Tri', you've gotta finish your shift. Don't get fired over my bullshit."

"I just smacked Bryan Cavanaugh in the face with a dinner napkin," Trina says. "It's my bullshit, too."

"He *so* had it coming," I say. The more I stare at the railroad ties that scantily border the drop into the canal, the more I wonder why they didn't just put a fence here, so no one could drive off the edge. I wrap an arm around both roommates and lead them away from the brink.

"Can I be the one to tell that shithead you're not going to Cape May?" Trina asks, shoving up her sleeves.

"Be my fucking guest." Audrey laughs. "But I think he got the memo just now."

I sense the two of them sliding back toward normalcy, pulling themselves over the tipping point where things will get resolved. That glint of a second chance.

In that moment, I remember that Drew is leaving for California next week. I promised to meet him on the beach back in New York.

"Trina?" I ask.

She presses a hand against her forehead. "What?"

"Is this a bad time to tell you I need a ride to the Trenton rail station, to go see Drew before he abandons me?"

Trina wipes her face.

"This is the worst possible moment to ask me that," she says.

"I know."

On Sunday, she brings me anyway.

CHAPTER 23

AUGUST 1984—Long Island
Bizarre Love Triangle

Long Island's North Shore looks like some extra-terrestrial mystery at night; blue and pocked, like the surface of the moon. Drew walks with me along the pebble-laden edge of Cedar Beach. This is the same stretch where we used to dig beer bottles into the sand in high school, blasting Aerosmith tunes from a boombox with dented mesh speakers. I inhale the gentle scent of sea salt.

"Kimmer says the first time she saw the ocean, she couldn't believe there was that much open space in one place, anywhere," I say. Baby waves nudge against the shoreline of The Sound. "She's never been to the beach after dark in her life."

"We're jaded," Drew says, looking out at the dark surf. "I've spent so much time in the ocean this year, my fingerprints are eroding."

A plane of sand stretches from under the black water, reflecting the inky night sky. Pebbles draw a perpetual S curve that outlines the rhythm of the surf, tinkling like a piano each time the water pushes on it.

Drew wears a new pair of John Lennon spectacles. "When did these come along?" I say, lifting them off his nose. "So studious for summer break." The wind sends his cocoa-colored hair blowing across his eyes. His hair is longer than it's ever been but is brushed away from his face. "Careful with those," he says, taking the frames back from me. He rubs the lenses with his Giants jersey.

"Did you ruin your contacts?" I ask.

"Maybe I'm tired of contacts. They bother me."

The breeze ripples Drew's jersey, plastering it against his chest. He has one of those V-shaped backs that come from high school wrestling matches, zipping down toward a flat waist. I miss knowing any guy's body this thoroughly. "So, you're honestly leaving?" I ask.

"There's not much to keep me here."

"Is this some kind of payback for me spending the summer away?"

He laughs. "Not everything is about *you*. How often do I get invited to UCLA? I've got to take my opportunities where they come."

Grit edges over the sides of my sandals as I step through the sand. "Will you be coming back?"

He nudges the glasses further back on his nose. "Jess, do you plan on coming back after that program in Europe you're so dead-freaking-set on?"

"I . . . of course I do."

Every vision I ever had of leaving was always for the purpose of applying that knowledge to my life when I got back. Yet a thought flickers in my subconscious like an ember: What if I'm searching for a city, a relationship, a *life* so fabulous, I might—

Not worth articulating. Chickens that will never hatch. "I live *here*," I tell Drew. "Yes, I'm coming home." A squiggle-trail of broken reeds draws itself down the length of the beach in front of us. I twist a cold reed in my fingertips. "How else will I brag about it to you afterward?"

Drew smiles. His every movement invites me back to a place I thought I might have outgrown. I wonder for a moment: If we'd just met today, would he hold the same tide-like attraction for me? Does that exist apart from our history together?

Would I fall in love all over again?

"Drew . . . tell me this isn't about another girl."

He laughs like I'm someone's silly kid sister.

"You're enjoying this entirely too much," I say.

"What if it were about a girl?" He swings my hand. "Would you have any right to be upset?"

"Absolutely not. I'm asking anyway."

A fallen tree blocks our path, stripped of bark and blanched smooth by the elements. We sit down on it. In the distance, a boulder the size of a beached whale sticks out of the sand, leading to a dark jetty.

"This isn't about a girl," Drew says. "Except you. You're the girl." He touches a long index finger along the bottom of my chin. "What do you have to report?"

The breeze gropes my clothing like a drunken party guest. I straighten the edges of my shirt. "I don't like these rules."

Drew lowers himself off the driftwood and stretches out along the sand. Moon-bathing. He reaches for me. "You wanted the beach. Come feel it."

I kneel into the grittiness. Drew slides his palm softly along the ground. "*Shhh.* If you listen closely," he whispers, "it talks to you."

Where do I find these people, engaging in dialogs with beach sand, consulting with cicadas for inspiration? Maybe I do seek out weirdness.

Drew pulls my wrist towards his face and tussles my studded leather bracelet with his finger. "Tell me who you're seeing."

I roll onto my back. The ground bleeds dampness through my clothing.

"It's me you're talking to," he reminds me. "*I know.*"

His arms smooth around me with the same touch he's always had: light and precise and gracious, as if he cherishes nothing as much as the moments he's in contact with my skin. I remember the Drew who held me, back when my hands shook at the very thought of fumbling with his body. Of having no clue how to reciprocate for the things he'd done to me. Of wondering how to master this ridiculously perplexing *sex* thing that the rest of the world already seemed to be on speaking terms with.

There was no textbook I could study, no course I could ace in preparation. But I wanted him. And I wanted *to be good* for him.

I was the Woody Allen of neurotic virgins.

Steady as Gibraltar, Drew closed his hand around mine.

Don't worry, he said. Whatever you do, I promise I'll like it.

I'll never have a moment like that again with anyone else for the rest of my life.

Back in the sand, my throat muscles tighten, recusing my vocal cords from answering Drew's question.

"So, who's the guy?" Drew talks in my ear, an entirely different voice than I'm used to now, making the conflict in my head boil over. His breath puffs against my neck. "I deserve to know."

I swallow hard, forcing the lump in my throat to flatten. "He's a musician. He's twenty-two. We met at a club in Philadelphia."

Drew takes off the John Lennon specs and folds them with one hand. "Does he mean something to you?"

"I don't know exactly what it means." I touch my fingers to my heart as that jagged pain tweaks inside me again, inches below my fingertips. *The Love Cramp.* "But yeah. He means . . . something." I squeeze my eyes closed, holding back the sting of salt. "That's all the details I can give you. I can't bring myself to be more duplicitous than that."

"I understand." The breeze is almost louder than he is.

"If you're so concerned, then why did you insist we had to see different people?" My voice wavers.

"Because it's what you needed. All I did was *articulate* it," he says. "Did you notice? When I asked if you were coming home from London, it took you a second."

"I don't have a frigging crystal ball to see how every moment of my life will fall into place." The wind picks up and I shiver. "Can you give me a break on that?"

"That's exactly what I'm doing." Drew props up on his elbow, leaning over me. "I've been in love with you a long time, Jessica. That's not going anywhere." I hot-swallow the wind as he talks. "If we're going to have some kind of future together, then neither of us should feel there were things we didn't get to do."

Drew brushes my cheek with sandy fingers. "This is not about some other girl," he goes on. "It's about us, becoming adults."

"*God*, is that what's happening?"

"It's what you wanted, Jess," he says. "And you're right. We have to let life happen. But understand, I'm coming back for this," he says, pulling me close, deep eyes swallowing me whole, pressing his forehead against mine. "There is no *me* without you."

And just then, I'm sure-as-shit that if he were a stranger who never so much as entered the same national airspace as me before, I'd fall in love with him.

Right.

Fucking.

Now.

He kisses me, and I know I'm toast. We delve impressions into the terrain that I'm happy I won't have to explain in the morning.

I may never get all the sand out of my hair.

I watch Drew climb to the top of the boulder that points to the jetty, his bare silhouette hovering over the black horizon of the water. He Tarzan-yells across the flatness of the Long Island Sound, arms waving.

It reverberates for miles.

As the sound drops off . . . lights blink to life in a palisade of houses hanging over the bluffs behind us. I hear the echo of slamming doors. I grope for my shirt in the sand. Both of us freeze as we hear voices grumble beyond the dunes.

Oh shit—oh shit—oh SHIT!

My clothes are scattered all around me. We shouldn't even be on this section of the beach; officially, it's private. I stretch my crumpled blouse over my chest.

Drew hops off the boulder and makes a run for his jeans as flashlights beam from behind the brush. I scramble to put on the rest of my outfit, spraying sand all over. I pull up handfuls of it with every piece of clothing. I can hear people clomping across their decks, heading down weathered wooden stairs towards the dunes.

My calf muscles burn as we sprint uphill toward the parking lot, me clutching pieces of clothing I had no time to climb back into. Drew's car is on an asphalt landing at the top of a bluff.

Once in a Lifetime

We throw open the car doors, and the interior vehicle light bounces off far too much flesh for my liking. I duck into the front seat, pulling the door closed barely in time for the soles of my feet to lift off the pavement. I'm a half-peeled banana, uncrumpling a ball of clothing in my lap, laughing as Drew finds his keys.

I get dressed behind his dashboard as we squeal out of the lot. Drew whips his head back and forth at me as the car pulls gracelessly up the road, headlamps white-washing rows of tall grass.

"What are you looking at!" he blurts at me.

He drives home in no pants.

I'll call this, *The Boulder Incident.*

Drew walks me to the Long Island Railroad platform the next morning. I press my face against the flat of his chest and whisper, "I love you."

Fingers slide through my hair. "I love you, too, Jess."

"*You better,*" I say.

Trina only mildly protests about picking me up from Trenton's fright of a transit yard. I smoke a Virginia Slim out the car window as thick elms fly past, tossing shadows over the station wagon's woodgrain paneling. The guitar jags of an INXS song prattle through the radio, pounding with drums.

"When does Drew leave for California?" Trina asks.

"Friday." I tap my ash out the window, which is immediately whisked away.

"And when's that Pretenders concert?"

"Same weekend." The wind pulls a tear out of the corner of my lashes. I push myself back against the seat and stub out the cigarette in the car ashtray.

Each minute, we drone closer to New Hope, to Whit, and to the unreconciled Love Cramp in my gut.

Sympathy whisks across Trina's face, ephemeral as the elm shadows. "You have it the-fuck *in* for the both of them, don't you?"

I clunk my head against the seat back. "What the hell do I do?"

Trina stretches an arm in front of my face and plays the tiny violin with her fingers, whining out the musical accompaniment you'd hear under a tragic silent film. "Poor you."

I drag tobacco. "You're ever-so-helpful."

"New subject," she says. "Good news in Trina land: I've been offered a real job at Fox and Rascowitz's Pittsburgh office, starting in the fall. Part-time, but with pay and everything."

"Congratulations," I say, wiping my face. "Aren't they downtown?"

"You mean *don-ton*?" she says, mocking a Pittsburgh accent. "It's a damn far ride from campus. But I'll swan-dive off that bridge when I get to it." She tilts her head out the window as she waits at a traffic light. "Would you get with the syllabus, pal?" she shouts at the hesitant driver in front of her. "Green means go!"

The ball compass that's suckered to the dashboard bobbles aimlessly, refusing to confirm our position. I smack it, setting its interior sphere awhirl. "What the hell is the problem with this thing?"

The compass makes an indignant popping noise as Trina wrangles it off the dash, whipping it into the back of the car. It bounces against the upholstery.

"That broken piece of crapola," she says. "We're on our own, now."

We return to an apartment that I'd swear has shrunk three sizes. Audrey comes out of the bedroom hugging a full laundry basket. I sling my gym bag to the floor and a sigh rumbles between my shoulder blades. I take a seat at our table.

"Did someone not take her happy pills today?" Audrey lets the basket whomp to the carpet. The rug needs more of a wash than her clothes, but it won't fit in the washer.

"Pity party, table for one," Trina says, stuffing her groundskeeper-size keyring into her purse. "Our unfortunate roommate has too many boy problems."

"Didn't you enjoy the sea air on Long Island?" Audrey asks.

I wrench my hair in my fists. "I wish I could meld Drew and Whit into one person."

"And in this dream, both of them adore her," Trina adds, heading for the bedroom. "Don't forget that part."

I lower my head against the Formica. "I'd be insulted, except she's right. I can't help it. I want the mosaic."

I want Whit's musical intensity and sexual voracity and that hyperactive fucking energy that makes him lead me down lamp-lit streets after midnight, contemplating the nature of art. I want Drew's soulful articulation and his whacked-out brilliant streak and his calm fingers. I want to scrape out the pain in my heart and keep the pure, centrifuged remains of both relationships.

I want it all. Isn't that what they told us we could have? We're the women of the '80s. We can have it all.

No one mentioned what would happen if we got it.

I smack the tabletop. "I do this with everything, don't I?" I say. "I force some combination of crap through my extruder-of-a-brain and try to mold it into something new. I even *pastiche* people."

"Too bad men aren't subject to artistic license," Audrey says.

I close my eyes. Audrey slaps something on the tabletop in front of me that smells of library. "The last time someone tried that, it didn't work out so well," she says.

I swoop hair out of my face. A copy of Mary Shelley's *Frankenstein* stares up at me.

It pounds against the sofa like a hockey puck when I toss it across the room.

CHAPTER 24

AUGUST 1984—King of Prussia
Birds Fly (Whisper to a Scream)

Whit and I finally spend the night in his bedroom.

The next afternoon, I spill earrings onto the countertop at his breakfast bar. The kitchen is so small we can't both stand in it at once.

Whit taps a button on his answering machine. A man's voice warbles on the tape, talking to Matt, something about coming to clean out his locker. And sorry it didn't work out. Man.

He pounds the button, cutting the message short.

I straighten in my seat. "What was that?"

Whit pulls open a cabinet that half-hides his face.

I slip a paint-splashed, masterpiece of a triangular metal earring through my earlobe. "Was that for the other Matt?"

"You want something to eat?" He tosses a loaf of bread onto the counter and slides it in front of me. Its wrapper screams *Fresh!*

Come to think of it, it's a Thursday and he's not at work. It didn't occur to me before.

"Whit, how did you get the day off?" I sweep earring number two off the tiled countertop. It makes a scraping sound.

"I gave myself the day off," he says.

"How does that work?"

He clinks two stoneware dishes against the tile. "It works like this: I didn't show up last week, so I lost my job."

My fingers struggle to keep an earring-back from shooting across the room like a BB. "I know it's none of my business," I say. "But, *what the hell?*"

Whit rolls his eyes and pulls open his refrigerator door, casting a vertical slant of light over his shirtless body. I feel myself tiptoeing into long-term girlfriend territory, that strange new terrain where I show an interest in his potential as a responsible adult. I'm not sure he's given me permission to do that.

I'm not sure guys ever do.

He slaps a plastic envelope of cold cuts on the tiled countertop in front of me. "It *is* your business. It happened so I could do *this*," he says, spreading his arms like he's displaying a banquet, instead of a Ziploc full of turkey roll. "With you. I called in sick a couple of times at work since we've been going out."

"I never asked you to do that."

"*Right.* I wanted to." He leans across the counter and kisses me, his tongue swiping my lips just gently enough to make it hard for me to stay on subject. "*Birds wanna fly*, you know?" he says. "Did you listen to that Icicle Works cassette I duped for you? Is 'Whisper To A Scream' transcendent, or what?"

"Holy *God*, yes. But you're changing the subject." Not to mention distracting me with some serious tongue action. I shake it off. "We could have worked around your schedule like we do mine."

He steps back. "That's the thing, Jessica. I'm more willing to change my shit for you than you are for me." He digs back into the refrigerator for a tube of brown mustard, which I hate. Even the color is bitter.

"Come on—you can't lay that on me," I say. "You quit a good company."

He slides the mustard my way. "It was a warehouse job. And I didn't quit. They *uninvited me back.*" Whit presses both palms against the counter, leaning in my face. "I told you, babe. Business sucks."

His full-on stare is something I have to look away from, even when he's not trying to melt me like a Hershey square.

"Eat something." Whit grips the overhead cabinet with both hands, arms suspended, looking mildly like the Soloflex guy, but with a punked-out haircut. "I've seen how empty your refrigerator is."

My foot catches on the floor mat of the Camaro on the drive home, flipping back its rubbery corner. A flake of metal catches under my sandal, so I reach down to see what it is. My fingers find a crooked stud earring in the shape of a letter "D." It's been tromped by a combat boot.

I raise the earring in the air. "Excuse me?"

Whit squints at my fingers, then his eyebrows rise in recognition. "*Shit*. God knows how long that's been there." He looks back to the road. "Throw it away."

"That's all you've got to say?" The gold "D" captures a flash of sunlight as the car rumbles over a pothole.

"*I want it out of my sight.*" Whit snatches the earring in his fist and flings it out the driver's side window, where it disappears into traffic.

Other than the thrum and pounding of that other-worldly Icicle Works album, it's quiet for the rest of the ride back to New Hope, where I have to get ready for Tye's first Miami Night show. I get to attend as a guest. I even invited Audrey.

Kimmer emerges from our bathroom shower in a thread-bare Disney Cinderella beach towel, prepping to work Tye's show. "Holy hell," she says. "That ceiling almost reached down to scrub my back." She tightens the terrycloth around her little body.

Audrey wedges herself into a corner of her foam mattress under a pile of covers. "I can't go. I don't have the energy to decide what's fashion-appropriate for a drag show."

"You're in serious need of some coffee," Kimmer says, pulling a brush through her wet hair. She studies herself in the bathroom mirror.

"Please just let me climb under a rock," Audrey mumbles. She crawls further underneath a pile of crocheted blankets, even though it's summer. "Coffee won't fix the fact that I haven't been on the schedule at The Rose all week."

I apply mascara, balancing a make-up mirror on one of our milk crates. "Is Lima on the rampage?" I pop the mascara wand in and out of its tube. It can't dry out now—not on drag show night.

"You'd think Lima'd be thrilled at how things turned out," says Kimmer. "Bryan's all hers now. That pecker."

"She didn't even know Bryan and I were a thing until I made a freaking show about it," Audrey says. "Now she's pissed as all get-over-yourself."

"They can't blame this mess on you," I say, separating my eyelashes with a tweezer. "Bryan's a renowned flirt."

"The whole staff hates me." Audrey shoves her face into her pillow. "I have a bullseye on my ass."

I crawl onto Audrey's egg crate. "Come out of there." My hands shake the lump of bedding that is her. "I'll buy drinks tonight."

"You're the brokest of us all," moans Audrey, muffled by enough crochetwork to mummify an Egyptian.

"Is that like *The Fairest of Them All*, but different?" Kimmer asks.

"And Giorgio won't even let you drink," Audrey reminds me.

"I'll come up with the cash, and you can order for both of us," I say. Audrey barely moves. I hop out of her egg-crate bed and pull open the accordion slider door of her bedroom closet, yanking out a black linen shirtdress. I toss it on top of her. "Wear this thing."

She gathers it in her fist, finally rolling to face us. "I'd have to put on heels." She pitches the dress back at me. "I can't deal with being taller than every guy in the room. And all of them will be prettier than me."

"Even in your highest fuck-me pumps, you're not taller than Tye, especially as Babylonia," I say. "In stilettos, she's seven-foot-something." I drape Audrey's black shirtdress against my own body, stepping in front of the mirror. Kimmer's hairdryer whirs in my ear like a chainsaw.

"Trina's parents took her out to celebrate her new job," I call to Audrey as I examine the dress. "I need a dance buddy tonight."

"Paula from upstairs will dance with you," Audrey says. "I talked her into coming. That woman needs out of the house like nobody's business. Take her before she dies of boredom."

"Or something else," Kimmer calls, wrestling with a round brush.

"You invited Paula under your wing," I tell Audrey, "so you better come with us." I fish Audrey's arms out of her jumbled bedding and heave-ho. Her body obeys, but her head rolls forward, dragging her back to horizontal. I have no choice but to drop her onto the bedding.

"Somebody get me a shot of Scotch," Audrey says into her pillow.

"More like a shot of adrenaline," says Kimmer, hair billowing like someone just frightened the blonde hell out of her. "You shouldn't schlump in a corner tonight, Auge. Get your mind off The Rose."

Audrey pulls herself to sitting. She rustles her spiked hair and takes a good look at the concert tee she's been wrapped in all day. "All right. But I'm doing this under duress." She points to the shirtdress as if it's an alien being. "And I won't wear *that*. It's too short. You wear it." She shoves her pool of bedding aside, like Venus emerging from the half shell. But in a Siouxsie Sioux T-shirt.

"Fine. *I'll* wear the shirt dress," I say. "But now you have to pick an outfit. Getting dressed is the fun part, remember?" I lead her to the closet and guide her hand into the mess of clothing until she clutches something. She slides a one-size-fits-all tent of a shirt over her head, which camouflages any measure of waistline she ever had.

Kimmer shuts off her hairdryer, staring at Audrey's overblown silhouette. "I think you chewed the wrong gum at Willy Wonka's Chocolate Factory."

"Stop hiding your figure in that thing," I tell Audrey, turning her toward the mirror. "You know what I'd give for those boobs of yours?"

She stretches her neck and juts out her rear end. "I'm Ostrich City."

"You're hot," I grab another sash from her drawer and lasso her narrow waist. I fit a black-brimmed hat on Audrey's head. She yanks a few sprigs of red hair to stand high and stiff in the front, which contrasts against the brim. "This outfit does nothing for my disappearing act."

"My evil plan worked," I say.

I jump into a pair of teal tights, overlaid with black fishnets to complement Audrey's borrowed shirt dress. She joins me in front of the bathroom mirror and tugs the hem of the shirtdress toward the floor. I tug it back up again, puffing out the front to approximate boobs that I don't really have. Audrey spins away from me in fake protest.

She shrieks and I stumble against the coolness of the tub.

The bathroom ceiling is bent into a swooping "U," its panels saturated with concentric rings of brown. The ceiling is a giant, protruding inkblot test. The two of us back away.

"Holy God," I say. "Kim, was it like that when you got in the shower?"

Kimmer stuffs her hairdryer into the dresser and kicks her drawer closed. "Told you," she says. "Our bathroom's about to give birth."

Paula cheers when I open the door but gives a stare behind her as she steps inside. I peek into the hall. No one's in sight.

She wears a ruffled, drop-waist sundress. A locket on a dainty chain decorates the dip of her throat.

"You clean up nice," Audrey says.

Paula flattens the ruffles with her hands. "Not too flashy?"

"Cabbage roses aren't flashy," I say. "I'm sporting a Neon/Gothic look, myself." The belted shirtdress barely covers my ass.

"Hot damn," Paula says. "You're gonna need a bodyguard."

Audrey pulls Trina's stash of Johnny Walker out of the cabinet, right behind the Soloflex Guy's shadowy curves. She traces his rippled chest with her finger, unscrews the cap of the whiskey bottle, and swigs. "Want some liquid courage?" She offers it to Paula. "It's going to be that kind of night for me."

Paula rests her petite white clutch against our tabletop and holds the bottle gently, like it's the missing Indiana Jones idol. "Dean would bust a vein if he knew I was doing shots with *those downstairs girls*."

"Is that what he calls us?" I ask.

"Never mind what he calls you." Paula swigs Scotch and wipes her mouth. She sighs. "Wowza. Alcohol. This is all coming back to me."

"Has it been that long since you've done a shot of Johnny?" asks Audrey.

"I haven't been out with anybody except my husband in, well, forever and two years." She passes me the bottle.

"Maybe it's time for you to strike out," Audrey says.

"We'll back you up." I gulp down a shot that burns my throat like rocket fuel.

Audrey returns the Scotch to the shelf behind Mr. Soloflex and sighs. "That's the kind of chest that can get a girl all hot and bothered."

"You're not kidding," I say. "Now let's go watch a guy in a dress lip-synch."

CHAPTER 25

STILL AUGUST 1984—Capresi's
Purple Rain

Billie Holiday music floats up Capresi's garden stairwell. A foam-board placard on an easel greets us in the lobby. Tye's face glams up the sign, which reads *Babylonia!* in splashy script. Her eyelashes streak across the board, dark curls dangling past her bone structure like Spanish moss.

Teddy the chef nods hello as I step toward the kitchen pass-through.

"How are you holding up for Miami Night?" I ask.

"It's bringing in the crowds, so I'm diggin' it," Teddy says. "They're mostly drinkers, too. Hey, thanks, kiddo."

"For what?" The smell of sweet peppers drifts from the kitchen like a warm mist.

He waves his mighty wooden spoon at me and the girls. "I can always count on you to bring chicks in here." He winks. His hair is unexpectedly presentable and a collared polo shirt shows under his chef jacket.

I stick my nose further into the kitchen. "Teddy, have you lost weight?"

He bangs his stomach. "Maybe I've been sucking it in for you girls."

"I'm not touching that one."

Miz Nena Love sits at a table in the bar room in front of Trudie, the girl who sometimes works at the gallery upstairs. A vivid smattering of tarot cards decorates the tablecloth between them. Giorgio nods hello to me from the bar as Miz Love snaps a few cards against the linen. I notice an empty spot on the bar room shelf where my mosaic used to sit. It's missing.

The patio buzzes with brightly dressed men lounging in Giorgio's mesh chairs. One guy has beaded hair like he just jetted in from Jamaica. Another wears a collar around his neck reminiscent of Whit's studded bracelet. Sequins twinkle from all angles.

The tables each have glass bowls in the middle of them, filled with a rainbow of party favors. As I get closer, I see they're actually jewel-toned condom packets, wrapped in toile and ribbon like the pastel candy almonds at the last wedding we catered. One bowl has "SAFE SEX" scrawled on it in glitter nail polish.

Paula inhales as if she hasn't breathed the open air for months. "This place is pretty, y'all," she says. As far as I know, she's not from the south. She's from Germantown.

"Haven't you hit every restaurant in town by now?" I ask her.

"I've been to the ice cream café next to Dean's shop." She bunches her clutch in her fingers. "And Andrea's Bakery. Dean's not much for taking me out. But this place is adorable."

Kimmer strolls over to us, balancing a damp cocktail tray. "God," she says, "we could have used you today."

"You handled this all yourself?" I ask.

She flexes a bicep and drops into a cartoon Russian accent, channeling Natasha from Rocky and Bullwinkle. "I'm *strong like bull*." She gives Paula a hug. "Look at you!"

"I'm a little out of my element," Paula says, forcing out a smile. "But having fun so far."

Kimmer motions toward a thick-bodied man at a nearby table who clinks glasses with a group of sophisticates. "Randy Arville's here," she tells me.

"*The* Randy Arville?" I say. Capresi legend has it that Cher and Michael Jackson's press manager frequents the restaurant. "I wasn't sure he actually existed."

"He's real, all right. Tye convinced Giorgio to invite him for the show,"

Kimmer says. "But he owes a tab for his last three visits."

"Since when does Giorgio run a tab?"

"*Exactly.*" Kimmer picks up empty glasses and adds them to her tray. "Speaking of Tye," she whispers, "Babylonia's on in 15 minutes. Can you check on her in the winter room?"

As I travel past the bar, Trudie from the gallery dabs at her eyes and Miz Nena Love comforts her. Nena must have given a hell of a Tarot reading.

I spread my arms for balance as I cut around the winter fireplace, not used to navigating the slate in heels.

Tye sits in front of an electric make-up mirror, which is the only light in the room. She rises to her full height in monstrous Lucite platforms and adjusts a blaze of reddish wig cropped nearly to non-existence. A plunging white jumpsuit drapes her body, its neckline mirrored with glass chips. Her eyes pop with contact lenses in an other-worldly shade of teal. Her heavy lashes are accented with charcoal eyeliner.

She's an over-tanned Annie Lennox. Although I've never seen Annie in such a ladylike outfit.

"What do you think?" She spins and the bottom of the jumpsuit flares, gown-like.

"Holy Eurythmics. Stunning. But what happened to Diana Ross?"

"It always helps to expand the repertoire. How do you think I upped my fan base out there?" It's confounding to hear such a deep voice emanating from Annie Lennox's body. I shake myself back from surreality.

"Besides, Diana's right here." Tye gestures toward a mannequin head supporting a fall of dark spirals. "She'll be headlining tonight also." Toiletries surround a three-tier make-up case on the table. I see a shaving kit. A toothbrush . . . and a mammoth-sized suitcase open on a tray stand.

Tye whisks a collection of bottles off the table and tosses them at her suitcase. "I'm not much of a housekeeper." She dips a make-up brush as wide as a feather duster into a pot of iridescent powder, swiping the sides of her buff arms.

"Tye," I ask, "where are you staying these days?"

She freezes. "Very nearby."

"Are you living in the restaurant?"

She pulls me close. "Here, and at the gym. Don't let on." I inhale the powdery scent of eyeshadow, pancake, and classroom craft glue. "Nena and I got thrown out of our room at The Lodge," she says. "I haven't exactly made a fortune here, tending a half-empty bar and scheduling a couple of shows a month."

"Oh *shit*." My chest tightens. Poverty scares the crap out of me. I always feel I'm one mishap away from financial ruin myself. "What are you gonna do?"

"*I will survive*. And I mean that literally. I have my health, at least for now. The rest will work itself out. Being broke is the least frightening thing in my life at the moment."

"Jesus. I'm sorry." I can't even say the acronym she's alluding to out loud. It's like I have no right to put a sound to it and make the threat of AIDS a real thing in the room with us. "Are you scared?"

"Everybody's scared. But this is life. *The show must go on*," she says. "I've got condoms out there in every shade of the rainbow. Did you see? It's very stylish." I nod. The circular light of the make-up mirror rings her pupils. "You should grab a few," she tells me. "Are *you* scared?"

"Me?"

"I'd keep prophylactics in every room if I were you girls," she says. "Well, if I had a room."

I shudder. "Maybe. Hey, will you make enough money on tonight's show to get back into The Lodge?"

"Not really. I'm living on an emergency credit card I borrowed from my father when he wasn't looking." She winks a prolific eyelash at me. "As for Nena, she always finds a way to land on her feet, usually with a meal ticket. But if this place doesn't get real busy, real quick, Babylonia will have a very short career in New Hope."

"You're freaking me out a little here."

She shakes my shoulders like an Etch-a-sketch as if to swish the worry off my face. "Jessica, *relax*." She dips a petite make-up brush into a brown pot. "As for money, when I have it, I flaunt it. When I don't," she swipes the brush between her imaginary breasts, heightening the illusion of cleavage, "I fake it." She's an artist who paints on *herself*.

Tye opens my collar and flails the make-up brush between my minimal boobs like she's contouring a portrait. "A little help for you," she says.

I peer in the mirror at the illusion she just fashioned on my chest. "I can't believe that works."

"You're welcome." She turns me around, shoving me toward the fireplace. "Now get ready to applaud your girly little ass off." She swats my butt, grazing me with elegantly manicured fingernails. "Hot fishnets, by the way," she calls as I hightail it across the slate.

I join Audrey and Paula at a table back on the patio. The lights dim. A spotlight flares to life from behind us, clamped to a railing that I notice has been repainted white. I'm getting used to the overnight color transitions.

A recorded voice crackles through the ceiling speakers: "Here she is, the one, the only—all right, the many . . . *Babylonia!*"

The audience erupts in applause as Babylonia strides through the room in a sleek black tuxedo jacket fitted over the white jumpsuit. Her pant legs flutter. Five-inch Lucite platforms glide against the slate. The rugged synthesizers of the Eurythmics' "Sweet Dreams" pulse from the ceiling.

Babylonia draws a cane from behind the piano. She mouths precisely to Annie Lennox's vocals, *whack*-ing a tabletop with the cane with each break of the lyrics, burning a goddess glare into the audience. With every phrase, she spins into a new glamour pose.

Paula's mouth drops open.

"Let's get a shot of whiskey into our neighbor, here," I say in Audrey's ear. She flags Kimmer.

Babylonia twirls, sliding the cane along her shapely deltoids as she faux-sings the next verse. The synthesized bassline pounds through the room, vibrating the liquid in cocktail glasses across the patio. Babylonia's cane *smacks*. She drapes herself across a sculptured art-deco chair that I don't recognize, her cane gliding along her opalescent ankles. *Smack*.

Paula gasps with every bang of the cane. Babylonia transfixes, channeling

Annie's deep alto as if the singer's been cloned.

The song builds to a climax, electronic drums bellowing under Annie's sparse and emphatic vocals. Babylonia chucks the cane and pirouettes, spotting her head like a ballerina. She undoes the black tuxedo jacket and lets it fly off her body, still whirling, revealing the sparkle-encrusted cut of the V-neck underneath. Beams of light bounce off it like a disco ball.

Babylonia suspends her silver-nailed hands above her head, fingers aerodynamically arched. White pant legs spiral like a lily in the process of opening. Drums pulse. Babylonia's spin rivals that of the Olympic skater for whom she's named.

Even Audrey holds her breath.

Babylonia stops cold as the music cuts, white organza winding around her legs. The lights go out. The crowd screams with applause.

As the stage lights fade back up, Babylonia flips her palms upward, comically motioning, *give me more*! Laughter mixes with increased clapping.

Paula blinks. "Well, I never."

"Now you have," Audrey says. Kimmer reappears, placing a shot in front of each of us, then scurries away. Audrey flips back her shot glass. Paula downs hers and smirks.

"I have to tell you," Audrey says to me across the table. "Tye is quite gorgeous."

I place a hand on Audrey's shoulder. "Notice how tall," I say. "And what a long, graceful neck." I glance to make sure Giorgio isn't watching and gulp my shot, wincing as it fights its way down my throat. I place the glass next to Audrey's so it's not obvious it's mine.

Trudie from the gallery works the spotlight behind us as an illuminated Babylonia travels from table to table lip-synching to the Eurythmics' "Who's That Girl?" She runs her hands through men's hair and shimmies against the edges of tabletops until the music stops. A watershed of applause pours across the patio. Babylonia ducks through the archway and into the darkened bar room.

Miz Love sneaks in between Audrey and Paula at our table and introduces herself. "Isn't Babylonia marvelous?" She folds a palm over

Paula's hand.

"I'm downright overwhelmed," Paula says.

"Her act is so *fresh*," Miz Love says amid residual clapping. "She's maybe too fresh these days."

When the spotlight swings back to life, Babylonia is draped against the barroom archway in the Diana wig and long gloves. She flings ebony curls as she lip-synchs to "Love Child." After three Diana tunes and one Cher number, she completes her set on her knees, reciting the prayer-like drama of Donna Summers' "MacArthur Park."

Babylonia trots toward the bar room amid waves of applause. Before reaching the archway, she shoves the face of a studly young spectator into her V-neck, washing an ocean of curls over the guy's head. She then vanishes into the shadows of the bar room. The stud darts after her. Guests howl and rise to their feet.

During the crazy-ass applause, Kimmer carries a dinner check on a plastic tray to press agent Randy Arville's table and snaps it down next to him. She sprints toward us.

"Tye is super-duper talented!" Kimmer giggles as Babylonia's ovation echoes over the creek.

"And all this time I thought Tye was just a fashionable bartender," I say.

Behind Kimmer's back, I watch Randy Arville the press manager lift the check tray in the air. "Miss!" he calls.

Nena Love wraps an arm around Kimmer. "Don't even look his way, dear." Nena turns to us. "Kim has strict instructions not to take that tray back without money on it." Randy gets up and carries his check tray toward the bar room himself.

Nena takes Kimmer's hand and leads her away, shielding her from Randy the press agent's view. She and Kim move tables to the edges of the patio, making space for a dance floor.

Techno-tronic music explodes through the sound system as if beaming down from God. The ceiling fixtures vibrate. Multi-colored light machines spew rotating spots along the back wall, turning the place into a full-tilt disco.

Babylonia sprints to our table. "Time to burn down the house, girls." She turns to Paula. "Oh, honey, you need a dance partner." Paula's cheeks go cherry as Babylonia draws her to the center of the floor, whirling them through a routine. We girls dance along to funked-up numbers by Prince, Dead or Alive, Culture Club, and Vanity 6. Thunder clouds rumble in the background, in time with a Baltimora jungle anthem.

Miz Love follows Kimmer around the floor, asking about her gaggle of siblings, offering her piano lessons. I pull Kimmer aside in the middle of the sea of eyelinered men dancing their asses off. "Is Nena showing a little extra interest in you tonight?" I ask.

"She needs my help," Kimmer tells me.

"With what?" I bounce along to an irresistible George Michael song. "Her zipper?"

"Don't be ridiculous." Kimmer tucks her drink tray under her arm and pushes me away.

Babylonia introduces me to Tom Bronski, the owner of a club called Marauder, famous for its all-lavender interior and elaborate drag reviews. Judging by the guy's moves, he was once a professional dancer.

"Tom's my VIP guest," Babylonia shouts in my ear over Soft Cell's musical ode to Tainted Love. "And if things work out, maybe my rescuer."

"Congratulations," I tell her. She flashes a powerhouse smile at me and spins away.

Babylonia thanks the last of the dwindling crowd. Somehow her makeup is still intact, while mine is melted. "You're a fucking star, my friend," I tell her as the crowd ebbs.

"Did you expect anything less?" she answers.

"How could I have guessed your full level of charisma?"

Paula shakes Babylonia's hand. "It was swell meeting you," Paula says. "I'm coming back to steal those shoes."

"Don't even think about it," says Babylonia. "I keep them under glass in the back." She hugs us one by one, like Dorothy saying goodbye to her friends from Oz. "Don't worry so much, kiddo," she whispers in my ear. Her curls flex against the side of my face. "Life is too short for that."

Giorgio waves me over to him. Chattering guests in Lycra filter through

Once in a Lifetime

the lobby behind us. "Please dress your best on Wednesday," he tells me. "Don't spread it around, but Randy Arville is sending Michael Jackson to the restaurant for lunch."

"Did Randy say that to get out of paying his bill?" I laugh.

"We're *bartering*," Giorgio stresses, ticking a finger at me. Sweaty patrons file past, unsteady on their feet. "Think of the publicity if he comes through."

Michael Jackson isn't exactly my thing. But all freshman year, you could hardly pass a television without him spinning at you on MTV, a triangle of dancers racked behind him like bowling pins.

"Okay. I wouldn't miss it. Hey," I look toward the shelf that used to hold my mosaic. "It's fine if you don't like that piece of art I made. But can I have it back in that case?"

Giorgio knits his eyebrows. "Didn't I tell you?" he says. "It's in the gallery."

"You mean on a *wall?*" My head buzzes, soaring far beyond the damage tonight's whiskey has done. I want to smack one of the ceiling lanterns in victory.

"Let's say that it's on consignment," he tells me. "I'm being supportive of your career."

I hug him, trying not to wrinkle his De la Renta dress shirt.

As Audrey, Paula, and I gather ourselves together and clomp through the courtyard, the sky starts to spit raindrops. A few cafés still host late-night guests, basking in the tangerine flicker of netted candle jars. Jan's Pub harbors a row of gritty motorcycles.

"You girls are a hoot." Paula shelters her head with her clutch and lets out a too-much-Scotch laugh. "I've gotta get out more."

"Tonight was about as *out* as it gets," Audrey says.

I blink rain out of my eyelashes. As we approach our building, I notice a black pick-up truck parked against the bricks. A tarp is bungeed over an unwieldy collection of cargo on its bed.

All at once, a mass of biceps and camouflage lunges at us through the haze of wet streetlamps. A piston-like arm closes a fist around Paula's hair, yanking her away from me and Audrey so fast that I trip forward, whacking my knees against the pavers. Both legs of my tights shred open. Audrey braces herself against a sidewalk elm.

"*Dean!*" Paula screams.

Dean Clayton's shoulders are slick and his muscle shirt is stenciled with rain. He grips Paula's hair like a handle; her head lolls. She screeches "*Let go!*" like a wild bird.

I scramble backward and watch a scrape on my knee seep blood, which crawls across a hole in my teal Lycra tights. My pulse bangs in my teeth. Audrey pulls me up off the bricks.

Dean opens his fist and Paula drops to the pavement. She shouts for us to get away. He retracts his elbows and stares us down, muscles twitching like an over-wound toy.

"*You little girl-sluts need to keep away from my wife,*" he growls.

Audrey straightens. "Who're you calling *little?*"

My spiked-heel sticks in the grating around the tree trunk. "Holy fuck!" I yell, to no one in particular. "Somebody help us out!" Rain blurs Main Street into a murky watercolor abstract. Paula mumbles her husband's name repeatedly, on her hands and knees.

"You freaking Neanderthal!" Audrey shouts. "*Stay off her!*"

A pair of boots stomp in front of Audrey and me as a gray-haired man plants his feet wide on the pavement. A long ponytail trails between his leather-vested shoulder blades and a bandana flaps in his back pocket.

It's the Cigar Chomping Man from Jan's Pub. He pulls a silver weapon out from under his belt and points it level with Dean's head. The gun glints through a smear of rain.

"Back off, Clayton," Cigar Man says.

Dean doesn't budge. Water pings off the shelf of his shoulders. I yank my shoe out of the sidewalk grating.

"You ladies need to take Paula here inside for the night," Cigar Man tells us, holding his ground.

Audrey and I gather up Paula and shuffle away, pressing ourselves against our building. Paula reaches an arm toward Dean, whimpering, slumping back to her knees. I feel my hair separating into wet strings, sticking to my face like a dripping canvas.

"Clayton, you need to get out of town," Cigar Man says. "*Now.*"

"We can call the police," Audrey says, holding Paula.

"*No police*," Paula begs, trembling.

Dean stays rooted in place.

The rain bounces off Cigar Man's barrel. "You heard me!" His bass voice vibrates down Main Street. "*Git!*"

Dean marches around the bed of his truck and climbs into his driver's seat, thudding the car door closed. Headlights flood the side of the brick wall. He nearly sends his rear bumper through the clapboard of the next building as his truck squeals out of the narrow lot. The oversized tires spit water.

Cigar Man clicks his safety and stuffs the weapon under his vest. Paula sobs against Audrey's arm.

"I'm Chuck." Cigar Man extends a hand to Audrey. She shakes it, offering a numb smile.

My heart thrums in my ribcage. "Thank you, Chuck."

"You'll keep Paula safe at your place tonight, right Red?" Chuck asks.

Audrey nods, spiked hair deflated against her head.

"Come see me at Jan's tomorrow if you need anything," Chuck says.

He lumbers back to the pub, shrugging his leather vest higher on his shoulders.

We tuck Paula into Trina's meager bed, then call the restaurant and ask Teddy to drive Kimmer home. He offers to stay, but we send him off.

Audrey shoves a chair under the front doorknob and clicks the lock of her bedroom door behind her, for the first time since we've lived here. The Louisville Slugger serves as my bedmate. Kimmer curls up with the telephone. I listen to Paula sob Dean's name through the wall as I drift into a rough-hewn sleep.

The honking of a duck startles me awake at 7:12 a.m., my legs pretzeled around the bat. I push the hunk of wood aside.

Our front door is ajar. The kitchen chair that Audrey had wedged under the doorknob sits neatly against the foyer wall. I peek into our bedroom. Audrey's still sleeping.

There's nothing in the other bed but an empty comforter.

We girls tiptoe toward Dean and Paula's apartment. Audrey chokes the neck of the Slugger with two hands. Its stout end clinks against one of the hanging metal ceiling fixtures, sweeping light through the hall.

Dean and Paula's apartment door sits full-open. A rain-saturated curtain puffs to life on an open window.

There's not a stitch of furniture inside.

"Oh, for the love of Houdini," Kimmer blurts out. We inch our way over the threshold, poking our heads into the bedroom, whispering for Paula. No one materializes.

Audrey lets the tip of the bat clunk against the hideous floor tiles and starts to cry, shoulders rattling. "*What the fuck did I do?*"

"We tried to help, Auge," Kimmer says.

Audrey splays her fingers over her eyes. "What if I helped her to the bottom of the river?"

I take Audrey by the shoulders. "Paula cried herself to sleep calling Dean's name, and we didn't hear a bit of struggle," I say. "What if that means she went back to him on her own? There's only so much we can do to stop her."

"I talked her into coming with us," Audrey says. "I told her to *strike out*." She raises the bat over her head.

I pull Kimmer backward as Audrey clubs the floor, chopping into the tiles. A flake of linoleum spits toward the wallpaper as if trying to escape. The bat leaves a softball-sized hollow in the floor.

Audrey backs away, one step, then another, bat in hand. She stomps down the hall, toward the front door of the building. Kimmer and I follow her, still in sweats and sleep shirts.

We march down Main Street toward Dean's smoke shop, the bat tucked under Audrey's arm. Kimmer and I can barely keep pace with her.

"That fucking ogre better be able to produce Paula." Audrey's voice cracks. "Or I'm calling the cops."

"We're behind you. Literally," I say. "Slow down before you lose us."

I almost sprawl into Audrey's back as she stops short, blocking me and Kimmer with her arms.

Yellow police tape draws an X across Dean's storefront. One windowpane is covered in cardboard. As we get closer, we see the inside of the shop is void of everything but a counter stool rolled on its side.

I point to a panel of vinyl siding. Two blackened bullet holes mar its surface. "Somebody wants Dean to know he's not welcome back." I squint toward Jan's patio, where the serene, pink half-light of morning falls innocently over the deck. Chuck the Cigar Man is nowhere to be seen.

A few parking spaces further down Main Street, a cop leans against a squad car jotting notes. Kimmer grabs the Louisville Slugger from Audrey and stashes it under her arm. I nudge Kim toward the ivy-covered retaining wall of the adjacent property. "This is the second time I've come *this close* to being in a police report," I remind her. "Maybe it was a mistake for me to come down."

"Right. Get out of here." Kim slides the Slugger into my hands. "While you're at it, hide this somewhere." I sprint back to our apartment before anyone catches sight of me.

When Kim and Audrey tell the story to the cop, they leave out any mention of Chuck.

CHAPTER 26

AUGUST 1984
When The World Is Running Down

Kimmer sits next to Audrey's foam mattress, balancing a bowl of Rice Crispies in her lap. Audrey is bundled back under multiple layers of crochet work. She's barely been out of bed for four days except to pee and change the David Bowie record. I smoke a Virginia Slim at the edge of the mattress, ashtray in hand. We haven't heard a thing about Paula. The police are looking into it.

"Auge?" Kimmer shakes Audrey's camouflaged shoulders. Not even her spiky auburn head shows. "You have to eat something," Kimmer says. "It's cereal. It won't bite back."

The blanket cocoon shifts. Audrey winds the bedding more tightly around herself. Kimmer rests the cereal bowl on a wooden crate and places a hand on Audrey's covered head.

"Sweetie," she tries again. "It will make you feel better. Even mole-people need to eat, eventually."

"Not hungry," Audrey moans.

I stamp out my unappetizing cigarette and head into the living room, plucking Bowie's *Heroes* album off the turntable. It makes a zipping noise as the needle scratches across its surface. I cringe.

"*Heeeyy!*" Audrey calls from the bedroom. "Don't hurt my David!"

"Sorry," I say. "But that's enough *Music to Overdose By*. It's not helping."

Kimmer presses a hand to Audrey's forehead as I come back to the bedroom. Audrey recoils against the wall. "Don't be my mother," she grumbles.

"We'll have to call your mother if we can't get you out of this funk," says Kimmer.

Audrey peels a coverlet off her face. "You wouldn't dare."

I pull back our window curtains to get some light into the apartment and the entire rod comes off in my hand, sending my glass suncatcher spinning. Gray afternoon light spills into the room. The rain is back.

Audrey shields her eyes. "You really know how to hurt a girl."

I toss the entire window dressing into the corner and sit next to her, inching the blankets off her shoulders. "Audrey, come out of there. We need you."

She rolls to face me. "For what?"

"To be Wendy, Mother of the Lost Girls. None of this works without you." I dig through the covers for her hand and squeeze it. "You're our glue."

"Are you saying you're stuck with me?"

"I'm saying you brought us together," I say, "and you keep us together."

"Come to think of it,"—Kimmer takes a slurp of the cereal—"you invited me to lunch my first year at Pitt when I didn't know a single person in the dorms."

"Then there's Trina," I add, "who you've known since, what, age 12?"

"Not my fault. Our parents vacationed at the same motel," Audrey mumbles.

"But you kept in touch every year, even though she was on the other side of the state," I say. "Who does that?"

"Face it," Kimmer says. "Jess is right. You're to blame for this whole unseemly foursome, Auge. I hope you're happy."

Audrey sits up, hair bending in all directions. She motions for the cereal bowl, which Kimmer hands over. Milk plunks onto a square of patchwork blanket.

"If I'm the glue in this operation," Audrey says, "you girls are in worse shape than I thought." She slowly raises a spoonful of Rice Crispies to chapped lips. "I should have a T-shirt made." She points to her chest. "*I Am Unglued.*" She crunches the cereal. At least she's halfway out of her covers.

"Let's get some coffee going," Kimmer says, heading to our turquoise sink. "I'll find an extra-big mug for you, Auge."

I search the room as Kimmer fills a carafe with water, extracting two cassette cases from Trina's drawer. I breach the seals of the rattling cases with a pen, then dump the contents down the toilet. I double-check for prescription vials in our rusted, 1960s medicine cabinet. God forbid, we don't want any not-so-accidental accidents to happen.

Coffee dribbles into the carafe as I round the corner to the living room. I pull a notebook from my storage box, plop myself on the couch, and begin to write:

> *Dear Audrey,*
>
> *I'm your new and loyal confidant, Ned the Notebook. Think of me as a friend who wants to hear your every thought and would never breathe a word of your secrets. I have a talent for making people feel a little better about this sorry-ass world when they use me. You deserve that gift.*
>
> *However deep the darkness goes, however horrifying you convince yourself you are, please write to me about it. When you're staring down the rabbit hole, that's your cue to scribble the fuck out of me. No one else has to know.*
>
> *I promise to still love you when it's over.*
> *Ready? GO.*

I tuck the notebook under her pillow when she's not looking.

Audrey's empty cereal bowl sits askew on the rug. She snores, curled with her blankets.

Kimmer pours herself some coffee. She takes a peek into the bedroom to see that Audrey's fast asleep. "Great. A whole pot, all for *moi*. I'm gonna be twitching." She clinks the glass carafe against the base of Mr. Coffee. "Did you want me to make you some tea, Jess?" she asks.

"No caffeine for me," I say. "I need to relax. Time for a hot shower, straight into tomorrow."

Forty minutes later, the bathroom is steamed like a Greek bathhouse. I climb out of the shower and slip into a T-shirt silkscreened with a Day-Glo image of Debbie Harry, which I left for myself on the sink.

The ceiling rumbles like Vesuvius.

I wrestle open the bathroom door. Steam sprawls into the bedroom, a confused version of the genie of the lamp. I grope the door jamb as our bathroom ceiling shreds like an overtaxed bargain paper towel in front of me. Blocky brown triangles nose-dive into the tub, hitting the floor like artillery. "Holy *SHIT!*" I yell.

Kimmer sprints in from the kitchen as I fall against the bedroom rug. Audrey tosses her covers and stands upright for the first time in hours.

Pulverized plaster drifts through the steam in ribbons, like fairy dust. I heave in a couple of raspy breaths and wipe plaster chips off my shins.

"You okay?" Audrey asks me.

"I think so. Maybe." I kick away a chunk of wet plaster.

Kimmer gazes into the hole that is now our bathroom ceiling and coughs. "Chicken Little was right."

Audrey waves floating particles out of her face. "I'll get a trash bag."

I wiggle my toes. "Get two."

Audrey and I gather damp chips of ceiling into a Hefty bag. I wipe schmutz off the perfume atomizer Drew gave me, which is looking a little emptier than I remember. This is strange, since no one would dare use the stuff but me.

"Kimmer says cleaning is therapeutic." I sneeze, mold spores tingling my nose. "Is it working for you?"

"Maybe," Audrey answers, cleaning dust off the toilet with a progressively graying towel.

I move on to sponging the inside of the tub. "At least it got you out of bed."

"Speaking of which." Audrey heads to her foam mattress. Instead of climbing in, she straightens her blankets and makes the bed. I join her in the bedroom, sponge still in hand.

The yellow notebook peeks from under Audrey's pillow. She plucks it up and flips it open, reading the passages I scrawled. She presses the book against her chest, standing barefoot in the middle of the room.

She hugs me, warm like she just came out of the dryer. My still-damp hair frizzes between us. Audrey's voice rattles like someone scraped it over a washboard. "If you could live in my head with me, I wouldn't need a shrink," she says.

"That's the most beautiful thing anyone's ever said to me." I spit a lock of damp hair out of my mouth.

Keys jangle in our front door as Trina returns from a lunch shift. I hear her discarded shoes ricochet off the wall before she gets to the bedroom. Audrey and I stand there clinging to each other like a HAPPINESS IS poster.

"Wow, a made bed." Trina peels her waitressing shirt over her head. "Welcome back from your own Private Idaho, Audrey." Trina points to the eyelet granny window panels wrinkling in the corner, from when I knocked the rod out of the window frame. "Are we redecorating?"

She sees the bathroom apocalypse and freezes. She tip-toes over a maze of plaster chips that still litter our floor and stares into the void of the ceiling.

"God damn!" Trina's voice echoes against the bathroom tiles. She stands there in just a bra and a waitressing skirt. "What the hell do you girls *do* when I'm not here?"

CHAPTER 27

STILL AUGUST—Capresi's
Wanna Be Startin' Somethin'

It's Wednesday, otherwise known as Michael Jackson lunch shift day. I'm dressed in my drop-waisted, kick-pleat skirt and a hand-beaded vest depicting Van Gogh's *Sunflowers* for the occasion.

Before I head down the stairs to Capresi's, I slip into the Milano Gallery to search for my mosaic. I inhale the scent of oil paint, delivering a mini rush as it absorbs into my bloodstream. Trudie waves from the front podium.

Sure enough, my mosaic glitters among the other artwork, its fragments refracting the clear story light from above. A placard underneath the piece reads, "*Godzilla vs. The Wizard of Oz*, Jessica Addentro, 1984."

Elated, I trot down the stairs to sling lunches. As I turn on my tenny runners, I feel five pounds lighter than before.

When I push through the lobby door, Kimmer is sitting at the bar in a pink A-line dress with embroidered trim. Tye leans against the bar in crisp khaki trousers and a spangled belt buckle big enough to festoon the grill of a truck. His lithe frame looks *built* under a double-breasted shirt with bulky shoulders.

Giorgio paces through the lobby in designer menswear accented by a cranberry paisley tie, *très Givenchy*. Out on the patio, Nena straightens sheet music at a piano draped with a velvet runner.

We hole up and wait for Michael Jackson.

And wait. . . .

Rain spatters low-grade white noise on the edge of the patio all afternoon.

A lone tourist materializes as lunch hour draws near to a close, an SLR camera slung over his raincoat. Rather than mope, I bring the guy a complimentary glass of red and recite the specials with panache, as if serving an MTV icon. My fingers swirl in front of the chalkboard that sits on the chair next to him, highlighting each delectable item. I flash a smile that might inspire game-show theme music.

"*Char*-ming, love," the man says in a choppy British accent, eyeing his lunch options on the chalkboard as it balances on a white mesh chair in front of him. The menu board slips. I kick the chair to straighten it. The man laughs.

"Do the guests fancy the slate board?" he asks.

"The menu is new every day, like a living being. Most people appreciate its uniqueness."

"Do you appreciate it?" he asks.

I raise my eyebrows. "This place has sharpened me up. It's taught me things I've been hoping to learn about the world. It's a regular wonderland." Rainwater tumbles through the ivy along our railing. "Too bad you couldn't have visited on a nicer day. New Hope is beautiful in the sunlight."

"Fair enough." He tilts his glass of Bordeaux at me, jostling the wine around. "Is that a New York accent, then?"

"You guessed it. I came here to waitress for the summer. I'm an artist saving for study abroad."

He extends a finger toward my sunflowers. "Brilliant waistcoat. That's my favorite work by Van Gogh."

"Mine, too." I tug at the vest. The weighty beads smoosh down what little boobs I have. "Hopefully I'll get through my art career without cutting off any appendages, though, like he did. I'd hate to have wasted all this money on earrings." Although you never know what insanity I'll face before my training is over. Suffering seems too big a part of success for me to escape it.

The man chuckles. I'm happy to have made him laugh, despite the dank weather and his apparent lack of a lunch partner.

"What's good today?" He sips his wine.

I recommend the curried chicken and Teddy's lightly dressed but heavenly Portobello and arugula salad. "Oh—and don't leave without experiencing Capresi's Neapolitan cheesecake."

He accepts my advice, although he points out that they don't actually serve much cheesecake in Naples.

I lean on the edge of his table, which rocks only slightly. "As a world traveler," I say, steadying the table with my fingertips. "I'm glad you won't need me to point out New Jersey." I salute him, gather my chalkboard, and head off, leaving him to contemplate the rain.

Kimmer and I rest against the bar room archway. My new tourist friend with the English lilt raises his camera and snaps a few shots from the patio: of the gazebo, his wineglass, and our fresh, white brick columns, complemented by waxy vines and wrought iron.

I hear him *mmmm* out loud when the cheesecake finally touches his lips.

He taps my arm on his way through the lobby after I cash out his table. "Here's for some nice paints, love," he says, stuffing a wrinkled bill into my palm. "Keep your head about yourself. And your ears." He pushes through the red lobby door, setting off the sleigh bells.

I uncrumple a twenty in my palm, which was more than his entire check. No one else materializes for lunch.

The front door jangles as Tye rushes up the garden stairs and out of the restaurant, coughing like a chain smoker. Kimmer changes the chalk boards over to the dinner menu.

Nena Love sidles next to Kimmer's bar stool. "See what I'm talking about with Tye?" Nena places a hand on Kim's embroidery-laden thigh. "He barely speaks to me now. All he ever does is excuse himself and leave."

Come to think of it, he's missed two days of work this week. I look up from refilling the silverware bin. "He's not sick, is he?" I ask.

Suddenly, Nena realizes I exist. "Learn to live and let live, dear. I'm sure he's fine."

Kimmer dabs a mistake off the slate with a wet dishtowel wrapped around her pinky. "We're all in the dumps today, what with Michael Jackson being a no-show," she says. "I guess we're not special enough for him to make an appearance."

I move to smooth the bar room tablecloths, even though no one has sat at them. "Nena, maybe Tye had other plans after lunch." With any luck.

"I'm sure I'll catch up with him." Nena dramatically adjusts the shoulders of her white gauze blouse, ready to swing the emotional spotlight back towards herself. "Kim, I can't tell you how much our little talks are helping me through this," she says, resting her weathered, piano-player fingers on Kimmer's thigh. "I need someone on my side." The piano isn't the only thing this woman knows how to play.

"There are no *sides*. I'm glad I can make you feel better," Kimmer says. "Sometimes I think my name should be Kimmer At-Your-Service Thorson."

I lift my eyebrows, trying to convey through our psychic roommate telepathy that maybe she shouldn't be quite so supportive of *everyone*. Especially when that person is momentarily homeless, and in the middle of a power struggle with her protégé.

Teddy slides a tray of newly-baked sour dough rolls at me through the pass-through. He waves at me to come closer. "Does Kimmer realize Miz Lovey-dovey is looking for a new victim?" he whispers.

"I've been trying to tell her." I accept the tray of rolls, which smell like my grandmother's Sunday baking days. "Kim is so darn eager to please. She's a nurturer."

"One problem with that," Teddy notes. "There's no shortage of people who wanna take advantage."

I unload the loaves into the bread warmer. They tumble with a series of thuds. "Wow. You really *get* her."

"If only." Teddy runs a spoon over a set of pots that hang above his head. They chime like a clock tower. "A guy can dream, though."

A cloud gives way in the overcast blanket of a sky outside, sending sunlight through the restaurant interior for the first time all week. The bar room animates, blooming like a diaphanous flower. I notice the once-brown bar room wall has been redone in a luscious shade of crimson.

I approve.

Kimmer rifles through her purse for our door key and her wallet topples to the floor. We use my keys instead.

I stamp mud off my tenny runners. Good thing for puddles or these things would never get washed. "*Man*, I'd trade my rarest bootleg EP for a vehicle at this point," I say.

"You'd never do that." Kimmer wipes her wet soles on our doormat.

"I might. Our walks in the rain together just aren't as sexy as Prince makes things sound."

"Sorry, you're not my type." Kimmer laughs, shaking raindrops out of her hair. "You're missing an essential piece of anatomical equipment."

"Miz Nena Love will be so disappointed." I open the fridge, hoping to steal some of Trina's leftovers. Empty shelves stare back at me.

Kimmer stops fluffing her hair. "*Nena?* Come on, she knows better."

"You still won't admit she's been hitting on you?" I kick my tennies under the kitchen table. The linoleum is cool under my feet.

"She just needs a shoulder." Kimmer steps out of a pair of ballet flats. She went fancier than I did for Michael Jackson Wednesday.

"Nena and Tye are broke," I say. "She's scheming a way to stay in town."

"So she thinks *I'm* her new sugar momma?" Kimmer heads to the bedroom to wiggle out of a pair of pantyhose. "She knows I don't do the Big V." Kim twirls the hose and tosses them across the bedroom. "And what makes her think I've got any money?"

"We've got an apartment, and she needs one. You better set some boundaries." I pick up Kimmer's pantyhose and flip them into her laundry basket. "Remember when Tye and I warned you about Joseph?"

Kimmer scratches her head. "You did, didn't you?"

A set of knuckles rap on our door. "And don't forget about *Ray*," I say, heading to the foyer. "Remember you were 'just helping him get his act together'?"

I pull open our thick green front door. A dampened Miz Nena Love stands there, still in her gauze outfit from this afternoon's prissy lunch shift, gripping the handle of a damp Louis Vuitton suitcase. Tye stands behind her, his marvelous hair impervious to the rain. He's changed into a more casual shirt, losing a layer of shoulders.

Kimmer adjusts her skirt and pops her head through the bedroom doorway. Nena extends her hand like royalty, waiting to be invited in. "Kim! Giorgio said we could find you here."

Tye shakes his head at me, mouthing, "*Not my idea.*"

Miz Love's luggage drips on our doormat. "Are you going on a trip?" Kim asks Nena. "Please say yes."

Tye shakes a black umbrella. "This whole summer's been a bit of a trip, hasn't it, girls?"

Nena drops her outstretched hand since no one has taken it. "Sadly, no, I'm not going anywhere. Truth is, I have no place to stay."

Kimmer pulls out a kitchen chair for Nena. I step behind Kimmer and squeeze her elbow. "*Boundaries,*" I whisper in her ear.

Nena strolls to our table, staring around the room. "What a lovely . . . compartment," she announces.

"*Apartment,*" I say, whisking away a smattering of toast crumbs that speckle the Formica.

"If you say so, dear." She sits in our rickety kitchen chair.

Tye makes himself at home, leaning against a kitchen counter. "I'm not advocating any of this, ladies," he says. "I'm just here for moral support."

"You see, Nena?" Kimmer clasps her hand. "Tye's still your buddy. You were imagining things. Now, why don't you two move back in together?"

"Because we can't *both* sleep next to the fireplace in Capresi's winter room," Nena moans, glaring at Tye from under her severe black bangs.

Tye folds his arms. "I got there first. Possession is nine-tenths of the law."

"How long do you think you'll need?" Kim says.

I clear my throat.

"I can't say, exactly," says Nena, who's mastered the art of ignoring me.

I open the cabinet door that's adorned with Mr. Soloflex, revealing the waning bottle of Johnny Walker inside. "We don't have much to offer around here, but I'm willing to share what's left of this with you two, as our guests." This is sporting of me since it's Trina's bottle.

"I never refuse hospitality." Nena daubs the feathering lipliner at the corner of her mouth. I pull juice glasses from the cabinet, holding each up to the plastic ceiling fixture to make sure they're clean. Not a single glass matches the other. I pour a slug of Johnny Walker in front of Nena.

Tye eyes Mr. Soloflex as I close the cabinet door. "Oh, look," he says, "there's *Scott*. Are you girls fans?"

I blink. "*Scott?* You're on a first-name basis with The Soloflex Man?"

"Sure. He's from Portland," Tye answers. "I ran into him at a few calls."

"You *call* the guy?" Kimmer's jaw slacks like a porch swing. "You're my hero."

I plunk a glass in front of Kim. "He means auditions," I say.

"That's right," Tye says. "Nobody had ever heard of Soloflex back when he first did that shoot."

I offer Tye a Welch's jelly glass. "Then he took off his shirt," Tye goes on, "and suddenly *everybody knew Soloflex*. The company got rich. Scott was freaking pissed, though. They paid him next-to-shit for that gig." Tye inspects the grape embossments on the glassware I handed him, then shrugs.

"Do you have his number?" Kimmer smiles.

Tye stares down his sculpted nose at us. "*I don't think so.*"

A terrifying notion dawns on me as a smirk shimmies across Tye's face.

"*No—*" I clunk my forehead against the kitchen cabinet door. Darkness descends as I close my eyes. "*Please don't take Mr. Soloflex away from us.*"

"Sorry, girls." Tye gulps Scotch. "Take my word for it. He's not pumping iron on your side of the bench."

Kimmer collapses against the chair back and rests a hand over her heart. "Please be joking."

Nena lets out a low laugh. "Oh, girls. You don't know much about the Portland lifestyle." She sips her Scotch with a finger sticking out like she's up for English scones next.

"Excuse me while I mourn," I say. "I'm going to change into something black. Forever." I reach to untape Scott the Soloflex Man from his place of honor.

Tye grabs my wrist. "Oh, leave him. He looks fabulous up there. I don't think he got too many other ad jobs, though. The competition for that shit is fierce."

I choke down my drink, wincing at the scorch in my throat. Kimmer points out the 800 number on the ad. "Can we order him wholesale from the catalog?"

"One size fits all," I add.

"I envy you, girls," Nena says, helping herself to another finger of Scotch, pouring the bottle almost empty. *Trina's gonna kill me.* "When I was a young girl, it was against the rules to objectify men like this," Nena goes on. "You're the first generation to get away with it."

"I never thought of it that way," I say. But she's right: Wrap him in a bow. Serve him on toast. *I wouldn't kick him out of bed for eating crackers.* It's weird to think this range of expression was off-limits not long ago. My grandmother never talked like this.

"Isn't it *delightfully wicked?*" Nena adds. "Turnabout is fair play."

"Speaking of turnabout, you'd be surprised," says Tye. "Plenty of the women you see in ads aren't even women." He transfers his empty Welch's glass to our sink, next to an overturned Winnie-the-Pooh cereal bowl.

"I knew all those Amazing Thighless Women in *Vogue* were too good to be true," I say. I think of Babylonia's photobook. A couple of the images could have been ads. "Wait—is Babylonia one of those women?"

Tye grins. "Some boys glam it up for the cameras the whole day as women. They make the big bucks." Tye flicks his head as if to toss a hank of imaginary Cher-hair over his shoulder. "I made some nice pocket change in my day. But performing live is more my thing."

"Can I ask a question, so I don't have to be stupid about this until the end of time?" I ask.

"Shoot," Tye says.

"Why not just live as a woman?"

He strolls to our couch and lounges against the cushions. "At the end of the day, some guys still want to be able to whip it out and,"—he gives us a Michael Jackson crotch thrust—"*fuck somebody.*"

Kimmer blushes. "Well, that'll do it."

"I'm not saying me." He fluffs a pillow, arranging it gingerly in the crook of the sofa.

Nena fingers the saltshaker on our table. "Whatever you say, dear."

"I don't want to live as a woman," Tye confirms. "I want to *perform* as a woman." He shifts on the convertible sofa, which is too short for his formidable height. "It's not an easy life. But it's the way to go, ladies. I'm free."

"What do you mean *free?*" says Kimmer. "We charged twelve-fifty a head at your show."

Come to think of it, that's almost what I paid to see The Police at Shea Stadium last summer.

"Take a hard look, girls," Tye says. "I'm a guy who wears a dress for a living. When your lifestyle is misunderstood by the masses, it's a fucked-up little gift. It doesn't matter whether you're a wallflower, or you do coke off the bartender's chest—you've already broken all the rules just by being you." He stretches against the couch, crossing his legs like Audrey Hepburn settling into a chaise. "So you might as well do whatever the fuck you want. It hurts. It *sucks.*" His eyebrows raise, pulling at my heartstrings. "And here's hoping I live through it. But, *voilà.*" He rolls one hand in a circle. "I'm *free.*"

Not that it's the same thing, but sometimes I get that feeling about punk. When you enter a restaurant in a leopard-print skirt and fishnets, with your bleach-streaked date in combat boots and a studded leather wrist guard, no one questions you. You've outstripped the confines of polite society, and people are just happy you don't smash the windows on your way out. Meanwhile, you're just a five-foot-tall student artist who's afraid to dye her hair.

I understand, though, that Tye can't strip free of his orientation the same way I wiggle out of the miniskirt. Mine's not as hard-earned a badge as his. And I don't necessarily have the same kind of considerations as he does when it comes to living to see my future.

"On the subject of free," Nena interrupts, eyes pleading like an over-linered puppy. "I do so need a place to drop my bags."

"*Uhhhhhm*," Kimmer stammers.

I clench her shoulders like a boxing trainer. *"Boundaries,"* I repeat in her ear.

Kim gets up from her chair and breathes deep. "Nena, I'll put on some coffee. You can pour your heart out, and I'll help you find a new place. But you can't move in here." Kimmer turns to me and flexes a bicep. *"Strong like bull,"* she says in her *Natasha* accent. Then she reaches into a low cabinet and pulls out a book.

She thuds the fat Bucks County phone book onto our tabletop. "As it is, Jess and I play 'Duck the Landlord' every day. Neither of *us* are even supposed to be living here."

Nena's damp black bob tumbles sideways with a tilt of her head. "I suppose I understand."

"You're not ticked-off?" I ask.

"At my age, you roll with every kick in the balls," Nena answers.

Tye taps his nails against our end table. "This is why you get mistaken for my opening act at the drag reviews, Nena."

"That, and my eyeshadow palette," she says.

"No comment," adds Tye. "But remember I give make-up tutorials."

I'm learning a lot on this subject. If you want to know anything about make-up, ask a drag queen.

Kimmer flips through the phonebook, one of the few items in the apartment that has avoided damage from some kind of leak. "Time for some research. Let's find out if someone in town needs a roommate."

"Black," says Nena.
"Sorry?" Kimmer asks.
"I'll take that coffee black."

CHAPTER 28

AUGUST 1984
Love My Way

It's still raining.

The Delaware races under the Lambertville Bridge, carving eddies around its pillars as I shuffle home from a lunch shift. The river has swallowed the rocks that formerly served as islands for the duck community.

Rain or not, I'm going to a Pretenders concert tonight.

The Camaro's engine rumbles outside our living room window, momentarily drowning out the strains of Joe Jackson's *Night and Day* album.

A bang against the window makes me jump. Audrey drops a library copy of Orwell's *1984* to the floor and loses the ash of her cigarette.

I throw back the curtain and there's Whit, crouched in the dark, wearing black boots and a leather jacket.

"Nobody here but us ducks!" Audrey calls.

I slide open the screechy pane to greet him. "Can't you go around the front, like a regular person?"

"It's wet out here." He twists his body through the window frame, boots smearing the wall. I wipe the streak with a towel we've been keeping on hand to block rain leaks.

Whit kisses me with a tongue so soft I lose my sense of direction, him holding the small of my back. Audrey gathers Orwell off the kitchen floor and waves it at us. "*Whoa, get a room.*"

"This *is* my room," I say, motioning to the pull-out sofa. Whit laughs.

"Oh, right." Audrey taps her Virginia Slim on the edge of our ashtray. "Feel free to swallow each other, then."

Whit slides a hand against my thigh, under the hem of my black jersey mini dress, which I bought at a Boho shop down the street. "Why don't you wear the, uh—," he makes crisscrosses against the skin of my thigh with his fingertip, approximating a fishnet pattern.

I promised him costuming for this occasion.

"Those got ruined, sorry," I say.

He grumbles. "Do I want to know how?" Then a beat, and he pulls me closer to him. "How?"

"Don't worry." Audrey blows a stream of smoke, twisting in the air like magic. "It was at a drag show. You missed the Diana Ross and Eurythmics Spectacular."

Whit's heavy boots clomp to the kitchen table, where he pulls out a chair. "Sorry. Maybe next time," he says.

I excuse myself to give my hair some extra spray, teasing the front with my fingers. Tonight calls for more-than-typical muss. Joe Jackson croons *Stepping Out* on our stereo as I double up on eyeliner pencil.

I see Audrey swing open our refrigerator. "How impolite of us," she says to Whit. "Would you like something to drink? Flat coke? Leftover creamer packets? What's ours is yours."

"I'm good," he says. "Sorry I forgot to bring a bottle of wine for the hostesses."

"All you need to bring around here is a sense of humor." Audrey adds, "Because as hostesses, we suck."

I chuckle, screwing up the smudge of my eyeliner.

Audrey squints at me as I come out of the bedroom. "Raccoon eyes are a new look for you," she says.

"It's a Chrissie Hynde concert," I remind her, stuffing my bare foot into the scrunchy cowl of my black leather ankle boot.

Audrey turns back to Whit. "As a musician, do you ever do the guyliner thing?"

He drums his hands against our garage sale kitchen table. "Once in a while."

"I might like to see that," I say. Maybe I've been watching too many Cure videos, but the look has become sexy to me now, especially when it accessorizes a guitar. I get entranced by all the dark, angst-ridden eyes staring from under masses of all-over hair. All those brooding post-punks crooning on video screens at dance clubs—they know how to stare their way through my whole being. It's a look so intense, it could fry me to a crisp like a zucchini slice.

Whit can do that. He can do that *stare*.

"Problem is, that make-up crap melts," he says, "and you can't get it off."

"Welcome to our world," says Audrey.

"This won't come off 'til Monday." I flutter my lashes and slide a palm over Whit's shoulders. "Look at us, bonding over eye make-up." This ironically makes me breathe more heavily.

"That eyeliner thing was passable when my hair was still dark," Whit says. "But only on stage." He shoves up the sleeves of his black leather jacket, catching the fact that I'm getting steamed over him, right there across the Formica.

I picture him all-brunette, blue eyes streaming past dark spikes of hair. Maybe. But that wouldn't be my Whit. I can't express the sense of ownership that falls over me when I'm near him, since that first night on his floor. A piece of him is just *mine*.

He takes my hand and leads me toward the living room window. "You ready?"

"I'm not climbing through there." I pull my hand out of his.

"Come on," he says. "It's raining, and this jacket is leather." He runs his palm along the curve of my ass. "I'll give you a boost."

"Like hell," I say. "Who told you to wear leather in the rain?"

"It's a *Pretenders' concert*," Audrey calls.

"I bet you can do it." He sweeps me in his arms, swinging my legs toward the window. A panel of my skirt flies up my thigh and I'm afraid the point of my heels might punch a hole in the drywall. I let out a mini-scream.

Audrey springs upright, her chair scraping against the Linoleum.

I scramble out of Whit's arms and smack the already-clammy shoulder of his jacket. "You are *warped*," I say, marching him through our foyer, both sets of our boots clomping the carpet flat. "Whit, this is a door. Door, Whit. This is what normal people use when they want to enter and exit the apartment."

"What was that about a sense of humor?" He laughs as I push him into the hallway. His damp jacket squeaks.

"Humor is one thing," I say. "Dating one of *The Dangerous Brothers* is another." Visions of the two wailing British guys from Whit's "Comic Strip Live" bootleg VHS tape bounce across my memory.

"I promise not to shoot you out of a cannon," he says, tossing his car keys in the air and catching them again. "Tonight."

My stellar fake ID is successful once again, like a magic passkey.

The Fall Out Club is wall-to-wall subversive types who have come to hear the heated, lovelorn rantings of the Pretenders. Everyone's in some tone of black, spattered with rain. It's like a goth fashion parade: Long, button-down shirts are on every other person, their collars topped by antique-looking rhinestone brooches, layered with vests and chains and black Frankenstein blazers with bulked-up shoulders. I watch medieval crucifixes hang like weighty, gothic albatrosses, sweeping back and forth across various breasts. Mesh gloves, ankle boots, and ripped fishnets are everywhere, making my pulse race with a sense of danger.

A ghostly cast of cigarette smoke clings underneath the stage lights as if we anti-establishment types have created our own weather system.

I teach Whit my strategy of elbowing to the front of the stage. This comes easy to him since he's more massive than I am. And having played this venue himself, he's not intimidated by the hardcore, torn T-shirted concertgoers that colonize the floor. I edge past girls with thick stripes of bruise-purple eyeshadow that stretch far past their temples and practically out the door.

The noise of the crowd nearly drowns out the Romeo Void sex anthem that's pounding through the club's speakers. Whit fits himself against my back like a puzzle piece. His teeth close on the jersey halter ties at the back of my neck, which hold up my whole dress. "What happens if I pull this?" he says, stretching the fabric.

"It's knotted."

"Damn you." He nudges my fist-sized earrings with his lips and his hands run along the sides of my body. "Nothing underneath here?"

I tilt back my head. "Just me."

"*You're awesome.*"

The stage lights flare to life. The band bursts into "Talk of the Town." Chrissie Hynde's spoken voice is as deep as her singing voice. She's a God. Not even a Goddess—a God. I can barely see her eyes under thick, bedraggled hair, eyeliner looking like she crossed herself out with a charcoal briquette.

Whit rifles his fingers through my bangs. "You look kind of like Chrissie tonight. You've got the eye thing going. And the hair." I feel *Preeee-cious*.

The band plays for almost two hours. When I'm not fawning over Chrissie, I've got Whit's tongue down my throat, keeping me good and dizzy. Colored spotlights whisk their way through my eyelashes; slam dancers with black jackets, studs, and metal-tipped combat boots blur all around me during the moments we come up for air.

After the last encore and a kick-ass version of "Brass in Pocket," the crowd files onto the gritty asphalt of Chestnut Street. The sky drips all over us as we try to remember where Whit parked. He takes off his leather jacket and slides it over my shoulders.

"Someday you'll wish you invited me to join your band," I tell him. "You said yourself, I do a mean Chrissie."

"You do. But then you'd have to stay here, instead of taking off to London," he says, "and we know that's crazy talk. Right?"

"Like you'd let me sing with you guys." I edge his jacket collar over my head, to keep the rain out of my hair. I peer down a cross street, looking for the Camaro.

Whit starts walking faster. "You didn't answer the question. Is staying in one place such a suck-ass idea? If it's the right place?"

What is it that motivates men to want to attach you to a single location, like a bulletin board pushpin? *Secured.*

"Do you have to shit-up this very cool night?" I ask him.

He turns to me. "It's just that . . . once in a while, a fucked-up miracle falls from the sky and people in the world *change their minds*, Jess. I swear, I've seen it happen."

"You're getting delusional now." I laugh.

"You still didn't answer me." His bleached hair is becoming wiry and weighed down by the rain.

"To hell with that answer." I grab his face and kiss him, right there in the middle of the road, sucking him into near-incoherence. His body heats up like a road flare against me. Whit's wet leather jacket tumbles off my shoulders and his hands draw paths in the rainwater on my exposed back.

Some half-buzzed skinhead in a studded jacket whistles from the curb. "Get a trailer, man!"

A Mustang flashes its high beams at us, its struggling muffler noise getting far too close. Whit breaks away from me, stumbling backward.

"*Shut up* now," I say. "Okay?"

I win the argument.

My boot heels teeter as I grab his jacket off the ground. The hubcaps of an old-model Mustang breeze past my skirt.

Whit's car is actually a block over from where we thought it was. He has a job interview in the morning, so I can't stay with him in King of Prussia.

He drives me back to my brick apartment building on Waterloo Street.

By the time we get to New Hope, the rain has hit full storm mode. We sprint to the front of the building through sheets of rain. As my hands fidget to unlock the slick glass door, Whit smacks his palm against it. His tongue attacks my ear and his fingers spread across my stomach from behind. I spin to face him, my back against the wet glass. His shirt is plastered to his skin. His hair is saturated.

He pulls one of my thighs up toward his waist. Hands run under my dress, free in the knowledge that there's nothing underneath the fabric to slow him down. It's nothing but me under there. Me making enough noise that he reminds me not to wake my neighbors. The sky flashes. The glass panel fogs and smudges behind my back.

I can barely remember my name.

He walks me to my apartment door. We trickle rainwater in the hallway. I root through my purse for my keychain and wrangle a key off the loop.

"Take this," I say. "You shouldn't have to crawl through the window."

"Really?" He turns the key in front of his face.

"Come get me tomorrow." I push wet hair out of my eyes. "I'll call off work. I'll buy new fishnets. Pick a color."

"I don't give a fuck what color," he breathes in my ear. "Just wear them." He gives me one more deep kiss. "You blow me away," he says, teeth clicking against my shoe-buckle of an earring.

He steps backward, receding into the late-night camouflage of the hallway, his boots scuffing against the filthy vinyl tiles. He leaves wet footprints.

Kimmer stirs a box of mac and cheese on our range top as I make my way back inside the apartment. A frayed beach towel is squished along the living room windowsill. A water streak darkens the wall underneath it, turning the drywall a more ominous shade of eggshell than usual.

I run a brush through my hair and collapse onto the pull-out, where Trina lounges with our ashtray.

"You're supposed to shower *before* you go on a date, not during," she says.

My hair crackles with remnant hairspray as I try to rake the brush through the back. "You're smoking in my bed?" I ask.

"*Whose* bed?" The sofa springs whine as she shifts toward the end table. "Dry off, before you ruin the sheets. Especially in punker boy's wet jacket."

"Geez, someone's in need of an attitude adjustment." Kimmer laughs, stirring the muck in our camping pot with a semi-burned wooden spatula.

Our five-alarm telephone rings to life.

"I got it!" Trina lurches. I practically climb into her lap trying to beat her to the phone, but I lose.

"Sorry, Whit," Trina babbles into the receiver, "but our heroine Jessica just rolled in from the rain and has to dry her hair—"

"Give me that phone!" I shout. She pushes me away, mid-rant. The sofa mattress bends as if it might snap closed with us in it.

"—So did you miss her when she was in New York last week with Drew?" Trina blurts into the phone.

Cold sweeps over my body like Niagara Falls. "*Are you out of your mind?*"

Trina stares at me, a millimeter of smile curling up the side of her lip like an infection. "Someone wants to speak to you," the receiver dangles from her fingertips. She drops the hunk of plastic onto the bed. "He deserved to know."

My pulse bangs in my teeth as Trina sashays out of the room, high on self-righteousness. I wonder for a moment what heavy object in the room I could kill her with. If my body weren't busy going numb.

I lift the phone to my face, slowly. "*Hello?*" The line is silent except for wind whipping in the background.

"At least I know his name now," Whit finally says.

"Holy God," I murmur. "*I'm so sorry.*"

Rain spatters white noise over the line. He's at another payphone, in the downpour. Without his jacket. "You were in New York last week?" he asks.

The muscles in my throat strangle down to a blistering little tube.

I cry.

It's not because I've been dishonest. He knew the status of this from the start. He asked me not to tell him anymore. I cry because I know what thought is going to bash him in the gut . . . any . . . *second*.

Fucking dammit, I don't want to be the one to make him feel that way. And I don't want him to disappear.

I can't stop the thought from hitting him now. I feel my insides twist, nerve endings uncoupling as I wait for him to contemplate what I did in New York. With another guy. Fuck, fuck, *FUCK*.

"*Last week?*" Whit repeats.

DIAL TONE.

I sling Whit's jacket on the kitchen chair and march after Trina, who's hiding from me in our tiny bathroom.

"What the *hell* is your problem?" Raccoon eye makeup drifts halfway down my reflection in the mirror.

"Me? You're the poor bitch with the over-complicated love life." Trina leans against the sink. "How long did you think you could keep that up?"

"None of your fucking business, that's how long!"

"You could use a few consequences in your life," Trina says. "The universe isn't all concert tickets and boy-toys." She wraps her palm around my atomizer and clanks it closer to me against the porcelain. "And *L'air du Temptress* perfume." The liquid swishes like a tidal wave in the bottle and then settles, unchanged—no sign of its typical frothy bubbles.

Trina lifts an eyebrow. "Notice anything?"

I raise the bottle to my nose to find there's not a whiff of alcohol-tainted prom smell left. I spritz my wrist and tap my tongue against the damp swath of my skin. All I taste is water.

"*What the fuck?*" I yell. "You dumped Drew's perfume?"

The bathroom mirror of the medicine cabinet lolls open. "Weeks ago." Trina and her reflection hiss at me in unison. "Like you give a shit. You tossed Drew aside like a stained shirt." She presses the mirror closed, rattling the metal cabinet.

"That's not even true." I stumble backward, barefoot in my wet dress, clutching a baby-pink atomizer full of plain water. Audrey and Kimmer show up in the bedroom behind me.

"Sure it is," Trina says. "You blew him off for fame and fortune. And London. And hot nights with punker boy." A vague memory of my accepting responsibility for the break-up with Drew bubbles to mind like the froth on a tap beer. I wanted to venture out. I made that decision.

Trina swings the bathroom door shut between us, locking herself inside.

I storm through the kitchen, smacking the atomizer on the counter. I shudder as someone pounds on the front door.

Whit shouts my name from the other side of the wood, no longer worried about waking my neighbors.

I bundle his jacket into one arm and open the door. His fingers close around my wrist. "Come with me."

I slip my feet into a pair of Kim's sandals just in time for him to lead me into the hallway. Audrey and Kimmer shuffle through the doorway as Whit and I stamp through the puddles we left in the hall half an hour ago.

"Jess, wait a minute," Audrey calls. "Is this smart?" Her voice reverberates in our wake.

Smart? No, I think. My feet keep moving anyway, though. Because I owe him an explanation. Or not. I don't know.

We shove our way through the glass front doors and Whit pitches the key I gave him against the cement. It jingles in the rain. I pull his leather jacket shoddily over my shoulders. The sandals suck water from the puddles as I shuffle.

"Where are we going?"

He throws open his creaky car door. "Driving."

My seat in the Camaro is clammy and his jacket is sodden as a wet cow. I bunch it in my lap. Whit K-turns out of the lot, zooming onto Main Street. I grip the door panel with my palm.

"I didn't mean to hurt you," I mumble. "That wasn't the plan."

"What the fuck *was* your plan, Jessica?" The Camaro rumbles into the winding darkness of Route 202, past the end of Main Street. I don't know where the hell I am after that.

"I tried to be honest with you from the beginning."

"Yeah. *You're a regular open book.*" His transmission whines unforgivingly.

"You said you didn't want me to tell you about him anymore."

"That was before—" he stops himself, teeth grinding under rigid jaw muscles.

"Before what?" I ask.

"That's when he was there, and you were here," he says, stomping the clutch, shirking the gear shift. The car lurches. "New York's not as far away as I thought."

"If it means anything, he's not there anymore," I say. "He left for California."

The Camaro takes a curve like a cougar in chase. Headlights flare through the gloss of the back windshield. "I get it," he says. "The guy in New York threatened to blow you off, and you ran to him."

"I did not." Although maybe that's what I did. "And *take it easy*."

"Did you tell him about me? Some idiot waiting for you back in Philly? What are we doing here, Jessica?" he shouts.

"Isn't that what we're trying to find out?" I grasp the dashboard with both hands. "Or have I already had all the relationships I'm allowed in my life? Two whole guys. Ever. I guess that makes me the fucking heartbreaker whore."

"Don't pretend you're the one being jerked around here."

"We both walked into this with our eyes open," I say. "Why don't you tell *me* what we're doing? You haven't exactly offered up that information."

"How about this?" he says. "How about you do one guy *at a time*."

"Oh, don't you *even*." The guillotine of the windshield wipers slash through sheets of rain water, whomping back and forth. "Take me home, Mister *Earring Under My Floor Mat*."

"I can't do this, Jessica. I can't be a piece of your screwed-up little Rubik's Cube of a life. I'm confused enough as it is."

"Fucking God," I shout, "you're breaking up with me?" His jacket rolls off my lap and to the floor.

"I'm not a *worn pair of shoes*," he says.

"Where are we driving to, then?" I ask.

"RIGHT!" he shouts. "You're going home!" He palms the wheel. The car spins into a U-turn, tires wailing against the flooded road. He curses all over the place.

The Camaro revolves past the 180-degree mark he was aiming for, swinging across the asphalt and into the opposing lane. Headlamps beam at us. A truck horn blares. I scream, a full-throated girl-siren.

We veer off the pavement, his fender slicing through a guard rail, metal screeching. The car shunts down a ravine, headlights bleaching skinny trees as we lumber sideways. I lift out of my seat to the sound of the windshield *snapping*. A crack zigzags from one side of the glass to the other like a streak of lightning.

I wonder how close the river is. I can hear it. Rushing. Silver fizzles across my vision, even when I close my eyes.

CHAPTER 29

LIMBO
It's The End of The World As We Know It

My grandmother repeats something to me through the soup of a medicated dream. "*Jess,*" she says. It must be time to wake up. Her hand closes over mine, warm like family. Peaceful.

My grandmother never calls me Jess, though.

It's not her voice.

Reality cuts through the fog like a swath of wind. There's no way I could be in the cramped Long Island bedroom at my grandmother's—I don't even remember going to sleep. That means I must be lying on my back in public somewhere. It's like fainting in seventh-grade health class all over again.

I adjust focus on a poorly-lit metal ceiling. "*Oh shit!*" Palms wrangle me from both sides as I pull myself upright.

"Hey, it's okay." Audrey sits next to me in a dim van with equipment along the walls, rain gliding down the windows.

She holds my hand, same as she held Trina's the night she spewed beer at Brent Fox, the fraternity vice president. That night, when Brent threatened to expel Trina from the Phi O house, we Little Sisters stood firm. If one of us had to go, we vowed, we all would.

The brothers showed us the lawn.

"We're in this together," Audrey said as the four of us sniffled, arms laced around each other, kneeling in the grass like Capri-wearing vagrants. "No matter what happens, *we'll be okay*."

My best friend Audrey.

"*Lie back, please.*" A gaunt man in a white coat shines a penlight in my eyes, all-business. An antiseptic smell tingles in my nose. "How do you feel?" asks Serious Medical Man.

I notice a throb that matches up with the part in my hair. "I have a headache. What the hell happened?"

"We're on our way to the hospital," Audrey says. Her clothes are wet, her hair slicked back.

"Miss Addentro, can you wiggle your toes for me?" Serious Medical Man asks.

I bang my bare feet against the gurney like it's a kettle drum. "Where are my boots?"

"You borrowed Kimmer's sandals. Don't worry about them," Audrey says, swishing my bangs out of my face. The jersey of my dress has sucked up rainwater like a chilled sponge.

"Audrey, what are you doing here?" I ask. "I was in the car with—" A shudder rolls over me. "Wait—WHERE'S WHIT?!" Numbness shakes through my body. I try to sit up, but Serious Medical Man insists I have to stay on my back. He's a handsy guy.

"*Shhh.* Whit's all right," says Audrey. "I mean, he's a freaked-out mess, but he walked away. Or out of the car, anyway. He's in a different ambulance."

Flashes flicker back to my memory: A Titanic screech, headlamps, a moment of zero gravity. "We slid off the road," I say.

"You sure did," Audrey confirms. "Luckily, you seem okay. Does anything hurt you?"

"I'm *fine.*" The ambulance navigates a pothole and a muscle in my neck pangs. *I'm almost fine.*

Serious Medical Man scribbles on a clipboard. "How old are you?"

A siren whirs. I try to think. The answer's not immediately apparent to me, but it comes. "I'm twenty."

"And what year is it?" he asks, talking to the clipboard.

"Did I die and come back to life or something? Am I in the fucking Dead Zone?"

"Not unless Bucks County is the Dead Zone. But you scared the hell out of us," Audrey answers, squeezing my hand. "Now will you behave, please? This nice man wants to make sure you don't have a concussion."

I try to squint away a tear or two, but they roll out anyway. "Audrey, how did you? How did you?" My questioning capability isn't quite functioning.

"*We followed you.* There's no way I'd risk another friend going into the river," she says. Rain prattles against the roof. "Trina and Kimmer are behind us in the station wagon."

"I can't believe you came after me." I press the cool back of her hand against my cheek. "You're the best."

"*As long as you're okay.*" Audrey's voice twitches. "And it wasn't just me. When Trina heard you guys pull away, she made a freaking mad dash for the car. Kimmer and I could hardly keep up."

"Trina did that?"

"She almost drove away without us." Salt stings the corner of my eye.

Serious Medical Man grills me all the way to Bucks County General. He asks who the president is, what ten times two is, the year I was born. As I answer, it occurs to me:

A guy just broke up with me and sent me to the hospital.

🎸

I don't have a concussion. The green cinder blocks of Bucks County General make me feel like maybe I ate a bad plate of fish, though. Audrey and Kimmer brought me the clothing I asked for so I wouldn't have to leave this place in a wet, backless minidress and hospital slippers. And no fucking underwear. My neck and shoulders ache every time I move.

Once in a Lifetime

Audrey sits in the blocky guest chair next to my bed. Kimmer studies the medical equipment. The whole place smells like industrial liquid soap.

"Did you call your grandmother?" Audrey asks me.

"She'd take me home this instant," I say. "Besides, I've got you and Doctor Kimmer here."

"Nurse Kimmer," she says, examining a clicking piece of machinery.

"Maybe it should be Doctor Kimmer," I say.

I wonder what's going to happen to the lot of us once we no longer have college keeping us tight as a hemp braid. I wish there was some commitment we could make to all stay together. Like a marriage, but different. For friends.

"Don't go skidding into any more trenches, okay?" Audrey tells me. She draws a circle in the air around us. "None of this works without you."

"Tell that to my driver." I reach for the waxy soda cup the girls brought me, chomping the straw.

"You can tell him yourself." Kimmer pulls a clipboard full of paperwork out of a pocket attached to my bed and starts flipping through a series of carbon copies. "Whit's four rooms down."

"Is he okay?" I poke my fingers through my hair, still kind of crunchy with leftover hairspray.

"He's got three stitches over his eye, but he's all right, fundamentally," Kimmer says. "I'm not sure he still has a driver's license." I recall the scar that already grazes his eyebrow and wonder if he got it the same way.

"Hey, I want your opinion on something, Jess." Audrey pulls the yellow notebook I gave her from below her chair. "Don't laugh."

"You used Ned the Notebook?" I say. "That makes me happy."

"Don't thank me yet." She clears her throat. "I call this, 'Gone.'" Audrey holds the book against her flattened palm and reads.

A line strikes, like a slip of paper cutting skin,
A wisp between the world and insanity.
A film of panic vibrates, waiting to be broken like a cobweb, or a womb.

Each phrase is punctuated by the soft bleeps of a monitor. A passing nurse is drawn through the proscenium of our doorway. I hold up a hand, warning her not to disturb the reading. Audrey goes on:

> *I sink into the nightmare, tasting an anger without mercy.*
> *My head is ballooned and blue and numb and*
> *Thoughts can barely siphon through this narrow sieve. . . .*

The words echo softly against the sterile cinder blocks. The nurse taps a hand to her heart.

> *. . .And I know where it's all headed:*
> *One moment foaming into the next,*
> *Threading through a fracture*
> *Where the last flicker of reason slides down a drain, past a hairline,*
> *Under a crack in a door*
> *And is gone.*

Audrey thumbs the spiral notebook closed. My jaw falls open. Our nurse-visitor claps her hands with baby softness.

"That was powerful," says Kimmer, her voice halting as if it hit a speed bump.

"Oh, Geez," I say, motioning for Audrey to lean closer. I wrap an arm around her neck. "Is that what it feels like?" I whisper. "When you *leave us?*"

"Sort of," she says. The nurse comes closer and pats Audrey's shoulder.

"I knew things got dark for you sometimes," I tell Audrey, "but I didn't realize you believed all that terrible shit you always say about yourself when you're in that condition. I guess because I think you're great." I bounce her hand against the hospital-issue mattress. "Audrey, do you know what this means? You're not an economist. You're a poet."

She looks at me like I just announced the world is trapezoidal. "Since when?"

"Maybe since always," I say. "All that classic literature has rubbed off on you."

She shakes her head. Her T-shirt gaps in the front where she recently created a scoop neckline with scissors. Clothing reconstruction is another vehicle for her creativity.

"Maybe this is why we've always gotten along so well," I add. "Maybe it was more than A Flock of Seagulls and our mutual need to run Beatrice out of the quad. You're an *artist*."

Audrey runs a finger over the dog-eared notebook cover. "I never thought about it that way."

"Welcome to the Tortured Soul Society," I announce.

"Now *that* sounds familiar." She pats the notebook. "I'm a master of self-torture."

Kimmer laughs. "Is that like '*Welcome to The Plaza*,' but different?" She tucks sections of the scratchy hospital bedsheet under my thigh and straightens my blanket as if I'm her patient.

"Very different," I say.

Audrey and Kimmer head downstairs to buy lunch, leaving the room quiet except for a clicking monitor. The nurse who stopped to listen to Audrey's poem shows back up at my bedside.

Her nametag reads *Barbara*. I see a distant memory of my mother in her smile. "Maybe it's none of my affair, but this is for your friend. The poet." She slips a business card into my palm.

I turn the slip of cardboard over in my fingers. It's information for a psychiatrist.

"*Help her*," Nurse Barbara stresses.

I nod and shove the card into the yellow spiral like a bookmark.

The hospital won't let me leave without the girls to accompany me. As the three of us head for the elevator, I ask Kim and Audrey to wait for me in the lobby. There's something I have to do.

I sneak down the hall, which smells like baby wipes. The flecked tile floor rolls under my feet as I count the doors leading to Whit's room.

I find him sitting up in a bed by a window, the sun slanting across his shoulder. A skinny guy leans over him in tight jeans with a studded belt. The guy's inorganic black hair is marked by a thick streak of violet, like a paint swatch.

The two of them smack lips.

I freeze like a salt pillar. My eye twitches. I feel spritzed with liquid betrayal, running down my body.

"*Holy God!*" I shout. It was bad enough when I thought his ex, *Delilah*, was calling his answering machine.

Whit and the guy snap apart as if I cleaved them with an ax. A gold-toned George Michael hoop earring glints in the guy's ear. The front of his hair screams purple at me.

The guy's finger gravitates my way. "Let me guess," he says, earring trembling. "You're the girl who draws."

I gape at them. The skinny guy shifts his weight as if he doesn't know whether to run.

Step away from the boyfriend, I think.

He shuffles back from Whit's bed as if he heard me. "I should go," he mumbles, eyes to the Linoleum, like the tile is far more important than what's going on here.

He slides past me, hands swiping back hair far more varnished and daringly punked-out than mine. His cool presence rips through me like shrapnel.

I stare at Whit. I can't feel my fingers. "You *shit*."

"It's not what you think." Whit taps his finger against the butterfly bandage above his eye and sucks a quick breath of pain past his teeth. "How are you doing? Are you all right?"

"How am I *doing*?" I lunge against his metal bedrail and grip the cold piping in my palms. I shake the bed. "My bullshit ex-boyfriend drove me into a ditch. And now he's making out with another fucking guy behind my back! *That's* how I'm doing. How are *you?*"

The fingernails of a rugged RN dig into my forearm.

"Jess, calm yourself," Whit says.

Nurse Brawny pulls me away from the bed, *shushing* me like a deranged librarian. "Miss, you're not allowed to visit another patient."

"At least I tried to be honest with you!" Unwashed hair falls in my face. "And I thought your slutty *ex* was sneaking around your apartment. Have you been seeing that guy this whole time?" I suddenly hear my own New York accent. It's light-years from attractive.

The nurse stamps her orthopedic loafer. "You have to leave right now!"

"How could you not tell me?" I wrench an arm out of Nurse Brawny's vice grip. "Did you have to make me into this much of an idiot? Is it a *rule?*"

Whit covers his face with his hands, curling himself into a ball like a poked spider.

A doctor materializes out of nowhere: a big wall of lab coat staring me down. He physically ushers me into the hall. I walk into a corner of the nurses' station, knocking a ceramic mug full of pencils off a desk. It smashes to shards and pencils scatter like Pick Up Sticks, pointing in all directions.

I hear Whit call my name just once, a sound that absorbs into the ammonia-scrubbed cinder blocks. The doctor follows me down the hall like a relentless slasher-movie villain to make sure I get into the elevator.

At the desk downstairs, I show my wrinkled discharge papers to the check-out nurse, as I huff air in big breaths. "Can I go now?" I glimpse Kimmer and Audrey on a bench at the other side of the lobby. They seem a mile away, in soft, rack-focus.

"Are you all right, ma'am?" asks the desk nurse.

"I'm fine." I swallow hard, humiliation going down my throat like a viscous gulp of tar. "Why does everyone keep asking me that?"

"Your insurance information?"

"I don't have insurance."

The nurse slides a pink invoice at me. "That will be $300 for overnight admittance."

I have less than 700 bucks saved for study abroad. This aggrieved sheet of paper says I owe nearly half of it to the hospital.

My head whirrs as I contemplate the ramifications of sleeping with a guy who's been doing another guy. Risk. Reality. My body. My future. I count condoms in my head, an AIDS-colored panic sliding through me like a ghost I thought was only haunting other people.

Tears bend the numbers on the wall clock across from the tidy, partitioned check-out desk as I sob, right there in the lobby, my fingertips jittering against the chalky hospital bill. My guts heave like a manual transmission in traffic.

Kimmer is suddenly there, pulling me into a bear hug.

I'm so fucking done.

We unlock the apartment door to see Trina wringing out a towel in the kitchen sink, wet with flood water. The windowsill is a grayer shade of scummy off-white than it's ever been. The distorted guitars of The Psychedelic Furs sift their way through our stereo speakers as she works.

"Anyone know how to build an ark?" Trina heads to the window and wedges the towel against the track with her fingertips.

My storage box sits on the couch, looking soft and fetid with water. My sketch of Whit sits drying on a cushion. It looks like someone smudged it in a spasm of anger. I realize this is the only physical image I have of him since none of us owns a camera.

Trina moves toward me, her fingers fidgeting. "I tried to save your box, I swear to God. It was mush by the time I remembered it was behind the couch."

I dig into the box and pull out a few sopping notebooks, including a folder full of blurred charcoal sketches I'd been saving for years. The purple nylon wallet where I've been stashing my money is squishy in my hands. An unruly pile of bills inside it have congealed like melted slices of deli cheese. "Pulp. My cash is now pulp."

My throat tightens. The wallet leaves a wet print in the middle of my mural when I throw it against the wall. I surrender into a mound on the spongy carpet.

I always thought tough chicks like me didn't cry, but the water lets loose like a flash thunderstorm. I crack, and it pours. For the second time today.

The Psychedelic Furs screech to a halt, the needle on our stereo grating as Trina yanks the album off the turntable. She joins me on the floor. "*I'm sorry.*" She wraps her arms around me. "I almost got you killed."

Audrey and Kimmer flop to the carpet to join us. "No, Whit almost got her killed," Audrey says.

"I helped," Trina says. "Can you forgive me? I'd like to blame this on my vindictive evil twin, but she's me."

I sniffle. "Is it too corny to say, *Water under the bridge?*"

"Not in New Hope," Kimmer says.

There on the oatmeal-colored shag, I recount the whole screwed-over narrative: The break-up in the car, the violet-streaked guy in Whit's room, my depleted savings. My sudden health concerns.

"You know what I can't believe?" I ask.

"That Whit got bent out of shape over some George Michael wannabe with purple hair?" Trina asks.

"That two guys in your whole life makes you an At-risk Heartbreaker Whore?" asks Kimmer. "I don't think so."

Trina dabs her eye. "If that's the criteria, I am so fucked."

"No," I say. "I can't believe that Pretenders concert was *yesterday.*" We laugh as a single unit, a gaggle of girls shaking on a moldy carpet.

Audrey flips open the top of her Virginia Slims pack, plucking out a cigarette. "We'll get you through this, Jess," she says, passing me a butt. "You're fine. You've gotta be fine."

"Tye says life is like show biz." I wipe my eyes with the back of my hand. "It goes on."

"It better," says Trina.

I light the cigarette. "How did I fuck this all up?" Dampness from the carpet seeps through my shorts as I pass Audrey back her lighter. I move to the semi-dry couch. "Am I a terrible person? Could I have worked any harder this summer?"

Kimmer lifts our plastic ashtray up to me and I flick the cigarette against its rim. "At least you have time to make more tips if you still need money," she says. "I'll have Giorgio get you back on the dinner schedule. As for guys, it's like my father used to say: There are more horses' asses than there are horses."

I dissolve into sketchy laughter, not sure how much longer I'm supposed to cry.

"Dad was a great philosopher." Kimmer rests her head on my shoulder, waves of gold hair spilling over my arm. "Too bad he couldn't straighten out his own life."

Trina pulls in a breath. "I guess this is as bad a time as ever to tell you this, girls," she says, "but I can't live with you guys in Oakland when we go back to Pittsburgh. I'll be working three days a week at Fox and Rascowitz, *don-ton*."

"*Shit*—are you going to live by yourself somewhere?" says Audrey.

"My dad set me up in an apartment. It's a decent drive from campus," Trina says. "His partner's daughter needed a roommate, so he volunteered me. I've been a little . . . on edge about it."

"More like over the edge," Kimmer says, stealing a drag off my cigarette.

"Ok, guilty," Trina admits. "I know it doesn't fix things, Jess, but how about I buy you lunch?" she offers. "And a stiff VO and ginger. If you're still the forgiving type."

"You're fucking lucky I like you." I sniff.

Trina and I change into fresh clothes and head out. As we scale the stairs, we see our landlord yacking with an upstanding-looking couple who cart boxes into Paula and Dean's old unit. I wonder where the hell Paula ended up. Is she dodging the back of Dean's hand in some new cigar store, doling out PA Lottery numbers to compulsive gamblers? Or worse? The police came up with nothing for us.

I duck into the building's front vestibule, since I'm not officially supposed to be living here.

Trina raises a wait-a-minute finger and shoves up her sleeves. "*Mr. Del Vecchio*, I need a word." She barrels down the hall.

CHAPTER 30

STILL AUGUST 1984
Mystery Achievement

Familiar sleigh bells jangle as I push through the door of Capresi's. Tye leans against the bar, dressed in black-and-whites. Through the archway, I watch Kimmer turn over a tablecloth on the patio, which is buzzing with guests. This many people haven't populated the slate since the day I dumped five wedding cocktails on my head.

Tye emerges from behind the bar, a serving apron tied around his waist. Giorgio and Kimmer wander in from outside.

"*There's* our indestructible waitress," says Giorgio. Tye applauds. Kimmer smiles, folding a linen napkin over her arm.

The suncatchers in our ceiling space glint like fireflies.

"We're glad you're all right." Giorgio takes my hand. "How do you feel?"

"*Eh*, my neck is still sore." I rub behind my collar.

Tye comes in for a hug, despite being far too tall for comfort. As his shoulders awkwardly surround me, I smell the sultriest cologne ever to grace my senses.

"Are you a waiter now?" I ask him, coming down from my toes. "That sucks balls, huh?"

"Waiter. Bartender. Headliner. Gotta scrape together a living somehow," he shrugs. "Maybe they'll let me back into The Lodge, now."

Teddy pushes through the kitchen out-door, a collar and tie showing under his chef's jacket. His hair is blown straight and neat. He reaches below the waitressing station and heads toward me and Kimmer with a collection of flowers. I'm bewildered, not having taken him for a zinnias-after-your-boyfriend-almost-kills-you type of guy.

He hands me a single stem from the bouquet. "I'm glad you're all right, Jess," he says. "Told you that guy was too pretty."

"Bite your tongue," says Tye. *They're never too pretty*, he mouths at me, shaking his head.

Teddy's cheeks pink-up. He tugs at the knot of his tie and extends the rest of the bouquet. But not to me.

"Kim, I know I'm not the kind of guy you usually hang around with," he says. She accepts the flowers in both hands. "But we've spent a lot of time in that kitchen together. You deserve better than some monster jock who lands you in the river."

Kimmer stands with her mouth agape.

Teddy takes her hand. "What do you think of spending your time with someone who thinks you're great? And smart. And gorgeous."

Kim shifts on her heels. Teddy continues. "We want you to stay here and manage the restaurant because you *know food*. You're like the perfect woman."

"*What?*"

"We want you to stay here." Teddy gets down on one knee and lowers his head. "Would you consider running the kitchen with me?"

"Oh, get up!" She laughs.

Giorgio steps forward. "You mentioned you were having problems with your loans," he says to Kim. "If you have to take a break before you finish college, you can manage things here with us until you figure out what to do. We take care of our own."

"Wow. I never thought of that, but . . . maybe it's not such a bad fallback position," Kim says. "At least until I save for my next semester."

Teddy scrambles back to standing. "Seriously?"

Kimmer laughs. "I'd have to think about it, but how can I refuse that speech? Besides, my father ran a restaurant. Why not carry on the tradition until I finish my degree?"

"Plenty of schools here in Bucks County, too," Teddy adds.

"*Think pre-med*," I faux-whisper to Kimmer over the patio noise. "So, how'd the dining room get so full?" I break into a British accent. "Is it a *luncheon par-ty?*"

"It's a party as far as I'm concerned," says Tye. "Thanks, by the way."

I wonder if my brain's a little mangled from the whack in the head. "For what?"

Giorgio hands me a copy of *The Philadelphia Inquirer* folded open to the Food page. It features a photo of a wine glass on a deuce, a white column . . . our wrought-iron trellis . . . our gazebo. The headline reads, "The Neapolitan Cheesecake Experience: Capresi's Continental Restaurant."

The article describes a shady outdoor dining room with a rustic slate floor, nestled between the Delaware Canal and the meandering creek. Sidled next to the Towpath, in view of the Main Street bridge. The restaurant with a uniquely evolving, handwritten menu, an epiphany of a Portobello salad, and a refreshingly frank New York waitress with a love of Van Gogh.

An owl-shaped suncatcher flashes light in my eye.

"My friend Randy couldn't produce Michael Jackson," says Giorgio. "He sent a food critic instead. The one you waited on."

Tye taps the newspaper. "Everyone from here to Princeton has been coming in for dinner and cheesecake."

"Especially since half the restaurants on the river have water damage this week," Giorgio says.

"Wow—you mean I *communicated the essence?*" I ask.

"You communicated something, all right." Tye undoes his apron and wraps it around my waist. "You're going to need this for the dinner shift. We're full-up with reservations. You'll make some good tips."

"I better," I say. "Otherwise I'll have to leave here London-less."

I earn back half my hospital bill in tips that night.

As the patio quiets, Giorgio lounges in the bar room in his red kimono. Miz Love shuffles her tarot deck after a reading with the Mechanic Street leather craftsman. The waxy cards reflect light from our lanterns.

I pull out a chair in front of Nena and Giorgio. "How much for a reading?"

Nena stops shuffling. "My in-house discount is ten dollars."

"I'll buy." Giorgio slips Nena a bill. "I'm impressed that you've become a believer, Jessica."

"We'll see about that," I say. "But New Hope makes a person more open-minded."

Nena straightens her cards into an orderly stack, then snaps an assortment of them against the wine-colored tablecloth. Their backs feature filigree patterns in shades of indigo and midnight and burgundy. She closes her eyes and breathes a mystical sigh, turning three cards face-up.

The center image shows a pale girl in a white dress, a castle lurking out of focus over her shoulder. Attendants shield her with a rough-hewn canopy. Nena pats a fingertip on the blonde girl. "The Four of Wands."

"Is that supposed to be me?" I ask. "She looks lost."

"Not lost. Searching for guidance. It's the card of home," Nena explains. "It means you have a strong foundation."

"That's funny, since this is the first time I'm on my own, outside of college." The concept of home feels nebulous to me now, like something I can barely feel under my feet. I don't know if it's ever felt solid since my mother died. And I was 12 then.

"You're moving through a fairy tale, in your own world, like Alice in Wonderland." Nena taps the canopy in the image. "But you're protected by the people who love you."

I think of my grandmother, sitting at her dressing table, dabbing oh-so-regal Prince Matchabelli perfume behind her ears, my nostrils tingling as the spicy smell reached them. The chime of the bottle settling back on the mirrored tray with the gold filigree trim that sat on her vanity. The way her smile bolstered me, knowing the hopes she had for me to conquer a world of options that she and my mother never had.

The way she reached across the chipped marble tabletop and held my hand, the very warmth of which was a promise that she wouldn't let me make the same mistakes as my mother. Ones that made Mom so intensely unhappy that it set off a time-bomb of a tumor in her brain.

And I think of my friends, who rushed after me in the shimmying station wagon, straining to keep up with Whit's Camaro, even in a torrent of rain.

I sigh. "Protected. Okay. I can see that," I say to Nena. "But what else have you got for me?"

Nena points to the next card, where a downtrodden knight faces an ashen sea. "You've had losses," she says. "The Five of Cups." Three fallen chalices roll against a jetty behind the knight. The other two cups stand upright. "You can either be defeated or realize there's still promise in the remaining cups."

"Can you be more specific?"

"A tarot reading is an interpretation," says Giorgio. "You have to add your own perspective to make it meaningful."

"In other words, you don't know," I say.

Nena laughs. "In other words, it's *unforeseen*." She raises a finger. "There's a difference. But I see plenty of experiences still in front of you, if that's what you're looking for."

"Good to know," I say.

We move on to the third card, where a woman sits on a throne, her lamé gown spilling into the foreground like ripples of lava. "Who's this lady?" I ask.

"The High Priestess," Nena says. "One of the most mystical figures in the deck. She's a guardian of mystery. Insight. Creativity."

I remember the first day I sat at this bar room table, when Giorgio reviewed my job application. *Ad-den-tro. Full of insights. Does that sound like you?* he asked. Maybe Nena's more intuitive than I was expecting.

She slides the card closer to me. "The High Priestess means change. Growth. Maybe she's the Jessica of the future."

"I'm working on the Jessica of the future."

Giorgio reaches across the table for my hand. "You'll get there," he says.

"Don't give up," Nena says. Her eyes flicker with an earnestness that goes against her usual dramatic flair. Ironic, since this portion of her act is two steps from roadside fortune teller.

As the bar room sifts to empty, a man slips in through our lobby door. It's the gray-haired attendant from the art gallery. Giorgio ushers him onto the patio and introduces him to Kimmer. They collect stray drink glasses.

I point to the gray-haired man as Giorgio returns to his seat. "Is he a new employee at the restaurant?"

Giorgio waves my question away with his hand. "Long story," he says. "He's helping out for tonight." I suppose it makes sense since Giorgio owns the gallery, that he might use people in both places.

Nena clears her throat. "Any other questions for me? Go ahead, dear. Let's get Giorgio's money's worth."

"Will I get to London?" I ask. The trees surrounding the patio rustle in the evening breeze.

"You will if you want to," Nena gestures toward the skipping blonde girl on the card. "Nothing will keep you in one place."

"Will I be a famous multi-media artist?" I ask.

Nena drags a pointy fingernail over the Five of Cups card. "You're hanging your head, holding onto the past." She leans toward me. "Let go. Move forward." Her black bob swings. "Don't let your setbacks keep you down. The only thing that can stop you is you."

My shoulders slump. I want a guarantee of fame and fortune to make this all worth it. All the studying. The wandering. The combat and heartbreak and indignity and terror of *life-as-it-is*.

Nena stares more intently. "Just between us girls, you have one more question, don't you?"

She's good at this. Because the guy I thought might help usher me into the punked-up, semi-famous artsy world I've been dying to join just landed me unconscious in a ravine. And I'm hoping that's the worst of it.

"How could Whit lie to me like he did? Did he actually ever care about me?" As pissed and shell-shocked as I am, a dull pain flushes through me when I imagine not seeing him again, not being able to retrieve that fragment of him that I thought belonged to me.

Nena exhales loudly. "It was a control issue, Jessica. *You're my girl. Do what I say. Put me first.*"

Aha. I know that song. Although it's all the more ironic now since Whit was screwing around behind my back.

"You're an extremely focused and independent girl," Giorgio tells me. "You're stronger than he is, emotionally. That much is obvious."

I roll my eyes. "Will I *focus* myself into being alone?"

"Maybe for now," Nena says, "so you can pursue the things you want. But not forever." She reaches across the table and tilts up my chin with her fingertips. "You'll hear this your whole life, my dear. Ambitious women always do. You can't let it stop you." She winks at me. "Maybe there's someone else out there already. Someone who's not afraid to admit he loves you."

Giorgio musses the cards with his palm, sending The Priestess askew. "Jessica, some things don't need a crystal ball."

Nena peels the cards off the table, assimilating them back into the deck, and gives me half a smile. "Was that helpful?"

"More than I would have guessed," I say.

"I'll take that as a compliment." She taps the deck straight. Christmas lights twinkle in the trees beyond her.

I make another $32 in tips from the last two straggler deuces on the patio. For the first time, I notice tinges of yellow mixed in with the willow leaves that drape toward the Main Street overpass. Their branches stretch like witchy fingers casting a spell over the creek.

We girls find ourselves fortressed by boxes again. It's still strange to see my life compacted into less than 20 cubic feet of cardboard.

Audrey and I spritz every crevice of the apartment with the last of our 409 cleanser. Instead of packing everything, we decide to fill a trash bag with crap to toss out. It's time to let things go.

Coffee perks on the counter. The coffee maker is one of the few things we haven't boxed up yet, along with some mugs and a few odd consumables. And our record albums. Those and the stereo have to wait until last.

Audrey delicately peels the Soloflex Man off the kitchen cabinet with her fingernails. "If we leave so much as a strip of Scotch tape on the cabinet door, Mr. Del Vecchio will bill us," she says. "Which means you've also gotta paint over your mural."

"Sure, cut out my heart," I say, sponging a countertop. I accidentally knock a stray can of soup off the Formica, which just misses Audrey's toe.

As she jumps away, our lovely mascot tears apart in her hands. His shadowy torso flutters to the floor in two sections.

Silence. *Shock.*

I rescue one side of Mr. Soloflex from the Linoleum.

"We could tape him back together," Audrey says, handing me the other side of Scott. I think of the Six Million Dollar Man. *We can rebuild him. We have the technology.*

I take a hard look at his literally ripped torso. "No. It's time for him to retire." I wad both pieces of the ad into my fist, tossing Scott's remains into the trash bag.

Audrey salutes the garbage.

The apartment door thuds and a guy's voice calls through the wood: "Somebody lookin' for a vacuum?"

Audrey opens the door to Russell Lee from upstairs, leaning on the handle of a Hoover.

"What would we do without your small appliances?" she says, swinging the door wide. He rolls the vacuum into our living room.

"Heh, heh. Nothing small about my appliances." Russell pokes his head around the place. "Is Katrina around?"

"*Katrina?*" Audrey repeats, reaching for one of our few remaining coffee mugs. "No one calls her that except—" She stops.

"Yeah," I say. "Get the picture?" No one calls her that except *her father*.

Russell thumbs his eyeglasses and straightens his plaid shirt. "I was hoping to say goodbye for real." I smell cologne. For once, he's scented with something he didn't grow in a terrarium.

"Wait . . . you and Trina?" Audrey asks Russell. He takes a step back, crunching his head into his shoulders like a turtle.

"I figured Jessie here told you since she caught us," he says, backing toward the door.

"You asked me not to." I bend to pick up the dented can of tomato soup, which rolled under our kitchen table.

"I didn't think you'd *listen*," Russell says.

My head pops back up from under our table to see Audrey shake her head like something just flew into her.

"*You knew?*" She yanks the soup can out of my hand. "Holy fucking Toledo. Why was she sneaking around?"

I pull out a chair at the table and sit. "She says we judge."

Audrey bangs the can against the counter.

Russell's face goes pink. "I'll come back later."

"*Ooooh*, no." Audrey pulls out a chair. "You. Coffee. Sit. *Now*." He does what she says. She puts a mug in front of him and pours him a cup of Joe. "How long have you two been . . . on each other's radar?"

"Um, since last month. But only when she feels like it. Which is whenever she's pissed at you girls."

"Do you think we're judgmental?" I reach into the drawer and hand Russell a spoon, plus a sugar packet from Capresi's.

He hides behind his mug. "I don't wanna say."

"*Spill your guts*," says Audrey, clonking the carafe back into the base of the coffee maker. She pulls a cardboard pint of milk from the refrigerator and places it in front of him. "We can take it."

Russell rests his mug back on the table and takes a breath, his skinny shoulders slumping. "You girls say you're open-minded and all, reading your college books," he gives Audrey's copy of *1984* a toss on the table, "hanging around with the Boy Georges and the swanky waiters, listening to punk music..."

"Yeah, so?" I ask.

"You're only open-minded when people like the same stuff as you." He stirs milk into his coffee. "If a guy listens to The Dead and watches the Steelers around here, he's shit outta luck."

"That's not true!" I say.

"Sure it is. You girls look at me like I'm Sammy the Sorry-ass Stoner." He sips. "Meanwhile, I grew up in this town. It's not some sideshow to keep me all ... entertained."

Audrey's mouth gapes. "Russell, that's just not how we think."

"Come on, girls. I *am* Sammy the Stoner." He smiles like a schoolboy, looking over his shoulder at Audrey. "It's just that I like it that way. Maybe Trina catches some of that vibe from you girls, too. Like you're better than her. And her getting some with your pothead neighbor wasn't gonna cut it with you."

"No one's ever said anything like that to us before," I say.

"Well, no *guy* is ever gonna say it." Russell shakes his feathery head and pushes back into his chair. "All four of you girls together? That's too much pretty to piss off."

Audrey swings open the cabinet door where Mr. Soloflex used to hang. She chokes the neck of Johnny Walker and places Trina's new bottle in front of Russell.

"Damn, we owe you one," she says.

Maybe we owe Trina one, too.

Late summer heat hangs like a muggy shawl over Main Street. I sit on the cement bridge that crosses the Canal, hanging my feet over the ledge where Whit and I did our balancing act, me afraid of falling.

I want to remember this view.

The Love Cramp in my chest perks up as I inhale the scent of hot algae and decomposing leaves. It's the smell of summer ending, and other things ending that I didn't plan. Like my belief that Whit could be what I wanted him to be. Safe. Loyal. Emotionally forthright.

Adoring.

Decisive.

I can't make him what I want, any more than I can make the phone ring by staring at it. Maybe I'll have to live with people as they are, not as I want them. Maybe it takes more than the scant weeks of summer for two people to figure out if their relationship is worth the investment. Maybe some people are facing much bigger decisions than I am when it comes to who to love.

Water pours its way behind the playhouse, making an incessant murmur as it flows into the river. The brown current pushes through the churn of the watermill and goes on to meld with the Delaware.

It's time to pick up my final check from Capresi's.

I swing my legs off the concrete and head up Mechanic Street, in a blindingly yellow tank top and parachute shorts. I've hardly had the chance to wander this way wearing anything other than a monochrome penguin outfit all summer. It feels good to reflect a different spectrum of light.

As I come to the top of the hill on Mechanic Street, the door of The Milano Gallery sits propped open. *Hi there, Jessica*, it says to me. I stroll past the blanched driftwood door frame, smooth like the tree that Drew and I rested on at the beach. A ceiling fan rotates lazily inside.

The rainbow birch painting still brightens the wall, its burst of teal light beaming through the back of the forest. Yet the piece looks different to me now, as if something's emerging from the forest, instead of lost in it.

"Hell-ooo," says the gray-haired gentleman at the podium. It's the same man who helped Kimmer clear Capresi's patio the other night. The terrarium in the oversized brandy snifter sits on the desk in front of him, growing bamboo shoots.

I shake my finger in recognition. "Do you work at the restaurant permanently now?" I ask him. "Giorgio wouldn't tell me."

The man's natural wool cardigan makes me perspire just looking at it. "Giorgio doesn't talk about me much." He walks toward the birch painting. "I see you're still taken with this work. Isn't it magnificent?"

"Absolutely." Of course, $5,300 better buy a whole fuckload of magnificent.

I do a quick scan for *The Wizard of Oz vs. Godzilla*. It's missing. "What happened to the greenish glass mosaic that was over here?" I ask. "Did Giorgio give up on it?"

"Hardly." His fingers tap against the wood podium, cheekbones lifting his oversized glasses. "It sold."

"*No shit!*" My voice echoes in the sacred-looking rafters. The colors of the room start to dance in front of my eyes, happy blotches floating through a field of periwinkle. I want to do handsprings, but God forbid I should disturb anything expensive. "I can't believe it!"

"That piece was yours, correct?" The man plucks a business card from a brass stand on the podium. "Jessica, hold onto this." Faint crimson paint is visible in the crescents of his fingernails.

I gather myself together and take his card. It reads, *Ernest Toradello, Curator, Artist*.

"Wait, you're *Ernest*?"

"In every way," he says.

"The Midnight Painter!" I shout.

He stretches his wrists to accept an imaginary pair of handcuffs. "Guilty. The restaurant was sorely in need of a makeover."

"I love the new red wall in the bar room," I admit. "It's so *rich*."

"I'm glad someone appreciates the aesthetic," he says. "Why don't you go downstairs and talk to Giorgio about a check."

His sweater prickles my fingertips as I rest a hand on the side of his arm. "You don't know how much I need this."

"I do, actually." He smiles.

Once in a Lifetime

I sprint down the steps to Capresi's, practically skipping through the courtyard. Without customers or the glow of lanterns, the bar room looks like someone's neglected 1970's den. Rows of books line the shelves, waiting for Woody Allen and Diane Keaton to sit down and kvetch.

Giorgio peeks at me over a folded copy of *The Philadelphia Inquirer* as I get to the patio. "There you are," he says. "We're going to miss your special brand of sunshine around here. When are you headed home?"

"In a few days," I say. "Trina agreed to drive me through Jersey and hand me off to my grandparents somewhere towards Newark. By September, I'll head back to Pittsburgh with the girls."

A grin marches across Giorgio's face. "I remember the first day you stumbled in here," he says, shifting in his patio chair. "You almost lost a finger in the bread warmer, you were so frazzled."

"I'd hoped you missed that."

"You bled on the counter." He drops the newspaper to the burgundy tablecloth. "But we needed a waitress. And you stepped up. You've learned to finesse the guests in a way I never imagined you would. Lately, I've watched you flutter around this patio like a ballerina."

"I thought I was more like a tumbler in the Russian Circus." I pull out a white mesh chair to sit next to him. It screeches on the slate—a sound I suddenly realize I'll miss.

"I know you've hit some rough patches lately." Giorgio lifts a finger. "I've got something for you." He heads for the bar room. It's unlike him not to clear away the nearly empty beer glass on the table.

He comes back with two envelopes and hands me one. "Here's your check for the last two weeks, plus a bonus for sticking with us all summer."

I thumb open the envelope to find a check for my salary plus a bonus of $400—that's more than I typically make on a good weekend's double shift.

I bounce in my chair. "Thank you so much!"

"So many girls start at one restaurant and go elsewhere before the season ends. You've got an outstanding work ethic, Jessica. And we take care of our own here," says Giorgio. "There's also this." He pushes the second envelope at me.

"Is this about my mosaic? I was just upstairs." I rip into the paper. "Who bought it?"

"That's a secret," Giorgio says. "I have to respect the anonymity of my patrons."

"No, you don't." I pull out a check for $450 from The Milano Art Gallery. Between that, the bonus, and my salary, I've made more in this moment than I did the whole month of August.

I count figures in my head. 700 . . . 800 . . . 900. . . .

I've hit my goal. Maybe a little over. Between this and student loans, I can afford the study abroad program in London.

A tear slips from a corner of my eye, probably dragging liquid eyeliner with it. "You don't know how much this means to me."

"I know what it means, Jessica." He takes my hand. "You only get one life. Make it worthwhile. Make your dreams happen."

I sniffle. "I wouldn't blame Kimmer if she decided to stay here."

"Kim might stay. But not you. You have a wanderlust," he says. "Remember, you'll be protected by the people who care about you, everywhere you go. That's what your loyalty buys."

Tye enters the shadowy bar room, a duffle bag slung on his shoulder. "*Hey*, you," he says, securing the duffle under the bar. "I was hoping to give you an official goodbye." He joins us on the patio, lifting a chair and setting it on the slate next to me without making a sound. He's so much more graceful than I am. "What's that you were saying about Kimmer?"

"She's still trying to work out her student loan problem," I say. "She's not sure if she can come back to Pitt this semester."

Tye taps his knuckles on the tablecloth. "If she's looking for a housemate, maybe we could talk. Tom Bronski offered me a regular show at Marauder. I can afford rent now."

"Oh my God," I say. "Congratulations! What about Nena?"

Giorgio smooths a wrinkle in the tablecloth. "Nena's heading back west."

"It's time for her and Babylonia to make a clean break," Tye says.

"One more thing." Giorgio tilts the mostly empty beer glass in front of me. "Remind you of anyone?"

I stare at the chestnut-colored puddle in the bottom of the glass of . . . lager.

I pull in a breath that makes my teeth ache. *"When was he here?"*

"About a half-hour ago," Giorgio says. "He went to your apartment, and they sent him here. I asked him to wait, but he wanted to find you himself," Giorgio says. "He's not much for sitting in one place."

"He's not." I straighten my bangs with my fingers. "You guys have been awesome. I can't thank you enough. But I should go find him."

"I expected nothing less," Giorgio smiles.

The two of them rise from their chairs. As I press against Tye's chest in a hug, I'm reminded that no guy I've ever held in my life smells as swoon-worthy as he does, awash in a cloud of designer perfection. "Not to get all Studio 54 on you," he says, "but *We Will Survive*, kiddo."

Giorgio hugs me next. He whispers, "Wander well, Alice."

Sleigh bells jangle as I push through the door and past the salvia flowers that guard the path, their purple heads bobbing in a shot of wind. I run my hand along the bricks of the wishing well, painted smooth and white, one last time.

As my apartment building comes into view, I wonder who that dark guy is sulking against our etched glass door. Buzzed hair. Hands pushed into his pockets, wearing heavy boots even in this heat. He hunches the same way Whit does.

Because it *is* Whit, his hair now fully dark and shorn to almost show scalp. Without his flopping, bleached fringe, he's suddenly has a military look to him—less up-start musician, more severe grunt. It's amazing what a fight with an electric razor can do.

No more blonde streaks.

He pushes off the building to his full, six-foot stance. A chill sparks through me as if I've never met him before. I stop on the barely populated sidewalk. "Look at *you*."

"Yeah." Whit taps his fingers gingerly against the black stitches that lace above his eyebrow. "Painful reminder."

"I'm glad you're okay," I say. "But I was talking about *this*." My fingers stretch toward where his hair used to fall over his eyes, wondering what the new texture of this close-cropped style might feel like. He darts his head away from my hand. I pull back.

A pang beats in my stomach; the Love Cramp comes back to life, reconfigured with a painful twist.

"I needed a change," he says, staring at the cement.

A version of him stands in front of me that I hardly know. Someone who resists my touch, who's able to zero down his attraction to me as abruptly as kicking a cord out of the wall. Someone with sexual apprehensions he never trusted me enough to truly confide in me about. A guy who'll barely look at me.

Funny how you can miss someone who's right in front of you.

My throat tightens as I try to establish eye contact. "Why did you come all this way to see me?"

He taps the metal toe of his boot against the ground. "I couldn't leave things the way they were. I had to at least tell you I'm sorry about the crash," he says. "It was reckless and fucked up." He looks down the street, and then to the cement. Not at me.

A hot breeze blows hair across my face and I toss a hunk of it over my shoulder. "I have to admit, that wreck was pretty fucking scary. But apology accepted."

"And about Daniel. . ."

"*Hmm*. At least I know his name now," I say.

Whit's eyes flicker up toward mine long enough to make my gut somersault, and he laughs uncomfortably. Then he returns his attention to the sidewalk. "He just came to visit in the hospital. It wasn't—"

I wince. "So that's where the studded 'D' earring came from."

"Things never went that far with him, Jess," he says to me. "You should know that."

"Is that the truth?"

"Swear to God. I wish I was confident enough for that. I don't fucking know what I want." He squints down Main Street. "Life is confusing."

I want to be consoling. I planned to be the understanding and supportive girl who helps people through these kinds of scenarios. I could have been that girl if he came to me with this outright. But instead, I'm aching, like an asshole who just had a restaurant tablecloth pulled out from under her, broken glass and screwed-up left-overs sprayed all around. Tossed on my tailbone.

"I just don't get it, Whit. Why didn't you talk to me about this from the start?"

"I didn't know," he says.

"Oh, *bullshit*—if you don't know then who the hell is supposed to know? How could you not know?"

"*Jesus*, Jess!" He straightens himself off the wall and grabs me by the sides of the arms. "Not everyone has their freaking life mapped out the way you do. Not everybody can spit out what they're thinking every minute." His palms are hot. "I don't work that way."

"You made like I was the duplicitous one, though."

"Yeah, well, maybe you're not the only one whose life is a fucked-up puzzle." His grip loosens. "As far as you and I go . . . New York. Pittsburgh. London. . . . You're here, you're there, you're all over." His whole body looks as tender as the stitching in his forehead. "You're gone." He goes back to squinting into the afternoon haze. "I can't deal with it."

Air stokes in my lungs as I prepare to yell at him, to insist this is all bullshit. That he's flat-out afraid of what he was starting to feel.

Then I hear Giorgio's voice in my head, gazing over a set of medieval illustrations that urged me to *let go*. To move forward. *You're stronger than he is, emotionally*, Giorgio said, shoving the Priestess card askew. I see Nena Love, lifting my chin. *You'll hear this your whole life.*

Lucky me. The decisive one.

"*Okay*," I finally say.

Whit pulls me against his chest, folding his arms across my back. He feels overheated from the August sun, black T-shirt having absorbed its rays. I smell the same gently scented soap that I know sits in a ceramic dish in his shower. I can't help still feeling a connection to him that buzzes in my chest like a fallen electrical wire.

Cold sweeps into the space Whit leaves as he unwraps himself from me and steps away, quiet, slow . . . then he shows me his back. I realize that maybe I can't crack guys into fragments like thrift store tumblers, trying to mold them back together like my own personal art projects.

Maybe that's my own brand of recklessness.

I watch his body shift, walking in a gait I didn't realize I'd memorized. He disappears behind my building, leaving the mystery of his future in his wake.

I let him go.

Have a nice life, I think.

CHAPTER 31

ALMOST SEPTEMBER 1984
My City Was Gone

Our record albums are the absolute last things to be packed. It's sad to divvy them up to their respective owners. I get A Flock of Seagulls, Joe Jackson, and The Police. Audrey gets multiple Bowies and the Pretenders. Kimmer gets back the Madonna album we hid under the sofa.

I try to negotiate Roxy Music's *Avalon* away from Trina since it has meaning for me now. She promises to make me a dupe on cassette but won't give up the vinyl version. Avalon is the name of a Jersey Shore town where she and Tony used to go dancing.

We all have our memories.

I wrestle on our shag rug with a cardboard box and a disorderly roll of packing tape. Trina stands over me, her outstretched arm offering me a yellow slip from the New Hope Post Office. "They're holding a package for you. Message in a bottle, maybe?"

I unstick a piece of tape from between my fingers. "Just what I need. Another box."

She shakes the slip in my face. "*You'll want to get this one.*"

A collage of fliers blot the windows at Lopito's music club as I stroll past. Drazine's New Wave dance club watches over the river; the glass panes in its front stairway are black with inactivity. The post office has gray concrete columns outside that could have jumped out of Bedford Falls in "It's a Wonderful Life." Museum-worthy tapestries hang on the walls inside.

A middle-aged clerk hands me a parcel the size of a shoebox. It's rock-heavy and postmarked UCLA, California. I rip the seals with my lousy fingernails.

Inside, a layer of foam peanuts cradles a delicate box decorated in peach and white floral. In Drew's handwriting, a tab of paper taped to the box reads, "Trina said you needed a refill."

I spritz a fresh cloud of Anaïs Anaïs, otherwise known as *Eau de Prom,* into the air of the well-appointed post office. Without the years-old twinge of decay, the scent is first-love in a bottle. I sigh.

A brightly colored corner of something else pokes through the foam chips. I pull a long slab out of the box.

It's a hand-painted rock, depicting an ocean scene in acrylics. The sea stretches to meet a blue, amorphous sky. A caption runs along the top: "Venice Beach, California, August 1984."

Two words streak across the bottom in black calligraphy:

You Better
--Drew

The next day, we girls cross the bridge into Lambertville, New Jersey, for one last round of drinks. The Seville House is very French Quarter, an antique building with black wrought iron accents, filigree metal tables, and a garden fence. The Delaware River gallops below us as traffic crosses the bridge's metal grating.

Audrey swishes her wine goblet as if comparing the viscosity to her regular Scotch. She gazes through Tony's beat-up Ray Bans, which Trina let her have back.

Trina tilts a fat wine glass to her lips. "Which do you want first, the good news or the bad?"

I gulp low-end house chardonnay and cringe. Indulging in cheap wine is like drinking fancy turpentine. Kimmer futzes with her fluffed-up hair.

"Give us the good news, please," I say.

"First, parting gifts." Trina pulls three envelopes out of her purse and deals them around the table.

"Is this cash?" I ask, turning the envelope in my hands. "Are you tipping us out? You couldn't have made out *that* well this summer, Trina."

"You know I'm not that generous," Trina says over the din of passing cars. "What I am, though," she folds her arms, "is an awful-talented litigator."

"*Katrina Moran, Esquire,*" Audrey feigns, fanning herself with her envelope. "What did you do?"

"I cornered our landlord." She takes another gulp from her goblet. "Thanks to the collapsed ceiling, our water-damaged carpet, and the poison ivy outside our bedroom window—"

"Don't forget the violent wife-beater upstairs," adds Kimmer.

"Him, too," Trina says. "All told, I threatened Mr. Del Vecchio into refunding our final month's rent and security deposit."

"Even with the mural?" I ask.

"He'll have to paint over *Attack of the Wall*," Trina says. "He just doesn't know it yet."

"Good job, Tri'," says Audrey. "Here's what scares me, though. Who are we going to stick in your place in the dorms at Pitt if you'll be living downtown?" The metal scrollwork table rocks. It seems no table on either side of the river is capable of balancing evenly on the ground.

Trina clears her throat. "Speaking of that, here's my *for-shit* news." She runs her fingers through her hair, mussing its razor-slick edges. "I got a call from Fox and Rascowitz. Turns out they 'can no longer use me.'"

Kimmer twists her envelope. "What the hell happened?"

"You remember Brent Fox from Phi Omega?" Trina says.

"As in, Fraternity Vice President Brent Fox?" Kimmer chimes-in.

"As in, kick-us-to-the-curb Brent Fox?" Audrey asks.

I cut to the chase. "The guy you spit on."

"That's the one," Trina says. "He's also Brent Fox, as in *Fox and Rascowitz*." She slurps a double mouthful of wine, slapping the glass back down. "He had a few discussions with his dad about me."

We each sink into our chairbacks. "Aw, fuck," Audrey says. A car horn bleats on the Jersey side of the bridge. Probably a tourist.

Trina lowers her head against the scrollwork of the table. "If I knew his father was a partner in a law firm, I'd have bought him a new shirt."

Audrey rubs Trina's back as she pounds the table with her fist. Kim and I stabilize our glasses.

"That so sucks," I say. Wine swishes across my brain, enhancing the shocking blue of the sky, set against the bridge's severe gunmetal fretwork. "But hey—doesn't that mean you can live with us again?"

"Nope. My father already signed an apartment lease with his partner and canceled my housing assignment," Trina moans. "And guess what? I have no way to pay for it now. Karma's a bitch, and then you die."

Kimmer straightens her blousy collar. "I have news for you guys, too," she starts. "My loan situation is a capital 'M' mess. I can't go back to Pitt this semester."

Audrey pulls the Ray Bans off her nose and shoves them into her hair. The lenses half-disappear into the field of red spikes. "Is *everybody* leaving me?"

"I've decided to take Teddy up on his offer to manage the restaurant for a while." A smile rises as she says Teddy's name. "He's turned into an honest-to-goodness, okay guy."

"I have to admit, I've been impressed with him lately," I say. "He's gone from undershirts and untidy hair to polos and a neat comb-out. And he's barely told a rude joke in weeks."

"Kimmer, is he *in like* with you?" Audrey asks.

"Maybe. Lower case 'l'," Kim says. "We're going to work together for a while. It'll be a nice change to spend time with a guy who doesn't need me to *fix* him."

"Or do his bidding," I say. "Even better."

Trina raises her head. There's a scrollwork dent in her forehead. "At least somebody's life isn't completely fucked."

I take Trina's hand on one side, Audrey's on the other, and Kimmer joins the daisy chain. "Is this the last time we'll be out together, as a unit?" I ask.

"You better still let me hang out with you guys when I live downtown," says Trina.

"If you promise to write me when I'm in England." I get a little choked. "Now that I've got the money to go."

"Enough of this crap!" shouts Audrey, breaking the circle of hands. "Wherever we land, we'll still get together if I have to call in the armed forces, get it?"

I toss my head toward Audrey. "See? *Glue*."

"Damn straight!" Audrey punctuates with another gulp of wine. "Now let's stop being sap-heads and get drunk."

"Here's a toast, then," I say. "To the real 1984."

"Orwell's version, or Bowie's?" Audrey asks.

"Apparently, we're surviving both," I say.

"Speak for yourself." Trina swipes at her smudged cat-eye make-up.

I let the girls leave The Seville House without me, since the three of them have more packing to do than me, and I've got a few errands in mind. I stop at the drug store on my last stroll through town, then at the Boho dress shop, where a palisade of rowdy-looking Doc Martens are aligned in the window.

Sometimes, we girls wear a pair of shoes far too long, even when they leave us in full-throttle pain. Even when we know that at any moment we might trip and break our freaking rear ends. Girls can be suckers for a shoe-full of excitement.

This time, I choose a pair of defiant-looking black leather combat boots with next-to-no height in the heels. I use some of the money from Trina's envelope and call it a leaving-town present.

Back at the apartment, I rest the boot box among the cartons on the floor and tap a palm against its sturdy top. *London Calling*, I think. I've got a lot of walking in front of me. Sometimes a girl needs a pair of shoes that won't hurt her.

Then I grab a roll of Scotch tape and the *New Hope Gazette* and head into our bombed-out bathroom with my purchase from Rite Aid. I lock the door and paper every surface I can around the sink and mirror to keep from bleaching the walls and the lousy tile with spots of hair dye. After a half-hour of rubbing and rinsing, I pull my head up out of the sink, throwing sparks of water around the newsprint like a dog after a rainstorm.

I look into the glass. I'm staring back at myself with a fresh spray of white-gold bangs.

Saturated. Limp. But an undeniably, defiantly punk-blonde swath sits in front of my eyes.

My impenetrable hair, defiled. Now I'm *committed*. And if I'm going to commit to anything, it should be myself.

I frisk Kimmer's Kermit the Frog towel through the newly lightened bangs, making the wet tendrils spike.

I'm gradient. I'm ready for an authentic future.

And then, just like that, New Hope isn't my home anymore.

I wrap my arms around my last carton, labeled *"Jessica's Crap,"* and pull the fat green apartment door closed behind me. As I leave the building, the sun slides through my eyelashes and I have no free hand to block it. Trina's station wagon is waiting for me.

I shove my box into the car. The finality of the squeak it makes causes my throat to tighten.

I'm not exactly sure where home will be next, whether Audrey and I will have to find a new roommate or even venture off-campus. Who knows if Kimmer will join us again, or if Drew will gravitate back from California?

I'm moving on anyway, taking that step onto the proverbial staircase you aren't sure exists yet. You have to trust it will materialize under your feet, someday when this weird whirl of a life decides which route you're destined for.

Kimmer and Audrey help me rearrange a couple of cartons to make more room for me to sit. Trina waits in the driver's seat, looking uncharacteristically patient. My life is stuffed once again into the way-back of a station wagon. I'm a newfangled pioneer.

Once we finish shoving boxes, I take a step away from the car and inhale the murky perfume of the riverbank. I want to keep the smell in my head for a while.

I remember the musk of the creek as it drifted past Giorgio's patio, mingling with a hint of fresh latex paint. And the smell of Kimmer's almost-drowned sneakers, not much different from the swampy scent of the towels Trina squeezed out during the flood.

I remember the murmur of water rushing under the Main Street overpass, where Whit slid his Army jacket around me as if I were part of his body. We balanced on a thin concrete precipice, willow leaves streaking downward in the background like a curtain, the two of us suspended over a drop. Listening for creative inspiration.

"You ready, Jess?" Trina calls through the driver's side window. "Our next reality awaits."

"Ready as I'll ever freaking be."

Audrey leans through the window and taps her palm against the most precious box: my portion of our record collection. "So long, Seagulls."

"Can we trade places, Jess?" Trina asks. "I'll go to Long Island. You tell my dad I fucked up."

"Wish I could help," I say, "but that's all you. I've got my own life in front of me."

Trina slumps over the steering wheel. "*Fuck-and-a-half.*"

I cross to the front of the wagon. Kimmer swipes at my newly blanched bangs. "Welcome to the Platinum Club."

"I'm only a half-member so far," I say. "But it's a statement, at least. I needed to commit to the scene, you know? With London on the horizon and all."

Kimmer hugs me, smelling vaguely of roses. "Whatever floats your boat, blondie."

"If you don't visit us," I mumble into her shoulder, "I'll come out here and carry you to Pittsburgh on my back."

"Sure. But let's rent a car, okay?" She steps back.

Audrey wraps an arm around my neck. "I know you're bummed about Whit," she says, easing her grip. "But if he had said, *Forget about London. Stay here with me.* Would you have done it?"

A breeze nudges my bangs into my eyes, delivering a moment to stall. I flick them out of my vision. "*No*," I say. "For a lot of reasons, no."

"Now you know why he didn't ask," Trina grumbles.

My shoulders stiffen. "That's too much *guy shit* to contemplate right now. I need to be by myself for a while." I climb into the seat and notice the abandoned ball compass on the floor of the car. Fluid has drained out of it, staining the mat.

A half-yellow leaf drops to the car's water-beaded hood. Audrey reaches through the open window and clutches my hand, the same way she did the day I woke up in the ambulance, wondering whether I had passed into The Dead Zone.

It's time for the canopied girl on the mystical wands card to move forward, shielded by the people she loves, even if they can't always be along for the ride.

I know my priorities.

Trina turns over the engine, and the Talking Heads blast to life.

The End

Acknowledgments:

Unlimited thanks to all the startlingly unique people who spouted clever dialog at me throughout my post-adolescence and on through my entire life, especially Susan Sofayov and Suzi Kroll of the many Sues (and Dianes), and John Mattaboni. At the risk of being repetitive…

Thanks to my mother, who hasn't disowned me yet over anything I've written. Hail the Giant Wrench that chases us both. Thanks also to Dad, my ridiculously talented brother Jim, and my amazingly supportive and terrifically fun crew of Mattatelliazzo in-laws.

Thanks to my Lehigh Valley Critique Group: Laura (Elle) Weller, Jennifer Laden, and Charles Kiernan. Thanks to the Team Peppermint girls on Twitter: Lauren Blackwood (now a best-selling author!), Jade M. Loren, Katie King, Heba Helmy, and Raina Xin. Thanks to Loriann for being my buddy forever. Thanks to Dave White, Scott Compton, and Rose Fullerton from Banzai Retro Club for all the great nostalgia talk. www.banzairetroclub.com. Thanks to DJ Jake Rudh of Minneapolis and the new wave Transmission "Manatees" for inspiration and that great spot on the show. A nod to Kristen and the New Wave Will Tear Us Apart Facebook Group.

Thanks to editor Jennifer Haskin for her perceptive take on how these events truly fit into Jessica's life—and into America's publishing scene. Thanks also to Olivia McCoy of Smith Publicity for the PR boost. Thanks to novelist J.D. Barker for his marketing insights and to Jonathan Maberry for further short story advice.

Kudos to the terrific podcasters I've met on this journey, including Steve Spears from Stuck in the '80s, Paul and Erika from That Aged Well, Wilnona and Jade of the And I Thought Ladies, Ben and Chris from '80s High, Juan Aleman from The '80s Hour, and Patricia Friberg from Learned it From an '80s Song. Lyndsey Parker, let's talk!

Thanks to those outrageously creative types whose contribution to the 1980s were profound, yet sadly they are no longer here to enjoy the spoils of what they brought into this world. Especially:

- David Bowie, whose death occurred in the middle of my writing the original version of the record store scene that referenced his Aladdin Sane album on the wall. I still feel sick.
- Joe Strummer, who dripped sweat on me from a stage in a gym at Carnegie Mellon University during a general admission concert, 1982. Student tickets cost eight bucks.
- The Ramones, one of whom threw me a pick from the stage at Hammerheads bar in Islip, NY, in 1983, which some jerk stole out of a ceramic box on my dresser years later.
- Andy Warhol, who grew up in Oakland (Pittsburgh). Whose cousin Pat Warhola took engineering classes with a college boyfriend of mine, who got Andy to sign a copy of *Interview* magazine for me in 1986 only months before he died.
- Rik Mayall, the people's poet, who made us outcast American students at the City of London Polytechnic in 1985 feel for brief shining moments like we belonged, because *everybody* loved "The Young Ones."
- Ric Ocasek, whose cool, mysterious musical poetry from The Cars still makes me reel. When I remember the big black blazers with the shoulder pads, I think of you first.

Thanks for an awesome and inspiring youth.

A message to Chrissie Hynde, David Byrne, Debbie Harry, and Sting: THANKS FOR STAYING WITH IT! Don't stop any time soon.

Thank you to: The East Side Club. The Kennel Club. The Ritz. The Palladium. The Limelight. The Lone Star Café. The Upstage Lounge. The Mad Hatter. The Angle. Hammerheads. Paris NY. Spit. Camouflage.

Thanks to everyone who ever stepped foot in New Hope in 1984.

Special not-so-secret recognition to New Hope locations including: The Towpath House. Zadar's. Fran's Pub. Jon & Peter's. Chez Odette's. Havana. The Hacienda. The Logan Inn. The Bucks County Playhouse. The Canal House. Zoli's. The Prelude. The Lambertville House.

And to the guys, shades or more of whom worked their way into this narrative, whose names I won't commit to the page so I don't embarrass

Once in a Lifetime

them. To those guitar-playing, wild-haired, poetry-writing, concert-going, motorcycle-riding, star-studying, fabulous, weird guys: It was great knowing you.

We did sort of have it all, didn't we?

About The Author

Suzanne Grieco Mattaboni is a fiction writer, essayist, pop culture podcaster, journalist, and former community service and education reporter for *Newsday*. Her work has been published in *Seventeen*, The Huffington Post, *Mysterious Ways*, Guideposts.com, *Child*, 50 Word Stories, *Dark Dossier*, Motherwell, *Long Island Weddings*, *The Best of LA Parent*, and SixWordMemoirs.com.

Suzanne's short fiction, essays, and poetry have appeared in anthologies including *Chicken Soup for the Soul – Miraculous Messages from Heaven*, the 2023 Howard Jones concert "Fanthology" *We're In This Together*, the 1980s-themed horror anthology *Pizza Parties and Poltergeists*, *The Future of Us*, the forthcoming *Ever After* mythological creatures anthology, The *Hard Boiled and Loaded with Sin* noir anthology, *Little Demon Digest*, *Running Wild Anthology of Stories*, *What's a Nice Girl Like You Doing in a Relationship Like This?* and *2017 Stories Through the Ages*. She was the chair/editor of the GLVWG *Writes of Passage* 2021 anthology, which debuted at #17 on Amazon's top sellers' list in the anthology category and won a First Place 2022 BookFest award. One of her short stories was nominated for a Pushcart Prize.

Suzanne is a past winner of *Seventeen* magazine's Art and Fiction Contest and a National Council of Teachers of English Award. She won honorable mention in the 2018 *Writer's Digest* Writing Competition and was a finalist in the 2018 New Millennium Awards. Her work has appeared in a multitude of high-tech trade publications and business journals. She has two talented children, one hysterically fun husband, a ravenous cat.

www.suzannemattaboni.com

www.onceinalifetimenovel.com

Author Q&A

Originally published on the *Jean the Book Nerd* blog

The following Q&A appeared June of 2022, outlining some of author Suzanne Mattaboni's thoughts about life, creativity, the past that shaped her, and the feminist themes in *Once in a Lifetime*.

What's the greatest thing you learned at school?

I learned a lot of terrific academic stuff at college, but what I learned most was to depend on myself and pave my own way in the world, which is invaluable. College for me was one long moment of Mary Tyler Moore tossing her hat in the air with joy, thinking, "You're gonna make it after all!" During that time, I made some of the best friends I ever had. We learned a ton from each other.

When/how did you realize you had a creative dream or calling to fulfill?

I was four or five. I used to practice being a talk show host in front of the radiator cover in my apartment, because it had this curved cut-out that looked like the proscenium of a stage. So I was always picturing myself interviewing someone or telling the world some kind of fascinating story, if not literally performing it for people. I was writing before I could write.

I used to cast all the kids in my neighborhood in little plays and musical numbers (they usually chickened out), or I'd act out long, involved storylines with Barbie dolls where Barbie and Skipper were a single mom and daughter with a tough road ahead. I'd act it out in installments, like it was an ongoing saga. I have notebooks going back to second grade in my basement with song lyrics in them, and crude attempts at writing music.

Beyond your own work (of course), what is your all-time favorite book and why? And what is your favorite book outside of your genre?

My all-time favorite book is *Jitterbug Perfume* by Tom Robbins. Read it—time will stop for you. An ancient, deposed Eurasian king and a doomed, sexy Indian widow decide they're going to run away together. She creates a dreamy-smelling potion that stops them from aging, so they skip through thousands of years of history, all crazy in love, fooling townspeople, living adventures, and having amazing sex.

I adore those irreverent, warped novels from guys like Douglas Adams (*The Hitchhikers Guide to the Galaxy*), Kurt Vonnegut (*Cat's Cradle*); and Robbins, who could sustain a whole book about a girl who dreams she's living in a pack of cigarettes. The '70s were an insane time for literature.

Outside my genre? I really don't read historical fiction, but *The Guernsey Literary and Potato Peel Pie Society* was beautiful. And I'm not a teenager, but I loved *Eleanor & Park* by Rainbow Rowell. I also have an affinity for cyberpunk-y writers like Harlan Ellison and Philip K. Dick. I recall a story Ellison wrote from the sixties where a villain drops thousands of jellybeans onto a city to cause havoc. That's just brilliant. And Dick wrote the novel that became "Blade Runner," which is the world's greatest movie.

Tell us your most rewarding experience since being published.

It's hugely rewarding talking to people in interviews, especially hearing someone quote lines of the book back to me. It's this surreal feeling of someone being in your head and knowing how you think, because you had that thought and committed it to paper, and then threw it out there into the world. Now it belongs to someone else.

Also, one really cool thing that happened lately: I got a DM on social media saying, "I'm looking for an author who wrote a poem called 'Someone' in *Seventeen* magazine. Is that you? I saved your poem in a memory box and just found it." Yeah, that was me. Except that poem was published in the 1980s, when I was in high school. Somebody remembered it.

I got an IM from a woman a few years ago who said she bought a Utopia album at a vintage record store, and a clip of that same poem fell out of the record jacket. At the time, girls—strangers—sent me letters saying stuff like "The poem meant so much to me. I put in on my mirror. It got tattered and torn and I laminated it." Etc. The effect that you can have on people as a writer is truly a phenomenal thing, if you're willing to lay your heart on the line. I hope *Once in a Lifetime* has as much impact.

If you could have written one book in history, what book would that be?

The Bible. What a bestseller! No, I'm only kidding.

Maybe *A Clockwork Orange*? What a masterpiece, although the violence is sickening (but necessary in that story). Or how about *The Great Gatsby*?

What was the single worst distraction that kept you from writing this book?

A successful career as a corporate PR person. But that's financing my fiction marketing budget!

Has reading a book ever changed your life? Which one and why, if yes?

All of them changed my life.

Can you tell us when you started ONCE IN A LIFETIME, how that came about?

Once in a Lifetime is loosely based on things I went through as a young person, although events and people are amalgamated and exaggerated and such for effect. I've had the basis for a few scenes that would become *Once in a Lifetime* sketched-out in spiral notebooks for years. But I think I officially sat down and started putting it together in 2018. I had a first draft in about seven months, but went through a lot of revisions and pitching and such. When you're diving into the Beta read/pitch process, you get so much conflicting advice that your brain swirls. So, I changed a bunch of things—and then ended up reverting some of it back to the way it was in the earlier versions anyway. Yet other things found their way in that created those perfect "Why didn't I think of that before?" moments of revelation.

What was the most surprising thing you learned in creating your characters?

The fluidity of them, how they change when you don't even realize it, as you write them. And how sometimes other people read things into them that you never intended, and it actually fits the story.

Your favorite quotes/scenes from ONCE IN A LIFETIME?

Our main character Jessica finds herself very conflicted over men. After a steamy, late-night make-out session with her hot new post-punk guitar player boyfriend, Jess gets a drunken, love-sick call from her brilliantly weird ex-boyfriend Drew, who asks her why the universe is here. Still coming down from the guilty high of having someone else's hands all over her, she frustratedly blurts out, "Because it's got no place else to go!"

At the restaurant where Jess is desperately trying to earn enough tips to fund a semester in London, chaos is always the first item served. She becomes friends with a bartender colleague named Tye who doubles as a drag queen. At a private party that devolves into a drunken brawl, Tye emerges from a back room modeling a spiral-curled wig, a sparkly Goddess gown slit-up-to-there, and Lucite platforms—just in time for rowdy guests to start throwing stoneware coffee cups across the dining room. Tye (a former Marine) barrel-rolls Jessica behind the bar, shielding her from flying crockery. "My nose is stuffed into the fake bosom of a seven-foot-tall guy in a spiral perm and a sequined dress," Jess says to herself. "Thank God."

And as Jess gets into her relationship with Whit the bass guitarist, she puts forth the "Men are Like Shoes" theory:

"Finding the right guy is like finding the right pair of shoes," she says. "You don't need to own a ton of shoes to know a great pair when you see one. But once you find them, you want to wear them. All the time. Because they make you feel fabulous."

Whit point-blank asks her if she's using him for sex.

"You don't understand," she says. "With shoes, it's not so much that you love the walking. It's that you love the shoes."

What is the first job you have had?

I was a day camp junior counselor. It was the best job ever. I wish I could do it professionally. Although I spent a lot of time yucking it up with the other counselors, which was almost a requisite of the vocation. You lived for your breaks, after-hours parties, and staff softball games.

Best date you've ever had?

Once in a Lifetime

I grew up on Long Island, so a couple of great dates involved the beach, including one mostly spent with my future husband's tongue in my ear. That was a really good date. Although one guy cooked me a lobster, cheesy bread, and Little Neck clams then took me for a ride on his motorcycle. Sometimes the best dates, you don't really even make a "date," you just come upon an opportunity to take off with that guy that you've been flirting with forever, and you do something spontaneous, like maybe partying under the giant iconic Iguana sculpture on the roof of the Lone Star Café in Manhattan, or eating French fries together at 3:00 in the morning at Primanti's in the strip district in Pittsburgh.

What's the first thing you think of when you wake up in the morning?

Have any of my PR clients emailed me yet?

What's your most memorable travel experience?

You should read my short stories for these kinds of rantings. I once jumped on a ferry from England to France to meet some friends when I was doing a semester abroad. On the boat, I met a team of Ultimate Frisbee players on their way to a tournament, who had a BIG thermos of rum and coke. They noticed me because I was wearing an American football jersey, and they were fans. When we got off the boat, they started tossing the Frisbee back and forth over commuters' heads on the transit platform. We started hanging out together after that, once we all got back to London. At my dorm, they were known as "Suzanne's Frisbee team."

What's your most missed memory?

Even with all the fun things I tried to do in my life, like traveling and clubbing, singing on stage, writing, the whole thing … you know what moments I would go back to and stay in if I could? The years of being a young mom with my kids. My most comforting memories are with my family when my kids were cute little munchkins, us all piled up on the couch, watching "Mulan" and "Toy Story" together for the bazillionth time. You don't have to train for that, or study or interview. You don't have to have the right clothes or the most advanced equipment or the coolest car to have moments like that. You just have to love each other. As corny as that sounds, it's the freaking best.

Have you ever stood up for someone you hardly knew?

I don't know about hardly knew, but here's a situation that unsettled me. My daughter once decided to be "campaign manager" for her friend down the street who was running for elementary school president. Let's call her Dorothy. Unfortunately, Dorothy came from a family that was troubled, with a mom who didn't pay much attention to her kids, to the point where it was common knowledge within the school administration.

One day my daughter came to me all upset, because the school said Dorothy couldn't run for president. I went to the principal to ask why. He said the student body president needed to have a parent that would be involved in school activities, and it was well known that Dorothy's mother was troubled.

I was shocked. I said, "Are you kidding? Here's this girl with a rough home life who's stepping up to be a leader, and you want to take that away from her? What if that could change her life?" I promised that if Dorothy won, I would do all the parental things they would need her mom to do, like a proxy.

So they let her run.

Which would you choose, true love with a guarantee of a heart break or have never loved before?

I've already made this choice; see the "First Love" section.

What do you usually think about right before falling asleep?

Every stupid thing I didn't get done that day.

First Love?

I grew up in a not-so-great school district, in a neighborhood on the district border. The street right behind my house was in a different, more upscale district. We stayed away from those kids; they were the "others" from the Shoreham School District. But when I was 15, I got invited to a 17th birthday bash for a guy who lived on that other street.

I dipped my finger into the icing of the sheet cake that guy had set out on his pool table, because I was really just a kid, and I had a sweet tooth. That guy grabbed my hand before I could get it to my mouth, and he licked the icing off my finger. I'll never forget: Blondie's "One Way or Another" was playing in the background.

I fell so hard. And it was for a guy who had lived around the corner from me since I was seven, but I had never met before.

Wait, maybe there's a story there...

In reality, it didn't work out so well. Once the summer was over, he went back to the girl he had been dating in the nicer district. I could barely look at another guy for most of tenth grade.

What event in your life would make a good movie?

I can't tell you that, because I hope to be writing it at some point! It's enough that I gave away the meet-cute story with the birthday cake on the pool table already. [© Suzanne Mattaboni 2022]

What is one unique thing you are afraid of?

Poverty. I always feel like I'm one mistake away from being homeless, even now with a stable, long-term career. I grew up in a tenuous financial environment. I don't know if I'll ever get over feeling like any minute that could come back to claim me. That's why I'm a workaholic, I think.

THANKS, JEAN!

https://www.jeanbooknerd.com/

Other Works by This Author

BONUS STORY: From the upcoming short story collection *Gore, Lust & Kin,* by Suzanne Mattaboni

THE WORLD IS LAVA

Even stoplights made me dizzy.

Every light source turned into a glowing blob of liquid phosphorescence that stretched apart and rubber-banded back together, beaming in cyan and amber, or fuchsia, or bright lemon. The sun itself looked like a clump of lava-lamp wax that gravity had pulled into a brilliant sphere, hovering in spitting-hot oil.

When I set out in the morning and stared into the street, orbs of color pulled and bobbed in front of my eyes, torturing me. The faces of strangers distorted and erupted. When I swallowed, I imagined an invasive blob being squeezed down my throat.

The cosmos churned *ad nauseum*.

I couldn't get away from it…

Daniel Griffin flicked on the two blown-glass pendant lights that hung over our heads like fancy clock chimes, illuminating the kitchen island where we sat. Two circles of light reflected off the black slab of granite counter. One halo spotlighted my clipboard full of paperwork like it was a work of art.

"Wait 'till you see what I'm going to turn this place into now that Mom and Pop kicked it," he said, not a wisp of sympathy in his voice. "This is gonna be an epic party house."

"Epic indeed," I parroted. Charlene had told me you need to nearly murder people with sweetness before you go in for the kill. I mean *the sale*. You have to scratch their eyes out with honey.

Charlene knew everything about everyone in town. She said it was part of the business. There were no secrets from the undertaker.

After a decade of being the estranged, rebel son who ran off to follow the Grateful Dead, Daniel Griffin suddenly found himself in charge of his parents' assets. Charlene said he was two steps away from being a vagrant until this week. Now that his parents drove their Mercedes off an overpass, he has this tremendous house all to himself.

Charlene was showing me the ropes on how to make sales for her family's funeral home. Selling coffins and burial plots was the only thing above minimum wage I could find, and my sister swore she'd kick me out of her apartment if I didn't get off my screwed-up ass and start paying my share. I also needed this due to VISA's unbridled penchant for extending credit to under-employed people.

Daniel's red and teal tie-dyed shirt looked thoroughly out of place in this shiny white kitchen. Like Jerry Garcia the day after hitting the lottery.

"So about your parents'... *final arrangements*," Charlene cooed, leaning over the granite counter. "I'm sure you'd like to do them justice, especially considering the resources they set aside for this purpose." *Scratch, scratch*. Scratch their eyes out with honey. She twisted a ringlet of her spider-black hair around her finger with one hand while nudging the clipboard full of contracts toward Daniel.

"To hell with doing them justice," he said. "Time to do things Daniel's way, Mom and Pop." He gazed around the room as if some spectral beings might answer. No one did.

"We appreciate that you'd trust us to take this burden off your shoulders, now that you're in charge. Dan, if you'd…" She tilted her head and a waterfall of black ringlets spilled over her shoulder. She leaned closer to him. "May I call you Dan?"

He sat up straighter in his chair. "*Heck yeah.* Dan it is," he said. Charlene slid a brochure toward him against the black granite countertop, one of the few things in this wide-open kitchen/living room that wasn't some shade of platinum or brushed nickel.

Charlene looked at me as she unfurled the trifold brochure. *Watch and learn, little one*, her arched, Morticia Addams' eyebrows told me. A smirk spread like a garter snake across her face.

The images of elaborate coffins looked appropriate against the thick slab of kitchen island countertop. The headstones in the Ryerson graveyard looked just like this countertop, the main difference being that the grave markers were engraved with powdery matte letters and laser-cut designs.

"We already discussed some fine options on our call yesterday," Charlene said to Daniel. "Why don't we finalize your choices? I remember there were several environmentally friendly selections you seemed to appreciate."

"*Right*," Daniel swiveled in a high, wrought iron bar stool pulled against the island. He leaned ever-closer to Charlene. A lock of greasy hair fell over his eyes as he bent toward her, smiling under his scraggly, forked beard.

"I kind of like this one here," he said, pointing to a hefty wooden box with gleaming silver handles and a particularly intricate silk liner. "But this ruffle thing inside is so washed-out, *dude*," he said. Charlene swallowed hard; she was far from a dude. "D'you have it in multicolor?" he asked.

I bit back laughter. "I've never seen multiple colors used in a coffin interior," my rookie mouth said.

Charlene's boomerang-shaped elbow suddenly found my ribcage and made me hunch. I clutched my side and gulped hard.

Charlene sneered at me through tight teeth, then turned back to

Daniel, all smiles. "We're never against entertaining custom options. What did you have in mind?"

"Let's go *psychedelic*," Daniel said.

"We can do that. Especially with your generous means." She winked at me from the side of her face that Daniel couldn't see.

I cleared my throat and tried to redeem myself. "Of course, sorry. There's plenty of room for personalization."

"*Ex*-cellent," Daniel said, revolving in his swivel bar stool. "I mean, look at this place—pale, pale, and MORE PALE!"

"I see what you mean," I said. "Your personal style isn't reflected here."

Charlene nodded at me. "Lilly, get this paperwork filled out for Mr. Griffin. I can discuss the rest of the details with him." She tapped her nails against the clipboard. I began filling in his name, address, parents' names.

"It's true," Daniel said. "This room is dull as shit. Reminds me of a hospital. You should see what it looks like when I'm vegging out in here with my party lighting, though," Daniel said. "It's *sweeeeeeet*."

"Sounds good," said Charlene. "Why don't we sew up the boring details first though, Dan, and get your John Hancock on the contract?"

Daniel chuckled as Charlene spun the clipboard to face him, loosening the pages out from under the metal clip. An arrow-shaped sticky note marked the all-mighty signature page. She offered him a thick ballpoint that read "Ryerson Funeral Home – We've Got Dirt on Everyone."

Daniel eyed the pen as she floated it in front of him.

"Wait, this is the first contract I've ever signed," he said. "Let's make a thing out of it. I've got all the lighting to make this a Class A celebration." He reached under the countertop, yanking out a long lava lamp, like a two-tone test tube. Then came another, clunking against the granite. "I want you to see the full set-up."

He pulled six lamps out from under the island, their cords hanging over the side of the counter like tails. He slid open an outlet that was built into the side of the kitchen island. But with only four sockets, he couldn't fire-up his whole collection.

"This one's USB powered," he bragged, switching on an electronic-looking thing that belonged on top of a cop car. It shot neon green LED spots across the blank cabinets and bedazzled the vaulted ceiling.

"Very impressive," Charlene sighed.

The lava lamps glowed. Bright globules that started out misshapen began oozing to life. One in fuchsia, one in brazen tangerine, one in electric indigo. The floating blobs were mesmerizing.

"Wait until they're all going, man!" Shavings of silver glitter in one of the lamps began to flurry in heated circles. Daniel backed against an amazing gas range with metal grates heavy enough to secure a prison cell. His face took on a ghastly grin.

He swung around and switched on the two front burners. Blue and orange-tipped flames whooshed into action.

Charlene's pen still dangled in the air.

"*I always wanted to try this.*" Daniel reached past her for the blue/violet lava lamp and balanced it carefully on one of the burners. He did the same with the bright yellow. "I heard this is mega-cool once it heats up on the stove. *Urban legend.* Let's see which one boils first."

"Are you sure that's a good idea?" I said, shielding myself from Charlene's scarecrow elbow before it could spring at me.

"Lilly, the customer's always right," Charlene said. "I'm good to finish up this contract under the glow of the party lights."

"K!" Daniel climbed back up onto his bar stool. He accepted Charlene's pen and settled over the brochure. Charlene leaned in, guiding him through the listings under the trippy effervescent haze of the lamps.

As Daniel and Charlene flipped their way through pricey carvings and finishes, the LED lights played against the ceiling. Various glass cylinders glooped in slow-motion, casting jewel tones against the granite. Charlene giggled like a middle schooler as she flipped through the pages, leaning closer to Daniel all the time.

A clinking came from behind his back. I peeked around him to see the violet oil in the lava lamp on the range bubbling like Pompeii.

"*Umm*, not to interrupt, but—"

Charlene's elbow cut into my ribs, doubling me over just in time for the kitchen to explode in a thunderous—

BLAMMM!!!

A noise like a tractor trailer blowing its tires echoed through the room, laced with screeching shards of glass. Charlene curdled-out a scream as the blast shot her off her bar stool and over the back of a white leather couch behind us. Contract pages flew like fierce birds. I was tossed to the floor, my jaw slamming against cold marble tile.

When I looked up, nothing was white and spotless anymore.

My ears rang as I lifted myself off the floor. The kitchen was sprayed with color like a Mardi Gras gone ballistic. Neon blue, violet, and yellow streaks were already cooling into mutated strands of waxy, expelled glut.

Daniel Griffin was strewn face-down across the granite counter, with staggered shards of glass sticking out of his back like a skyline. The tie-dye spiral of his t-shirt had morphed into a bullseye of ketchup-bright blood. A slick of the vile red liquid was creeping across the kitchen island.

Charlene climbed off the leather couch and crawled across the floor, gathering up the scattered pages of our contract, smearing lava lamp oil as she moved.

I blew hair out of my face and coughed. *"What the hell are you doing?"*

Charlene clutched the pages of the contract to her chest, her curls sticking out like a corkscrew crown around her face. Dribbles of blue wax clung to one ringlet. "We have to get out of here," she whispered, climbing to her feet, "*with* this contract."

Blood started to roll over the lip of the countertop and ping against the marble floor.

"Are you *insane*?" I fumbled for my phone. "I'm calling 911." The phone slipped out of my jittery fingers and smacked against the tile.

Charlene's eyes widened as she *stomped* her black spiked heel against my phone, *again,* then *again,* crunching glass and digital guts under her sole. She grabbed the fabric of my collar into her fist and yanked me close enough to practically kiss her.

"This was the biggest sale I'd ever had, and Shaggy here just added one more to it." She jerked her pointy chin toward Daniel, splayed on the counter. Her breath burned against my skin. "You're not saying a word about this. As far as you know, he signed the papers this morning."

"*What?*"

"You'll swear to it. Unless you want to lose your job and have me report you as a murderer. I'll say you dared Griffin to boil that lamp, so he'd croak and bulk-up the sale," she hissed at me. "My family's got goods on everyone in this town—the police commissioner, the county judge, they're all in our pockets." Her knuckles bit into my neck.

"*But I—I never—but!*" I struggled to peel away her hand.

"Grab your shit, shut your mouth, and *you might get away without jail time.*" She twisted my neckline so tightly the dots of LED lights on the ceiling took a swirl around my head. I fell back to the floor after she let go, left staring at her oil-stained stilettos.

She yanked back the pen that stuck out of Daniel's tight, motionless fist.

Daniel Griffin's casket was accented with white-gold overlays and a custom tie-dyed liner. Color-changing LED bulbs were installed in its interior. His family's triple funeral was right out of the Ryerson's top-tier, Eternal Platinum package, including memory drawers, carvings, and engraved plates.

The next week, Charlene bought a black vintage Porsche that matched her hair.

After that, every step I took, the world looked like neon lava. Streetlamps gurgled with stunning, daisy-yellow globs, reconfiguring themselves in slow-motion. The eyes of mourners at the funeral home were illuminated blue orbs suspended in boiling oil, tears streaming like dribbles of wax.

The stars twinkled in a shower of silver glitter every night, whirling

against a viscous, indigo sky.
Lava, seething.
Everywhere.
Everywhere.

The End

Made in the USA
Middletown, DE
07 December 2024